The Consorts of Death

GUNNAR STAALESEN was born in Bergen, Norway in 1947. He made his debut at the early age of twenty-two with *Seasons of Innocence*. In 1977 he published the first book in the Varg Veum series. They are immensely popular and have been translated into twelve languages including French, German, Dutch, Italian and Russian. Gunnar Staalesen has twice won Norway's top crime prize, the Golden Pistol.

DON BARTLETT lives with his family in a village in Norfolk. He translates from Scandinavian literature and has recently translated, or co-translated, novels by Ingvar Ambjørnsen, Lars Saabye Christensen, K.O. Dahl, Roy Jacobsen and Jo Nesbø.

The Consorts of Death

GUNNAR STAALESEN

Translated from the Norwegian
by Don Bartlett

Arcadia Books Ltd
15–16 Nassau Street
London W1W 7AB

www.arcadiabooks.co.uk

First published in the United Kingdom by Arcadia Books 2009
Originally published by Gyldendal Norsk Forlag AS, Oslo as *Dødens drabanter*
Copyright © 2006

This English translation from the Norwegian
Copyright © Don Bartlett 2009

A catalogue record for this book is available from the British Library.

ISBN 978-1-906413-38-5

Typeset in Minion by MacGuru Ltd
Printed and bound in Finland by WS Bookwell

This translation has been published with the financial support of NORLA.

Arcadia Books supports English PEN, the fellowship of writers who work together to promote literature and its understanding. English PEN upholds writers' freedoms in Britain and around the world, challenging political and cultural limits on free expression. To find out more, visit www.englishpen.org or contact
English PEN, 6-8 Amwell Street, London EC1R 1UQ

Arcadia Books distributors are as follows:

in the UK and elsewhere in Europe:
Turnaround Publishers Services
Unit 3, Olympia Trading Estate
Coburg Road
London N22 6TZ

in the US and Canada:
Independent Publishers Group
814 N. Franklin Street
Chicago, IL 60610

in Australia:
Tower Books
PO Box 213
Brookvale, NSW 2100

in New Zealand:
Addenda
PO Box 78224
Grey Lynn
Auckland

in South Africa:
Quartet Sales and Marketing
PO Box 1218
Northcliffe
Johannesburg 2115

Arcadia Books is the *Sunday Times* Small Publisher of the Year

1

A phone call from the past. 'Cecilie speaking,' she said, and when I didn't react, she added: 'Cecilie Strand.'

'Cecilie! Been a long time. How are you?'

'Could be worse.'

'Are you still in social services?'

'Some of us are still hanging in there, yes.'

'Must be at least ten years since we last saw each other, isn't it?'

'Yes, I crossed the mountains. Went to Oslo five years ago. Summer of 1990.'

'You're not ringing from Oslo now then?'

'No, I'm in Bergen. Visiting my old mum in Munkebotn. Don't know if you remember her?'

'No, I …'

'Well, that's not so strange, but … I've got something important I need to talk to you about.'

'OK.'

'If you've got time.'

'Time is what I have most of, as I usually say.'

'Could we meet?'

'Of course. Any suggestions where?'

'What about in Fjellveien?'

I looked out of the window. The rain this morning had not exactly been a foretaste of autumn. Now the September sun was drifting like liquid honey over the town. Mount Fløien looked green and inviting, with Fjellveien as the equator and not a storm warning in sight. 'Whereabouts?'

'Shall we just see where we bump into each other? I'll be leaving here in under half an hour.'

I checked my watch. 'Great. Let's do that then.'

Five minutes later I had put the answerphone on, locked the office door and set off. I crossed the Fish Market, passed the Meat Bazar at the bottom of Vetrlidsallmeningen and took the steps up towards the district of Skansen and the old, white fire station there. The first yellow leaves had appeared, but there were not many of them yet; green leaves still dominated. From the nursery in Skansen Park came the excited shouts of children banging mud cakes out of their plastic buckets. The last pair of magpies of the summer screeched shrilly from a chestnut tree still bearing its fruit. Finally, I cut up the tiny side street to Hesten and found myself in Fjellveien, where we had arranged to meet.

Fjellveien was Bergen's number one street for promenading. Generations upon generations of people had taken their Sunday walks up there, enjoyed the view over their beloved town, pointed to the house where they lived and said, as if confiding a state secret: 'That's where we live.' Hesten [The Horse] is the local name for the sign reading *Husk at hesten trenger kvile* [Remember the horse needs rest] which had been erected next to the drinking fountain, where there had once been a water trough, on the occasion of the Fjellveien centenary celebrations.

I started walking. A male pensioner with knee breeches, an anorak and a spring in his stride was on his way up to the mountains. A school class was jogging past the forester's house with a sporty PE teacher at their head. The young children bobbed towards me, a slow wave-like motion, like the ripples on the sea of life they still were, a comfortable distance from the height of the storms even now. I moved to the side as they passed, not to be dragged into a futile dream of youth, into yearnings for long past lap times and the smell of perfumed T-shirts.

I looked at the clock on Mon Plaisir, the old temple-shaped summer house that backs onto Fjellveien and faces the sea. She should have been here by now. There was only the last bit of Fjellveien to go, by Wilhelmineborg and Christineborg, names that conjured up a time when every man was free to chisel his wife's name into the landscape, if he could afford to. Here Sandviksfjell's steep slopes rose to the arrow on top of the mountain telling you which direction the wind was coming from, if your eyes were sharp enough to see that far. Here the trees were tall and erect with trunks like brown columns, and the tree stumps and scree were testimony to the wind and landslide hazards.

I met her by the green telecommunications station directly up from a street called Sandvikslien. She was walking towards me wearing a denim jacket and jeans, with sunshine in her hair and a shoulder bag hanging down by her side. On seeing me, she stopped to wait, squinting through her oval glasses to make sure it was really me. Her hair was short and dark blonde with a veneer of grey that had not been there last time I saw her.

We hugged quickly and looked at each other in mild surprise, the way old friends do when the tattoos of time, carved with a sharp knife into your face and other places, cannot be denied.

She smiled fleetingly. 'I'm sorry I'm a bit late. My mother … now and again it takes time.'

'We're still in Fjellveien. No problem.'

She pointed to a bench. 'Perhaps we could sit down? It's lovely in the sun.'

'Why not?'

'I suppose you're wondering why I phoned?'

'After so many years, yes.'

'Well, it's only ten.'

'A lot has happened in my life in those ten years.'

'Really?'

She looked at me, waiting, but I didn't follow it up.

'You had something important to talk to me about, you said.'

'Yes.' She paused as we sat down. 'Do you remember Johnny boy?'

That gave me a jolt. 'How can you ask me that?'

'Well … it was actually a rhetorical question.'

'For six months it was like he was … ours.'

That made her blush, but that was not why I'd said it. It had been like that.

Johnny boy. At six, at seventeen and now …?

'Tell me what's happened.'

She gave a faint sigh. 'He's done a runner. In Oslo. Wanted for murder.'

'Oh Christ. Again? How do you know?'

'Yes, Varg. Again. And that's not all.'

'No?'

'He left behind him a kind of death list.'

'A what?'

'Or … well, he's made it known there are a few people he's going to take out.'

'Oh yes?'

'And one of them is … you.'

'What! Me?'

'Yes.'

I sat in silence. Slowly my eyes wandered down to Byfjord and back a quarter of a century. I felt the sun weakly warming my face, but inside I felt frost, the frost that had somehow always been there and had never let go. The frost from the missing spring.

2

The first time I had met Johnny boy was one hot, sultry July day in 1970. Elsa Dragesund and I had been sent on a home visit to a flat on the Rothaugen estate, the massive grey blocks of flats near Rothaugen School. Some neighbours had reported the matter to the council and the social security people had passed it on to us.

Out of the two of us, Elsa was the one with the most social services experience. She was a sharp but good-natured woman, just turned forty at this point, with carrot-coloured hair and a tendency to dress in colours that were a bit too bright. I was completely new to the job.

The stairway was dark and damp even on a day like this; it was almost twenty-five degrees in the shade. There was no sign of any kind on the brown first-floor door. Through the matt glass panes we could hear the sound of loud music. We had to press the doorbell several times before shuffling steps could be heard inside; the door was opened a little way and a sallow face stared at us.

'What d'you want?' came the response, in broad local dialect.

Elsa put on a pleasant smile and said: 'Mette Olsen. Is that you?'

The woman in the doorway gave us a vacant look. She was blonde, but her hair was greasy and unkempt. She was wearing a T-shirt with holes and threadbare jeans that had not been washed for the last month at least. She was thin, haggard and stooped, as though trying to dull chronic abdominal pains. Her lips were dry and cracked, and under the thin material of the T-shirt sprouted two small breasts, like children's buns, flat and uneven.

'We're from social services,' Elsa said. 'Can we come in?'

For a second or two, a sudden fear flared up in her eyes. Then the channel closed, she stepped aside docilely and held the door open for us.

The smell that hit us when we entered the narrow unlit hallway was a delicate blend of acrid cigarette smoke, refuse and alcohol. On top of that, there was a smell of untended toddlers – something I would become depressingly used to during the years I was employed by the welfare authorities.

Without waiting for our host we followed the sound of the loud music into the sitting room, where a portable radio cassette player was playing a hissing cassette at full volume. I couldn't place the music; it was rock with a heavy bass line which made the walls vibrate. Elsa resolutely strode in, saw the radio and pressed the right button.

The silence was deafening. Mette Olsen had trudged after us. She was gesticulating with her arms. Her eyes were blank and glassy. The explanation was not hard to find. On the worn coffee table and floor was a glorious selection of empty bottles, mostly beer bottles, but also wine and spirits, and the characteristic plastic containers used by homebrew suppliers. On a small chest of drawers were several empty boxes of pills, upside down and without lids, seemingly discarded after a last desperate search.

'Where's your little boy?' Elsa asked.

Mette Olsen gazed around helplessly, then nodded towards a half-open door at the other end of the room. We stood listening for a moment, but not a sound reached us. Carefully, we walked towards the door, Elsa first, and pushed it slowly open.

A broad unmade bed filled one wall. A wooden drying rack had been shoved into one corner, loaded down with laundry. Clothes were scattered across the entire room, with no apparent system or pattern. There was a cot beside the bed, and in it was sitting a small boy, two and a half to three years old as far as I could judge, in a stained vest that had once been white and a swollen, soaking wet paper nappy under a plastic liner. He hardly reacted when we entered the room, just looked at us with blank, apathetic eyes. His mouth was half-open and dribbling, and in one hand he held a sandwich with what looked like chocolate in the middle. But worst of all was the silence. Not a sound came from him.

Elsa took a few steps forward before turning on her heel and staring at Mette Olsen – thin, shadowless and with an aggrieved expression on her face – in the doorway behind us.

'Is this your child?' Elsa asked with an audible tremor from her vocal cords.

Mette Olsen nodded and swallowed.

'What's his name?'

'Jan.'

'Jan?'

'Jan Elvis.'

'How long is it since you changed his nappy?'

She sent us a blurred look and waved her arms around. 'Yester-day? I don't remember.'

Elsa sighed loudly. 'You're aware that this is unsatisfactory? That we will – have to do something about it?'

The young woman looked at us with sadness in her eyes, but she did not react, giving us the impression that she had barely understood what had been said.

Elsa looked at me. 'Classic case of clause five. Mother needs treatment, the child acute referral.'

The front door slammed and a coarse local voice resounded round the flat. 'Meeette! You there?'

No one answered, and shortly afterwards we heard loud cursing and the sound of bottles rolling around the room behind us.

'Where the fuck've you hidden yourself?'

We turned to the doorway, from which Mette had nervously retreated towards us.

'What the fuck are you all doin' here? Who are you? What are you doin' here?'

The man was big and strong, closer to forty than thirty, with tattoos over both forearms. He was wearing a dark brown polo shirt and light trousers; the blood vessels in his forehead were visibly swollen.

'We're from social services,' Elsa said coolly. 'Are you the child's father perhaps?'

'That's got fuck-all to do with you!' he snapped and stepped into the room.

Elsa stood her ground. I moved forward a pace, between them. That made him turn on me.

He clenched his fists and glowered at me. 'What was it you wanted? Wanna bit of this, do you?'

'Terje,' sobbed Mette Olsen. 'Don't ...'

'What the fuck is it to do with you whether I'm the father of her kid or not? We're old enough to vote, aren't we.'

I shrugged. 'Social security asked us ...'

'Social security can go to hell. Piss off, the pair of you!'

I looked at Elsa. She was the one with most experience. She summoned up all her authority and said: 'This child is in a critical situation, *herr* ...' She sent him a quizzical glance, but when he reacted with no more than a snort, she continued: 'He requires emergency treatment and we're going to have to take him with us. Your wife ... She also needs help, as far as I can see. Should you have any objections, may I ask you to contact us through the appropriate official channels and then we will confer on the matter.'

He opened his mouth wide. 'Tell me, do you understand all the words that come out of that slippery gob of yours? If you and that prick with you are not out of here this minute, you'll get a taste of this.' He brandished a clenched fist in front of her. 'Have you got that?'

I could feel I was beginning to simmer inside. 'Look, big mouth ... I may not have as many tattoos as you, but I went to sea for long enough to learn a few tricks, so if you were thinking of attacking anyone, then ...'

He focused his attention on me again, his eyes a little less secure now. He cast a quick eye over my physique.

Elsa broke in. 'I assume that you are – *herr* Olsen?'

'My name's not fuckin' Olsen! Hers is, and she's not my missus, either. My name's Hammersten. Remember that!' he said with a menacing look.

'If you don't let us take the child, we'll be obliged to call the police,' Elsa said.

'Terje,' Mette Olsen appealed again. 'Don't!'

'But first we'll have to put a dry nappy on him,' Elsa said, looking at Mette. 'If you have any?'

She nodded. 'In the bathroom.'

'Then I'll go and get them.'

Elsa walked right past Terje Hammersten and out. The rest of us stayed where we were. I could feel the tension in my body and was ready for anything. Then he gave a snort of contempt, kicked at the air and left the room. I followed to make sure that he didn't attack Elsa, but nothing happened. She returned with a bag of unused nappies and directly afterwards we heard the door slam shut.

'So you're not married?' Elsa asked.

Mette Olsen shook her head.

'But he's the father of the child?'

She shrugged her shoulders.

Elsa sighed. 'Oh, well … We'll have to deal with this one bit by bit, it seems.'

The same evening Johnny boy, or Jan Elvis Olsen, which was his official name, was placed in a home for infants in Kalfarveien. The mother, however, was placed in a rehab clinic in Kong Oscars gate where they did their damnedest to get her to agree to a full course of treatment.

When I went home to Møhlenpris that evening, Beate glanced up ironically over the edge of the book she was reading. 'Food's in the fridge,' she said.

'Yes, I'm sorry it took such a long time. If you could only imagine how some people treated their children …'

'Don't you think I know?'

'Yes, of course ...' I bent forward and kissed her. 'Had a good day?'

'So so.'

In October I heard that Johnny boy had been placed in a foster home. He had suffered terrible emotional damage, I was told, and it was difficult to communicate with him. According to the reports, the mother was not too good, either, and Terje Hammersten was up in court on a GBH charge. He was found guilty: six months' unconditional imprisonment. Life on the outside went on as before. I didn't expect to see any of them again. Which just goes to show how wrong you can be.

3

The next time I met Jan, he was six years old. It was early 1974. I had just separated from Beate and had had far better periods in my life. We had been called to a crime scene, to see to a little child, we were informed, and Cecilie and I were the ones given the task.

At that time I still had my old Mini and we squeezed into the front seats, me at the wheel, Cecilie beside me. Driving a Mini felt like trundling round in a tiny bathtub, with such small wheels that you felt your backside was touching the road as you sped over Bergen's cobblestone streets. You were so perilously low over the tarmac that any head-on collision would put you well in the running for the flat-as-a-pancake award. On the other hand, you could almost always tuck yourself into a parking gap however tight it looked and petrol consumption was not a lot more than for a medium-sized cigarette lighter.

The crime scene was in Wergelandsåsen, a hillside dotted with large detached houses lying like a buffer zone between Landås and Minde, Landås with its fifties and sixties blocks of flats, Minde with its sedate twenties residences. The house we were called to was brown and had a wintry grey garden with faded rosebushes, patches of snow in the shrubbery beds, apple trees with long-established mushroom-like growths in the bark and rhododendrons in their hibernation phase, with hanging leaves and brownish-green winter buds.

Several cars were parked outside the garden gate. The front door was open and a handful of people had gathered on the steps. I recognised many of them from Bergen Police HQ as they stood there drawing their very first conclusions over thin roll-ups. We opened the gate and stepped inside.

Cecilie had briefed me about the case on our way there. A six-year-old boy had been at home with his father. On her return, the mother had discovered the boy crying in the hallway and when she shouted to her husband, there was no answer. She started to look and found him at the bottom of the cellar stairs. His neck was broken. The man was dead. She had managed to ring for help before breaking down. For the time being she was being held at Haukeland hospital, heavily sedated and with a female police officer at her bedside in case she needed someone to talk to when she came round. 'What are their names?' I had asked. 'Skarnes. Svein and Vibecke Skarnes.' 'Background?' 'That's all I know, Varg.'

We entered the house, where Inspector Dankert Muus gave us a grim welcome nod. Muus was a tall man with grey skin, a small hat screwed down on his head and the burning stump of a cigarette in the corner of his mouth, like an amputated limb. I hadn't said more than hello to him before, but he clearly recognised us. He pointed towards a door on the left of the cosy white hallway. 'He's in there.'

We went into a simply furnished modern living room with dark bookshelves, a TV cabinet alongside the shortest wall, potted plants in the windows and light, shiny curtains. A policewoman, a round-faced Bergen-blonde, was sitting on a sofa with a little boy in her arms. In her hands she was holding a blue transformer with a red button, while on the floor in front of them a small Märklin train was running round an ellipsoid track carefully laid between the rest of the furniture. The boy sat watching the train without any visible signs of pleasure. He resembled a doll rather than a small boy.

The constable smiled with relief and stood up. 'Hi! Are you from social services?'

'Yes.'

As she put down the transformer, the train came to a halt. The boy sat watching. There was no indication that he wanted to take over the transformer.

We introduced ourselves. Her name was Tora Persen. Her accent revealed roots in Hardanger, maybe Kvinnherad. 'And this is Johnny boy,' she added, lightly placing her hand on the back of the tiny boy's head.

'Hello,' we chorused.

Johnny boy?

The boy just looked at us.

Where had I heard the name before?

Cecilie squatted down in front of him. 'You're going to be with us. We have a lovely room for you which will be all yours. You'll meet some nice people there and some children you can play with if you want.'

Then it struck me: *But it couldn't be … that would be too grotesque.*

The scepticism in his eyes remained. His lips were clenched together and his gaze was big and blue, as if frozen in a cry, in a terror that still had not released its grip.

'Is there anything you would like?' I asked.

He shook his head.

I glanced at Tore Persen. 'Has he been like this the whole time?'

She nodded, half-turned away from him and whispered: 'We haven't had a word out of him. It must be – the shock.'

'He was with his mother when you arrived?'

'Yes. A grisly situation of course.'

The boy did not move. He sat staring at the electric train as though waiting for it to start of its own accord. There was nothing to suggest that he had heard a word of what we had been discussing. There was not the slightest hint of a reaction.

I felt myself wince inside. It had been exactly the same with the other boy, whose name was also Johnny boy.

But it couldn't be …

I looked at Cecilie. 'What do you think? Should we bring in Marianne for this one?'

'Yes. Could you ring her?'

'OK.'

I went back to the hallway. A constable was standing by the entrance to the cellar.

'Was this where it happened?'

The constable nodded. 'They found him down there.'

'Is he still there?'

'No, no. He's been moved.'

'When did it happen?'

'About midday.' He looked at his wristwatch. 'We received the report at two thirty.'

I looked around. 'Is there a telephone we could use?'

He sent me a sceptical look. 'I think you'll have to go outside and use one of the car phones. We haven't examined the telephone here yet. For fingerprints.'

'I see.'

The front door was still open. I walked over to the parked cars and asked the plainclothes officer in one of the cars whether I could use his phone.

He put on a surly expression. 'And who's asking?'

'Varg Veum. Social services.'

'Veum?'

'Yes.'

'Right. I'll get you a clear line.'

He tapped some numbers into the dialling pad and passed the phone to me through the door. 'You can dial the number there,' he explained.

In the meantime, I had found the number for Dr Marianne Storetvedt, the psychologist, in my address book. I called.

After a few rings, she picked up. 'Dr Storetvedt.'

'Marianne? Varg here.'

'Hi, Varg. How can I help you?'

'We have an acute situation here.' I gave her a brief summary.

'And the mother?'

'Has been taken to Haukeland. Nervous breakdown.'

She sighed. 'Well … what are you planning to do with him?'

'We were going to take him to Haukedalen. To one of the emergency rooms there.'

'Sounds wise. But do pop by here first. How soon could you be here?'

'Barring anything unforeseen cropping up … in a half an hour's time?'

'That's great. I'll be waiting. I don't have any more patients today, so that's fine.'

We finished the conversation and I passed back the phone to the officer in the car, who switched it off for me. Then I returned to the house. In the hallway I stopped by a slender bureau. On top was a framed photograph. It was a family picture of three people. I recognised Jan in the middle. The other two must have been his parents. Svein Skarnes looked older than I had assumed. He was almost bald with a narrow, slightly distant face. His wife had dark hair and a nice, regular smile, an everyday beauty, the type you see six to a dozen. Jan looked a little helpless sitting between them, with an expression of pent-up defiance on his face.

In the living room the situation had not changed. Cecilie had taken a seat on the sofa with Jan. Now she had the transformer and the train ran in fits and starts; she wasn't used to this kind of activity. The policewoman stood to the side with a pained air.

'All done,' I said. 'We can go to Marianne's right away.'

'And she is?' asked Tora Persen.

'A psychologist we consult whenever necessary. Marianne Stortvedt.'

'I suppose we ought to check with Inspector Muus first. To make sure it's alright that we're taking him, I mean.'

'Of course.'

She disappeared.

I looked at Jan. Six years old. I had a boy of two and a half, Thomas, living with his mother now, after things had gone wrong for Beate and me six months ago. For the moment we were separated, but the outcome of the waiting period was a foregone conclusion. I had tried to change her mind, but she had given me a look of despair and said: 'I don't think you understand what's behind this, Varg. I don't think you understand anything.' And she was right. I didn't understand at all.

I gazed at the vacant, apathetic look on his face and tried to summon up the photograph of the tiny boy on the Rothaugen estate from three or four years ago. But my first impression had been too hazy. I remembered the awkward atmosphere in the small flat, the loudmouth who had burst in, the mother's despairing eyes; and I remembered the tiny boy in his cot. But his face … it still had not taken shape; had hardly done that now.

I crouched down beside the sofa where they were sitting, to be on the same level as him. I put one hand on his knee and said: 'Would you like to come in my car, Johnny boy?'

For the first time a glint appeared in his eyes. But he said nothing.

'Then we can go have a chat with a nice lady.'

He didn't answer.

I took his hand. It was limp, lifeless, and he didn't respond. 'Come on!'

Cecilie rose to her feet, carefully took him under the arms and warily lifted him onto the floor. He stood upright, and as I led him to the door he offered no resistance. He tentatively placed his feet in front of him as if he were setting out across a frozen pond, unsure it would bear his weight.

Then we were brought to a halt, all of us. Inspector Muus filled the doorway. Behind him I glimpsed Tora Persen. The tall policeman stared down at the boy in a surly manner. 'Has he started talking?'

'Not yet.'

'Well,' he growled. 'And where had you been thinking of taking him?'

'First of all to a psychologist we use, then to an emergency shelter organisation in Åsane.'

He nodded. 'Just let us know its whereabouts. I suppose it's not impossible that some of us might have to interview him.'

'Interview!' exclaimed Cecilie.

'He's the only witness,' Muus said, sending her a measured glare.

'I'll keep you posted,' I said. 'But now we have to think about Jan. Could we pass?'

'Less haste, young man. What name did you say?'

'Veum. But I didn't say.'

'Veum. I'll make a note of it,' he said with a faint smile from the corner of his mouth. 'We could have an amusing time together, we two could.'

'But not today. Can we go now?'

He nodded and stepped aside. Cecilie and I led Jan into the hallway and headed briskly for the door. From the corner of my eye I saw Muus turn quickly and return to the cellar staircase while Tora Persen remained in the hallway, looking as abandoned as a passing headlight on an ice-bound road.

Outside on the steps I took Jan in my arms and carried him the last part of the way. He didn't object; I might just as well have been carrying a sack of potatoes. By the car I said to Cecilie: 'I think you'll have to sit at the back with him.'

She nodded. I sat Jan down and pushed the right-hand seat forward so that they could get in. Cecilie clambered in and eased herself into the seat behind the driver. I lifted Jan up and she held out her hands to take him. Suddenly he turned his head round and looked me straight in the eye for the first time. 'Mummy did it,' he said.

4

Dr Marianne Storetvedt was a somewhat old-fashioned-looking beauty, around forty years old. Her hair fell in loose cascades over her shoulders. She had an attractive, narrow face with high cheek-bones. Her sharp eyes were softened by the adjacent laughter lines. She was dressed simply, a bright twin set and a brown skirt with a pearl necklace.

Her office was at the far end of Strandkaien and looked over the docks, Rosenkrantz Tower and Haakon's Hall or towards Skansen and Mount Fløien, if she cast her gaze in that direction. I would not have minded an office there myself, had anyone offered me one.

The Åsane-bound line of traffic in Bryggen had come to a standstill, as usual at this time of the day, and on the archaeo-logical dig site after the 1955 fire, the new museum building on the slope down from St Mary's Church was beginning to take shape.

Marianne Storetvedt was in the waiting room to greet us. She had immediate eye contact with Jan, who, after the statement he made while being lifted into the car, had been as silent as a trapeze artist. 'Hello,' she said, smiling at him, then laying a friendly hand on his shoulder. 'We're going to be good friends, you and I.'

He looked at her without saying a word, without any visible reaction.

She turned to Cecilie and me. 'I think I'd prefer to speak with him on my own, but … do you have anything to tell me first?'

'Yes,' I said. 'If we could have a few words undisturbed.'

'I'll look after Jan in the meantime,' Cecilie said. 'We'll find our-selves a magazine to look at, won't we.'

She sat down with him on one of the upholstered benches in the waiting room and took a weekly from the shelf under the coffee table. I followed Marianne Storetvedt into her office.

The room was as simply kitted out as she was herself: a desk with a chair, a very comfortable leather armchair on the other side of the desk and a leather couch along one wall for those of her clients who preferred to be lying down during the consultation. On the walls hung a handful of beautiful, unpretentious landscapes – sea, mountain and forest – broken only by one of Nikolai Astrup's pictures of Jølster, the well-known spring evening motif, where a man and a woman were on their knees working in a meadow, the apple tree in blossom and the moon reflecting off the lake beneath them.

We stood, and she looked at me with a little smile. 'Well?'

'Well, we don't know much. He'd been at home with his father who was found dead at the bottom of the cellar stairs. He was standing in the hall crying when his mother returned home. He didn't say a word to us until …'

'Until?'

'Well … when we were getting in the car to drive here he said …'

'Yes? Come on!'

'"Mummy did it."'

'"Mummy did it?"'

'Yes.'

'Did you tell the police?'

'No, we haven't yet. She's still at the hospital and … I suppose it'll all come out at some point. Anyway …'

'Is there anything else I should know about?'

'I'll have to get it checked out first, but I was wondering whether Jan could be … whether he might've been their foster child, and I've met him before.' Briefly I told her what I could remember of the flat on the Rothaugen estate that July day three and a half years ago.

'What's the background of the foster parents? Do you know anything?'

'No. We haven't been told anything as yet. They're called Skarnes. Svein and Vibecke. That's all I've been told. But they live in a detached house in Wergelandsåsen, so we're not talking about a low-income family here.'

'No one else? No brothers or sisters, I mean?'

'No, not as far as I've been informed.'

'OK, so let's get cracking. I'll see if I can get him to loosen up. But I don't want to push him too much. If you and Cecilie wouldn't mind waiting out there, then ...'

We walked into the waiting room together. Outside the windows it was getting dark. The street lighting had come on and the car headlights in Bryggen resembled a torn necklace, the pearls falling off one by one as they headed for Åsane. After a further, unsuccessful, attempt to establish contact with Jan, Marianne guided him into her office and closed the door behind her.

Cecilie and I sat outside. She was flicking through the same weekly magazine. It was hardly her taste. I had known her since the summer of 1970, and a periodical like *Sirene* would have been more up her street, workaday feminist that she was.

Some people would call her the classic social worker: short hair, metal oval-framed glasses, no make-up, white blouse under a bright little waistcoat I guessed had been manufactured in a Mediterranean country, dark brown, somewhat worn velvet trousers and short black winter boots. Her accent revealed that she came from south of Bergen, more Røldal than Odda. We were chums; we had a great relationship that had moved in two directions since Beate went for separation. On the one hand, we had become more open, on an almost personal level, and, on the other, a new distance had sprung up because her sisterly solidarity demanded that Beate should be seen to be right. But when Beate had complained that I spent too many nights away, on business, in fact it was Cecilie I had spent most of them with, and truly on business: on the streets looking for children and youths who had upped sticks.

'What do you think?' I asked.

She looked up into my eyes, as though she could see down to the very bottom of them, and shrugged.

'I don't know. Hard to imagine that he's making it up.'

'The stuff about his mother?'

'Yes.'

'Do we know anything about – the parents?'

'No. It all happened so quickly.'

'Perhaps we should delve a little deeper?'

'Really we should just hand him over to the Haukedalen centre, shouldn't we.'

'Yes, but …'

She gave a weak smile. 'You always have to dig deeper into cases, don't you, Varg.'

'Well, that's the way I am. A bit too nosy perhaps. Anyway …'

'Yes?'

'Mm, I'm frightened that I may have met him before.'

'Met – Johnny boy?'

'Yes.' Once again I told the story about the hot July day in 1970.

After I had finished, she said: 'Yes, we'll definitely have to do some digging into this one. I agree with you.'

She flicked through the magazine without really reading. It was obvious that I had given her something to ponder. I walked round studying the pictures on the wall. They were old photographs of Bergen, most were of the area around Vågen, the bay, some of down from Murebryggen wharf, others of the market square. It was a town in black and white with busy people in motion, something the camera of the time had not always been able to capture, some of the figures were fuzzy at the edges, like apparitions. In the bay the forest of masts revealed how many boats there were. Down on the quay, delivery boys and porters passed by with sacks over their shoulders and barrels on their handcarts. Another town, another time, other problems.

Almost an hour passed before the office door opened again.

Marianne Storetvedt carefully led Jan through the double doors into the waiting room. She shot us a look and gave a quick shake of her head. Then in a friendly tone, while patting him on the shoulder, she said: 'Johnny boy doesn't feel like talking to us today. That's his right. I think what he needs most now is something to eat and perhaps a nice cup of hot chocolate.'

I nodded. 'If I could just use your phone …'

She pointed to her office. 'By all means.'

I went in, alone. The desk was nice and tidy, and there were no notes about what she might have got out of Jan. I leafed through my address book and dialled the Haukedalen Children's Centre, an institution which was mainly for children at risk.

The manager himself answered the phone, a colleague of ours called Hans Haavik. I explained the predicament to him and said we were on our way. He promised to have a hot meal ready for us when we arrived.

I took the opportunity to search through Marianne's telephone directory.

Skarnes, Svein was in the book, no mention of a profession. His wife was not listed. Above the surname I found something called Skarnes Import with General Manager Skarnes, Svein mentioned, giving the same private address and telephone number. The text did not detail what he imported.

I went out to join the others. Marianne Storetvedt and Cecilie were standing by one window speaking in hushed voices. Jan stood behind them with the same distant expression. When I came in, his eyes sought mine, and for a moment I had the impression he wanted to say something. I smiled encouragement and nodded, but not a sound emerged after all.

'Are you hungry?'

He gave a slight nod of the head.

'Shall we go in the car again?'

He nodded again, with a bit more energy this time.

'I've been talking to someone called Hans. He'll have a meal ready for when we arrive,' I said, including the two women in the conversation.

Cecilie said: 'Well, I could do with something to eat, too.'

Marianne Storetvedt said she would like to talk to Jan 'when he was in the mood', as she expressed it. We thanked her and took our leave, then went down to the car which I had parked in the quay area across the road from the building.

Not long afterwards we had joined the traffic queue to Åsane as though unable to keep away, despite all our efforts. An anthropologist might have called it the eternal longing to migrate that all humanity has in its blood.

We were like a small family unit as we wended our way, and not that untypical: no one said a word. For myself, I had more than enough to ponder. Not least – and in vain this time round – Jan's mother's real name. If it was him, that is.

5

Haukedalen Children's Centre lay discreetly set back from Hesthaugvegen on the ridge leading to Myrdalskogen and Geit-anuken, one of the mountains screening the central parts of Åsane from the sea. The area, originally considered countryside, had been included in the town at the local council merger of 1972. At this time it was the setting for huge building projects, from rows of detached houses to tall blocks, schools and shopping centres. Road extensions had not managed to keep pace with develop-ments, and the proposal for an urban railway that had been put to the council had been rejected by the majority as economically irresponsible. They had decided to build motorways instead. Until these plans were realised we all sat in jams, if we were intending to go in that direction. It wasn't until we reached the top of Åsavegen, by the turn-off to Tertnes, that the traffic began to flow without any further delays, and by the time we were in Haukedalen, Hans Haavik had had plenty of time to prepare the meal.

Hans Haavik was a big man, around one-metre-ninety tall, as broad as a barn door, in his mid-thirties, with a good-natured temperament that inspired trust in all those who, for a variety of reasons, sought shelter beneath his wing. Cecilie's need for food was met. He had set the table for us all in the refectory, a bright room with large, vivaciously decorated wood panels against the grey concrete walls behind. On the way in we had passed two thir-teen- or fourteen-year-old boys standing and kicking a ball to each other in the car park by the entrance. From the lounge we could hear the characteristic sounds of an ice hockey game with the puck whizzing between the one-dimensional mini-players like a bullet.

The meal consisted of a thick stew, served with fresh slices of wholegrain bread and delicious butter. We were given cold water from a jug, and Hans promised us hot chocolate, coffee and home-made cakes for dessert.

Jan did not eat much. He sat picking at his food, regarding the bits of meat with suspicion, but tried the slices of sausage. We left him in peace, but so long as he was sitting there, we couldn't talk about him.

So we talked shop instead. We were all social workers, Hans had been in harness for ten years, Cecilie and I came into service later, she a couple of years before me. When we had finished eating, Hans glanced across at us and said: 'It might be a good idea if one of you stays here until he has fallen asleep.'

Cecilie nodded and looked at me. 'I can stay. After all, you've got …'

She caught herself in time, and I returned a stiff smile. I knew what she had been going to say, but, well, I didn't have anyone waiting for me any more.

'Fine,' said Hans.

I observed Jan. Six, six and a half. Thomas was two and a half. It was strange how dependent you became on such small creatures. As soon as the daily routines were broken, there was a void in your existence, a hole which if you were lucky could be filled with something else, but not necessarily, and not always.

I sighed, and Cecilie sent me a dejected smile as if to apologise further for her tiny slip of the tongue.

'Well, then I'll be off.'

A telephone rang and Hans went to answer the call. Cecilie came over to me. 'Sorry, Varg. I didn't mean to open up old …'

'Not at all. Relax, it's not your …'

Hans returned. 'Police on the line. They're wondering whether one of you could talk to them.'

I looked at Cecilie, who nodded towards me. 'OK, I'll take it.'

I went into the hall, to the coin-operated telephone on the wall. 'Veum speaking.'

'Inspector Muus here.'

'Yes?'

'The situation has changed.'

'Uhuh.'

'This woman, Vibecke Skarnes. We went to the hospital to see whether she could receive visitors, but she couldn't.'

'What do you mean?'

'Er … she wasn't there any more. She had gone.'

'Gone?'

'Hopped it without leaving much more than her imprint on the mattress.'

'But I suppose you've started to search for her?'

'What do you think we are? Idiots?'

'Not all of you.'

'I beg your pardon.'

'No.'

'But we think it might be handy if someone kept an extra vigilant eye on the boy. Until she reappears.'

'I see. I'll talk to Haavik. If he can't, I'll stay here myself. Keep us posted.'

'Fine.'

We hung up, and I rejoined the others. I looked at Jan and smiled. 'Don't you think it's time to head for bed?'

He watched from somewhere far away, a land where adults were refused admission. Sometimes I wondered whether that wasn't a better place to be. But the way back was closed – for most of us, anyway.

Over some brisk activity, carrying out the soup bowls and plates in two trips, I managed to update Hans and Cecilie on the latest developments. We agreed that Cecilie would stay as planned, but now she would sleep in the same room as Jan, while Hans would inform those on the night shift about the situation.

'But she can't know where he is, can she?' Cecilie queried.

'Not as far as I understand things. I wonder whether I should pop up to Wergelandsåsen again in case she turns up there.'

She looked at me in surprise. 'But isn't that the police's job?'

'Yes, it is.'

She rolled her eyes in response.

We went with Hans while he showed Jan where he was to spend the night. It was a room on the first floor with two beds, a table and two chairs in the middle, a double wardrobe and a view onto a mountain face. The only picture on the wall had been taken from a book I vaguely seemed to remember from my own childhood. It showed some children lost in a forest of gigantic toadstools that grew high above their heads. I was not so sure how reassuring that would be.

However, Jan appeared to be at ease there. He still gave an impression of apathy, and I said to Cecilie that if he hadn't snapped out of it by the day after, we would have to summon further medical support. She nodded indulgently, as if to say that she didn't need to be told.

Cecilie stayed upstairs to help Jan with preparations for the night. I followed Hans back down to the refectory. From the adjacent room the sounds of the ice hockey game had died away. Now the TV had taken over, although I was unable to identify the programme.

Before leaving, I went upstairs to say goodnight to Jan. He had been given a pair of pyjamas from one of the wardrobes. Cecilie had found a book on the shelf over her bed and was reading aloud from it. The boy lay in bed with his eyes open, staring up at the ceiling and giving no obvious sign that he was listening.

'Goodnight, Johnny boy,' I said.

He didn't answer.

To Cecilie I opened my palms, gave her a pat of encouragement on the shoulder and was off.

Hans accompanied me out. He laughed when he saw my vehicle. 'Is there really any room in that sardine can, Varg?'

'More than you would imagine,' I answered. 'But it would have been a size too small for you.'

He stood watching as I got in. I peered up at him. He wore an air of concern.

'Anything bothering you?'

He shrugged. 'It's just an occupational disease, Varg. You'll get it, too, after a few years in this line of work.'

'And it has what effect?'

'A slow accumulation of disillusionment regarding what some adults do to the children they brought into the world.'

'Well ...'

We nodded to each other, then I put the car into gear and set off. I glanced at him in the rear-view mirror as I turned out of the car park. Standing where he was, he looked strangely forlorn: a big, good-natured teddy bear forgotten by a child who had long grown up, slightly at odds with the times.

Beate had kept the flat in Møhlenpris. I had found myself two rooms and a kitchen in Telthussmauet, in Fjellsiden. But I didn't go there. I did what I had told Cecilie I would do, and drove back to Wergelandsåsen.

6

February was dark and this year there wasn't much snow. It wasn't cold, either. It had been an unseasonably warm winter, and in January the föhn winds had swept through the town for such long periods that man and beast had smelt spring in the air long before it was due. No one would have been surprised if the first migratory birds had arrived a month or two early.

Wergelandsåsen was an almost noise-free zone this evening. All you could hear was the distant hum of cars down in Storetveitvegen, a cat meowing furiously in a garden and an aeroplane passing overhead towards Flesland airport.

Behind the hedges, the houses were lit and peaceful. I pulled in, got out of the car and carefully put the car door to, without closing it. I stood taking stock of the area.

The street was narrow and surrounded by withered brown hedges, most of them neat and tidy. A few cars were parked down one side. I bent forward to see if anyone was sitting in them, but there was no one.

I closed the car door quietly and moved forward. There wasn't a hedge around the brown house but large dark green rhododendron bushes, the biggest of them at least twenty years old. I paused by the gate. The police had cordoned off the house with red and white plastic tape, a measure which did not prevent anyone from entering if they wished. I looked towards the house. It had a dark, closed air. An outside lamp was on. That was all.

A car door further down the street was slammed. I stared after it. Two men were coming towards me. Neither of them wearing a uniform, but they didn't need to. I recognised them by their gait, and when they were close up I recognised Ellingsen and Bøe.

Ellingsen because he had married an ex-girlfriend of mine; Boe I had seen at the police station.

'Something we can help you with?' asked Boe, the older of the two, weasel-faced, lean and wiry.

'I know him,' said Ellingsen, a bit chubbier, dark-haired with visible bristles.

'Hello, Elling,' I said. 'Everything alright at home?'

'Yes, thanks.'

'You know him, did you say?' Boe asked.

'Just by repute.'

'His wife,' I began.

'They were in the same class at school,' he added with alacrity.

I gave a thin smile as though I knew something he would have preferred not to know.

'And what the hell are you doing here at this time of night?' Boe pressed.

I studied him. 'The fact is I was here earlier in the day on business. Social services, if you're curious. I just felt like – seeing how things were up here, during the evening.'

Ellingsen expelled air through his nose and Boe sent me a suspicious glare. 'Seeing how things were?'

I opened my mouth to answer as a car turned into the narrow street. When the driver became aware of our presence he switched off full beam. For a second, time stood still. Then the two policemen began to walk towards the new arrival, a BMW of the sporty variety as far as I could see, as muscular as it was lowbrow and in an unbelievably indecorous colour, the closest relative to which was orange. Before they had closed in, the driver had opened the door and got out. He was slim, wore a short jacket and was only visible as a silhouette in the distance.

I followed Ellingsen and Boe.

'Who are you? What are you doing here?' asked the man with natural authority in his voice.

'We should ask you the same,' Boe said, showing his police ID.

'My name is Langeland and I'm the family's solicitor.'

'Which family?'

'Skarnes. Who did you think?'

Ellingsen looked sheepish. 'Well, we had to ask, didn't we.'

'Not necessarily.'

The two policemen introduced themselves. Langeland looked at me. 'And this is?'

Ellingsen and Boe turned round in astonishment, as if they had never seen me before.

'Veum,' I said. 'Social services.'

'Are you responsible for looking after Jan?'

'He's in safe hands.'

'That's good to hear. Where?'

'I don't know if I can divulge that information.'

'As I said to the policemen here … I'm the family's solicitor. You can tell me everything.'

'I've learnt that you should say as little as possible to solicitors.'

Boe gave a crooked grin. 'Perhaps you should take Veum with you for a ride in your car, Langeland. Make him an offer he cannot refuse.'

'You've seen the film, too, have you?' I said.

'What is in fact the problem?' Langeland said.

'What's what problem?'

'What are you doing here?'

'Perhaps I should ask you that question. Are you expecting to find your client in?'

He sent me a chill look. 'My client?'

'Vibecke Skarnes. You're the *family's* solicitor, didn't you say?'

'Yes, I am … Isn't she in hospital?'

'In which case wouldn't it make more sense if you were visiting her there – rather than here?'

Both policemen focused their attention on Langeland as if they shared my view of the matter.

He glowered at us. 'I came here to see what the situation was. I hadn't received a report back on what had happened before this evening.' With a sidelong glance at the policeman, he added, 'I was working on a case in Kinsarvik, but I understand there is nothing else to be done here.'

'Never say never,' I said.

'And that is supposed to mean?'

I turned to Boe again. 'I don't know how much I'm allowed to disclose. To be on the safe side, I'll leave an assessment of that to our friends here.'

Boe took stock of Langeland. Then he said succinctly: 'It turns out *fru* Skarnes has disappeared.'

'What! Disappeared?'

'Yes.'

'From the hospital.'

No one said a word. Boe just nodded in silence.

For a moment, Langeland stood mesmerised. 'Well, I never!' He turned to me again. 'Do you know anything about this?'

'No more than has already been said.'

An apparently dumbfounded solicitor was such a rare sight that I was distracted for a moment. Then he had himself under control again.

'Well, I'll have to go up there myself and find out what could have happened.' He looked from me back to the policemen. 'And you?'

Boe gazed at him from under weary eyelids. 'We've been assigned to surveillance duties outside the house. In case she turns up. Veum's going home to bed.'

I winked at Ellingsen. 'Yes, if Elling's here then ...'

His face instantly went scarlet. 'Veum! I've warned you!'

'You have indeed. But has that scared me off? Not yet.'

'One day I'm going to hit you so hard you'll ...'

'We'll be in the papers?' I looked at the other two. 'Now I have witnesses anyway. Will you take the case, Langeland?'

'Alright, alright,' Boe said, with impatience. 'Since neither of you has any official reason to be here, I suggest you leave – now!'

'Fine,' I said, looking at the dark garden around the house.

'I'm going to the hospital,' Langeland said.

I followed him to his car, which stood next to mine, an appropriate demonstration of the difference between our respective monthly salaries. The Mini blushed to its rust stains and pointedly looked away when I came to a stop beside it.

Before getting into his polished chariot, Langeland turned to me once more. 'Why won't you say where Jan is?'

'I certainly will, Langeland. It's no big deal. He's staying at the Haukedalen Children's Centre.'

'With Hans Haavik?'

'Yes. Do you know him?'

'We're old friends. From university.'

'Well, in that case you'll know where he is. But before you go, Langeland ...'

'Yes?'

'Is there a possibility that Vibecke and Svein Skarnes are not Jan's biological parents?'

He sent me a hostile glare. 'Where have you got that from?'

'Did you catch my line of work? I think I've met Jan before, when he was two or three years old. And in a very different home.'

He averted his eyes, looked across the car roof at the two policemen. 'Well ... I can't see any reason to deny that. But Vibecke and Svein had adopted him. They have full parental rights.' After some reflection he added: 'Well, Vibecke, anyway.'

'Does Jan know, do you think?'

'That he's adopted? I doubt it. You'll have to ask Vibecke about that. Why do you ask?'

'Well, I ... it was just a thought.'

'OK ... I'm off then.'

After a final nod he got into his car, closed the door, started up and reversed out of the side street, so quietly that you could hardly hear the sound of the tyres on the tarmac. I stood watching him before I got into my own car, ill at ease.

Mummy did it, he had said. Which mummy? I wondered.

7

I had an uncomfortable night. Waking up next morning, I could remember fragments of a dream in which the boy sitting on the other side of my kitchen table eating chunks of bread with Norwegian goat cheese was Thomas, and he was suddenly six years old and had Jan's eyes: expressionless and thus accusing.

I rang Haukedalen and got Haavik on the line. 'How was it?'

'He's up anyway. He and Cecilie are having breakfast.'

'And the mother … You haven't heard from her?'

'Not a peep. Would you like to talk to Cecilie?'

'I could have a quick word.'

I waited while he went to get her. 'Hi,' she said, taking the receiver.

'Slept well?'

'No. I had one eye open the whole time. I was worried that if I fell asleep he would try and run away.'

'But he didn't?'

'No. He slept like a log. Really. He had the odd nightmare, was sobbing and thrashing around, but he didn't wake up. Not even when I sat on the edge of the bed stroking his hair.'

'And now? Have you got him to say anything?'

'No. He's just as distant. If he doesn't improve, I'm afraid a Child Psychiatry Centre will be the next stop.'

'Let's try Marianne one more time. I'll see if I can get her to come out here. And then I'll try to find out what's happened to his mother. Or mothers.'

'You haven't checked that out yet? Whether it's the same boy or not?'

'No, but it's top of my list of things to do. Of course, it would have been useful to know whether he himself knows that he's adopted. But I doubt it. And if he won't speak anyway, then …'

'Then it must have been the foster mother he meant?'

'On the face of it, yes.'

'Have you told the police what he said, Varg?'

'No. Not yet.'

'But … why not?'

'I don't know. Client confidentiality maybe.'

'But … well, I understand. A potential murder case, though.'

'The most likely scenario is still an accident, isn't it.'

'Yes, but nevertheless.'

'I'd like to carry out a few investigations of my own first.'

'You're just so incredibly nosey, Varg! This is way out of line … the best is to go to the police – and tell them everything. That's what we've got them for.'

'I'll think about it.'

'If you don't, I will.'

'Give me a few hours first.'

'OK! You're just absolutely hopeless.'

I thanked her for her confidence in me and we concluded the conversation. I promised to call back later. In the meantime she would try to find out something about Jan.

From Telthussmauet I took the quickest route down, straight across Vetrlidsallmeningen and past the Fløien funicular. The weather had turned. Outside it was bitingly cold with specks of frost in the air. The low cloud cover hung like a taut drum skin over Bergen valley, a snare drum ready to be used.

I dropped in on Elsa Dragesund. She had been promoted to assistant director since we had last met, but her office door was always open and she waved me in when she saw me in the doorway.

I went straight to the point. 'Can you remember the summer of 1970 when you and I were sent to the Rothaugen estate to take care of a neglected child? The mother was a drug addict and a man turned up while we were there.'

She nodded, deep in thought. 'Yes … vaguely. There have been quite a few of those cases unfortunately.'

'The boy was placed with foster parents who later adopted him.'

'Right …'

'He was known as Johnny boy. But he'd been christened Jan Elvis.'

She grinned. 'Yes, I do remember that bit.'

'You wouldn't have the adoption papers, would you? I'm afraid I may have bumped into him again, in perhaps an even trickier situation.' I explained the background to her and I observed that not even twenty years in social services had taken from her the ability to be visibly moved.

'My goodness … Mummy did it! Did he really say that?'

'Yes, he did.'

'Talk to Cathrine. She'll find you the papers. But … what is it exactly you're after?'

'Most of all, confirmation that it is the same boy. After that … well.' I shrugged. 'I suppose, strictly speaking, it's a police matter.'

'It certainly sounds like it. I don't think we should get ourselves caught up in the criminal investigation anyway.'

'No, no,' I said, thanked her for her help and went to see Cathrine Leivestad, three offices along.

Cathrine was fair-haired and attractive and as fresh to the job as I had been in 1970. 'No' didn't exist in her vocabulary, at least not in a professional context. As for her private life, I hadn't gone there yet.

She produced some papers from a drawer in the filing cabinet, cast a quick glance over it and passed them across the table for me to peruse for myself.

It didn't come as much of a surprise. Nonetheless, my heart seemed to sink even deeper in my chest, like a leaden weight in polluted waters.

The papers were factual and bureaucratic in style. The only thing that caused me to react was the new middle name.

Skarnes, Jan Egil, born 20.07.1967 was a child of *(mother) Olsen, Mette, born 29.03.1946* and *(father) unknown.* In June 1971 he was adopted by *Skarnes, Svein, born 03.05.1938* and *Vibecke, born 15.01.1942.* From the papers it emerged that he had been placed with foster parents, Vibecke and Svein Skarnes, since October 1970. There were two medical certificates attached. The first, dated August 1970, attested that Jan Elvis was under-nourished and suffered from severe emotional trauma. The other, dated December 1970, stated that his general condition was a great deal better, but the boy had several symptoms of what in clinical terminology were called reactive attachment disorders. He was anxious, restless, impulsive and a constant attention-seeker.

You hardly had to be King Solomon to appreciate that the two mothers were key figures here. The question was whether they could be traced, a question which I transported a bit further down the corridor where Cecilie and I shared an office, for space rather than practical reasons.

I made two telephone calls. The first was to the police, where I got Inspector Muus on the line and he didn't seem all that well disposed towards me. 'Yes?'

'Veum here. Anything new?'

He permitted himself a pause. 'What do you want?'

'I was wondering whether … Have you found her?' For lack of an immediate reaction, I added: 'Vibecke Skarnes.'

'Oh, you mean Vibecke Skarnes, do you?' he said sarcastically. 'No, Veum. We haven't found her yet. You haven't, either, I take it?'

'Well, I'm not out looking …'

He interrupted me. 'No, I certainly hope you are not! For your own sake. Was there anything else you required?'

'No, not at this moment.'

'Right, well, I think we can continue with today's duties then, Veum.' And with that he hung up.

I took a grip on myself before dialling the next number on the list, Karin Bjørge, my friend at the National Registration office.

A couple of years ago I had brought her sister, Siren, home from Copenhagen and got her back on an even keel. At the time Karin had said that if there was anything she could help me with – *anything at all*, she had said with an expression in her eyes that had caused my brain to go into a tailspin for a moment or two – I was to ring her. Later I had, several times in fact, and she was always just as helpful, fast and efficient. If I ever started up on my own, it would do no harm to have a loyal friend at the NR office.

It didn't take long to trace her. Mette Olsen had an address in Dag Hammerskjölds vei in Fyllingsdalen, a tunnel away from Bergen town centre. 'I think this is the house number of one of the high rise blocks out there,' she added.

I added quickly: 'What about someone called Terje Hammersten … Can you find his address as well?'

She flicked through, then located it: 'The last address given here is Bergen Prison. It may be out of date, though. The last official address before that is Professor Hansteens gate, but in fact it says here he'd moved.'

'Right, I'll check that. Thanks very much.'

When I rang the social security office, Beate answered. 'What is it now? I'm sitting here with work up to way over my ears, Varg. Can't we talk outside office hours?'

'This is a business call.'

'Oh yes?' She sounded more than sceptical.

'We're looking for someone who by all accounts is in your system.'

'Really? And that is …?'

'Hammersten, Terje. Would you mind checking him out?'

She emitted a loud sigh, but I could hear her getting up from her chair and straight afterwards there was the familiar sound of a stuffed filing cabinet drawer being opened and then the efficient leafing through of a great many case files, like the flapping of heavy wings.

Then she was back. 'He has to report regularly to the police and his finances, except for unemployment benefit, are under administration.'

'Well, that's something. Have you got an address for him?'

'Just a c/o.'

'And that is ...'

'Mette Olsen, Dag Hammerskjölds vei, if that's ...'

'Yes, thanks, but – I'll catch you another day, okay?'

'Fine,' she said. 'Take care.'

'You, too,' I said, but she wasn't listening. She had already put down the phone.

I went to the window and looked out. Snowflakes were slowly fluttering down and settling on the black tarmac outside, like dandruff on the lapels of a dark dinner jacket. I didn't linger long and was soon on my way.

8

The party at Mette Olsen's was in full swing. I could hear it from the stairwell. Her flat was on the second floor and her next-door neighbour – a well-filled out lady wearing a brown coat and grey hat as if on her way out – came to the door when she heard me ring. She scrutinised me suspiciously and said with irritation in her voice: 'Are you going in there as well?'

'Well, I …'

'If so, just tell them, if they don't quieten down soon, I'm going to call the police! They've been at it since five.'

'Five o'clock this morning?'

'Yes, they woke me up when they arrived. They weren't exactly quiet, I can tell you.'

The door in front of us opened and the noise level rose appreciably. The man standing in the doorway was in his forties, a rough character, unshaven and dressed in clothes with an unmistakable Salvation Army cut: solid and timeless. His eyes swept the stairway. 'What's yer business?'

'Mette Olsen,' I said politely.

He sent me a baffled look.

'The person who lives here. Is she in?'

'Oh, Mette. What's yer business, I asked.'

'Are you her guardian or what?'

'What's it got to do with you! You from the social?'

'Something like that. May I come in?'

He didn't answer, just stepped back into the flat. The inauspicious music that was belting out was Swedish dance band. It sounded like a Danish ferry in there. 'Meeette!' came the cry, like a delayed echo from 1970.

'What's the problem?' answered a high-pitched, reedy voice from inside the room.

'Someone wants to talk to you!'

'Send him in then, for Christ's sake!'

The next-door neighbour, who had moved so close to me now that it felt like I was under guard, gave a loud snort. More in hope than anything else, she said: 'Are you really from the social services office? I suppose you're going to evict her, aren't you? You know things can't go on like this, don't you.'

'I belong to a different department,' I said as the man in the doorway slowly turned his head back in my direction.

'You heard what she said. Come in!' He beckoned me in, and I had never felt so welcome.

The neighbour seemed to be about to enter too, but she stopped on the threshold. The thug didn't need any second bidding; he slammed the door in front of her so hard that she literally had to jump back a step to avoid being struck.

Inside what was supposed to be the sitting room there was the raucous babble of varying shades of inarticulate human voices in a bad-tempered struggle to drown the music. The smell of alcohol and smoke from roll-ups mixed with a not insubstantial dash of dope wafted towards me as I stood by the door squinting through the sea of fog for Mette Olsen.

There were eight people in there, nine including the doorman from Rent-an-ape. Three women and six men. The oldest of the men must have been close on sixty, the youngest eighteen or nineteen. I had my money on him as the dope-smoker and the others as the musical directors. Their faces were unshaven, undefined and unfocused, both with regard to their vision and their pattern of movement. Everything seemed eerily sluggish, as if their whole nervous systems were so shot through with alcohol that they moved in slow motion, powered by a controller who was even drunker than they were.

The women were not much more presentable. All three were

in that slightly diffuse age-range between twenty-five and forty. The one with most years of service, in drunkenness terms, had fiery red hair with an extended grey patch from the roots upwards. Another's hair was so black she could have been a gypsy, but the colour had come from a bottle and her dialect from the coastal region around Bergen. The third was Mette Olsen.

She was half-sitting, half-slumped over the table. Her gaze came from deep inside her narrow, thin face and she had become ten years older in the three years that had passed since I last saw her. She had light streaks in her hair, although they made little difference, and the make-up she had applied ten or fifteen hours earlier had now turned to black smudges around her eyes and a red stripe from one corner of her mouth like a frozen sneer. Her blouse had come undone at the front and in the opening I could see a dirty, grey bra stained light brown from coffee or beer.

One hand was holding a kitchen tumbler full of what looked like neat alcohol, for it was hardly water. Slowly her eyes focused on me. 'Waddywan?' she asked in slurred dialect.

I asked myself the same question, but it was neither the appropriate place nor the time. 'I don't know if you can remember me.'

She studied me without a spark of recognition. 'Where from?'

'I was at your house a few years ago. From social services.'

Instantly the room seemed to change character. Even the music took a break and stopped and the needle rasped its way to the end. Several of the competing monologues died away. The Danish ferry veered round in a huge U-turn and everyone's attention came with it. 'Social services! He's from social services,' I heard pass from head to head. One of the men stood up and began to roll up his sleeves. Another pulled him back down. 'Hang on. We'll deal with him afterwards ...'

Mette Olsen looked at me, her eyes swimming. Her lips trembled. 'From social services? There are no kids here!' A shiver went through her body. 'You yourself saw to that ...'

Steely, hostile looks struck me from all sides.

'Well … this is about – your son.'

'Johnny boy?'

'Yes.'

'What's up with him?' For a moment a sudden fear flared up inside her. 'He hasn't …?'

'No, no. Is there somewhere we could talk, alone?'

She blinked, trying to get me in focus. 'I dunno.' She slowly turned her head. 'In there maybe.' She was looking at a half-open door.

One of the men called out: 'Yep, take him to the bedroom, Mette, then there may be more children for social services to take care of!'

Rowdy laughter filled the room.

Mette Olsen stood up and tottered on unsteady legs round the table. 'Don't listen to them. Come with me, you.'

She grabbed the underside of my arm, more for support than anything else, and led me with a solemn countenance into the bedroom, where the unmade bed and all the clothes scattered to the winds made its first indelible impression. I left the door behind us ajar so as not to feed any unwanted reactions. Behind us the volume of voices resumed and someone put on another record, although they may just have returned the stylus to the first track.

Inside the bedroom, she let go of my arm and flopped down on the edge of the bed. The look she sent me was of indeterminate character, on the frontier between fear and loathing. 'Wozzup with Johnny boy?'

I adopted a serious expression. 'When did you see him last, Mette?'

Tears filled her eyes. Large, red flushes appeared on the side of her neck. 'You ask me when I saw him last? You were the one who took him from me! I've never seen him since – since the day you came to my house …'

'Not at all?'

'Never!'

'But you know he was placed in a foster home?'

She closed her eyes as if thinking. Her face quivered. 'I know, yes. Some snooty sods who couldn't have kids of their own. Foster home! Right. They stole him from me! That's what they did. Stole him! Terje said I should sue them, but that was no help, and Jens advised me not to. He said it would be my ruin. As if I had anything left to ruin …'

'Jens?'

'Jens Langeland! The solicitor. I'd had him before …'

'Langeland?'

'Yes. The first time I was charged with … but that's a long time ago now. I was pretending to be a hippie and played with the bad boys. But he was so young then, straight out of school. Just a stripling. Well, mm …' She blinked again.

'So you haven't had any contact with Jan or the foster parents since 1970?'

'That is … I should've had visiting rights. I was s'posed to visit him at the weekend, and if I'd recovered I'd've been able to take him home. But he was in the foster home for such a long time and … well … I didn't recover. Things went downhill! I was so bad I couldn't even visit him. It wouldn't've done him any good, they said. Jens had me admitted – to Hjellestad for rehab. But what help was that? We had dope smuggled in there, too. Dealers were in the forest outside our windows throwing ropes up to us. We tied them to the window catches and then we hauled up the goods. We just had to promise on our word of honour that … well, you know, when we got out again … If not, we'd've been beaten up. And I must say they kept precise records. I was on my back being screwed by anything that moved for six months without getting much more than pocket money. Then I had to keep going for even longer to earn what I needed every day. I'm tellin' you, I didn't even have time to think about him … about Johnny boy, I mean.'

From the next room came a familiar siren. 'Meeeette!' But it wasn't the doorman this time. It was Terje Hammersten.

'She's in there, Terje,' a voice said.

'They're screwing!' It was one of the women, who burst into hysterical laughter afterwards.

'What?! I'll bloody …'

The bedroom door opened with a bang. Hammersten stood in the doorway, and he did not look well pleased. He was ready for trouble, and I was not left in any doubt that I was the trouble, and this time there was no escape.

9

One of the first things you learn in social services is to blather your way out of even the trickiest predicaments. Often children are present and they must be spared head-to-head confrontations between parents and other adults.

But this time there were no children around, and Terje did not let me get a word in before he went for me.

'Tryin' it on with my girl, are you?' He rushed towards me at great speed with one fist raised. I jumped back, careered around the bed and started to speak. But he wasn't listening. He leapt up onto the bed, the base gave way with a crack, and Mette tumbled forward screaming. He staggered in my direction and this time he got close. The first punch hit me in the shoulder and I felt as if I had been struck by a sledgehammer; when I saw the left hand swinging towards me I levered myself off the wall and hurled myself in the opposite direction.

'Hammersten!' I yelled. 'You're impeding a civil servant in the performance of his duty!'

That stalled him for a moment. Like a heavyweight boxer he stood with both fists raised, half on tiptoes. 'D'you know who I am?'

'I know who you are, and I've met you before. I'm from social services, and if you hit me one more time, you will be reported and end up in clink again. If you stop now, I'll forget …'

He scowled at me, unconvinced. 'Then you won't report me?'

'No. You have my word on it.'

'I could crush you with these hands. You know that, don't you?'

'Don't be too sure. I can take quite a bit of punishment, if I have to.'

For a second he gauged me with his eyes. My hands hung down

by my sides, ready for action if he launched another attack. But I seemed to have taken the edge off his fury.

He looked down at Mette, who was sitting on the floor beside the bed, while she stared vacantly up at us both. 'What d'you reckon, Mette? Did he touch you?'

She slowly shook her head. 'We were just – talking. He had some news, about Johnny boy.'

'Some news? What?'

'We didn't get that far.'

'There was no news,' I said. 'I just wanted to find out if you had seen him recently.'

'And that's what you were asking her? I call that harassment!' Again the fury in him rose. 'You were the one who took 'im from her.'

'You think this would be the right surroundings for him to grow up in, do you.'

'You …!' He took two steps forward and raised his fists again.

I held up both my hands, palms outwards.

'Hammersten! Remember what we agreed!'

'Terje! Don't …' whimpered Mette from behind him. 'I can't take any more. I've lost him for ever. I know I have …' She slowly dissolved into tears.

Hammersten took another step closer. 'D'you know what I'm gonna do? Tomorrow I'm gonna go with her to her solicitor, Langeland, if you know who that is, and ask him to complain to the local council about you, whoever you bloody are and whatever your bloody name is!'

'Veum is my name, and I can save you the bother. I'm going to have a chat with Langeland myself, I reckon.'

'What about?'

'It's none of your … It's absolutely no concern of yours.'

He glowered at me while obviously fighting with himself. One moment he was going to knock me senseless, the next he was shaking like a leaf, angst-ridden and dying for a drink.

'Veum …' It was Mette mumbling my name.

'Yes?' We both turned towards her.

'When you meet Jan, could you say hello from me and …' She began to sob. 'I still love him! I miss him so much! Oh, Jan my boy … my Jan … Johnn …' Her words were smothered by sobs.

'I promise you, Mette. I'll say hello from you.'

Terje Hammersten gave me a look of contempt. I turned on my heel and left the wretched bedroom with the two dysfunctional individuals.

In the sitting room hardly anyone noticed me pass through. Outside on the landing the neighbour had gone. I was glad. On returning to my office, I phoned Paul Finckel, the journalist, an old classmate from Nordnes.

'Hi Paul … guy called Terje Hammersten. Does that name ring any bells?'

'Loads! Have they let him loose again?'

'What was he in for?'

'GBH. If I were you, I'd keep well away from him, if I could.'

'Thanks for the advice. Got any more info?'

'Cost you a beer.'

'So long as it isn't too many.'

'I said one, didn't I. I'd better bring you some photocopies, so you know who you're dealing with.'

'Is he dangerous?'

'Dangerous doesn't begin to cover it.'

'But he hasn't killed anyone?'

'Not officially at least.'

'Not … What do you mean?'

'We can discuss this over a beer …'

'Usual place?'

'Usual place.'

10

The clientele of Børs Café varied according to the time of the day. In the morning, the majority were ageing alkies, seamen on home leave and pensioned-off harbour sweats. In the evening, you could meet anyone from petty criminals to Business School students with a penchant for field studies. At lunchtimes, when Paul and I met on this occasion, most customers were single men who valued the cooking at Børs over their own culinary skills. There had never been many women. Those that dropped in, however, became the centre of enthusiastic attention. No one took any notice of Paul and me raising our midday glasses of foaming beer.

Paul looked at me inquisitorially. 'What's going on, Varg? Have you started playing detective or what?'

'No, no. It's just this case we've been drawn into. We have to take care of a little boy. The mother kind of lives with Terje Hammersten, and that's why I was interested in his background.'

'My God. Living together? Poor woman.'

'What do you mean?'

'There's only one thing you can say about the guy. He hits like a hammer and he's hard as stone.'

'So I gather. When we got involved with these people three or four years ago, he was being taken in on some GBH charge.'

'That sounds about right. He has a dangerous temper, as I said.'

'But you were suggesting that ...'

'Yes?'

'On the phone. Off the record, you said.'

'Yes, it's the kind of rumour we newspaper people have to grapple with all the time, you know. We're never sure how much faith we can put in it. It was all to do with the great alcohol smuggling affair in Sunnfjord a year ago. I suppose it must have been early 1973. A boat was boarded by customs officials in one of the inlets between Verlandet and Atløy. Full to the gunnels with foreign goods ready for national distribution, so to speak, further down the fjord. A few days later one of the gang was found beaten to death with a baseball bat or something equally hard. Rumour has it that he was the snitch and that Hammersten was summoned from Bergen to deal with the matter. Pure Chicago, as I'm sure you appreciate.'

'Why didn't they do the job themselves, the people behind it?'

'I suppose they were in prison already, most of them. A message must have been passed out via alternative channels. Pretty clear message, let's put it like that. Blood had to be shed. But the odd thing was …'

'Yes?'

'Well, the person who was killed …' Paul tossed his notebook onto the table and opened it. 'A certain Ansgår Tveiten … was his brother-in-law.'

'Hammersten's brother-in-law?'

'Yep. Married to his sister, Trude.'

'Uhuh. And what did she have to say to that?'

He grinned. 'Nothing about that in the story. But he was never arrested for the crime.'

'I'll have to ask him face to face then, next time I bump into him.'

'You do that and in the meantime I'll order the flowers for your funeral.'

'Does he belong to any other gangs in town, this Hammersten?'

Paul took a quick scan around. 'You see the guys in the corner over there? Sort of semi-organised thieves. In Birger Bjelland's network, the new Mr Big, a fence from Stavanger. The buzz is he's building up quite an organisation, and Hammersten fits in there somewhere, I would guess.'

'Birger Bjelland?'

'Yes. Unknown quantity round here, but in Stavanger he's pulled off some impressive jobs, my colleagues there tell me, using false companies and false accounts, if you understand what I mean.'

'Not quite. But I get the gist. And where does Hammersten fit into this picture?'

'A sort of errand boy, to put it euphemistically. Send Terje Hammersten to the creditors' door and they beg you to be allowed to pay, the sooner the better.'

'I hope he never comes to mine.'

'Let's hope so for your sake, Varg.'

We raised our glasses and finished our beer. Afterwards it was not far to Langeland's.

11

Jens Langeland had his office in Tårnplass, across the street from the Law Courts. When they rang the bell for the first sitting, he could glance at his watch, stroll downstairs, cross the square and take his place on the bench before the judge had raised his eyelids to declare the court in session.

It was nearing the end of the working day and, as I stepped into the anteroom on the second floor, which he shared with two colleagues and a secretary, the secretary was on her way out, dressed as if she were on a charter trip to Eastern Mongolia: under the fur-lined anorak hood I could only just make out that she was blonde.

'Is *herr* Langeland in?' I asked.

'We're closed,' she said flatly.

'Yes, but I think it would be to his advantage to hear what I have to tell him.'

She examined me with a sceptical gaze. 'He's busy with a client.'

'You couldn't buzz through and tell him I would like a word with him, could you? It would be very quick, tell him. It's about – Johnny boy.'

'OK ...' Reluctantly she went to her desk and tapped in a number on the telephone. 'There's a man here who wants to talk to you. About someone called Johnny boy. – Yes. – No. – I'll ask him.' She looked at me. 'What was the name?'

'Veum. From social services.'

She passed on the information, listened in silence to what Langeland had to say and then shifted her gaze back to me. 'He's coming out.'

'Thank you very much.'

She sent me a cool stare. 'Not at all.'

The door to one of the offices opened. Jens Langeland came out, closing the door behind him. He was wearing a dark tweed jacket with leather patches on the elbows and dark brown trousers.

The secretary was quick off the mark. 'Can I be off now? I'd like to catch the half past four bus.'

'Of course, Brigitte. Have a good evening. See you tomorrow.'

She nodded briefly to me in passing and was gone.

'What's this about?' Langeland asked. 'As I'm sure you were informed, I'm busy with a client.'

'Yes, I … Not Mette Olsen, I trust.'

'Mette Olsen! What makes you ask about her?'

'Well, her partner – a certain Terje Hammersten – suggested that he might contact you.'

'Well, I definitely haven't heard from either of them.'

'I've come about Johnny boy.'

'So I understood.'

'You didn't mention yesterday that you were his mother's solicitor as well. The real mother, I mean.'

'No, and why should I? What's this supposed to be anyway? Don't tell me that social services have taken up criminal investigation as well! You have a strictly delineated sphere of influence, let me remind you. Social services, that's your remit.'

'Have you contacted Haukedalen?'

'I have spoken to Hans, yes,' he said, tight-lipped. 'Your colleague – something or other Strand – was there keeping a close eye on things, but progress was slow, he said. I assume you will put him in professional hands before very long.'

'We already have a psychologist in the team. Dr Storetvedt.'

'I see. But you wanted to talk to me, my secretary informed me.'

'Yes. This is about Mette Olsen.'

'Uhuh?'

'She said you recommended her not to proceed when she wanted to try to hold onto Jan.'

His eyes glazed over. 'Mm … I suppose that is a correct

interpretation, as far as it goes. But I'm not at liberty to discuss client issues, Veum. I'm sure you appreciate that.'

'Why not?'

'Why didn't I recommend her to proceed?'

'Yes.'

'Poor odds. That much I can say. And I also had the child's welfare to consider. The child was better off where he was.'

'You'd been her solicitor before, she said.'

'Yes, indeed, but only as a solicitor's clerk. A matter she got involved in during the mid sixties.'

'You were fresh out of school, she said.'

'We-ell, school … She was also a very different person then. Young, sweet and mixed up in something that had suddenly gone sour on her.'

'And that was …?'

'They'd been arrested at Flesland airport, she and one other person. Charged with trying to smuggle in a hefty stash of dope. But we managed to have her acquitted.'

'Mm?'

'But as you have discovered, it didn't end there. She drifted into the habit and when the Jan business blew up, she contacted us again. Then I was given the case on my own. But it was hard going and, as I mentioned previously, I had to prioritise his interests over hers, even though I was her solicitor.'

'But at the same time you were acting on behalf of Svein and Vibecke Skarnes.'

'No, no, no! Not at all. That came later.'

'Uhuh?'

'A coincidence. I knew both Vibecke and Svein from university. Svein contacted us – that is, the partnership here – in connection with a compensation matter, and the case landed on my desk.'

'What was his line of business?'

'Photocopiers. Not the big brands, but they were very competitive in the local market, in Bergen and south-west Norway generally.'

'But the fact that you'd been Mette Olsen's solicitor first, didn't that disqualify you from acting for Skarnes?'

'No, why should it? This was a business matter. And today … today the situation is quite different, for everyone. Now I have to assess what is best for Jan once again. But I don't have time for this, Veum. I have to get back to …' He faced the office door.

'Has Vibecke Skarnes contacted you?'

Something happened to his eyes, a brief flash of panic immediately replaced by frostiness. 'It's beyond my comprehension what this has to do with you, Veum.'

'It has nothing to do with me, except that the police would very much like to speak to her.'

'In that event, the police would have every opportunity – when the time comes.'

'When the time comes. So she has contacted you?'

'Veum! I'm afraid I will have to show you the door. I'm closing.'

He grabbed my shoulder with great determination and shoved me towards the exit.

'Just one more thing,' I objected on my way out.

'No, Veum, no.' He shook his head resolutely, pushed me into the corridor and, before locking up behind me, said: 'Mind your own business, Veum.'

I heard what he said, but for some reason I was not in an amenable frame of mind that day. I walked down towards Christian Michelsens gate, then decided to play detective for another hour. I stood in a house entrance and waited.

I didn't have to wait very long. Jens Langeland appeared after less than half an hour, and he was not alone. There was a woman with him, and I realised that the secretary had not been lying when she said he was busy with a client. She was wearing a light brown sheepskin coat, and her hair was concealed beneath a large woollen hat. Nevertheless, I had no problem recognising Vibecke Skarnes from the photograph on the bureau in her hallway.

12

From the gateway in Tårnplass I watched Jens Langeland and Vibecke Skarnes cross the square to the part of Fortunen Design offices that led up to Markeveien. They passed between Scylla and Charybdis: on the one side, the Law Courts and, on the other, the state-owned off-licence, the Vinmonopol. The former ate you alive; the latter sent you headlong into ruin, all according to personal predisposition and adversity.

They made an odd couple, he with his tall wading bird figure, she small and slender, but with a determined gait nonetheless. The notion that she was on the run from the police couldn't have been further from your thoughts.

I followed them far enough to see them getting into a car parked by the pavement in Markeveien. I recognised the car without any difficulty. It was Langeland's orange BMW. He held the door open for her and she got in. He walked round to the other side and surveyed the scene.

He seemed to hesitate before getting into the car. For a second I was frightened he had seen me. I flipped up my lapels and turned in the opposite direction, as though unsure where I was going. Glancing back, I saw the car was gone.

I walked down to the nearest call box, in Strandkaien, and flicked through the telephone directory. Jens Langeland had a comfortable address in Fjellsiden. Ole Irgens had been Bergen's first headmaster, he had been a central figure in Bergen's Timber and Tree Planting Company and one of the founders of Fjellveien. In gratitude, the winding road from Fjellveien right up to Starefossen had been named after him, and somewhere along this road Langeland had acquired accommodation of as yet indeterminate format.

I took the Fløien funicular up to Skansemyren and walked from there. Reaching Ole Irgens vei, I studied the street numbers and headed uphill. The orange-coloured car was unmistakable. It was parked outside the gate of a brown box-shaped property with a white basement floor that matched the address in the telephone book.

The house turned out to contain six apartments. According to the signs by the doorbells, Langeland lived on the first floor to the right. I peered up. The curtains were partly drawn and the lighting inside was muted. But, from a room at the side, harsh, naked light fell onto the winter-dark garden. I guessed they were in the kitchen; hopefully in front of the worktop and not on top of it.

I went through the gate, up some steps and followed the path round to the main entrance which was at the back of the house. The front door was open. I went in and up to the first floor. In front of Langeland's flat I hesitated for an instant. I stood listening, but no sounds carried through. So I rang the bell.

For the second time in a couple of hours, I was standing face-to-face with Jens Langeland. He didn't seem at all happy to see me at his door again. His face reflected extreme distaste, although there were clear signs of nervousness. 'Veum …'

'I'd like to speak to *fru* Skarnes.'

He gulped. 'And what brought you here?'

'Save me the hassle, Langeland! I saw you in Tårnplass. I know she's in there.' I angled my head towards the inside of the flat.

'That's correct,' he said with the same tight-lipped expression that I recognised from before. 'I do have a client in here. But I feel no obligation to reveal the identity of the person.'

'Of course not. But I suppose you would feel an obligation to do so to the police, bearing in mind the status of the client.'

'The status?'

'Yes, she's a witness in a case involving a suspicious death, isn't she?'

'Suspicious! What are you talking about, Veum? It was an accident. He fell down the damn stairs.'

I smirked. 'You admit this is the case in question then?'

He didn't answer.

'And that you have Vibecke Skarnes in there?'

He eyed me in silence.

'But you … If you don't let me in, I will have no choice but to ring the police. Now, this very minute. Could I use your phone or should I try a neighbour?'

He heaved a heavy sigh. Then he thrust out his arms and stepped aside. 'You'd better come in. I don't understand what you're after, but … We're in the kitchen.'

The hallway was long and narrow. It must have been just redecorated. The whole apartment gave the impression that he had moved in recently. A glance into the living room revealed a sparsely furnished area in which pictures had not yet appeared on the walls and books were piled up on the floor.

The kitchen was bright and modern. A pan was simmering on a red stove. Vibecke Skarnes stood in front of the worktop with a sharp knife in her hand, and leeks, carrots and celeriac on the chopping board. She was wearing a blue and white striped blouse she must have brought with her from the hospital and a short black skirt that set off her slim legs well.

'Hello,' I said, motioning towards the frying pan. 'Food for thought …'

She looked nervously from me to Langeland and said nothing.

'This is the fellow from social services. Veum. I think I mentioned his name, didn't I?'

She nodded and stared at me with enlarged eyes.

I sent her an encouraging smile and introduced myself properly. Then I said: 'I can assure you that Jan is in the best hands.'

'The best?' She didn't seem to grasp what I meant.

'Yes. But it would be very helpful to us if you could tell us exactly what happened …'

She still seemed perplexed. 'Happened?'

'Yes, from your point of view. I mean …'

Jens Langeland walked past me and stood beside her. 'There is no reason why my client should tell you anything at all, Veum.'

'Yes, there is. I want to!' she blurted. 'I – must …'

Langeland sighed with an expression designed to tell her that if she did, he would wash his hands of her. She put down the knife and perched on a kitchen chair. I remained on my feet. I saw my reflection in the kitchen window behind her.

Langeland turned away. He demonstratively collected all the prepared vegetables in a bowl, took the lid off the pan and carefully emptied them in. The aroma of Toro pea soup reminded me of how hungry I was.

'It was … Jan had been absolutely impossible for a few days. He refused to go out. And I had some errands that had to be done, I needed to go to the doctor's, amongst other things, and then Svein …' Her voice cracked and tears formed in her eyes.

Langeland interrupted. 'Don't put yourself through this, Vibecke! He has no right to interview you like this. I'm your solicitor. Let me …'

'You know the alternative yourself, Langeland. It's not certain they would be so understanding.' I turned back to Vibecke Skarnes. 'I do appreciate that it's difficult to talk about this.'

She nodded. 'Yes, it's … terrible! That that tiny … that he should be such a cuckoo in the nest …'

Langeland again signalled that she should desist. I said nothing. After a pause, she continued: 'Svein was supposed to stay at home with him until I returned. I didn't take longer than I had to! But when I … I knew of course that they were at home, so I just rang the bell when I arrived. But when no one opened up, I had to unlock the door and then …'

She raised her head and stared into the distance, a faraway look in her eyes. 'The first thing I saw was Jan. He was standing in the hall, right in front of …' She took a deep breath. 'The cellar stairs.

I didn't know, I didn't understand ... He was so strange. Just stood there staring at me as though he didn't recognise me. So ... apathetic, I would say. And I asked him: Johnny boy, what is it? Where's Daddy? But he didn't answer, and I walked past him and saw the cellar door open. I must have known then. That something terrible had happened. I went down the top steps and there ... then I saw him. He lay on the bottom step, twisted ... his neck.' She made an involuntary movement with her own neck. As she continued, her voice was forced, as if she were pushing herself towards the inevitable conclusion. 'He ... I knew immediately from the way he was lying ... he was dead. I ran down, bent over him, tried to lift him, held him tight, but I knew. He was dead, dead, dead ...'

She burst into tears again and I let her cry. Langeland sent me accusatory glares, leant over and put his arms around her. She turned, half-stood up from her chair and rested against him, sobbing. He patted her back, trying to console her. 'There, there, Vibecke ... There, there ...'

For lack of anything else to do, I went to the pan on the ring and lifted the lid, as if to make sure it wouldn't boil over. It all looked fine.

When I turned back to Langeland and Vibecke, she had let go of him. She was sitting slumped over the table with a handkerchief pressed against her face, staring at the table top.

Langeland said: 'I think you should go now, Veum.'

I nodded. 'Perhaps we'll talk again another time, *fru* Skarnes,' I said to her.

She gave an imperceptible nod.

Langeland followed me to the door. I whispered: 'And ... the police?'

'I'll contact them myself, Veum. You don't need to worry. I just wanted her to calm herself first. You could see for yourself how upset she is.'

'Not unjustifiably, I'm afraid to say.'

His eyes probed me.

'As we drove with Jan yesterday … as we got into the car … the only thing he has said so far …'

'Yes?'

'He said: "Mummy did it."'

He glanced over his shoulder to make sure she hadn't joined us and lowered his voice further. 'What?'

'And he knew nothing about any second mummy, did he?'

'Not as far as I know. Not unless Vibecke …'

'Shall we go back and ask her?'

'No! Not now … I'd rather … If she says anything, I'll ring you. I promise.'

'Hand on your solicitor-heart?'

'Hand on my – yes.'

I wavered for a moment. 'But there was one thing that made me wonder. I don't know if you also noticed.'

'What was that?'

'She didn't ask how Jan was. Not a word.'

He nodded in silence as he let the thought sink in. Then he shrugged, went to the front door, opened it and let me out. In the garden, I took a deep breath and wondered what to do next. First of all, however, I needed something to eat.

From a telephone box in Skansenmyren I called Cecilie. But she was not at home. Then I rang Haukedalen. I got Hans Haavik on the line. That was where she was. They were still struggling to get a word out of Jan.

'Come on over, Varg,' Hans said and uttered the timely words: 'We can even offer you some leftovers.'

I didn't protest. I walked straight to Skansen, got into my car and was on my way.

13

The row of windows in Haukedalen Children's Centre glowed with warmth as I got out of my car, locked up and walked to the entrance. It had started to snow again, slightly heavier snowflakes now, and a treacherous promise of a late winter and renewed life on the ski runs around the town. A few degrees higher, though, and it would tip over into rain.

Hans Haavik met me in the vestibule. He seemed concerned. 'Not a lot to tell you, Varg. I'm afraid we may have to recommend hospitalisation.'

I nodded. 'Is Cecilie still here?'

He pointed towards the refectory. 'They're sitting in there.'

Some youths passed us in the company of a male care-worker. They scowled at me with suspicion before disappearing into the lounge. I followed Hans into the refectory.

The light inside was garish and sharp. Cecilie and Jan were sitting at the same table as the night before. On the table in front of them there were bowls and pans with the evening meal: boiled potatoes, a mixture of greens, half a head of cauliflower, rissoles and gravy. And a jug of water to wash it all down.

Cecilie was eating. Jan was sitting passively on his chair, his hands on his lap, not a movement.

I went over to them. 'Hiya, Johnny. How's it going?'

His eyes glinted, his head quivered warily and, without turning, he looked in my direction. His eyelids trembled, as though in some discreet way he was semaphoring a distress call to the outside world: *Help! I'm being kept prisoner! I want to get out …*

I glanced at his untouched plate. 'You have to eat, you know!

It's snowing and when you've eaten we can go outside and – have a snowball fight or something like that.'

He moved his lips soundlessly, like a fish on land. I swallowed hard. At once I felt sympathy for this tiny mite who had had such an aberrant start to his life.

I sat at the place set for me. 'Well, I'm definitely as hungry as a wolf!' I began to load my plate. Cecilie and Hans watched, like two public officials checking the composition of my diet. 'I'm going to wolf this down. My first name, Varg, means wolf, you know. So perhaps I ought to say I'm going to varg it down, eh?'

I had his attention now. He looked at me from a closer distance than before.

'And you … You're going to jan it down, you are. I'm sure of that. As hungry as a varg and as hungry as a jan – that's about the same. Don't you think?'

He nodded.

Cecilie flashed a sudden smile and Hans sent me a nod of acknowledgement.

'So I think I'll swap your food around. Watch … back in the pan with this and a hot rissole in its place. There we are. Hot sauce. And then we shovel a potato onto there. Nothing better for small famished vargs and jans than a bit of gravy and potatoes, eh? And what a big boy you are. You definitely don't have any problems using a knife and a fork, do you. When you're even bigger you'll be driving a car, and if you drive a car you've got be able to lick the easy things, like eating with your knife and fork …'

With careful movements, he grabbed first the knife, then the fork. Slowly he pushed a bit of potato through the gravy onto the fork and, like a gourmet chef ready to sample, lifted the fork to his mouth, opened up and took the first tiny mouthful.

In silence, he continued to eat. He cut up the rissole into small pieces, and when the first one had been eaten, I put another on his plate. 'Jan-hungry boys always eat two rissoles,' I said. 'Minimum.'

I was almost fainting with hunger myself, so I used the

opportunity, while he was eating, to stuff down two or three rissoles. Hans, happy now, took a seat at the neighbouring table and poured himself a cup of coffee from a flask.

Cecilie eyed me across the table with a warm smile. 'Now we're almost like a little family, Varg.'

'Yes, aren't we.'

She was right. If anyone had peeped through the window they would have seen a peaceful little mini-family, Mum, Dad and small boy – and there was Uncle Hans dropping by – sitting round the meal table at the back-end of the day. None of us said anything, but I was afraid that was how it was at most family meal tables. Conversation had not been that lively when it was Beate, Thomas and I, either. The food was delicious, we ate, and there was more than enough for one sitting.

In the end, he was obviously full. He sat back heavily in his chair and a glow of satisfaction flitted across his face.

'Pudding?' Hans asked.

'What is there?'

'Prune compote with milk and sugar.'

'Sounds fantastic, if you ask me. What do you say, Johnny?'

He nodded with a smile on his thin, pressed lips.

'You heard what Johnny said,' I said. 'We would like prune compote!'

It arrived on the table, and everyone ate. Even Hans on the neighbouring table sneaked an extra dish. Unbidden, he topped up Cecilie's coffee and mine. The family idyll was so perfect that the catastrophe, from all statistical calculations, had to be imminent.

We three adults sat making small talk while Jan finished the whole dish of prune compote as well. Afterwards I asked: 'And what would you like to do now, Johnny?'

This time he turned his head. He looked me straight in the eye, offended that I had forgotten. 'You said … a snow ball fight.'

'So I did! Is that what you fancy?'

He nodded.

'Can Hans and Cecilie join in, too?'

He shifted his gaze from one to the other and at length he nodded. They smiled gently, happy not to be excluded from the game.

We went outside. It had stopped snowing, but luckily there were enough snowflakes left for us to be able to make a few snowballs, even though they were pretty flimsy and they disintegrated when we tried to throw them.

Nevertheless, we stuck with it for as long as Jan wanted, and he took part in the fight with a passion. When he got his first hit, a snowball that turned to powder on my nose, he laughed out loud, and when we aimed at him but missed, on purpose, he grinned with pleasure.

In the end, the fight flagged of its own accord. As we went back inside, I put my arm round his shoulder and said: 'That was fun, wasn't it.'

'Mm,' he said with a nod.

'What would you like to do now?'

He peered up with a start. 'Wanna go home.'

The door closed behind us, and both Hans and Cecilie held their breath.

I said: 'I was wondering if Hans had some hot chocolate for us today, Johnny …'

Hans nodded in confirmation.

'Then we can talk about that while we're drinking. Agreed?'

He sent me a sceptical look. Then a reluctant nod.

We went back into the refectory and Hans flitted into the kitchen. Cecilie and I sat down with Jan at the same table as before.

I patted him gently on the hand and said: 'Do you know why you're here with us, Johnny?'

He shook his head from side to side.

'You arrived here yesterday, you know …' As he didn't react, I added: 'We came here in my car. You remember that anyway, don't you?'

He nodded.

'But do you remember what happened … before that?'

He looked at me with big, shiny eyes.

'You don't?'

Again he shook his head, but with more hesitation this time.

'You don't remember … that you were alone with … your father? Your dad?'

Again came a few powerful semaphore signals from his eyelids. But he said nothing, just blinked several times.

'You don't remember … the accident?'

He shaped his lips. 'A …'

'Yes?'

He shook his head firmly. 'Nope,' he said.

Hans returned from the kitchen with hot chocolate for us all. Cecilie pushed one cup over to Jan, who grabbed it instantly and put it to his mouth.

'Careful!' she said. 'It's hot.'

He took a big swig, didn't react, but a shiver ran through him, and he put down the cup straightaway.

'But you remember your mum coming home?' I continued. 'That's what you told me yesterday.'

His face seemed to close again. 'Nope,' he repeated, looking down.

Cecilie sent me an admonitory glance.

'Well, so … let's not talk about that any more,' I said lightly. 'Is the chocolate good? For famished boys?'

He squinted up. There was a wary appraisement in his eyes that had not been there before. Then it was gone, and he nodded in silence, raised the cup to his mouth and took another swig, more cautious this time and still without saying anything.

'Well …' I motioned to Hans and we went into the vestibule, leaving Cecilie with Jan.

'I heard Langeland, the solicitor, had rung you.'

'Yes, he … we were at university together. Moderate rebels, both of us,' he said with a tiny grin.

'He told you everything?'

'Yes, I was given the whole story. But I had no idea that Vibecke and Svein were his foster parents. Her name was Størset when I knew them.'

'Yes, you must have been fellow students, too?'

'Yes. She and Jens were, I suppose, almost … an item for a while.'

'They were a couple?'

'Yes, but not for long. And later we lost contact, all of us.'

'Not her and Langeland though. He's their family solicitor, as I'm sure he said.'

'Indeed, so I understand.'

'But you didn't have any contact, I gather?'

'Not with Vibecke and Svein. Jens and I met up on the odd evening over a beer or two, but nothing more than that. As time went on we developed … in different directions. He became a law-abiding citizen, I …'

'Became an outlaw?'

He grinned. 'No, no. But you know how it is, Varg. You, me and the law are not always on the same wavelength, are we.'

'No, you may be right there. Did he say any more about … Vibecke?'

'No, he didn't. He was most concerned with Jan. And his state of mind.'

'Good. What do *you* think? He's thawed a bit now, hasn't he.'

'You've done a great job, Varg. But I still think we should consider hospitalisation.'

'Let's give him one more night, eh?'

'OK. I'll go with that.'

We went back to Cecilie and Jan. 'Must be bedtime soon, right?' I said. 'Are there any exciting books up there?'

Cecilie nodded. 'The one we started yesterday was nice, anyway. About Winnie the Pooh.'

'I'll come up with you.'

On the stairs I said to her: 'Shall I take this shift?'

'Would you like to?'

'One of us definitely ought to be here, and since you did last night then …'

She nodded. 'It would be nice to go home and change clothes anyway.'

She still helped Jan put on his pyjamas, wash and clean his teeth, though. When finally he was in bed, she sat on the chair beside him and asked: 'Should Varg read perhaps?'

He looked at me.

'I'm wolf-keen to read,' I said.

He lowered his head stiffly, and Cecilie and I exchanged places.

'Here,' she said, and I began to read. '"The Piglet lived in a very grand house in the middle of a beech tree, and the beech tree was in the middle of the forest, and the Piglet lived in the middle of the house. Next to his house was a piece of broken board which had 'TRESPASSERS W' on it. When Christopher Robin asked the Piglet what it meant, he said it was his grandfather's name, and had been in the family for a long time."'

Cecilie sat on the other chair and stayed there until Jan's eyes had begun to flicker. When he seemed to be falling asleep, we motioned to each other and crept into the corridor.

We were standing at the top of the stairs. In the distance other noises came from the house: the television set on the ground floor, the hissing in the pipes and excited falsetto voices from one of the other rooms.

She said: 'In a way, this has been a nice day.'

I nodded and smiled.

She came over to me, put her arms around my neck and gave me a hug. I could feel her warm, light body against mine as the door behind us banged open. Like lovers with a bad conscience we jumped apart and turned around.

Jan had opened the door and now he was coming towards us with his head down, not looking ahead. 'Don't!' he shouted before hitting me in the stomach like a battering ram. For a second or two I stood swaying. Then I lost my balance and fell backwards down the steep stairs.

14

So Cecilie had to spend the night there after all. I was driven to A & E by Hans who had only just managed to squeeze himself in behind the wheel of the Mini. There, they confirmed a bad strain and a pulled muscle in my right arm, but as the on-duty doctor laconically added: 'If you hadn't grabbed hold of the railing, things could have been a lot worse for you.'

'What the hell was that all about?' Hans had asked me on the way there.

'Don't ask me! But it's given me something to mull over ...'

Again and again I went back over the absurd moment when I lost my footing and lurched down the stairs. I struck out blindly with my right arm, grabbed hold of the railing, lost my grip, got hold of another support, gripped and held on so tightly that I broke my fall but pulled a muscle in my arm, which felt as if it had come out of the socket and would never settle back.

For a second or two I seemed to have passed out. Then I heard Cecilie from above: 'Varg! Are you alright?' – and Hans come charging out of the vestibule office: 'What the hell's going on?'

I turned over and crawled up into a kneeling position before slowly getting to my feet. I looked up the stairs. There were Cecilie and Jan standing together. She was holding his arms tight while both stared down at me as if they had seen a ghost.

I met Jan's gaze. It was black with fury.

'But, Johnny, I thought we were friends.'

'I hate you! I hate you!' he screamed, his face bright red.

'Now, now ... Don't say that,' Cecilie said in a consoling tone of voice, but who she was consoling I was not at all sure. 'Come on ...'

She led Jan back into the bedroom while Hans supported me

out of the building and to my car. When A & E were finished with me, he said: 'I can drive you home, Varg. I don't live that far away.'

'Well, I'm not going to say no. I'm not sure if I'm strong enough to change gear at this moment.'

That night I slept even worse. I lay brooding until the early hours, and when I did finally fall asleep I was drawn into a night-marish dream where once again I mixed up Jan with Thomas, and on waking I was confused as to which of them kept pushing me down the steep stairs again and again. And the matter was not made any better by Beate replacing Cecilie at the top of the stair-case, with a gloating expression on her face: What did I say? Even this is too much for you!

In the end, when I got up, my whole body hurt and a headache was pounding away behind my forehead. I rang the office and explained the situation to them. They wished me all the best and said I shouldn't concern myself about Jan. They had already con-ferred with Cecilie and relief was on its way. 'Besides Hans Haavik already has competent staff out there, so everything is in hand, Varg,' they comforted.

A little later Cecilie rang and said the same.

'And what about you, what are you doing?' I asked.

'After two nights at my post I will be taking a day off, at home,' she said. 'And you relax,' she added with an undertone I thought I recognised from the other woman with whom I had shared the last years of my life, intonation that bespoke mistrust and scepticism.

'And Jan, did he say anything – afterwards?'

'No. He fell into a kind of coma. Hans is getting Marianne out there this morning, and then it's up to her. I'm afraid it will be hospitalisation. But you …'

'Yes?' There was another sound in my head, as if I were in a concrete cellar.

'Neither Hans nor I have mentioned a word of this to the – police. But perhaps you ought to contact them yourself. I mean … with reference to what he said to you on Tuesday.'

'Yes ... I'll see.'

For an instant I could see them all together. Vibecke Skarnes and Jens Langeland. Mette Olsen and Terje Hammersten. Hans Haavik and Cecilie. Jan coming towards me like a torpedo: *I hate you! I hate you!* And what he had said to me on Tuesday: *Mummy did it.*

In my mind I balanced them against one another: Mette Olsen with or without Terje Hammersten in one pan of the scales and Vibecke Skarnes in the other.

I had only a vague image of Svein Skarnes from a black and white family photo. After forcing down a skimpy breakfast, I decided to do something about just that.

15

Skarnes Import turned out to be a very small company. They had offices on the second floor of a building in the part of Olav Kyrres gate that had survived the 1916 town fire. I was received by a secretary with red-rimmed eyes and a sniffly nose which she tended, throughout our conversation, with a tiny crumpled lace handkerchief that could hardly absorb more moisture than a stamp.

She introduced herself as Randi Borge and burst into floods of tears when I explained the purpose of my visit. Age-wise, I would have put her at about forty. She had groomed dark blonde hair and was wearing a tight-fitting black dress that, from where I was standing, on my side of her reception desk, put me in far from a funereal mood.

She kindly explained that, apart from Svein Skarnes and herself, the company had consisted of one technician, Harald Dale, who was out on a maintenance job that day.

'No one else? But they're heavy machines you import, aren't they?'

'Yes, they are. Photocopiers and franking machines. But we hire in extra help for when the biggest machines have to be positioned and installed.'

'And what were Svein Skarnes' duties?'

'But …' She sent me an angry look. 'That's obvious! It was his company. He'd built it up from scratch. First he worked for – one of the bigger enterprises. Then he realised there could be just as much money working for himself. And there was. All the contracts, all the marketing, all the dealing with customers … that was his responsibility. And he travelled a lot. We have customers up and down south-west Norway, from Ålesund to Flekkefjord.'

'I see. I didn't mean it like that. But what will happen now, now that he's no longer …?'

Her eyes widened as though the future was revealing itself in all its gruesome detail to her inner eye.

'Will his wife take on the company, do you think?'

'Vibecke!' It sounded like a trumpet blast, rich with contempt. 'Can't imagine that at all.'

'No?'

'No, she simply doesn't have – the capacity. So unless Harald can take over …' Again the tears burst forth. 'Well, then I don't know. I suppose I'll have to go to the job centre …'

I leaned across the reception desk. She looked up at me. Her shapely legs pointed flawlessly downwards beneath the short dress, and I had to concede that she made an extremely tasty impression, perfect bordering on almost painful. The only thing that spoiled the image was the tearful expression on her face and her red-rimmed eyes; however, that lent her an even more human aspect, a touch of openness and intimacy that invited closer attention.

'Tell me, *fru* Borge …'

'I'm not married …'

'Indeed?'

She met my gaze and blushed. 'What was it you were going to – say?'

'Yes, it was … In such a small company as this and with, if I have understood correctly, Skarnes and you alone here in the office for most of the time …'

Her eyes flashed and the redness of her cheeks assumed a more fiery hue. 'What do you mean?'

'No, no. No offence intended. I was just thinking … People talk. You may have had lunch together. You knew each other better than you would have done in a larger company, I would imagine.'

'Yes, we did. And so?'

'We at social services are most concerned about Jan. About how he's going to be. And so I wondered … if we could form a picture of what the relationship was like at home. With his foster parents.'

'But can't Vibecke tell you that?'

'Yes, but you know how it is. Often an outside view may be necessary. Those involved in the situation often become myopic.'

'Well, I didn't see much of either her or the boy. They very rarely came by the office. That's also one of the reasons there won't be any more … now that Svein …'

Once again her voice faltered. Her expression was distant. It struck me that she bore a slight resemblance to Vibecke. Or a roughly ten-year older version of her. They had the same regular features, the same well-groomed hair, they held their heads in the same slightly proud way. I wondered if it was Skarnes' taste in women that was being reflected, in both his secretary and his spouse. Not bad taste anyway, but a bit conventional, perhaps …'

'What was he like, Svein Skarnes?' I asked tentatively.

'I …' She searched for words, and when she eventually found them, there was a new warmth in her voice. 'He was a good person. Kind to other people. A good boss and one who never let the demand for maximum profit control the business. We had lots of small customers – small firms, many of them in outlying areas, and he insisted they were given the best possible deals and offered fair after-sales. In fact, Harald said that if things went on as they were doing, they would have to employ at least one more technician to take care of the more remote districts. Well, I think … Lots of problems can be solved over the phone, but of course it's Harald who's sent off if there's anything serious.'

'And, on a personal level? How long had you known him?'

'Right from the start.'

'The start of …?'

She rolled her eyes. 'When the company was set up, five years ago. We had the five-year anniversary last autumn. An anniversary dinner at Sunnfjord Hotel in Førde.'

'In Førde? Why there?'

'Well ... it was in connection with a sales meeting. Both Harald and I were up there anyway, and so Svein said: Today I think we'll treat ourselves to a decent anniversary dinner.'

'Aha. And Vibecke, *fru* Skarnes, was she with you?'

'No, she certainly wasn't! Why should she be? She hardly set her foot in here, as I said, unless there was something she needed copying.'

'And Jan didn't either, from what I understand?'

'No. I only saw him a few times. The boy was Svein's big worry, I can tell you.'

'In what sense?'

'Listen *herr* ... Veum, is that right?'

'Yes.'

'I don't have any ... any children myself. But I can easily understand ... the longing for a child. And I know Svein took it very hard, that he and Vibecke couldn't have ... their own children. So when the opportunity came along, he made a quick decision and said yes. First to the enquiry about whether they wanted to be foster parents, later to the adoption.'

'And how did it work out?'

'At first everything seemed to be going well. But it turned out that the tiny boy ... he was a time bomb waiting to go off. There were so many strange reactions in that boy, and thinking back to all the incidents Svein told me about ... once – well, no point covering it up – a few months ago, he came to the office in the morning and I could see that something was bothering him. In the end, I couldn't restrain myself. I went into his room – there ...' She tilted her head towards an open door behind her. Through the opening I could make out a large desk and a vacant chair. 'He told me that Johnny boy had bitten his hand the night before! And I do mean bitten. You should've seen the mark! When I was told on Wednesday morning what had happened and heard that ... You can imagine what thoughts went through my head, can't you.'

'Naturally.'

She looked at me, with insistent eyes now. 'Could that be what happened, this time as well?'

I met her gaze. Her eyes had a shimmer of green in the blue, like an ice wall in a glacier. 'To be quite frank, *frøken* Borge, I don't know. But, yes, it's certainly a possibility.'

She gave a faint nod, as if she had had her worst fears confirmed.

'But tell me ... He never mentioned anything about ... Did you have any impression of what the relationship was like, between him and Vibecke?'

Her face wavered between professionalism and personal feelings. The impeccable shell cracked and the teenage girl she had once been burst through. 'Not so good, I think,' she let slip with a tiny sob.

'And what do you base that on?'

'The evening in Førde I mentioned just now.'

'The anniversary dinner?'

'Yes. We sat in the bar talking, it was more personal than it had ever ... Svein and I.'

'Mm?'

'It was after Harald had disappeared with, er, well ... a woman he met at the bar. And that was precisely why ... I mean Harald lives with a really sweet girl, and that was the reason that Svein and I sat talking about ... that sort of thing. How some people can never control themselves, and how mortifying it must feel to be ... the one who is left on their own after it's all over, or the one who may have a suspicion that everything is not all as it ought to be ...'

I coated my voice with velvet. 'And that may have been the situation with Svein and Vibecke, too?'

'Yes. And it ... really got to him.' Instantly there were tears in her eyes, as if this was about her.

'And his own house was spick and span?'

She glowered at him. 'What do you mean? Of course it was!' Her cheeks flared up.

'Yes, by all means, but ... he was away a lot travelling. You said that yourself. And women are in bars everywhere, not only in Førde, aren't they.'

'Yes, that's true, but the way he put it to me … at that time … he was genuinely upset, Veum. He wasn't like that. Not Svein. I would've … noticed.' Again the distant look in her eyes, and the small, almost unnoticeable stiffening of the neck, as though she was unconsciously studying herself in a mirror no one else saw.

'So she had someone else? Was that what he was trying to say?'

'Trying! He … well …' All of a sudden her professional super-ego had taken control again. 'I can't see that this has anything to do at all with social services! They were tied to each other through their common responsibility for Jan, and that may have been what bothered him most of all, what would happen to Jan, if Vibecke … left him.'

'Well, he was a man in his best years. There may have been others who would have proffered a helping hand?'

Mirror-woman made one last appearance, and for a second she sat with closed eyes, as though to keep out all the brutality of the world. On re-opening them, she was a hundred per cent in the here and now. 'Was there anything else I could help you with, *herr* Veum?'

'No, I don't think so. Not for the moment.'

I had a question on the tip of my tongue, but I let it lie. I had no right to ask it. The question of how far her consolation had gone that anniversary night in Førde last autumn …

16

The time had come. I couldn't find any more excuses, neither to myself nor to others. There was nothing else to do but eat humble pie and call on the Muus that roared, in the lion's den, the new Bergen Police Headquarters, built in 1965.

From the telephone box outside the police station I rang Hans Haavik and received confirmation of what I already assumed would happen. He and Marianne Storetvedt had agreed that hospitalisation was the only solution, and Marianne and one of the assistants out there had driven Jan to the Children's Psychiatric Centre in Haukeland.

'But how are you, Varg? Can you feel anything after the fall?'

'Yes, I can but … I'm fine. I'm just a little bruised.'

'Right, well, hope you're better soon.'

I thanked him and rang off.

The duty officer informed me that Inspector Muus was in, and I took the lift up to his office, which was on the third floor overlooking Domkirkgate, where the cathedral was situated, and very little else. Muus himself towered up behind his desk, as fierce as a matron at the annual meeting of the missionary society. When I showed my face through the crack of the door, he seemed to be refusing to believe that this could be true. 'Yes?' he said brusquely. 'What is it you require?'

I sent him a disarming smile. 'I have a confession to make.'

'You, too?'

'Yes? Are there more?'

He swept this aside. 'Spit it out!'

'The day before yesterday, when we were driving Jan to Haukedalen, he said something to us.'

'Did he now?'

'He said: "Mummy did it."'

He didn't bat an eyelid. 'I see. And?'

'Well … I thought you might like to know.'

'And that thought took about forty-eight hours to reach base?'

'There was no one on duty, if I can put it like that,' I ventured, but it didn't meet with approval.

'And what's the reason for your coming here now with this?'

'Mm … she's at large, isn't she?'

'You have some idea of where she might be staying?'

For a second my eyes relinquished their hold on his. 'No, that …'

'But there's something you've missed, Veum.' He sent me a triumphant look.

'Really? And that is …'

'She's come forward.'

'Come forward! *Fru* Skarnes?'

'Yes.'

'When did that happen?'

'Early today, on the recommendation of her solicitor, *herr* Langeland.'

'Yes, I suppose I knew,' I mumbled.

'She's being questioned now, by Inspector Lyngmo.'

'Questioned? So you …'

'No, we haven't, Veum. And you haven't brought anything new to the case. In fact, she has confessed.'

I found it difficult to understand what he meant. 'Confessed?'

He raised his voice a fraction. 'Yes, she's confessed. Something wrong with your hearing? She admitted she'd pushed her husband down the cellar stairs that day during a marital row. The defence will, of course, plead involuntary manslaughter and that it happened in self-defence. But we'll see. We're making further investigations, naturally, but in essence the case is as good as solved. I doubt that comes as much of a surprise to you either, in light of the information you've just brought us. *Mummy did it.* Wasn't that how it went?'

'Yes, it … And if she's really confessed, then … I suppose it no longer has anything to do with me.'

He raised his eyebrows sardonically, the clearest indication of a facial expression since I had arrived. 'No, I suppose, strictly speaking, indeed it does not.'

'But you're aware he has another mother, aren't you? He was adopted.'

He looked at me without enthusiasm. 'And this mother …'

'Mette Olsen. Living with an old acquaintance of yours. Terje Hammersten.'

'Hammersten? But –'

'If I were you, I would …'

His voice rose a notch. 'What I was trying to say, Veum, before you interrupted me … This mother, has she also confessed?'

'No, of course not.'

'Exactly.' He stood up behind his desk. 'Do you know what you remind me of? You remind me of those bloody private eyes that swan around in American films thinking they're so much bloody better than the police.'

'Uhuh?'

'Yes. So now, would you be so kind as to hop it? We have more useful things to do here than exchange views with representatives of the social services.'

'Perhaps social services has more useful things to do as well.'

'I don't doubt it. Have a good life, Veum. I hope I never see you again.'

He was mistaken, sad to say. Sad to say for us both. Later I often wondered if it was then that the idea was first sown in me: if all else failed … start up on my own. But I never reminded him. That would have been taking the joke too far.

At nine that night there was a ring at my door. I went to open. Cecilie was standing outside, made up to the nines and wearing a slim dark coat I had never seen her in before. She held out a net bag. 'I've brought a couple of bottles of red wine. Can I come in?'

17

Twenty-one years later she asked me with a slight blush, on the bench in Fjellveien: 'Do you remember that we had a – fling at that time, Varg?'

I gave a wry grin. 'Is that so?'

Yes, I remembered we had had what she called a fling. I remembered the iron tang of the red wine she brought with her that Thursday night in 1974, with the case apparently solved and Jan in specialist care; I remembered her lips tasting of the same, and the compact little body that she could never quite keep still, but wriggling and squirming whether on top or underneath, so lively that I slipped in and out of her like an inexperienced plumber on his very first solo call-out. She had kissed me, hard and firm, and there had never been any doubt about what she wanted. Afterwards we were agreed that it had been our way of celebrating the end of the case. Later we repeated the celebrations on two or three occasions before the whole thing, for reasons I had never quite been able to articulate, just petered out, becoming fleeting memories, a quick raid on my recall faculties when later in my life I was served a red wine with a similar flavour.

Yes, I did remember. I had not forgotten. But there were so many other things that happened that year, far too many other agonising incidents.

The investigation ended with Vibecke Skarnes being charged with involuntary manslaughter. The case went straight to court where she was defended with great passion by Jens Langeland.

I was myself sitting on one of the court benches for several of the days and I was impressed by Langeland's performance. He used Vibecke Skarnes's confession to maximum effect, and in court a far more negative impression was given of Svein Skarnes than I had received from Randi Borge. Langeland presented the awkward home situation, with a very unstable adopted child requiring a lot of attention. Vibecke Skarnes claimed that her husband had made unjustified accusations of infidelity against her, accompanied with violence, and just such a row had ended with the fatal fall down the cellar stairs, a fall caused by her pushing her husband away so that she would not be beaten up in, what Langeland called in his final summing up, nothing less than self-defence. She also claimed that Skarnes, on several occasions, had shown unnecessary brutality towards their tiny adopted son.

These claims were rejected by the opposing side in no uncertain terms. I remembered one day in particular when one character witness after the other testified what a decent fellow Svein Skarnes had been, and that they had never seen a hint of maltreatment towards his wife or had any reason to suspect that anything of the kind had taken place. Randi Borge took her stand, even more attractively dressed than when I visited her in the office, and gave Skarnes the best possible character reference; it was so convincing that Jens Langeland had squeezed in a couple of well camouflaged but nonetheless quite defamatory insinuations about the kind of relationship there might have been between this magnificent boss and his secretary. He was soon called to order, but I could see that the jury had taken the point.

However, the court was never entirely convinced that the tumble down the stairs was a pure accident in an impassioned situation. Despite what was referred to as mitigating circumstances, Vibecke Skarnes was convicted. She was sentenced to two and a half years' imprisonment for involuntary manslaughter, and the subsequent High Court appeal from both sides did nothing to change the judgement. I was present at the court's final pronouncement, and it was with a feeling of sadness that I left the courtroom that day with a cursory nod to Vibecke Skarnes.

After emergency hospitalisation in Haukeland, Jan was given treatment for what Marianne Storetvedt termed reactive attachment disorders and placed in Haukedalen. In the autumn of 1974, on the initiative of Hans Haavik, he was transferred to a foster home in Sunnfjord, where the combination of a smaller community and life on a farm working at full capacity was assumed to be a good way to lead him back onto the right path, to make him a benefit to society.

Both Cecilie and I had kept tabs on him as well as we could during the six months he was in therapy. We went for walks with him on Geitanuken or other mountains in Åsane and around Bergen. We went out on the fjord with boat-savvy social workers and taught him how to fish. One June day in 1974 we went to Vollane to swim, and I can remember – yes, I remembered Cecilie in a very small bikini, white with green dots, and nipples that went erect after a cold dive. That was another of the times when we rounded off the day with a very private party in Telthussmauet. But it was a grey, rainy summer, and there were not many swimming trips.

We were like a little family, a bit maladjusted and dysfunctional, as families with such children often are. I also remembered the afternoon in September that year when Hans called us into his office after we had taken Jan on a trip to Akvariet, the sea centre in Bergen. He told us he had found a foster home for him in Sunnfjord and that he himself would travel up with him the day after. I could hardly look at Cecilie. In a way it was as if our own little child was being taken away from us, our own difficult little sprog. And perhaps that was the real reason it never came to more than the two or three celebrations between us: the separation we both felt when Jan was sent to Sunnfjord that September.

I remembered him the way he had been in those six months. From the apathetic tiny boy we had seen in the first days he had developed into an active and vigorous boy, a bit too vigorous at times. He didn't know where to draw the line and sometimes he seemed to be deliberately provoking us, to make trouble, to create an unpleasant atmosphere and evoke rejection. 'Extremely characteristic of children with early emotional damage,' Marianne informed us in a conversation we had with her. 'So what can we do?' I had asked, and she had looked at us with a tiny resigned smile: 'Hope the therapy helps, hope that he gets clear signals from the adult world and that someone sets new boundaries for the life he has to teach himself to live.' We had nodded in agreement, but after leaving her we felt as despondent as we had when we arrived.

'What are the people he's living with like?' I had asked Hans that September day. 'Decent folk. I know them personally. Klaus and Kari Libakk. Klaus is a cousin of mine. They run a farm in Angedalen, north-east of Førde.' 'Does he have local support?' 'Of course. Social services in Sunnfjord has put one of their own on the case ...' He flicked through a few papers. 'Grethe Millingen. That name mean anything to you?' 'No,' I said and Cecilie just shook her head sadly.

In the car back to town we had little to say to each other. We both sat enclosed in our own worlds, and when we parted neither of us saw any reason to celebrate anything.

It was a miserable year in general. The period of separation came to an end and the divorce from Beate was executed without mercy. We negotiated a visiting agreement for Thomas and it wasn't long before it came to my ears that she had got herself a new friend, some teacher, Wiik, whom Thomas called Lasse. In my welfare work I regularly became frustrated and there were a number of episodes that indicated that perhaps I was not the right man to tackle all the challenges I confronted. The whole thing came to an end the year after when, under strong pressure from above, I was requested to look around for something else to do.

I had a distressing feeling that life was passing me by before my very eyes, outside my windows, and that feeling was not exactly diminished when in August of that year I turned Muus's nightmare into reality and started my own little firm as a private investigator in Strandkaien, a street fronting the harbour and a block away from Marianne Storetvedt.

Nine years later, I received a phone call from Førde.

18

A private investigator's office can be a depressing place. It's not a lot better when the rains beat against the windowpanes, the floods start and there is only a limited number of tickets left for the ark. The call from Førde did nothing to improve my mood. Quite the opposite, it took the ground away from beneath me.

Her voice was both hoarse and pleasant, in an extremely sensual way. 'Veum? Varg Veum?'

'That's me.'

'Grethe Mellingen here. From social services in Sogn and Fjordane. I'm based in Førde.'

I had an unpleasant sensation in my abdominal region. 'Right! How can I help you?'

'It's about a client of ours. One Jan Egil Skarnes, seventeen years old.'

'Yes, I know who you're talking about. But ...'

'It's just terrible. I don't know if you heard the two o'clock news, did you?'

'No, I haven't ...'

'There's been a double murder here. In Angedalen. Both of Jan Egil's foster parents.'

'What was that?' The glaring ceiling lamp seemed to have grown, filling the whole of my head with intense light, an interrogator's lamp from my unconscious.

'Yes and ... I'm afraid there is every reason to believe that Jan Egil did it, because he's holed up in a neighbouring valley and refuses to speak to anyone except – you.'

'Me? But I haven't had anything to do with him since ...'

'And he's not alone. He has someone with him. A girl from the neighbouring farm.'

'As a hostage or what?'

'We don't know. They're about the same age, anyway. But the police have contact with him via a loud-hailer and he's told them he won't talk to anyone except … you.'

'I'm amazed he can remember me!'

'I was summoned there myself to negotiate with him, but … I'll only talk to Varg! he shouted. Varg? Who's Varg? we asked. Varg, he repeated, and I contacted Hans Haavik to see if he knew who he was talking about, and he referred me to you.'

I swallowed. 'So then …'

'The question is just … how quickly can you get to Førde, Varg?'

I looked at my watch. 'There are several hours till the afternoon boat leaves, and I have no idea about plane routes. But … if I jump in my car now, if I'm lucky with the ferries and ignore speed limits, I should be there in five to five and a half hours.'

'Can you do that?'

'I'll have to, won't I! How will I find you?'

'I'll meet you … Do you know where Sunnfjord Hotel is?'

'Yes.'

'Go there and I'll meet you in reception.'

'OK, let's say that. But it'll take me getting on for half an hour to leave. I have the car parked …'

'Yes, yes. Just come as quickly as you can. We're relying on you …'

People had had their fingers burnt doing that before, but I didn't say that to her. I switched off the lights, locked the office and hared off up to Skansen to fetch the car. Barely half an hour later, I was on my way.

It had turned dark by the time I reached Førde a little before nine that evening, and it had not been an easy drive. If it had been dark in Masfjorden before, the dense rain had not made it lighter. I stopped in Brekke to wait for the ferry, but once over the fjord I broke all the speed limits that existed in the hope that every available variety of local police official was in Førde and Angedalen on this dark October day which was to go down in the local history annals under the headline: *Double Murder in Angedalen.*

There is much that could be said about Førde and most of it has already been said. In many ways it is the centre of the Vestland region, south-west Norway, in reality it is a huge crossroads with a few buildings thrown in for good measure. I passed the bridge over the Jølstra River and bore left towards Sunnfjord Hotel. The rain was hammering down on the car roof and I pulled the hood of my all-weather jacket tightly over my head as I sprinted, bent-over, the few metres to the main entrance.

Grethe Mellingen realised who I was, got up off a chair and came towards me. 'Varg?'

I nodded and we shook hands.

'I'm Grethe. Come with me!'

She looked to be two or three years older than me and had sleek, golden yellow hair which hung in damp clumps on either side of her symmetrical face. I immediately noticed her eyes, light blue, as if made of glass. She was dressed in full rain gear, dark green from the sou' wester to the high wellies. 'We have no time to lose,' she added as we charged from the hotel entrance to the car and tore open the doors on both sides.

'That way,' she said pointing west, towards the main hospital. 'Just follow Angedalsvegen and we'll see the lights when we're there. We can only go on foot in Trodalen.'

'Trodalen?'

'Yes, you may have heard of it?'

'Vaguely.'

'Trodalen Mads – does that mean anything to you?'

'An old criminal case, isn't it?'

'Yes, I can tell you all about it – later.'

'But the old case has no connection with this one, I suppose?'

'No, no. Of course not.'

'Why don't you tell me – how Johnny boy is?'

'Jan? You call him Johnny boy, do you?'

'We used to call him that – ten years ago.'

The road climbed abruptly to Angedalen now, to the long valley that lay like a hollow in the countryside between the municipalities of Naustdal and Jølster. I had never been there before.

'Well, what should I say? He hasn't been so easy, but … we thought things were going better now. At any rate, this came as a shock to us all. Like a bolt from the blue.'

'What did he do?'

'Now we don't know yet if it was him who did it …'

'Don't we?'

'Well, it's like this. His foster parents are called Kari and Klaus Libakk. One of their neighbours called the police. He thought something must have been amiss because he hadn't seen either Kari or Klaus since Sunday, and the only person who went to the cowshed was Jan Egil. He made up some pretext about wanting to see the Libakks and asked after Klaus, but Jan Egil behaved so strangely, said they were away and didn't know when they would be back. So this neighbour, Karl on the Hill, as we call him, contacted the local sergeant, who sent up one of his officers. And that was when everything came out.'

'Mm?'

'Jan Egil must have seen him coming because after the officer knocked on the door he suddenly saw Jan Egil and Silje racing up the mountainside behind the farm buildings, towards Trodalen.'

'And Silje, that's …'

'Silje Tveiten, she's from a neighbouring farm. But the worst of it all is …'

'Yes?'

'When the officer tried to follow them, Jan Egil fired a shot at him. A rifle shot.'

'Oh, bloody …'

'Then he gave up. And when he went back into the farmhouse

it was a gruesome sight that met him. At first the place seemed empty, but when he went to the first floor, into the bedroom … Klaus had been shot in the chest while he was still in bed. Kari must have tried to escape, because she was lying on the floor right in front of the window, shot in the back. There was blood everywhere!'

'But … had no one heard the shooting?'

'It's mid deer-hunting season, Varg. There's shooting at all hours.'

'And now they reckon it was Jan who shot them?'

'There was no sign of a break-in, so for the moment they haven't got anything else to go on, I'm afraid.'

'When did the murders take place?'

'I don't know, but all the indications are that the bodies have been lying there for a couple of days.'

'My God!'

'Yes, there's not a lot else you can say! And now he's holed himself up in the scree on the eastern side of Lake Trodalsvatn, not far from Strand.'

'Strand?'

'Yes, or Trodalsstrand. Where the murder took place in 1839.'

We passed a farmyard, and I slowed down. Round the next bend we were met by a mass of lights: brake lights, courtesy lights, headlights and torches. The exhaust fumes drifted like patches of mist over several of the cars parked in a line winding its way up a narrow gravel path to the north of the main road. At the very top a patrol car was parked across the path, blocking any movement in that direction. There was an ambulance with the side door open, the driver in conversation with a policeman. Beside the patrol car was another constable with his arms crossed, staring sternly ahead.

'Pull in there,' Grethe said, pointing to a narrow gap between a large Mercedes and a four-wheel drive Mitsubishi Pajero. I rammed the Mini halfway up the slope. From the boot I took my waterproof trousers I had had the foresight to bring with me. I always kept rubber boots there, in case I went fishing.

We trudged up to the patrol vehicles and the ambulance. They had gathered around the two vehicles, the whole caboodle: photographers under wide rain capes with their cameras held against their chests; radio commentators with portable recorders held in shoulder straps and microphones sticking out, as if to measure the moisture in the air; and veteran reporters with soaking wet, lit cigarettes between their lips, sou'westers and rain hats pulled down over their foreheads.

Grethe ploughed a way through the media throng for us before she was stopped abruptly by the brusque police officer. 'No one passes here!'

She gasped for breath. 'But we're on our way up to – negotiate. This is Veum, the social services man from Bergen that Jan Egil demanded to speak to.'

The uniformed officer gave me a sceptical look, then turned to the car. There were two others sitting there. He motioned to one of them to roll down the side window.

'It's that welfare bloke. They should be let through, shouldn't they?' he said in vernacular.

'Yeah, but Standal said that everyone should be escorted.' The officer got out of the car. He stuck out his hand and introduced himself. 'Reidar Ruset.' His face was thin and pale, his handshake wet and cold. 'In addition, they have to wear bulletproof vests.' He stretched into the car and pulled out two stiff, greyish-black vests.

With a little difficulty, we put the vests over our all-weather jackets. If nothing else, they provided a little extra warmth.

Reidar Ruset pointed up at the dark, tree-clad mountainside. 'On that mountain.'

We began walking. Directly in front of us lay an old hay barn. As we passed it, Grethe said: 'This is where he lived as an old man.'

'Who?' I asked.

'Trodalen Mads.'

No more was said. In the heavy rain and with only Reidar Ruset's head lamp as illumination we had more than enough to think about just looking where to put our feet. We followed the path upwards alongside a stone wall. Then we entered the forest, a mixture of deciduous and dark spruce trees. Neither of us said a word. Thoughts were ricocheting around my head, completely out of control.

Memories of 1974 ... the call-out to the accident in Wergeland-såsen, which would later turn into a crime scene, Jan and all the work with him, the search for Vibecke Skarnes, the confession, the trial and the six months with Jan afterwards, before he was sent up here. All this merged with the impressions I had formed during the hectic hour since I had met Grethe Mellingen: a possible double murder with Jan as the principal suspect, a boy fleeing with a girl of the same age, a boy who ten years earlier had pushed me down the stairs in a violent fit of anger ...

We waded up through withered ferns, bare blueberry bushes and a path that regularly became a rushing stream through the dense undergrowth. Now and then we passed a clearing with bare rock face. If we had cast our eyes across we would have glimpsed the lights from the farms at the furthest end of Angedalen valley, already a long way down. After a good half an hour we were at the top of the incline. We continued through the forest until we could make out black water. On both sides of the lake rose steep mountainsides. Even in the daylight Trodalen had to be a fairly gloomy place. Now, in the dark and the rain, it was just one black abyss in the night, a slumbering volcano which could erupt at any time.

Reidar Ruset pointed along the eastern bank of the lake. A powerful searchlight lit up the scree where the rough terrain and the crooked old tree trunks formed troll-like shapes on the mountainside. Around the searchlight we saw the flickering light of less powerful lamps. 'Over there.'

We followed him up the slope from the lake, fast at the

beginning, slower as we approached. We were almost there when it happened.

The rifle shot rang out like a whiplash in the darkness. With a splintering sound the glass lens of the large searchlight was smashed, there was a scream, followed by more, and the flickering lights in front of us suddenly scattered in all directions, away from the area where the searchlight had stood. Then it was dark. Completely dark.

Through the darkness came the sound of piercing laughter from somewhere up in the scree. It was an eerie, almost supernatural sound.

Reidar Ruset switched off his head lamp and mumbled in local tones between clenched teeth: 'Yeah, isn't it what they've always said? That there are ghosts here …'

'That's because they never found the body,' Grethe mumbled, shaking the rain off her sou'wester with a swish of her head.

19

Reidar Ruset beckoned to us to move forward again. Without the light from his head lamp it was even more difficult to see where we should walk. The terrain was trickier now, the path overgrown, impassable in places. The darkness lay thick around us, and it felt as though the rain had penetrated all the fibres of our clothing. Grethe had grabbed my hand tight. I kept close to Reidar Ruset, if for no other reason than not to lose sight of him.

Somewhere ahead we heard voices: a hushed animated discussion.

'Hello!' Ruset whispered.

'Reidar?' came the answer.

'I've got the bloke from Bergen with me.'

Something came crashing through the birch trees in front of us. A well-built man in a police uniform with a nose reminiscent of a deformed potato filled the path ahead of us in the evening gloom. Reidar Ruset stepped out of the undergrowth so as not to stand in his way and half-turned towards me.

'Sergeant Standal,' said the newcomer, holding out an ample wet hand.

'Veum,' I said, passing him mine.

'Good you could make it. I suppose Grethe's explained the situation to you?'

'In rough outline.'

'We have what we assume is a hostage situation. A killer on the run who has taken a girl from the neighbouring farm with him and has now holed himself up in the scree here. You heard the shot, I take it?'

'Yes.'

'He smashed our bloody searchlight! But you know the boy, I understand?'

'I wouldn't say that. I was involved in … had some dealings with him ten years ago in Bergen. I haven't had any contact with him since then.'

He came closer in the darkness. 'You operate as a kind of private investigator, I've been told.'

'Yes, I –'

'You can make ends meet doing that in Bergen, can you?'

'I'm surviving anyway.'

'Well, well. Each to his own, as the bride said. At any rate, the boy has informed us that he won't speak to anyone except you.'

'So I heard.'

'In fact … he said *to Varg*, and we found out, with the help of a bit of detective work – we country constables can do that too, you know – it had to be you.'

'I don't share my name with many, shall we say.'

'No, you don't. My name's Per Christian, so that's more like the opposite.'

Grethe cleared her throat impatiently behind us. 'Shall we try to make contact then or what?'

'Yes, yes, yes, of course. We're just chatting,' said the sergeant, looking as though he would love to continue. He angled his head and said, 'We've got a megaphone over here.'

We staggered on through the dark. Half hidden behind a clump of trees stood a handful of policemen. The metal on their weapons glinted, several had night sights.

They greeted us in low voices. One of them had a large battery-operated megaphone in his hand.

'Give me it, Flekke,' said the sergeant.

It was difficult to see him in the dark, but Flekke appeared to be a relatively young officer. He passed the megaphone to Standal, who passed it on to me with a sweep of his arm.

I took the megaphone. The amplifier was designed to hang over the shoulder from a broad strap. I grasped the handle, which was attached to the amplifier by a flexible cable.

Standal pointed upwards in the gloom. 'He's up there. You'll have to see if you can make contact, but … move around a bit. Don't stand on the same spot for long.'

I understood what he meant by that and instantly felt a chill go down my spine. I had been elevated, not to a place in heaven, but to a moving target.

The only place on my body that was dry was my mouth. 'Anyone got anything to drink?'

'Just water,' came a chuckle from somewhere in the dark.

'And coffee, boiled to death.'

'That's what I was after. Bit of water perhaps?'

From the murk came a bottle of mineral water. It had been drunk from, but I relied on Sogn and Fjordane germs being no more deadly than those from Hordaland, and took a good swig. I rinsed my mouth thoroughly before swallowing.

Then I cleared my throat, raised the megaphone to my mouth and called: 'Jan Egil! Are you there?'

The sound was muffled, dead, and young Flekke leant forward to the amplifier. 'You have to turn it on first.'

'Can you do that?'

He performed the action with a little click. A green light went on and I raised the megaphone again. This time the sound reverberated between the mountain walls: 'Jan Egil! Johnny boy! This is Varg here!'

Everything was quiet, both around me and in the dark night. All we heard were nature's own sounds: the rain against the trees, dripping leaves, the trickle of rivulets between our feet.

'Can you hear me?!'

No answer.

'You remember me! Varg from Bergen! You asked me to come and talk to you!'

Suddenly there came a shout from above: 'There ain't nothin' to talk about!'

'But *you* asked me to come here! I've driven all the way from Bergen just to meet you!'

Again there was a silence, as if he was thinking.

'It'd be nice to see you again! It's ten years since you left, isn't it! You've grown up since then!'

From above came a sound that we could not decipher.

'What was that? I didn't hear!'

'Bullshit!'

I lowered the megaphone and had a think. Then I raised it again. 'Cecilie says hello. You remember her, don't you!'

No answer.

'Johnny boy! Is it OK if I come up to you?'

Standal shook his head and raised a flat palm in the air, as if to say he could not allow that.

'Are you so keen to snuff it?!'

'No! But it's so tiring shouting at each other like this! I can come up and keep my distance. Then at least we can see each other!'

After a short pause, the answer came. 'Just you!' But there was no warmth in the intonation. He sounded more like a big troll trying to entice me out onto the bridge and thence down into the abyss.

'I don't know if I can allow this, Veum,' Standal said with heavy authority.

'It's why I was called in, wasn't it.'

'But you heard what he said.'

'He's a big mouth. Believe me. I've worked in social services and I know the type. He'd rather shoot himself than me.'

'Yes, and we'd rather not have any of that! We've got a murder case to solve.'

I waited for a while. Then I said: 'Do you have any idea where he is, more or less?'

'Yes, it was light when we came up here earlier today. Follow the path for forty to fifty metres until you see an uprooted tree. Then go straight up the scree from there. He's holed up behind a promontory of large rocks.'

'Have they got any food? Drink?'

'Haven't the foggiest.'

Again he raised the megaphone. 'Johnny boy!'

'Stop calling me that!'

'Jan Egil!'

No answer.

'Have you got any food up there? Anything to drink?'

'We've got enough to be getting on with!'

A short pause. I wasn't sure, but I had the feeling I'd heard a higher-pitched voice up there.

Then it came. 'You can bring a bit with you!'

I sent Standal a contented nod. 'There you go ... He won't shoot me until he's had something to eat anyway. What have you got?'

'We have some iron rations.'

'Spam?'

'No, some nutrition bars and that sort of thing. Energy-rich dried foods. And we've probably got some Coke back there, haven't we, boys?'

'If you mean Coca-Cola, then ...'

Chuckles broke out around us.

'Be careful, Varg!' Grethe grabbed my arm.

I nodded dolefully. 'Well, at least something will happen now. I could imagine a lot more tempting places to spend the night rather than up here.'

'Oh yes?' she whispered, with a sudden glint in her eye.

'Mm,' I answered, turning back to the sergeant.

Standal had found a plastic bag. In it he had put a few emergency rations and a big bottle of Coke. 'I still don't know if I like this, Veum. On your own head be it.'

A voice from the dark said: 'Perhaps he ought to take a handgun with him?'

Standal fixed his eyes on me. 'Have you had any weapon training?'

'No, but I wouldn't have brought anything with me whatever. You don't solve conflicts like this with guns.'

'I hope not.'

I unhitched the amplifier and passed it to Flekke. But before switching it off I raised the megaphone and sent a last message: 'I'm on my way now, Jan Egil! Give me a shout when you can see me. It's as black as hell up here!'

He didn't answer. I shrugged and handed over the megaphone.

Grethe gave me a quick squeeze and whispered in my ear: 'Take care …'

Standal and the other officers nodded as I passed. Slowly I began to proceed along the narrow path. I could hardly see half a metre ahead of me, and I had no idea what awaited me. In my chest I had a kind of vacuum, a burial hole dug ready for someone to move in soon.

Once again I felt an unpleasant chill go down my spine. It was my brain sending warning signals up and down, forwards and backwards, without getting the answer it was waiting for.

20

Now I was alone in the black night. The only sounds I heard were the trickle of rain and the gurgle of streams.

I grabbed hold of branches hanging heavily over the path for support, put one foot in front of the other with care, moving one step at a time. Gradually my eyes became accustomed to the darkness. The contours of the countryside emerged, and a few stone's throws beneath me I could distinguish the vast black surface of Lake Trodalsvatn.

I peered ahead. I still couldn't see the uprooted tree.

There was a sudden movement in the undergrowth in front of me. I gave a start, but seconds later I heard the wings of a large bird flapping, driven from its repose by this unwelcome intrusion.

I breathed out and continued on my way. Wet branches slapped into my face, and I repeatedly had to swerve to the side or back to get past. Then I came to a clearing in the forest. Down to the left there was a little creek where the greyish white water foamed against the shore. Just ahead of me I could make out an uprooted tree, and against the slope there were more huge rocks, the remains of an earlier landslide. I allowed my eyes to wander upwards, but all I saw was a grey-black amorphous nothingness. There was no sign of movement, nothing that might reveal where they were hiding.

I stood hesitating for a second or two before taking the first step forward and entering the clearing. Consoling myself that if I couldn't see him, he could hardly see me, either. Swiftly I crossed the open area, stumbled forward against the fallen tree and, keeping my shoulders down, found shelter there.

Then I poked up my head and shouted into the scree: 'Jan Egil! Am I in the right place?!'

A second passed. Then came the answer. 'Come on! But slowly! And with your hands in the air!'

'All I've got in the bag is food – and a drink!'

'Come on!'

I walked around the tree and peered in the direction the voice had come from. I still couldn't see anything.

With my hands in the air, I started climbing. A few times I had to reach out with my arms to regain my balance on the wet rocks, and once I tripped and had to go right down on my knees and grope my way forward with my hands. He didn't react.

I stared upwards with such intensity that it strained my eye muscles. Now I could distinguish a raised edge, two or three larger rocks forming a kind of redoubt at the top of the scree. And there, just above one of the rocks, I saw the first sign of life: a head, a shoulder and the faint glimmer of something that could have been a weapon.

'Jan Egil?' I said, my voice at normal volume now.

'Move forward slowly!' he replied. 'I've got you in my sights.'

That gave me a shock. It wasn't the first time by any means. During the nine years I had worked as a private investigator I had found myself on at least two occasions in this same situation: on the wrong side of a gun. And I had survived both experiences unscathed. However, on the other hand ... at the back of my head I had the grim story Grethe had told me on the way into the long valley, the image of his foster parents, shot and murdered in their own bedroom. What if ... if it really *was* him who had done it? How far would he go?

My mouth had gone dry once again, and a shudder went through me. 'Don't do anything stupid, Jan Egil. I'm here to help you.'

'Do what I tell you!'

'Of course.' I couldn't see his face yet, but he seemed tall for a seventeen-year-old. The girl who was supposed to be with him was nowhere to be seen.

'Approach slowly until I say stop!'

Nature seemed to be holding its breath as I trudged up the last bit. It wasn't raining quite as hard any more. For some reason that made me feel even colder, as if the temperature had plummeted in the wake of the great quantities of precipitation.

I fixed my eyes stiffly on the silhouette above. Gradually he emerged from the darkness, but he had his anorak hood pulled down over his forehead, and all I could see of his face, when I was finally close enough, was the broad nose, the taut mouth and the drops of rain that had settled in the down over his top lip. It was impossible to recognise tiny Johnny boy from this angle.

I could see the weapon. It was a big Mauser. No longer pointing at me, it was down by his side, as if to indicate that if I behaved myself, I wouldn't come to any harm.

Now I could see her, too: a little cowering creature, also with her head covered by a weatherproof hood, a face with an open round mouth, like a fish in an aquarium, unable to escape through the glass, to get out and away.

I held up the plastic bag. 'Here's the food.'

He motioned with the rifle barrel. 'Throw it here!'

'There's a bottle of Coke inside.'

'Then bring it here!' he commanded impatiently.

I went closer. Now I saw that the skin around his mouth was pimply and uneven. When I had advanced far enough, he said: 'Stop!'

I did as instructed. Then I passed over the bag.

He removed the hand that had been resting on the trigger. As he held it out, our eyes met for the first time, and immediately I recognised him. Set far back in the oblong, pimply adolescent face, there was Johnny boy's wronged, defiant expression that we had grown to recognise in the period after Vibecke Skarnes's arrest, when the responsibility for him had been ours for six months. The round, not yet fully formed facial features of the small boy were gone, replaced by new, craggy contours, but the look and that particular set of the mouth were the same.

He grabbed the bag and took it. He cast a look inside. Then he threw it over to the girl who snatched at it greedily, opened the bottle of Coke and took a long draught before feverishly tearing the paper off the energy bars. Once the bars were out, she passed one to Jan who started eating without letting me out of his sight for a moment. Then he extended his hand for the bottle, raised it to his mouth and took a long, deep swig.

I could have rushed him then. I could have thrown myself on him, grabbed the rifle and tried to wrestle it from his hands. But I didn't. The risk of something going wrong was too great.

It was as if I could sense the presence and intensity among the police officers down in the woods. I knew that those with night sights on their rifles were keeping an eye on us. But I didn't want to give them the slightest reason for going into action.

I felt a strange calm seeping into me. The two young persons stuffing themselves with emergency rations in front of my eyes reminded me of starving whelps. This seemed to be what they had actually holed themselves up for: a last, desperate meal before they had to face reality head-on again.

While they were eating I saw that Jan Egil was paying less and less attention to the weapon. It was no longer pointing in my direction; it just hung loosely under one arm, hitched over a shoulder with a military-coloured strap, but out of action for no longer than the second it took to lift it.

'Do you remember what a great time we had in Bergen … Jan?'

'My name's Jan Egil!'

'Jan Egil,' I corrected. 'The fishing trips we went on, the walks in the mountains with Cecilie and …'

'Barely,' he sulked.

'But you must have had a reason to ask me to come all this way here?'

With an involuntary toss of the head, he fixed his gaze on me and his eyes were shiny, filled with tears. He swallowed and nodded. After a while he said in a strangulated voice: 'You were kind.'

I nodded. 'We liked you, you know.' As he didn't react, I went on: 'You had experienced terrible things, and we wanted you to have a good time. That was why Hans got you this home here, too. Everyone wanted the best for you.'

His lips trembled, and I saw him pursing them tight.

I chose my words with care now. 'But … something happened here, too, I understand.'

He gave a brief nod. A single tear ran from one eye, down the side of his nose, resting under one nostril as a teardrop.

'But whatever has happened … there's no sense in hiding up here with … what's your girlfriend's name?'

I watched him fight to speak. I turned to face her. 'You … can you answer me? What's your name?'

'Silje,' came the reedy response.

'You want to go home, don't you?'

As she didn't reply, I addressed Jan Egil again. 'This is horrendous weather, and the night's going to be long and cold. You can't seriously mean that you're going to stay out here all night?'

As he didn't reply either, I went on: 'I can promise you one thing, Jan Egil. You'll be given a hundred per cent fair treatment.'

He snorted with contempt.

'You will! I'll guarantee it. Perhaps you don't know, but since we got to know each other ten years ago, I have stopped working for social services. Now I'm a private investigator. A detective. I promise you that if there's anything at all doubtful in this case that you've got involved in, then I … I won't leave a stone unturned until I know everything. Together we'll find out what actually happened here, and you'll get all the help you need. It won't cost you a bean!'

I thought I could hear my creditors cheering in unison in the background, but I could see the message had got through. The word *detective* had been the key to make him listen, and it was also the first word he said, in that same slightly dumbstruck intonation most people adopted after being told: 'D-d-detective?'

'Yes,' I smiled. 'Varg Veum, private investigator, with an office in Strandkaien, just by the fish market. Next time you're in town, you'll have to pop in!'

'But the police …'

'The police have their job to do. But now that you've turned seventeen, social services don't have much say any more. You'll get some help from a solicitor as well, of course. You can be sure of that. No one down there is after you, Jan Egil! Everyone wants to help you.'

It had almost stopped raining now. I celebrated by pulling back my hood so that he could see all of my face. 'What do you say?' I carefully stretched out my hand. 'Give me the rifle, Jan Egil. Then it's all over. We can go down to the village, have a roof over our heads, put on dry clothes and get something nice and hot down us. Eh? Doesn't that sound good?'

I could see how his emotions were pulling him in all directions. But I knew that I had got through to him, that the thought of spending the whole night up in the valley, soaked, cold, without any food, other than what they had already made short work of, as compared with what I had promised him – dry clothes, roof over your head, hot food – was too much to resist.

He looked down at Silje. She nodded back enthusiastically.

Then he held out his hand, holding the rifle.

I grasped the barrel firmly and took it. Then I hurriedly examined the side for the safety catch. With some surprise I noticed that it was on. I stepped away in case he should change his mind.

I half-turned, looked down towards the trees, formed my hands into a loud-hailer and called: 'Veum here! Everything's fine. We're coming down.'

It took a bit of time for an answer to come. I heard the sergeant's voice, metallic in the speaker they had brought with them. 'That's great! We'll be waiting here!'

'Will I have to wear … handcuffs?' asked Jan Egil in a thin voice behind me.

I turned back to him. 'No, no. That shouldn't be necessary.'

'No,' said Silje. 'Because it was me who did it.'

21

'Wha…' I started.

'Shuddup, Silje!' Jan Egil shouted.

'But I …'

'Shuddup, I said!'

I took a couple of steps away from them. 'Now I think we should do what I said, OK? Go down to the village, put some dry clothes on, and then we can talk all this through properly in somewhat more comfortable surroundings than these, right?'

'I just wanted to say that,' she sobbed.

'Shuddup!'

'Now, now,' I said. 'Let's calm down a bit, shall we?'

They looked at me, both of them. For a moment it was as if they had united against me, a strict father, an angry teacher or an exacting confirmation priest. I was happy now that I had taken the rifle off them.

I thrust out my hand, smiled and motioned towards the bottom of the valley. 'Let's get moving. I'm freezing my arse off!'

They neither laughed nor smiled, but both nodded, and soon we were on our way down. I stepped to the side and let them pass. 'I'll bring up the rear,' I determined, without saying why. Neither of them objected.

Like a quiet, gloomy procession we stumbled our way down the scree, to the uprooted tree and from there into the forest. As we approached the others, I called out again: 'We're coming! Silje and Jan first, me at the rear!'

'Fine, Veum!' Standal answered, without the loud-hailer this time.

With which they were upon us. I heard the muffled sounds

of a brief scuffle in front of us as Silje was shoved aside and three to four policemen overpowered Jan Egil, then the click of handcuffs.

'Vaaaaarg!' Jan howled desperately as he kicked out in the dark. 'You said I wouldn't be handcuffed!'

I charged through the undergrowth. 'Nor should you be! I've got the rifle here!'

'Are you or the police in charge here, Veum?' the sergeant snapped. 'We obviously have to ensure that there are no further attempts to escape.'

'But for Christ's sake! He's only a child.'

'He's seventeen years old and responsible for his actions.'

'But I promised him!'

'And who gave you the authority to promise anything at all?'

'Bloody knuckleheads!'

At once his face was there, right in mine. 'Mind your step now, Veum – or we'll handcuff you, too.'

I looked around. We were standing in a tight clump in the forest. Silje had sought shelter in Grethe's arms, and I met her eyes over Silje's shoulders. She warned me with a glare and shook her head as a sign that I shouldn't attempt any further provocation. Around us stood police officers, tired and irritable. Jan Egil had given up. He was almost hanging from the arms of two officers, attached to one by handcuffs.

Silje suddenly turned round. 'But I'm the one who did it!'

Everyone focused on her. Standal barked: 'What?! What did you say?'

'I'm the one who did it!'

'Did what?'

'Shot 'em!'

'What did you say? Are you telling us the truth? Do you mean that?'

'D'you think I'm lying?' Her face was red with repressed fury. 'About something so serious?'

'No, no – I sincerely hope not,' Standal mumbled, caught off guard and perplexed.

'He was an old pig!'

Standal regarded her with a flinty look.

'You mean ...'

'Uncle Klaus!'

'Silje!' Grethe reproved.

An excited mumble spread through the officers around us. 'There's the motive!' I heard one of them say, looking around triumphantly. 'Isn't that what I ...?'

Standal seemed to have run out of words. He just stared down at the young girl, depressed, with that disgruntled expression of his.

'Now listen here,' I said. 'We're not going to stand here for the rest of the night, are we? For God's sake let's get back down to civilisation, get a roof over our heads, put on some dry clothes and then we can sort out this business down there.'

Standal visibly pulled himself together. 'Of course. You're absolutely right there, Veum.' Not without some difficulty, he took command again. 'OK, men!' He pointed to two of them. 'You go first. Then you ...' he pointed to the man handcuffed to Jan Egil, '... and him. You follow, Reidar. Then you ...' He pointed to some other officers. 'Next you three ...' That was Grethe, Silje and I. 'We'll form the rearguard,' he concluded, indicating himself and the young officer with the loud-hailer, Flekke. 'And ... Olsen! When we reach Angedalen ... make sure the cars come up to us and keep the bloody media pack a hundred metres away, at least!' As an afterthought he added: 'And when you get contact on the walkie-talkie, inform them that the ambulance can go back. We won't need it, I'm happy to say.'

He turned to me and held out his hand for the rifle. 'Veum ... I'll take that.' I passed him the heavy Mauser, and he beckoned to one of the officers, who conjured up a large black bin bag, in which the rifle was placed.

After some final instructions we set off down the path again. No one said anything. We had enough to do to find our footing and make sure we didn't crash into the person in front. I saw Silje's and Grethe's heads bobbing up and down ahead. Behind me I could hear Standal puffing and panting down my neck. There was a strange atmosphere in the group. Everyone was lost in their own thoughts. There was a marked sense of relief that the whole thing was over, but at the same time we knew that we had been given something new to mull over. *It was me who did it,* Silje had said and like an inner echo I heard Jan's own voice from ten years ago say: *Mummy did it …*

Were there any similarities? Were there any connections at all between these dramatic incidents?

I had promised him that not a stone would be left unturned until I was satisfied I had a result. But right now we were not talking about a stone or two but a whole landslide of complex events.

The first thing to do when I got down to Førde was to have the last ten years of Jan's life mapped out, from the time we parted in Bergen, to attempt to find out what might have led to the atrocity committed.

We were approaching the end of the gradient now. The path flattened out, and we were in open country again. By the old hay barn we came to a stop, while the two foremost officers went down to make sure that Standal's orders were being followed. From a distance we could see the throng of press people being pushed down the hill, and their protests reached all the way up to us, like the distant baying of a pack of hounds.

'I've got my car down there,' I said.

'You can pick it up tomorrow, Veum. Now you're coming with us,' Standal said.

When the area was clear, we continued on down. Jan Egil was put in the first car; Silje, Grethe and I in the back seat of the second, with the sergeant in the front and a police officer behind the wheel. It was only then that I looked at my watch. It was five minutes to one.

The press people had waited a long time, in vain. There wouldn't be many kind words for the Førde sergeant in the following day's newspapers, I guessed. There was a storm of flashes as we passed them, but it must have been difficult to see who was sitting in the cars, and both Jan Egil and Silje had jackets over their heads and were bent forwards in their seats.

As we swung onto the road, I cast a glance back. They were following in our wake in a line. A safari without a trophy and a funeral procession without a corpse, I said to myself, before closing my eyes and leaning back in the seat. But I didn't doze off. I didn't sleep for a second the whole night, and early next morning I staggered out of bed, as fresh as an ageing teacher on the last school day before the summer holidays.

22

I shuffled bog-eyed into the bathroom, had a thin pee and then went into the shower, where I stood with my head against the cold wall. A minute or two passed before I could be bothered to turn on the water. Once I had done this, I stood letting the water run and run as if there were little else to do on this depressing morning in a dark, miserable world.

Eventually, I unwrapped a small packet of soap, washed and rinsed, turned off the water and ventured back in front of the mirror. I was a man in my next best years, had just turned forty-two, but was hardly recognisable. My hair was standing up, like after a permanent shock, my skin was grey and wan, and even my stubble was pale and colourless, as if all the colour in me had leached out during the long hours up in wet Trodalen. This was not a cheery morning.

Taking shaving things from my toilet bag, I tried to improve my appearance. I covered my face with foam until it was nearly invisible against the white wall behind me and then went to work with a vengeance, resulting in a large number of cuts on my chin and neck. When I looked leprous enough to frighten the wits out of anyone, I concluded the abuse, rinsed off the blood and the last bits of foam, pressed a cold, wet hand cloth against my face and walked stiff-legged out of the bathroom.

I went to the window and stared outside. There wasn't much solace to find there.

Førde was, first of all, no metropolis seething with life and activity. On the other side of the river occasional juggernauts passed, some going to Jølster, others to Bergen. Today, the cloud cover between the mountains lay so low that cars on their way up the

Halbrendslia Mountain simply disappeared in the dense greyness. For a little while you could make out their rear lights, then they were gone. They reminded me of UFOs after a lightning visit to Førde, concluding that this place was hardly worth a stay and now they were on their way back to whence they had come.

I dressed and went down to the dining room where the staff were busy clearing up after breakfast, but not so insistent that I was not allowed to help myself to what was left before they finished their tidying up. I could take as much coffee as I wanted until it ran out. I did my best, but there was still some left. While sitting over my fourth or fifth cup I quickly went back over the very last part of the night's events.

The atmosphere in the car had not exactly hit the heights. Silje was crying silently between us, and Grethe had put a comforting arm around her and pulled her close. 'A solicitor from Oslo has rung to say he will be coming early tomorrow,' the officer behind the wheel informed Standal. 'And what's the name of this genius?' the sergeant wanted to know. 'Langeland,' came the answer, and I pricked up my ears. 'Langeland! But he's a top-class solicitor! What the hell does he want here?' asked the sargeant. 'A follow-up to his previous success maybe,' I mumbled. Standal turned to me: 'What do you mean by that?' 'Nothing, except that if it's Jens Langeland we're taking about, he was the one who took the case the last time Jan Egil was involved in something like this.' 'In Oslo?' 'No, that time he was in Bergen.' 'And is he good?' I smiled wryly: 'Better than you will like, I'm afraid.' 'Well ... we'll see. I'm just wondering who the hell tipped him off.' 'Well, it wasn't me, anyway.' Standal sent me a surly look: 'You report to the police HQ early tomorrow, too, Veum. We obviously need a bit of an update on this Jan Egil ...'

By the time we arrived back in Førde it was half past one. The car pulled up in front of the hotel to let me out first. Grethe went to the police station to support Silje and Jan Egil, as far as there was anything she could do. She had hugged me quickly before I got out of the car. She looked pretty careworn, too. But on the other hand … she had an official function to perform. As for me, I had just been brought in on the sidelines. 'See you tomorrow, Varg.' 'See you …'

And now I was sitting here, hardly able to move.

I walked over and took the fifth, or sixth, cup from the coffee machine. On the way back, I saw a podgy young man, red-haired with round glasses, striding energetically across the floor in my direction.

'Is your name Veum?' he asked.

'Who's asking?'

He held out a hand. 'Helge Haugen. Journalist for *Firda Tidend*. I would appreciate a few words with you.'

'I've got nothing to say.'

'No? They all say that, but … would you mind if I joined you?'

I was too tired to offer any resistance. 'Not at all. Take the weight off your feet, young man. You look as if you need to.'

He pulled out a chair and made himself comfortable with a contented smile. 'You're a private investigator, I've been told.'

'Correct …'

'But who hired you?'

'No, no, no, it's not like that.' I held his gaze. He was in his late twenties and bursting with energy on the other side of the table, he had the enthusiastic glint in his eye of a star reporter on the way up. 'Not at all. I used to work for social services in Bergen and the boy involved was one of my clients. I was summoned here because he had asked to talk to me.'

'Why was that?'

'Well, I can't actually answer that question. That was the message I was given.'

'So … what's his background?'

'You've heard of something called client confidentiality, haven't you?'

He smirked. 'I've heard of it, yes. But I don't suppose it counts for much when an Oslo newspaper opens its wallet.'

'And how much is there in *Firda Tidend*'s wallet?'

'How much do you want?'

I shook my head slowly. 'Mm … In fact I mean it. I'm not going to say any more than I've already said.'

He nodded matter-of-factly, as if taking note, and went on. 'What do you know about the Trodalen killing, Veum?'

'That's a good question. Not much more than I was told last night on my way here. A killing – in 1839, wasn't it?'

'Yes, shall I tell you about it?'

'That would be, if not useful, then at least interesting.'

Helge Haugen leaned back in his chair, interlaced his fingers on his stomach, instantly reminding me more of an old grandfather than a young ace reporter. As he began to tell the story, it was obvious that he enjoyed the sound of his own voice and I guessed that the majority of what he said would appear in print in *Firda Tidend* one day very soon.

'It was a hot, sunny June day in 1839. The snow still lay on the ground in huge drifts up in Trodalen, the narrow mountain valley that acts as a mountain pass between Øvre Naustdal and Angedalen. A man from Naustdal was passing the tiny smallholding in Trodalsstrand with a cow he was going to sell to a dealer from Aurland in Sogn, Ole Olsen Otternæs. They had arranged to meet at Indrebø Farm in Angedalen to settle the deal there, but when the man from Naustdal arrived, there was no sign of Ole Olsen. The Indrebø farmfolk were surprised because it was well-known that a few days earlier the dealer had been in Angedalen. And it was said that he had undertaken the long walk to Trodalen in the hope of selling a few goods there. On June 19th he had left some clothing at the neighbouring farm, and a message that he would be back. He was never seen again.'

'Really?'

'The Indrebø farmfolk began to worry that something might have happened to Ole Olsen. He might have had an accident on the way up or down. They set off from Trodalen to search for him.

At last they arrived at the only farm in the valley, Trodalsstrand. Neither the farmer nor his wife was there, only an elderly servant. But she had a story to tell … This was June 24th, and the servant said that, indeed, five days earlier Olsen had been at the farm, although he hadn't sold anything. So he had gone back towards Angedalen, accompanied by the farmer's son, Mads Andersen. Mads had returned later in the day, but the next morning she had been surprised to see that he had taken the boat and was on the lake, despite the fact that the master had given explicit instructions that the boat was not to go out before he returned.'

'Where was the father?'

'He was on his way to Bergen, and the mother had accompanied him down to Naustdal. She didn't return until late in the day on June 24th.'

'And where was she now?'

'Out in the field with Mads. They were drying hay.'

He waited to see if I had any more questions. I didn't, and he continued the story. 'Well, the men went there and began to question Mads. *No, Ole Olsen had left the farm alone*, he said. *That's not true*, the men said. *You went with him*, they said. *Well, part of the way maybe*, he said. *So where did you take your leave of him?* they asked. But Mads's answer was quite vague. *Over on the mountainside*, he said, with a flourish of his arm. But now the men pressed him harder, and the matter was not made any easier by the mother standing and listening. Opinions are divided as to what role the mother played in this business. Some say she was the one who went to the local policeman and reported her own son, and that she had suspected what had happened the moment she returned from Naustdal. Others claim she gave clear hints during the conversation with the men from Indrebø on June 24th, while others maintain that she never cast any suspicion on her son. Anyway, later that day Mads was paying for a skin he had bought from one of the Angedalen men. On the note he paid with there were some red stains. *There's blood on the note!* the man from Indrebø exclaimed. *Yes*, Mads answered, and not long afterwards he confessed his misdeed.'

'So easy?'

'It was said he was a bit simple-minded, this Trodalen Mads, as he came to be called in local gossip. Others insisted that he was a hardened criminal, that he had stolen before and that people had heard him say that he would kill again, if he survived this murder.'

'And he did?'

'In a sense. He was over eighty before he died, but he spent many years in prison in Kristiania, the old name for Oslo. Originally he was sentenced to death, to having his back broken on the wheel, but the sentence was commuted to imprisonment, and he did his term in Akershus for forty-two whole years. The reason he had to serve such a long term was that he threatened he would kill his parents when he got out again. But even after they were both dead, he was kept inside. He wasn't released and allowed to return home until 1881. Not to Trodalen of course. He lived in Angedalen where he earned his bread by making spoons from the horns he collected from valley farms. The young ones were scared of him, but older people considered him harmless after so many years of prison drudgery.'

'He did confess, though?'

'Oh, yes. I've read the court records of the time myself. He confessed to the men from Indrebø that evening, later to the sergeant and finally in open court. He had accompanied Ole Olsen part of the way with the intention of robbing him. At a suitable spot he had hit him over the head with a rock, and he had continued hitting the dealer until he lay dead in the scree.'

'In the scree?'

'Yes, perhaps towards the end of the lake. Afterwards he had taken his money and a few other objects of value, then had dragged him off the path and hidden him behind some rocks. The next morning he had gone back, carried him to the lake, put him in the boat and dropped him into the deep.'

'I heard yesterday the body was never found?'

'That's right. And there were no bloodstains found where the murder was supposed to have taken place …'

'In other words …'

'Well.' Helge Haugen studied me with a sardonic glint in his eye. 'A matter for a private investigator perhaps? Now it is said that the bottom of Lake Trodalsvatn can be tricky. A lot of big rocks from old landslides are supposed to cover the bottom, and perhaps it wouldn't take much for a body to be snagged down there. But it is a bit strange nonetheless. Most usually float to the surface when the body is filled with enough gas … There may have been some hungry pike down in the deep of course …'

'But the man was sentenced anyway, I understand.'

'It's a historical fact. No one can change that. And I assume Jan Egil Libakk will become one too when the case has been investigated.'

'Libakk? Did he use that surname?'

'As far as I am aware. However, I haven't had that confirmed. It's just that they were his foster parents, I believe.'

I nodded, distracted. 'Do you know anything about these people?'

'Klaus and Kari? Nothing special, yet. I'm working on the case, if I might put it like that. That's why, among other reasons, I came to see you.'

'Right … I'd hardly heard their names before yesterday.'

'And?'

'Nothing.' I sent him a disarming smile. 'If you're expecting something in return for the story about Trodalen Mads, I'm afraid you're wasting your time.'

He bent forward in a sudden movement. 'We could make a deal, Veum.'

'Mm?'

'We can keep each other posted. If I dig up anything of interest regarding … circumstances in Angedalen, I'll share it with you.

And vice versa. You won't regret it. I have lots of feelers out, in all sorts of areas.'

I nodded slowly. 'OK. It's a deal, on a non-committal basis. If I come across anything of interest, I'll pass it on … and vice versa. Where can I get hold of you?'

He handed me a business card. 'Here you've got my telephone numbers, home and office. But Førde is not a big place. I would guess we will bump into each other several times before the day is done. Where have you decided to start?'

'Start? The present situation is that the sergeant has summoned me to his office to talk through what happened yesterday.'

'Not a bad start, Veum.' He stood up. 'So we've got a deal?'

'Kind of.'

He seemed satisfied with that. He left the dining room with a cheery goodbye. I took the last cold mouthful of coffee, then stood up and followed.

23

At the police HQ in the Red Cross building, the atmosphere was sombre with a thin veil of control. The police rooms were on the second floor, with a view of the wetland area at the back of the hotel. The area by the reception desk was swarming with reporters. An impatient photographer stood with his camera slung over his shoulder, ready to snap away if anything were to happen.

As I arrived, a uniformed policeman announced that there would be a short press conference at eleven and another in the afternoon after national KRIPOS representatives had come and been allowed to make their first assessments of the case. The press took note without much enthusiasm. Some stayed in the room, others wandered off in the direction of the nearest cafés.

I had picked up a couple of newspapers on my way from the hotel. None of the Oslo papers had come to Førde yet, but *Firda Tidend*, *Bergens Tidende* and *Bergensavisen* had big front page spreads on what they called the 'Double Killing in Angedalen'. There were large photographs of the Libakk farm, deserted and abandoned with the exception of a couple of parked cars in the farmyard, and a few smaller, somewhat fuzzy shots of the police cars carrying Silje, Jan Egil and the rest of us as we passed the press ranks on our way down from Trodalen. In the press reports, the gruesome murders were portrayed in detail, based doubtless on sources within the police force. Jan Egil was described as a 'member of the family' who after a 'hostage situation' in Trodalen had given himself up to the police and for the moment was being 'questioned' at the local police offices in Førde. Kari and Klaus Libakk were described as 'decent folk' about whom no one had anything negative to say, and it was stressed that the tragedy had spread 'unease and horror' in the tiny rural community of Angedalen. In *Firda Tidend* Helge Haugen had concentrated on the Trodalen murder and I did indeed recognise several of the phrases he had entertained me with almost an hour earlier. In *Bergens Tidende* they had written a small parallel article about 'murders in the fjord county' in which they summarised the cases of Trodalen Mads, Hetle, the 'contraband murder' of 1973 and many others. *Bergensavisen*'s coverage was coloured by the fact that they didn't have a provincial correspondent and it was based mainly on the Norwegian News Agency's sober account of events. There would be enough other articles to digest when the Oslo tabloids caught up, I imagined. But I was pleased that none of them had named Jan Egil so far.

I elbowed my way through the throng of press reps and reported in at the desk, where I introduced myself and said that the sergeant had summoned me to appear.

'Really?' The officer behind the counter looked at me in bewilderment.

'He would certainly like to know what I had to say about the case.'

'A witness then, I think we'll say,' mumbled the officer. His hair was thin and his skin pale, and there wasn't a trace of enthusiasm in the way he spoke. But at least he opened the gate in the counter, let me in and showed me to a kind of waiting room further into the office area. 'I'll tell the sergeant you've come. The name was Veum, wasn't it?'

'It was.'

I took a seat in the lounge area and spread out one of the newspapers I had brought with me. I had a suspicion I was unlikely to be the first person in the queue, and I was right. I didn't see anything of the sergeant until he walked past, pursued by several other officers, on his way to the eleven o'clock press conference. He was almost surprised to see me but gave a quick nod and made a sign to say that we would talk when he was back.

Nevertheless I strung along with the others to the reception area to attend the brief, somewhat off-the-cuff press conference held there. I saw Helge Haugen and a couple of familiar faces from Bergen in the audience.

There was not much new to report, apart from what was already in the papers. The couple, Kari and Klaus Libakk, had been found shot and killed in their own home. There were no signs of a break-in. A close relative of theirs was in the interview room at this moment, and two KRIPOS officers were expected on the morning flight from Oslo to assist the local constabulary with the investigation.

'Has the person in question been charged?' one of the pressmen wanted to know.

'No,' said the sergeant before adding, almost involuntarily: 'Not yet.'

'But he will be?'

'At this moment in time I am unable to say.'

'Is it true that he took a girl from the neighbouring farm with him as a hostage?'

'I don't wish to comment on that.'

'Are there any theories as to what the motive might have been?'

'I don't wish to comment on that, either.'

They didn't get much more out of him, and Sergeant Standal concluded the conference by hoping they would return later that day, either at four or at eight o'clock. More details would be announced as soon as the timing was decided.

With that the conference was over. Some of the journalists tried, unsuccessfully, to set a trap for the local police boss with a few additional questions. The only ones to get a few words with him were a couple of radio reporters, who asked the same questions and were given the same answers as during the conference.

When he was safely on the inside of the counter again, Standal motioned to me to follow. 'Come with me, Veum. We'll take it in my office.'

The sergeant's office had a view straight across the wetlands to the tall cranes in the shipyards and the narrow landing strip. Standal indicated a chair, took a seat himself behind the desk and rested his pale blue eyes, with a slight squint, on me. 'Now tell me all you know about this Jan Egil Skarnes which, I am informed, is his real name. You knew him from before, I'm led to understand?'

'Barely, in fact.' In brief outline I told him about Jan Egil's unhappy life, from the first meeting I had had with him on the Rothaugen estate during the summer of 1970, while he still had Elvis as a middle name, until the tragic events of 1974.

The sergeant bent forward, eager to hear. 'So he was involved in a suspicious death then, too?'

'Involved?! He was six and a half years old. And the foster mother soon confessed that she had caused the accident.'

'I see.' He had jotted down the names of Vibecke and Svein Skarnes long ago. 'Any more?'

'No, nothing ... We in social services followed his case for six months afterwards, before he was transferred to a foster home up here, with Kari and Klaus Libakk, and that is, in fact, the last I'd heard of him until I was told yesterday to get here asap.'

'So you know nothing about how his life had turned out in Angedalen?'

'No. I thought you would be able to fill me in on that.'

He looked at me blankly. 'And why?'

'Well, don't you have any records on him? Hasn't he been in the police spotlight before?'

'Not at all. Like you ... to be precise, I'd never heard of him until yesterday.'

'But you knew about the Libakks?'

He trod water. 'I knew who Klaus was. This isn't a big region.' For a second he seemed to be in two minds. 'But nothing of specific importance to this case.'

I leaned forward a fraction. 'So he's never been involved in any indecency cases?'

His mouth tightened. 'Indecency cases?'

'Yes, we all heard what she said last night. Silje. He was an old pig, she said. And she called him Uncle Klaus. Was he her uncle?'

He nodded slowly. 'She comes from a farm further down the valley. Almelid. Her mother is Klaus's sister.'

'Has she been questioned, too?'

'Not yet.'

'Where is she then?'

'She was given permission to go home.'

'What!'

'Her parents collected her.'

'But … she confessed!'

He seemed to project his lips forward, forming a kind of funnel, supposedly perhaps to signal profound scepticism. 'I wasn't very convinced by that, Veum.'

'Why not?'

'Well …' He thrust a hand between us. From one finger to the next he counted his points. 'First of all, it was Jan Egil holding the weapon when the constable observed them on the way up the mountainside. Secondly, the murders were executed in such a brutal fashion it is difficult to believe that they were committed by a sixteen-year-old girl. Thirdly, it was Jan Egil who spoke up during the whole dialogue with the police, if we can call it that, and fourthly, there was nothing at all to suggest that anyone else was responsible for what had happened until she burst out with this, er, statement. Sort of hysteria, if you ask me.'

'She said the same thing to me earlier when I was negotiating with them up in the scree.'

'Nevertheless. It seems totally unfounded.'

'Even though we're assuming that this Uncle Klaus had abused her?'

'We know nothing about that, Veum. And why would she take Kari's life as well?'

I threw out my arms. 'She was in a frenzy. If you've shot one person … I assume you haven't released her for good?'

He gave me a condescending look and checked his watch. 'She's on her way now. We're going to have a long chat with her, Veum. And she'll be examined by a doctor.'

'Has she got herself a solicitor, too?'

'One of the local ones, Øygunn Bråtet. Furthermore, *fru* Mellingen from social services spent the night up there, in the same house as her.'

There was a knock at the door, and Reidar Ruset opened. He nodded to me before turning to Standal. 'The solicitor says Jan Egil is ready again.'

The sergeant acknowledged the information. 'Good, let's get going.'

'What shall I do?' I said.

He eyed me as if he wasn't quite sure. 'I can't see that we have an urgent need for your services right now, Veum. But if you're not too busy it would be nice if you'd stay in Førde for at least a couple more days.'

'Alright.'

'You'll have to do what you can to kill time.'

I nodded slowly. Fine by me. But I was not at all sure he would like the way I would do it.

'At any rate, I'll have to pick up my car. Can I pass you the taxi bill?'

'As long as you don't take the scenic route, yes. That's fine.'

Five minutes later I was sitting in the back seat of a taxi past Førdehus, the culture house, towards Angedalen. Halfway up, we passed a car with several passengers. For a second or two I met Grethe's eyes through one of the side windows, it was so quick that the smiles we sent missed each other.

24

I paid for the taxi and walked to my car. The contrast with the evening before was striking. Now the abandoned Mini was the only vehicle left, like a boat that had hit a reef and no one had managed to free yet. I patted the bonnet with encouragement to tell it the waiting time was over; soon we would be on the road again.

Angedalen showed itself from a different side now that it was bathed in daylight, although it was still enshrouded by the low-lying greyish-white cloud between the mountains. The very end of the long valley had been wide and open. Here the valley narrowed between Sandfjellet and Skruklefjellet to the north, and Tindefjellet to the south, according to the map I kept in the car. The first snow of the year lay up here, white stains, that is, if it wasn't from the previous winter which had not yet let go.

Farms lay dotted about, some of them right down at the bottom of the valley, others further up. In front of what I recognised from newspaper photos as Libakk Farm, I saw several parked cars, among them a police patrol car, and I saw two people in the forensic department's white overalls carrying a cardboard box from the farmhouse to the car before returning. It was impossible to say which farm was called Almelid, but I assumed the farm on the slope opposite Libakk must have been Lia.

There was a strange calm hanging over the whole valley, as if everything was as it should be and nothing dramatic had happened. Nonetheless, I sensed a tension, as if nature were holding its breath before the next eruption, and I guessed I was not the only person following the activity around the police car at Libakk; inside every house in Angedalen I was sure someone was walking to the window at regular intervals to check if the car was still there.

But there was not a great deal I could do here today without upsetting the apple cart. Instead I got into my car, reversed down the slope, turned round and drove back down the straight road to Førde.

I rang Cecilie from a telephone box in Bergen. She had already had an unpleasant feeling in her bones when she read the full page spread in the papers that morning, but it still came as a shock to have her suspicions confirmed. 'Thank you for ringing and telling me, though, Varg.'

'But … there was one thing I was wondering if you could check on for me.'

'Mm?'

'Could you try and find out where Jan's mother is staying, and how she is? I suppose someone has had the gumption to tell her.'

She hesitated for a second. 'Mette Olsen, you mean?'

'Yep.'

'I'll try.'

'And one more thing. You don't have Hans Haavik's number handy, do you?'

'Just a mo.' I heard her flicking through a telephone book, and straight after I got the number, which I jotted down in my notebook.

'Thanks. I'll ring you back in an hour or so to find out if you've tracked her down.'

We finished the conversation and I rustled together some more coins to phone Hans Haavik. He was still at the child reception centre in Åsane, but when I got through he wasn't available. 'He's in Førde,' a colleague of his told me. 'He left as soon as he was told.'

'Told what?'

'I'm not sure I can say.'

'Never mind. I know what it's about. I'm in Førde myself. You don't know where he's staying, do you?'

'He must be in one of the hotels there.'

'OK. I'll find him then. Bye.'

I came out of the telephone box. The low-lying cloud seemed to have advanced even closer. I was in the semi-dark in the middle of the day. It looked as if it wouldn't be long before it rained again.

I went back to the police offices and asked if Grethe Mellingen was there. The officer behind the counter could confirm that she was, and after a little to-ing and fro-ing I was allowed inside.

Grethe got up off a chair and smiled. 'Varg …' She came towards me and put her arms around my neck. 'Good to see you.'

'You, too. How's it going?'

She stood close to me, so close that I had problems focusing my eyes. 'She's being questioned now, accompanied by her solicitor.'

'Yes, I heard someone had been appointed for her. Is she sticking to her statement?'

'I think so.'

'And her parents?'

'They're being interviewed in a different office.'

'All systems go, I can see. Tell me … how was the night?'

'The little that was left, you mean?'

She pulled an ironic smile. Her face was drawn and pale. She hadn't put on any make-up, and her eyebrows looked light and blonde. Her lips were dry with narrow cracks in them, her hair still tangled after the rain.

'Well, I was given a sofa and a rug at Almelid Farm. The sergeant insisted I stayed with her, in case of any crises. But there wasn't anything. I dozed off for about half an hour, or that was how it felt anyway, but we had a tough job getting Silje out of bed. She refused point-blank. That was why we were so late arriving here.'

'And her parents? How did they take it?'

'They're in shock, pretty much. You can imagine. As if it wasn't bad enough hearing that Klaus Libakk and his wife had been brutally murdered, then they had to hear what Silje had said … They didn't seem to take it in, they seemed to be in denial.'

'But …'

'And there's one more thing you should know, Varg.'

'Mm?'

'Silje is not their daughter by birth. She's adopted, too.'

'What!'

'Yes.' She nodded several times, as if underlining what she had said.

'So … she and Jan Egil are in the same boat, in a way.'

'In more ways than one, I'm afraid.'

I studied her, waiting. 'In which ways then?'

'Her real father was killed … it must have been ten or eleven years ago. A row connected with some contraband case. Alcohol.'

A memory stirred faintly. 'And his name was?'

'Ansgår Tveiten.'

25

She met my gaze. 'Does the name ring a bell?' she asked.

'I'm afraid so. It certainly complicates the picture a bit further.'

'Do you remember the case?'

'No, but I was told about it, in the briefest of outlines, ten years ago.'

'In what connection?'

'Believe it or not, it was in fact to do with Jan Egil.'

Now her jaw was the one to drop. 'What! Tell me ...'

I had to ransack my brain. 'If I remember correctly, it was something to do with Ansgår Tveiten being killed somewhere round here.'

She nodded. 'It was near Bygstad, at the far end of Dals fjord. He was found by the water's edge, half-dragged under an old boat-house.'

'In 1973, I think it was.'

'Could well be right. But the case was never solved. It was obviously quickly written off as the settling of a score inside the province's criminal fraternity.'

'Right. The main suspect, however, was supposed to have been a hard nut from Bergen. Someone by the name of Terje Hammersten. The name mean anything to you?'

'No.'

'He was Tveiten's brother-in-law.'

'Really?'

'Tveiten was married to his sister. I don't recall her name, but I can find out.'

'Trude,' she said. 'Silje's mother.'

'My God! Are there any other connections? Where is this Trude now?'

'I believe she lives in Dale. That was the last I heard of her. She's supposed to have recovered, so they say, but there was never any talk of Silje going back … there.'

'No?'

'No. She never made a move in that direction, either. I mean … when her husband was killed, Silje was five years old and at that time Trude was totally unfit to take care of her.'

'A strange coincidence.'

'What's on your mind now?'

'Listen. This Terje Hammersten, in both 1970 and 1974 he was sort of living with Jan Egil's mother. His real mother. Furthermore, he's Silje's uncle, who was under suspicion of killing her father.'

'Yes, and so what?'

'In 1974 Jan Egil's foster mother, Vibecke Skarnes, was sentenced to two and a half years' imprisonment for having pushed her husband down a staircase during a row. She's been out for ages now.'

'But has this Terje Hammersten got anything to do with that case?'

'Not at all, as far as I know.'

She looked at me in desperation. 'Now you've got me completely confused, Varg!'

'Yes, but I can console you with the fact that I am no less confused myself. Now what I wanted to say was this … These two children, with their parallel fates, each end up on a farm in Angedalen … and today, at the police station here in Førde, where Jan Egil, from what I can see, is being charged with murder …'

'But … do you think there's some connection between all these events in Bygstad, Bergen and now Angedalen?'

'For the time being I don't think anything. But there are a conspicuous number of tangents meeting here, and the clearest of them all is Terje Hammersten.'

'Right …' She splayed open her arms. 'Then I think you should tell the sergeant that.'

'That's what I've been thinking of doing, as soon as I've got my head straight.'

We sat in silence for a while. Then I changed the topic. 'But turning to you … I think the sergeant addressed you as *fru* …'

She smirked again. 'Yes, I suppose he did.' After a short pause she added: 'But I'm not any longer, even though I've kept the surname.'

I nodded. 'Then we're in the same boat, too. Unless there was anything more dramatic than a divorce?'

'Not at all! No brutal death on my farm, Varg.'

She didn't say any more, and I didn't ask. From reception I heard a voice I recognised. Soon afterwards Hans Haavik joined us.

I hadn't seen him for some years, and he had put on a few more kilos. Otherwise he was the same, though in a somewhat emotional state. 'Hi, Varg … Grethe …' He shook hands with me, and Grethe received a hug. Then he fixed his eyes on me. 'This is one hell of a situation, isn't it. Have you any idea what happened?'

I shook my head. 'Nothing beyond the facts as they appear.'

'And they are …?'

'Well, I don't know much more than what's in the papers. But I went with them to get Johnny boy – Jan Egil – down from the mountain last night. For some reason it was me he had asked to talk to.'

He grimaced and nodded. 'He must have had positive memories of you from the last time. I came as fast as I could after Grethe called me yesterday. But the worst thing of all, do you know what that is?'

'No.'

'I was here last weekend and visited them. I'm going to be regarded as a bloody witness in the case.'

'You visited them?'

'Yes. I don't know if you remember, but Klaus was in fact my second cousin. I've always kept in touch with them. I've followed Jan Egil year on year, and it's been a pleasure to observe his behaviour.'

I hurled my arms in the air. 'And there was I … imagining I would have to travel round the district to make enquiries, but here we have the main man in our very midst. Come on!'

'Well, what should I say? There was nothing to suggest that there was anything brewing. As you know, it was me who arranged for Klaus and Kari to take him, but you can imagine what I think about that idea now!'

'Yes, but no one could guess that something like this would happen.'

'No, and he settled in quickly here. I'm sure you remember. I brought him here myself, in September that year. Later I popped by at least once every six months, even more often in the first years, to see how things were developing. And it was all positive. Of course, it could be pretty isolated here, especially in the winter, and there weren't that many children of his age around, either. But after a while a girl turned up in one of the neighbouring farms, and of course there were a few others, too. After he started school. But … well, I won't hide the fact that he was a struggle for them. Klaus and Kari, I mean. He was a restless fellow. Hyperactive you would call him nowadays, with huge emotional problems. Not much surprise, of course, with the trauma in his past, both from the children's home, if we can use such a sophisticated term for it, and from – well, you know. But it got better bit by bit, and now he had started upper school, a year behind, chosen his career path. Electronics, if I'm not mistaken.'

'And so you visited them that weekend?'

'Yes, I drove here on Friday after work and returned on Sunday night. I hadn't been here since around Easter time, but I finally pulled myself together and, well …' He opened his palms. 'I'm glad I did now. In fact it was the last time I saw them. Kari and Klaus.'

'And you didn't notice any cause for unease, an atmosphere?'

'No. Nothing.'

'Did you spend the night there?'

'Yes, I always did. The only thing I can say … Jan Egil was

hardly there at all. He came home on Friday evening, but then he stayed in his room as soon as we'd eaten. Said he was busy with something. On Saturday he went to a party and didn't come home until late. I heard him climbing the stairs.'

'Party?'

'Yes. At the youth club. Nothing more than that, I believe.'

'And on Sunday?'

'He had a long lie-in. Until twelve o'clock. After we'd eaten he was off again. But this time he went out. He was going to Silje's, he said.'

'On Sunday afternoon?'

'Yes. And I didn't see any more of him. I left at about eight, not to get back home too late, and by then he hadn't returned. You can imagine the shock I had when Grethe rang me on Tuesday and told me …'

'Yes, same here. But … did you see anything of Silje that weekend?'

'Nothing at all.'

'What's the relationship between her and Jan Egil? Are they sweethearts?'

He rocked his head back and shrugged. 'Possible. They've played together since they were very small. They went to school together, if not in the same streams. You'll have to ask …' He caught himself, and I knew what he had been going to say. We couldn't ask Klaus or Kari any more, though.

'Do you know that she …?' I stopped myself in the middle. As Hans Haavik had said himself it looked as though he was going to be a witness, and in that event it would be wrong of me to say too much. Instead I expressed myself as neutrally as possible. 'This cousin of yours … what sort of person was he?'

'Hmm, what can I say? They were very ordinary people, both Kari and Klaus. They ran their farm, and Kari did her night shifts at the central hospital here in Førde as a state registered nurse.'

'Night shifts?'

'That was the best way of combining work with the farm.'

'What kind of farming was it?'

'They had sheep, cows, calves, bit of fruit and berries. Milk subsidies were important, goes without saying. But they made ends meet. Why are we talking about this actually?'

'So Klaus and Jan Egil were often alone then? At night, I mean.'

He gave me an old-fashioned look. 'I hope you're not insinuating what I think you are, Varg?'

'I'm not insinuating anything at all. But my experience is that very few murders take place without some kind of motive and …'

He interrupted me. 'Oh yes! You don't need to expand. I've got the point. But does that explain why he killed Kari, too?'

'No. It's difficult to understand. Almost incomprehensible. But that's precisely why … there must have been some strong emotions under the surface.'

He sighed aloud and cast around desperately. 'Well, I don't know.' He looked at Grethe. 'Have you any ideas?'

She shook her head. 'None, Hans. None at all.'

We sat in silence. I looked at my watch and stood up. 'Excuse me for a moment. I just have to see if I can make a call.'

I went into reception, and, with extreme reluctance, the officer let me use his telephone. 'Make it snappy though!' he added with a stern glare.

I dialled Cecilie's number. When she answered, I said, half-turning to the officer: 'We have to be quick – did you find anything?'

'You won't believe it, Varg.'

I felt a stabbing pain in my stomach region. 'Try me.'

'Mette Olsen moved two years ago from Bergen to Sunnfjord.'

'To Sunnfjord!'

The policeman sent me a patronising look as though I didn't know where it was.

'Apparently to a disused farm belonging to the family.'

'Yes, everyone has a brother or a sister living in the Sunnfjord district, we all know that. Whereabouts?'

'It's in Jølster. I've got hold of a detailed description. The farm's called Leitet and is situated by Kjøsnes fjord. You turn off the main road at a place called Sunde.'

'I know where it is.'

'Well, you'll find her there.'

'As the crow flies, ten to twenty kilometres from where her son has lived for the last ten years … right, thank you very much. Did you find out anything else?'

'You didn't ask, but I checked out Terje Hammersten anyway.'

'And?'

'He still lives in Bergen.'

'OK. Thanks again. You're a brick!'

We rang off, and the officer behind the counter turned right round on the chair to face me. 'I couldn't help hearing what you said. You'll have to tell him … in there.' He signalled with his head towards the offices inside. 'Tell Standal.'

'Naturally. Have the KRIPOS officers come?'

He nodded. 'Yes, but they went to the crime scene first.'

'I see. Just tell Standal that I can talk to him when he's free.'

I walked slowly back to the others. Another surprising development to digest … But before I could say anything a door at the back opened and out they came in single file. Silje and what I assumed were her parents, a woman who must have been her solicitor, a policewoman, Reidar Ruset, Sergeant Standal, two further officers and bringing up the rear, Jens Langeland.

Standal fixed his eyes on me and said: 'He's asking to talk to you, Veum. Alone.'

26

Jens Langeland came over to me and we shook hands. 'Veum …
Long time, no see. But I heard about your exploits yesterday. It
sounds like you averted a disaster.'

'Hmm. He must have trusted me for some reason.'

'It's not customary for us to let you slip in to see him on your
own,' Standal broke in. 'But since he insisted with such vehemence,
and because of what happened yesterday, we'll take the risk.'

'I'll see what he has to say. May I exchange a couple of words
with Langeland in private first?'

Standal eyed me sceptically, and I added: 'Well, after all, he is
his solicitor, isn't he.'

'Fine, fine …'

'I need a bit of background info before I go in.'

Standal nodded, and Langeland and I walked off from the
others.

He had kept his characteristic wading-bird-like appearance:
tall, lean and slightly stooped. His nose had a pronounced curve.
His hair had thinned, with deep inroads, and there were the first
signs of silvering around his ears.

I had followed him from a distance. He had had a dazzling
career, thus far. The talent I had seen sprouting when he defended
Vibecke Skarnes had later blossomed. He achieved his great break-
through in what was known as the Hilleren case in 1978. After
confessing, a man was charged with murdering his neighbour. He
indicated where he had dumped the body into the sea, but the
body was never found, and Langeland had him acquitted, despite
the fact that he maintained his guilt to the very end. Langeland's
final summing up of the case had gone down in court history

as a dazzling defence plea using guilt and atonement as central concepts and emphasising the significance of avoiding a possible travesty of justice. After this Langeland was taken to the capital by a large firm of lawyers, and his career as a defence barrister had taken off in earnest. Today he belonged to the highest stratum of defence counsels, among the first to be called in when spectacular cases were mooted anywhere in the country. In this light, the double murder in Angedalen was not at all untypical, with the additional piquant minor detail that ten years earlier he had been the defence counsel for Jan Egil's foster mother in another but nowhere near as sensational murder case.

'I just have to ask you, Langeland. Vibecke Skarnes … how did she get on?'

'I know very little about her, Veum. I managed to trace her this morning to tell her what had happened before she read it in the papers.'

'You met her?'

'No, I told her on the phone. She lives in Ski, just outside Oslo.'

'How long has she been out?'

'She was released after a year and a half, and since then hasn't needed any legal help, to my knowledge.'

'So she didn't hire you for this case?'

'No, not at all. I was, of course, Jan Egil's solicitor even back then. It was quite a complicated case, let me tell you, from a purely legal point of view. Having a conviction did not relieve Vibecke Skarnes of the parental responsibility she had as a foster mother. Nevertheless, she chose not to insist on keeping it, primarily out of consideration for Jan Egil himself. She thought it would be untenable for Jan Egil to be looked after in a foster home in the intervening period and then return to her after she had served her sentence. That was why she asked me to take care of the case, both the legal and other aspects. I was myself here in Førde to assess the new foster home before it was approved.'

'So you met the two – deceased?'

'Yes, but just the once, in September 1974. Subsequently neither they nor Jan Egil had any need for my services until … well, now. The arrangement was that social services had registered my name, and they notified me last night about what had happened.'

'Does that mean that you've been officially appointed to represent Jan Egil?'

He flashed a quick smile. 'I'm certainly taking the case, Veum. This is a boy I will do my utmost to help.'

'Good. So we're on the same team. If you should need my assistance …'

He nodded and gave me a searching look. 'Don't rule out the possibility. Let's come back to that as soon as we've been given a rough summary of the situation.'

'So who actually has parental responsibility now?'

'Officially, it's still Vibecke Skarnes.'

'But she …'

'Yes?'

'I'm thinking about what happened in 1974 when she confessed to killing her husband …'

'No, no. She always claimed that it was self-defence, that it was an accident …'

'Yes, of course, but – Johnny boy – Jan Egil was the only person who was present at the incident, as far as we know. And now there is another murder – a double murder – here, again with Jan as the only person in the house at the time …'

'We need further information about that particular point, Veum. He tells quite a different story.'

'What does he say?'

'I assume you will hear it if he's asked to talk to you. Besides, there is, in fact, another person who has confessed.'

'I know, and that was exactly why I wanted to ask you: is it conceivable that the same thing has happened as in 1974?'

'I'm not quite with you there.'

'Is it conceivable that the mother assumed the guilt for what her own son – or adopted son, that is – had done that time, to spare him the psychological damage, in the same way that another girl is doing now?'

'No, no. That's just speculation, Veum. I thought you said we were on the same team?'

'A last question, Langeland. Did Jan Egil ever find out that Vibecke Skarnes was not his real mother?'

'Not as far as I know. The only person who can answer that is he himself. And I doubt if this is the right time to broach the matter.'

'Right, but then … let's talk later, Langeland.'

'Let's do that.'

I nodded and turned to go. Silje and her parents had gone into another office, followed by Grethe, the woman I presumed was her solicitor and the policewoman. Standal and Ruset stood waiting for us to finish.

'OK, Veum,' said Standal. 'Ready to go in?'

'I'm ready.'

'You did a good job up there last night. That's why I'm permitting this. But I expect something in return.'

'Oh?'

'A confession, Veum. It would be good if you could manage that.'

Jens Langeland gave an admonitory cough behind us. 'Er, I don't think you should be leading Veum on, Standal.'

Standal, peeved, glared at the nationally celebrated barrister. He had a fair inkling of what would be awaiting him if they ever met in court. 'Of course not, *herr advokat* Langeland. We will take note.'

Then he exerted his authority and led me to the partition door. And, without saying another word, escorted me in to see Jan Egil.

27

A uniformed officer stood to attention as we entered. Standal nodded to him. 'It's OK, Larsen. Veum may speak to the witness on his own. But I would like you to stay right outside. And, Veum, should you need assistance for some reason, all you have to do is say.'

I nodded. The two policemen left the room and closed the door behind them. I was alone with Jan Egil.

For the first time I had a decent look at him. The night before, up in Trodalen he had been wrapped up in an anorak and hood, and when we came back down to Angedalen he was put in the other police car. Now I saw an overgrown seventeen-year-old I would never have recognised if I had met him in the street. He seemed to be taller than me, even when he was sitting, with disproportionately long arms. He had red scars and fresh spots in the area around his mouth and down his neck, and his facial hair was blond and downy, which further strengthened the impression of a grumpy cockerel. It was the taut, slightly aggrieved, expression around his mouth that I seemed to recall, and when my eyes met his, I caught a glimpse of the demonstratively silent and aggressive Jan that was ingrained within him. He looked down with a scowl on his face. He sat hunched over the table with the palms of his hands on the surface as though he could launch himself any minute and dive forward. It was only when Standal and the other policeman had closed the door that some of the tension seemed to leave his body. He raised his head and scrutinised my face, perhaps in an attempt to raise me from his database, as I had done with him.

We were in a kind of interview room. There was a small window situated high up in the wall. All we could see through it was the sky over Førde, and that wasn't much to shout about from here, either. Scattered raindrops fell on the pane, becoming thin lines of tears between us and life outside. Now and then we heard the sound of passing vehicles and the odd scream of a child from Kyrkjevegen; distant everyday sounds.

I went to the table edge and held out my hand. 'Hello again, Jan Egil.'

He looked at my hand in surprise, without showing any sign of wanting to shake it.

I shrugged, smiled to signal it didn't matter, pulled out a spindle-back chair and sat down opposite him.

Again I met his eyes. The expression in them was let's-wait-and-see, wily almost, as though he was prepared for anything.

'You wanted to talk to me, they said.'

He gently tossed back his head, and averted his eyes. Then they returned and he gave a stiff nod.

'So what's on your mind, Jan Egil?'

I watched the muscles in his jaw swell. The blood vessels in his temple grew and his face went red. 'Nothing,' he mumbled, unconvincingly.

'Yeah, well, I'm sure you will have when you've had a think.' I gave him some space, but as he didn't react, I continued. 'Yesterday you said I was the only person you wanted to speak to. I've come all the way from Bergen to help you and would have come twice as far if it had been necessary. Langeland, your solicitor, has come all the way from Oslo. Grethe from social services. Hans Haavik. We're all here to help you. You can be sure of that. None of us takes what the police say happened as read. We want to hear it from your own mouth, in your words.' After a pause I added: 'What really happened.'

As he still didn't answer, I said: 'Silje has given her version of events. The same as she said up in Trodalen last night.'

His mouth twitched, but he still didn't say anything.

'Of course you know the story about Trodalen Mads?'

He nodded with a jerk. 'Heard about him at school.'

'It's not at all certain that he'd be sentenced nowadays. I mean, now even a middling lawyer would've got him off provided that the trader's body hadn't been found. And who knows what was behind it. No one knows. Perhaps it was a miscarriage of justice, too. There have been enough of them over the centuries. The Hetle case. You must have heard of that one as well.' He nodded, and I went on: 'What I'm trying to say is … that this case may not be what it appears to be at first glance. That's why it's so important that we hear the version of events of all those implicated.'

'Impli …?'

'Yes, all of those who are involved in some way or other.'

He nodded heavily. I thought I could discern a first glint of understanding in his eyes.

'So you tell me now … You do remember, don't you … The last time I saw you was almost exactly ten years ago, when you moved here in 1974. To Kari and Klaus in Angedalen. You were well looked after, weren't you?'

Again he tossed his head in that way of his. 'They were OK.'

'Yes? You were treated well in their house?'

'They were OK,' he repeated, as though I hadn't heard the first time.

'Good. You went to school. Now you're starting the final years, I've been told. Electronics, right?'

He nodded. '… Lectronics.'

'Right, but that's fine, isn't it?'

'Yup.'

'And then you got to know Silje.'

He didn't answer.

'How long have you known her?'

'From – kiddies' school.'

'She's a foster child too, isn't she …'

He nodded.

'So in a way you were in the same situation?'

He looked at me and tossed his head. 'Mm.'

'Did she become … your girlfriend?'

Again he went red. The corners of his mouth twitched, but this time it might have been a smile pushing through rather than anything else. 'She is now!'

'So when she went up with you to Trodalen yesterday, it wasn't because you forced her?'

His brow darkened. 'No! That's lies, something the sergeant cooked up.' Jan still spoke in dialect.

'OK, OK. I don't believe you forced her. I realised that as soon as I saw you. That she wasn't a hostage in any shape or form, I mean.'

'No! She wasn't.'

'Right.' I waited for a bit, until he had calmed down. 'But what she said up there …'

Again his eyes turned wary.

'You heard it as well, didn't you. It was me who did it, she said. Have you got anything to say to that?'

He pursed his lips, like a reflection of the six-and-a-half-year-old Jan ten years before.

'She blamed … Klaus,' I whispered.

He didn't answer.

'Was there anything in what she said?'

His expression smouldered and I could see him fighting with the words that just would not come out. For a moment I was afraid he would go on the attack, and I involuntarily tensed my stomach muscles, ready to get to my feet if it was necessary.

Then he seemed to shrink inside himself again, crumpled up, lowered his head and stared down at the table top. 'Dunno,' he mumbled.

I sighed. 'Perhaps we should take it right from the beginning, Jan Egil. Can you tell me what happened the day before yesterday, on Monday?'

His reaction was instant. 'I wasn't at home!'

'But … where were you then?'

'At Silje's house!'

'At night?'

'Yes!' he said with a defiant stare. 'We're old enough!'

'Yes, yes … but …?'

He suddenly looked almost pleased with himself. 'Her parents … Klara and Lars. They didn't hear anything. But we were sleeping together, all night.'

I smiled sympathetically. 'Through till Tuesday?'

'Through till Monday!'

'Through till … OK. But you had to go to school then, on Monday?'

'Yeah. I just popped by to fetch my bag. Popped home to Libakk.'

'And …what happened?'

He looked across at me. 'Nothing.'

'But … didn't you speak to them?'

'No.'

'You just …'

'I just shouted. But when I didn't get an answer, I assumed they were in the cowshed. So I just made myself a packed lunch and rushed off to the school bus. It wasn't until I came home, in the afternoon, that I – found them.'

'You found them! Where?'

'In their bedroom. Klaus was in bed, Kari over by the window. Shot, both of them.'

He told me this with the same intonation as if we were both sitting in a chair and reading a newspaper, strangely untouched, as if this had nothing to do with him at all.

'And the weapon?'

'It was on the floor, just inside the door. Klaus's rifle, the one he uses for deer-hunting.'

I studied him. His expression was hard to decipher. It was flat and catatonic, the way I remembered him in 1974.

'So this is Monday afternoon …?'

He nodded in silence.

'But you didn't ring the police?'

'No, I knew what it would be like. Knew who would get the blame … and that was how it turned out of course.'

'But what did you think you would do? Leave them lying there?'

He didn't answer, just pursed his lips tightly and tossed his head in his characteristic way.

'Silje. Didn't you tell her?'

He just shook his head.

'Did you talk to her at all that day?'

'No, not after school.'

'Tell me … you say you slept together the whole night. Through till Tuesday. Could she have nipped out while you were asleep and down to Libakk?'

His face changed colour. 'It wasn't Silje!'

'So who was it then?'

'How should I know! Somebody trying to rob them perhaps.'

'Well … we'll have to hear what the forensic examination turns up. So what then? Tell me what happened on Tuesday.'

'I didn't go to school that day.'

'Oh, what did you do then?'

'I went into the cowshed, Monday night and Tuesday morning. Someone had to look after the animals.'

I nodded. 'So you've taught yourself to milk?'

'We've got a machine.'

'Right, of course. But when you'd finished that?'

'I just sat there, in the sitting room, waiting for something to happen.'

'Uhuh? With Klaus and Kari lying dead upstairs.'

'And then Silje came. Because I hadn't been on the bus.'

I waited.

'Then I told her.'

'And how did she react?'

'She was scared, of course.'

'Nevertheless she didn't say –'

'How many times do I have to tell you? It wasn't her!'

'No, of course not. But didn't she say you should ring the police?'

'Yeah, she said that.'

'And?'

'That was when they arrived! I panicked. I didn't know what they would think, and I was right! I grabbed the rifle and took off with Silje, out the back of the house and up the mountain, towards Trodalen.'

'But the sergeant says you shot at him?'

'Yes, I did, when he shouted for me to stop! I didn't want to stop. I knew what they would say, and now … Now I'm sitting here, just as I had feared, accused of something I didn't do!'

'But the rifle … you say you grabbed it. The bedroom's on the first floor, isn't it?'

He nodded.

'And you were sitting on the ground floor waiting for something to happen, as you say.'

'Yes.'

'You'd taken the rifle downstairs?'

'I had to have something to defend myself with if they came back!'

'If they came back! Who came back?'

'The robbers!'

'But it was the police who'd come …'

'Yes! You know the rest. I hid up in Trodalen, together with Silje. I should never have given myself up. I should be sitting up there now … then they would have had to shoot me, if that was what they wanted.'

An eerie silence fell over us. There was something unreal about the whole thing. I found it difficult to visualise. The two dead people, Klaus in bed, Kari by the window, both in a pool of blood. And then the perpetrator … I tried to imagine Silje, but it was hard. Such a young girl … Jan Egil, on the other hand, if he had strong enough reason to do it. But it could easily have been someone else, or several others. Robbers, as he put it. Nothing had been reported stolen, though, and there were no signs of a break-in. What could the motive have been?

The perpetrator, standing by the bed with two dead or dying people in front of them. What was he thinking? Or she? What did they do? Run off? Drive away? Did anyone observe any cars in the yard that night? On their way in or out of the valley? And if it had been Silje or Jan Egil, had she or he just run back to Almelid, gone into the bedroom and cuddled up to the other person without anyone noticing?

Or … could they have been in on it together?

What if Silje was telling the truth – about the motive at any rate? In that case perhaps it wasn't so strange that she had confided in the person who had become her boyfriend, and who even lived in the house of the possible abuser, although he was not related. Had they conspired, or had he become her avenger, the person who carried out the action she herself could not? In that case Klaus was the target and Kari had the misfortune to be in the same room as him when revenge was exacted; that is, if she hadn't known what was going on and thus made herself an accomplice, at least in the eyes of the two youngsters.

When they had to give themselves up, Silje did what she could to protect him and assumed all the guilt herself …

Yes, I had to admit it. Until there was proof of anything else, there was a lot going for this version of reality.

I cleared my throat to attract his attention again. He looked up from the table.

'Listen, Jan Egil. What Silje said last night, when she called Klaus an old pig, we all understand what she meant by that. But even though neither you nor she had anything to do with the murders themselves … could there be anything in it? Could he have tried it on her?'

He shook his head sullenly. 'Not as far as I could see. She never said anything to me, about stuff like that.'

'Well, I'm afraid that's the way it often is. You keep it to yourself for as long as possible. My question was: could he have done it? Could it have happened without your knowing?'

He shrugged. 'Anything's possible, I s'pose.'

'He never tried it on you?'

'No!' He looked at me with an expression of horror. 'What do you think I am?'

'Sexual abusers are not always bothered about gender. I had to ask. I'm sorry.'

I thought briefly about what the sergeant had proposed. He wanted a confession, he had said. But I had the feeling we were further from that than when I had stepped into the room.

I studied him for a long time, then said tentatively: 'Something quite different, Jan Egil. Now I would like you to think back ten years.'

His eyes narrowed and he seemed to be holding his breath.

'That was why it was me you wanted to talk to, I assume. Because you can remember what a great time we had, Cecilie, you and me, the time you had to move from … where you were living at the time.'

He eyed me warily.

'Can you remember any of what happened at that time?'

He just gawped.

'I'm thinking of …' I was unsure as to how far I should go. 'Do you remember an accident taking place? Your father … fell down the staircase and broke his neck. Your mother said it happened during a row. But at first you and your father were alone at home. Do you remember any of that?'

He pinched his lips together, but made a faint negative movement with his head.

'Not even that you and your father were alone at home? You were playing with your train, I think.'

For a moment he brightened up. 'My Märklin train. I've still got it!'

'Exactly. I remember how well it ran.'

'There was a ring at the door.'

I bent closer and nodded, gestured for him to continue. But he stopped there.

'There was a ring at the door,' I repeated.

'Yes. Someone came in. I heard them quarrelling. But I was playing with my train. I didn't want to hear!'

'They were quarrelling? Your mother and father?'

'It wasn't her! It was a man. A man's voice.'

A shudder ran through me. 'What! What did you say?'

He looked at me in bewilderment. 'That's all. I don't remember any more. Not until I was standing there, at the top of the stairs, and he was lying at the foot. There was a ring at the door, and she let herself in. She screamed out loud. Looked at me horror-stricken, as though I had done it. But it wasn't me! I always get the blame!'

His eyes were open wide. For a second it was as if he were six and a half again and was going to be told off for something he hadn't done. 'The last thing I remember is her scream. Then I remember nothing until we're at Hans's place with you and me throwing snowballs.'

'But why ...?'

It suddenly rushed in over me, like a wave reaching the shore all too late. Why didn't he say anything about this at the time? Why had no one asked him? Or had they, without getting an answer? Had he not told anyone till now? Was I the first person to hear? For a moment my mind went giddy. What would Jens Langeland say to this? I wondered. Should Vibecke Skarnes have been acquitted in 1974? And ... did this have any repercussions for this case, ten years later? Did death follow in his footprints, or was this all just a network of coincidences?

I threw out my arms. 'I don't know if we're going to get much further today, Jan Egil. Have you got everything you wanted to say off your chest?'

'I think so.' All of a sudden he stretched out one hand and grabbed my wrist hard, the way a drowning man grasps a branch before he is inexorably dragged down by the current. 'Help me, Varg! You have to help me!' There were tears in his eyes. 'It wasn't me! Not this time, either ...'

I patted his hand with the one I had free.

'I promise, Jan Egil! I'll do everything that's in my power. If you're lucky, something will turn up that can underpin what you've told me. Forensic evidence, a witness's statement, whatever. One thing you can be absolutely sure of, Jan Egil. We'll help you as much as we can, all of us.'

His eyes implored me. 'You have to help me! You do!'

'Yes, of course.' I felt almost ashamed at the trust he was showing me. 'I will help you, Jan Egil. I will, too. As much as I can.'

I didn't dare promise him any more. I was frightened it was too much already. But I felt a strong urge to have a detailed conversation with Jen Langeland; and not only about the double murder in Angedalen but perhaps just as much about the accident in Wergelandsåsen ten years before ...

Gradually he let go of my arm. Then he withdrew his hand. But his eyes were still locked on mine, intense and pleading.

For a moment we sat like that. Then I nodded, got up, made a gesture with my hand and walked towards the door. Before opening it, I turned back to him. 'Bye for now ...'

He didn't answer. And he was no longer looking at me, but down at the table.

I quietly opened the door and left.

28

The constable on duty outside got up off his chair as I was leaving, nodded briefly and went in to Jan Egil. I heard him say something before closing the door behind him. Straight afterwards he opened it again and shouted down the corridor. 'He's hungry! Can anyone go and get a pizza and a Coke?'

Standal came into the corridor, nodded, then passed on the order to one of the other officers.

Jens Langeland and the person I presumed was Silje's solicitor were sitting at the coffee table in the corner of the waiting area. Both stood up as I came out, and all three looked at me with an expression of anticipation.

I was introduced to Langeland's colleague, a woman with cropped dark hair, small and sprightly, almost a bit French in style, wearing a short grey skirt and a tight black top. She was from Trondheim. 'Øygunn Bråtet,' she said with a little smile. 'I'm Silje's solicitor.'

'Yes, so I gathered. Varg Veum, private investigator.'

Standal sniffed behind me, and I turned to face him again.

'Well, Veum. What did he want?'

'To be quite frank, I'm not entirely sure. But I think I'm going to have to disappoint you. I didn't get a confession. More the opposite.'

'In other words, he served you up the same pack of lies we had?'

Langeland reacted instantaneously. 'I reject such leading comments, sergeant! So far the police have not adduced one single piece of evidence, and another person has confessed to the misdeed.'

'A confession not one of us believes, please note!' Øygunn Bråtet said sharply.

'Absolutely!' Standal concurred. 'We have questioned the young lady, you see … Silje Tveiten. And we were not very impressed, Langeland. To put it mildly. When we asked how she dealt with the gun, her descriptions became somewhat vague. She had no idea how she had released the safety catch, nor loaded the gun. If you ask me, the girl has never had a rifle in her hands.'

'And you're sure the old Mauser is the murder weapon?' asked Langeland.

'The pathologist's and the forensic examinations will make that clear very quickly. But I would be very surprised if it wasn't.'

'The only thing you know for certain thus far is that this was the weapon Jan Egil took with him when he ran off.'

'Yes, exactly. Ran off! And why did he do that, if I may ask, if he was so innocent, as you wish to claim?'

'He's had a traumatic childhood,' I interceded. 'As I explained to you earlier today.'

'Yes, yes, yes. We've noted that, Veum, but …'

'Besides, Grethe Mellingen told me something I didn't know. About Silje and the murder of her father in 1973.'

Langeland nodded in confirmation. 'Yes, my colleague has just informed me about that. A very important piece of information, I have to say.'

The sergeant glared at him. 'In what way, if I might ask? She was no more than five years old when that happened.'

'Nonetheless …' Langeland assumed a didactic tone, as if he were already well into his courtroom procedure. 'We are dealing here with a double murder. We have a brutal murder in 1973. We have a suspicious death in 1974. Both children are implicated.'

'And Terje Hammersten,' I added.

Standal looked as if he would explode. 'Terje Hammersten! Who the bloody hell is that?'

'I understand the police up here were interested in him in 1973. Isn't that correct?'

'I wasn't here in 1973, but I will, of course, dig up the files.'

'So you haven't done that yet then?' Langeland commented caustically.

'We have other business to take care of!' the sergeant barked.

'And in 1974 he was still living with Jan Egil's biological mother, Mette Olsen.'

Standal stared at me. 'In 1974!'

'Yes, his foster father was killed.'

'But that case was solved, Veum,' said Langeland sharply. 'There are no loose ends.'

I met his gaze. 'Are you sure? Now in fact I have some new information about what happened at that time. From Jan himself! Maybe Vibecke Skarnes should not have been found guilty at the time.'

Langeland blanched. 'I beg your pardon. What did he ...?'

I sent him a knowing look. 'Let's come back to that later.'

'Yes, we certainly aren't interested in cases solved years ago,' Standal said.

Langeland eyed me pensively before nodding in silence and wagging his index finger: *We have a deal.*

I shifted my attention to Øygunn Bråtet. 'Where's she now, Silje ... and her foster parents?'

'They've gone home.'

'Home!' I turned to Standal again. 'You've let her go free today, too?'

He looked at me with unease. 'So young she is ... After consultation with her solicitor and *fru* Mellingen, and because we have no confidence in her statement, we have let her go home. But there is a policewoman with her, and we expect Silje to come in whenever we need her.'

'Strikingly different treatment!' Langeland commented. 'Or were you thinking of letting Jan Egil out, too?'

'He doesn't have any home to return to now,' Standal said coldly. 'Besides he's still our main suspect, and if you don't mind, *herr advokat*, I would suggest we see him now and continue the interview.'

Langeland sighed. 'Yes, let's do that. We can talk later, Veum. You're staying at the Sunnfjord, aren't you?'

'Yes, just get in touch when you're back.'

Langeland nodded. Standal clocked me with an expression of hope that he would never see me again. They went back to Jan Egil.

Øygunn Bråtet and I stood back, a little perplexed, like two castaways on a reef after the storm has passed. Then she shrugged and went over to a hat stand to get her outdoor clothing, a natty little cape the same length as her skirt.

'I'll have to get back to my office,' she said. 'We're going to be busy in the coming period. But we'll see each other again, I imagine.'

'Hard to avoid. And should you ever need a private investigator then …'

'I know who to turn to. Yes, thank you,' she said, with a brief nod and a smile that lasted a tiny bit longer before departing.

Before I left, I was addressed by the officer behind the counter. 'Veum? We've got a message for you here.'

'Really? Thank you.'

I took the small handwritten note. It was from Grethe. *Going home to rest*, she wrote. *Ring you later.*

When I got down to the street, Øygunn Bråtet was gone. I went back to the hotel to have dinner. Alone.

29

When I arrived at the hotel, a message was waiting for me there, too. But it was from Helge Haugen of *Firda Tidend*. *Ring me asap*! it said, and I did. I unlocked my room, sat down by the telephone table and rang him at the newspaper.

'Veum … thanks for phoning. I've got something I'd like to discuss with you. An interesting point that no one has brought out yet.'

'Oh yes?'

'You know … this Klaus Libakk, one of the murder victims inside the house, I've been doing a bit of enquiring about him. There's some evidence to suggest that the police have had him under suspicion.'

'Really? What for?'

'Well, now you can guess!'

'Not an indecency affair, I assume, since he was approved as a foster parent by social services.'

'No. Indecency …?' He was quick on the uptake. 'Has there been any talk of anything like that?'

'I can't comment on that.'

'We agreed to exchange our information, didn't we?'

'Agreements only go so far, Haugen, I'm bound by an oath of client confidentiality.'

'Client confidentiality! A private investigator?'

'If not to others, then to myself, if you understand what I mean.'

'OK, OK. I won't insist. Not yet. But then listen to this … you may have heard of the great smuggling business that was all the local news in the 1970s?'

I felt my whole body tense up. 'Yes. It even culminated in a murder, I remember.'

'Bullseye, Veum.'

'Did Klaus Libakk have anything to do with that?'

He let the question hang in the air for a moment. Then he said: 'He was never charged with anything. But the information I've unearthed says he was responsible for distributing illegal alcohol, to everyone in Angedalen!'

'Wow! Where did you get that from, and why was he never taken to court?'

'The thing is, Veum, I'm afraid to say, that the case was never properly followed up. There are lots of loose threads left dangling, if I can put it like that.'

'And why not?'

'You know how it is in small communities. Rumour has it that various persons high in the top echelons of local administration were involved – yes, even high-ranking police officials, at least they were on the customer list, and this led in the end to the matter being hushed up. Those behind the actual smuggling were snapped up, but the middlemen by and large went free. In addition, many considered this a political matter, as good as. I mean, Sogn and Fjordane is the only county in Norway not to have its own Vinmonopol – we still have to go to Bergen or Ålesund to buy alcohol.'

'But … the matter was hushed up, you say. For Christ's sake, there was a murder! Ansgår Tveiten.'

'You're well informed, Veum. I'll give you that. But Ansgår Tveiten himself belonged to the criminal fraternity hereabouts. No one missed him.'

'He left behind a little daughter …'

'What? Right … perhaps he did. But no one else. It proved to be difficult to get anyone from this milieu to talk and … anyway the case was dropped. No one was even charged with the murder.'

'Right. Back to Klaus Libakk. You're saying he was responsible for distributing alcohol to everyone in Angedalen, aren't you?'

'Yes, to those who were interested in buying the product, that is,' he said, marginally modifying the statement.

'Like those at Almelid Farm perhaps?'

'Almelid? I haven't checked the case in such detail yet. Why do you ask?'

'OK, I'll give you a tasty titbit in return, Haugen.'

'Yes? I'm all ears!'

'This girl who went up to Trodalen with Jan Egil last night …'

'Yes, she was from Almelid, that's right.'

'Yes, but she was a foster child, too. Her name is Silje Tveiten. Daughter of Ansgår Tveiten.'

'What! By Christ, that is tasty!' After mulling this over for a second, he added: 'That could almost give the girl a motive, Veum. At least if Klaus Libakk had been involved in the murder of her father. Have you thought about that?'

No, I hadn't. Not until now. And I didn't tell Helge Haugen, either. All I said was: 'But how on earth would she have found that out, if the police had dropped the case?'

'Well, that's a point. But it's worth thinking about, isn't it.'

'You'll have to do what you think best. But don't make any references to me in this.'

'We always protect our sources, Veum. You can be sure of that. Even if you should decide to break what you call your oath of client confidentiality …'

'Anything else?'

'No, just what I told you, and I've been richly rewarded. We'll talk again as soon as there is anything. See you!'

'See you.'

I rang off and sat staring at the telephone.

Ansgår Tveiten and Klaus Libakk. Terje Hammersten and …

I sensed a pattern beneath all of this, a vague outline of things unsaid and unseen which were slowly rising to the surface.

But what? And where? I asked myself, then made a decision: the next day the search would start in earnest.

30

All roads lead to Rome, they say. But they were wrong. In my part of the world, all roads lead to the bar at Sunnfjord Hotel. Especially during these days when Førde is at the centre of news in what must be the biggest sensation since Ålesund burnt down, judging by the media frenzy. The place was swarming with reporters, inside and outside the hotel, and most of them ended up in the bar, as they are wont to do.

After dinner in the hotel dining room – roast venison with sprouts and cranberry sauce – I took a pile of newspapers and slunk off to a free table in the spacious bar. I started carefully with a pot of coffee and a glass of Line aquavit. It wasn't long before I had company.

Jens Langeland came into the foyer, looked around ignoring all the press people who started waving their arms to attract his attention, caught sight of me, made a gesture and came in my direction. 'Alright if I sit here, Veum?'

'Course. We have a lot to talk about.'

He nodded. I noticed that he looked tired, and I wondered how early he had set off from Oslo today. He signalled to the bartender and ordered a coffee and a cognac. He glanced at my glass, which was as good as empty. 'Can I offer you another, Veum?'

'Certainly can. Thank you.'

'What are you drinking?'

'Løiten Line. They didn't have my regular tipple.'

He raised his eyebrows, but made no further comment about the choice. For himself, he chose a cognac from the top shelf, from where he was used to gathering his trophies.

'Now,' he said. 'You had something new to tell me about the events of 1974, you said.'

'Yes. You didn't ask Jan Egil about it?'

'No, not with the sergeant present.' He ran his hand across his face. 'It was the same as always. Flogging a point to death. The police asked the same questions again and again, in the hope that the witness would contradict himself. On top of that, we had the KRIPOS officers with us.'

'I see. Did they have anything to bring to the case?'

'It's too early to say. They're still at the information-gathering stage. Detectives are going from farm to farm to ask if people have anything to say, if they have seen or heard anything, and alongside that they're making general assessments of Jan Egil, the Libakk couple and Silje Tveiten. But what we're all waiting for now, of course, is the results of the forensics examination.'

'And when are they expected?'

'We haven't been given a clear date yet.'

'But I have something to tell you, Langeland.'

'Yes, you said that.'

'Yes, but about this case, too.'

I paused as the bartender came over to serve us. When every-thing was in place and we had said *skål* for the first time, I went on: 'The murder victim Klaus Libakk was involved in the big con-traband racket in 1973 when Silje's father was murdered and Terje Hammersten was being fingered as the culprit.'

'Whoa there, Veum. One thing at a time. Klaus Libakk was involved in the smuggling affair?'

'Yes.'

I suddenly became aware of a guy in his late thirties sitting alone at the adjacent table. He was dark-haired with a bloated face and drunken eyes. He was clinging to a glass and staring ahead, with such rigid attention that I drew the conclusion he was either pissed and/or intensely following our conversation.

I lowered my voice still further and leaned across to Langeland. In succinct terms, I repeated what Haugen had told me an hour and a half earlier.

Langeland listened until I had finished without commenting. Then he got down to brass tacks. 'This would actually suggest that Silje Tveiten can be said to have a motive.'

'That presupposes at least three things, Langeland. First of all, that the rumours are true, about Libakk's involvement, I mean. Secondly, that he had something to do with the murder of Ansgår Tveiten, and thirdly that Silje had somehow discovered this connection, and this was a case that the police had been forced to give up on. Pretty unlikely, if you ask me. The last presupposition, anyway. We'll have to investigate the first two, of course.'

Langeland bent forward with an intense expression in his eyes. 'Could you see your way to doing that, Veum? For me?'

'Investigating these questions, you mean?'

'Yes.'

'No problem. I've worked for lawyers before, Langeland.'

'I pay well. Money is no object.'

I passed my hand over the table. 'We have a deal then. When shall I begin?'

He quickly shook my hand. 'The sooner, the better.'

'Regard me as hired from this minute. In that case I can tell you something else. You remember Mette Olsen, Jan Egil's real mother?'

'I certainly do. I represented her years ago. Where is this leading?'

'Did you know that she's moved to Jølster?'

'To Jølster!'

'Barely an hour's drive from here. By Kjøsnes fjord. I'm planning to look her up tomorrow. Are you interested in what might come out of the visit?'

'Mette Olsen, so close to her own son ... but have you checked? ... This has to be a coincidence. Perhaps she has family up here.'

'Most people in Bergen do. But I don't believe much in coincidences, Langeland. Not when there's a murder in their immediate vicinity anyway.'

'No, of course not. No stone left unturned. You have my full support to visit her, but … tread warily. She's had a tragic life.'

'You aren't her solicitor any more, I suppose?'

'No, no. When I left Bergen, she must have found someone else. At any rate, I haven't heard anything from her since then.'

'So we have a deal on that point, too.' I raised my glass for a *skål*, to seal our agreement.

'But it was 1974 you were going to tell me about,' he said, putting his glass down hard.

'Yes. Jan Egil, when I was talking to him today, told me something I had never heard before. It's about the day that Svein Skarnes died, if I can put it like that.

He leaned forward and watched me with those intense blue eyes of his, as if I were the prosecution witness in a case he was leading.

'Jan Egil told me that on the day of Skarnes's death in February, 1974, he was sitting in the lounge playing with his Märklin train when there was a ring at the door. The father opened and immediately a row ensued.'

'A row. With whom?'

'He doesn't know. He was sitting and playing. He didn't want to be disturbed.'

'But there was a ring. So it wasn't …'

'No, probably not. In fact, Jan Egil said the same. His mum had a key after all. She wouldn't have needed to ring.'

'No, but she said herself at the time, I believe, that she rang first and then unlocked the door, as no one would open up.'

'Yes, but that was later – after the fatal fall had occurred. And Jan Egil said, so far as we can trust him of course, ten years later, that it was a man's voice he heard, apart from his father's.'

'A man!' He paled visibly as the consequences of this dawned on him. 'But then …'

'As I said earlier today, Langeland, Vibecke Skarnes should probably have been acquitted.'

'But why the hell did she confess? She did confess, Veum, and I never managed to persuade her to retract this confession.'

I nodded and leaned back in the chair. The man at the adjacent table waved to the bartender and ordered another whisky and soda. In ringing Bergensian tones, I noticed. 'Just put it on the tab!' he added.

'There was a confession in the Hilleren case, too.'

'Yes, but no body, Veum! We had one here. Besides ...' He hesitated.

'We must both have wondered why she confessed, didn't we?'

'Indeed.' He nodded. 'To protect the boy. She was convinced he had done it.'

'In fact he pushed me down the stairs straight afterwards, so the notion was not inconceivable.'

'No, and he had bitten Skarnes until he bled a few months before. I'm sure that was the main reason why she decided not to maintain parental responsibility when she was released.'

'She was frightened of him?'

He shrugged. 'I'll have to contact her. It may become relevant to consider a retrial, in my view. But ... I don't see any significance it may have for the current investigation.'

'No, but that's something I could examine as well, as I work my way into this case.'

He nodded. The bartender brought the glass of whisky to the neighbouring table and we took the opportunity to replenish our glasses. Langeland kept to expensive cognac. I switched to a Bloody Mary.

Several reporters were circling our table, but Langeland sent them all packing. He refused to comment on anything at all. The Bergensian at the neighbouring table seemed more alert now, as if the new drink had resuscitated him. A couple of times I saw him looking in our direction as though keen to say something. But I didn't encourage him. On the whole I had had bad experiences with this kind of relationship in late night hotel bars.

A large shadow fell over our table, and we peered at the top of this towering figure.

'Hi, Hans!' said Langeland. 'Sit yourself down before anyone else does.'

'I'm not disturbing?'

'No, no.'

Hans Haavik turned to the bar, gestured that he wanted a glass of beer and then sat down heavily in the free chair at the table. He glanced at me and shook his head. 'One helluva story!'

I nodded back and looked at Langeland. 'Hans was Libakk's cousin and had kept tabs on Jan Egil the whole time. He was up here visiting them as late as last weekend.'

'So I hear. We had a chat while you were in with Jan Egil.'

'What's your line of attack going to be then?' Hans asked.

'The way it looks now, there are two possible lines. The first is to take Silje at her word and exploit her confession as far as we are able. But she may have a job sticking to it herself, from what the police say. The second is to opt for unknown killers, burglars, robbers who go too far and, when they realise, flee without the spoils, terrified of being caught in the act. Not so unusual in rural areas, I regret to say. The problem is that there are no signs of a break-in, of course. It will be very interesting to hear the results of the forensic examinations, both at the crime scene and of the weapon, as well as the pathologist's report on the bodies. In a nutshell ... everything is in the air for the time being.'

Hans seemed thoughtful. 'This Silje ...'

'Have you met her?'

'I've said hello, yes. Several times. But why would she confess if she hadn't done it?'

'Hmm.' Langeland sent him an inquisitorial look. 'Why did Vibecke confess in 1974?'

'Because she'd done it, I suppose!'

'But now new information has emerged which suggests that was perhaps not the case. That she simply took the blame because she was sure Jan Egil had done it.'

'Well ...' Hans glanced at me. 'I think we all thought that was a possibility, even at the time. But she stuck to her confession with such determination.'

'You remember yourself how headstrong she could be!'

'Yes indeed ...'

'You both knew her from university?' I broke in.

They nodded.

'What did she study?'

'She drifted a bit. Took psychology foundation, but she fell at the next hurdle and couldn't get in. It can be terribly difficult without top grades. So she started law, but didn't finish. That was where she was when I got to know her. And in the end she moved into your subject, didn't she, Hans?'

'Related. She took sociology foundation.'

I looked at Langeland. 'Someone intimated that you and she had been a couple for a while ...'

He glowered at Hans. 'Have you been opening your big mouth again?'

'Me?' Hans feigned an innocent expression, which was partly torpedoed by the pink tinge to his cheeks. 'He must have got this from a different source,' he grumbled.

'Veum?'

'I protect my sources, Langeland,' I said with a little grin. 'But it wasn't a million miles from the truth, was it?'

'It was a short affair a long time ago when I was a student. It didn't have any significance, neither for ... at any rate not for the case I took on in 1974.'

'No, because you were the family solicitor, weren't you? I think you told me something like that.'

'It was Svein who needed legal assistance generally. But I knew Vibecke best. She got to know Svein through Hans.'

I turned quickly to Hans. 'But you and Vibecke never had a thing going, did you?'

His mouth fell. 'Vibecke Størset? Well, that was her name at the time. No, Veum, we never did. She never looked in my direction as far as I can remember. Besides Svein and I were … pals then.'

For a brief instant the table went silent, and I sensed a sudden tension between the two old university chums, only for it to dissolve and us to grab our glasses, all in one movement, it seemed.

Jens Langeland put on a disarming smile. 'But there were enough others, weren't there, Hansie, eh? When you were sowing your wild oats at the end of the course? Swinging London and wonderful, wonderful Copenhagen, city of sin … I think we got to hear the odd story or two, we stalwarts left in the old country, didn't we.'

Hans forced a rigid smile. 'I returned home safe and sound, didn't I.'

'Yes, yes. Let's hope so, Hans. I've never heard anything to the contrary …' he smirked over his glass.

'Listen,' I said. 'Something completely different. Your second cousin, Hans. Klaus Libakk. From a very reliable source I've heard that he was supposed to have been smuggling alcohol in the early sixties. Do you know anything about that?'

It was an evening of surprises for Hans Haavik. He shook his head. 'Klaus? I find that hard to believe. Who said that?'

'Well, it was mentioned as hearsay.'

'I didn't have much to do with Klaus and Kari at that time. It was only when Jan Egil moved in that I began to visit them regularly. After all, we were only cousins, and in my childhood I as good as never came to the Sunnfjord district. My maternal grandfather grew up here, and he moved to Bergen right after the First World War.'

'But when you visited them, were there drinks around?'

He shrugged and grinned. 'Well, we had a drink on Saturday nights. They weren't teetotallers, neither Klaus nor Kari.'

'And that was drinks from the Vinmonopol?'

'Varg, I didn't study the labels that closely. There has to be a limit. You know how these things are. Up here it's often a bit of both. The result of many years of a restrictive alcohol policy, as we all know. Large production of home brew and a hotbed of smuggling. Think of the significance the prohibition period had for the development of organised crime in the States.'

'Well, apropos of …' I looked at my watch. 'Time to drink up maybe? We've sorted out tomorrow, Langeland, haven't we. I'll report to you when I get back. And you, Hans, what's on your agenda?'

'No idea. I'll try to contact a few more relatives. Hear what's going on. I suppose it'll be a long time before the bodies are released for burial, but … we should organise some kind of memorial service. And then I'll help Jan Egil, of course, if need be. We'll see. I'm staying here over the weekend, anyway.'

I glanced over to the nearby table. The Bergensian had come to the same conclusion as we had. Time to hit the hay. Stiff-legged, he staggered out of the bar. But he didn't head for the part of the hotel where the rooms were. Instead he went into the foyer, opened the front door with difficulty and then disappeared into the Sunnfjord night, wherever that might take him.

Both Hans and Langeland were staying at the hotel. We parted company between the lift and the stairs. The first thing I saw when I entered the room was the message I had received from Grethe earlier: *Going home to rest. Ring you later.*

I dialled the reception number and asked if anyone had called for me. A grumpy night porter said no one had.

I looked at my watch. It was too late to ring her now, at any rate. I didn't have her number, either. Perhaps she was still asleep. The sleep of the innocent, I hoped.

I let it go, undressed and crawled into bed, alone, the same as almost always. Some things change very little, no matter where in the world you are. All roads lead to Sunnfjord Hotel, I had decided, but to my room all the mountain passes were closed. There was not much else to do but wait for spring.

31

The stretch of road alongside Lake Jølstravatn must be one of the most beautiful in Norway. The vast lake lies there, extending into the far distance, blue and looking as though it could last for all eternity. The mountain formation is beautiful and majestic, and against the arch of the sky you can glimpse Jostedal glacier, dazzlingly white in the daylight. An atmosphere of timelessness and calm rests over the countryside, the north-bound traffic on the main road the only disturbance.

It was no longer raining. There were patches of blue in the ceiling of cloud where the sun broke through with compact bundles of rays, like a harbinger of better times. The trees were rusty brown, specked with green and red. In a little boat in the middle of the lake sat a man with a fishing rod in his hands, patience personified. If he waited long enough he would undoubtedly get a bite. If I was lucky, his good fortune would rub off on me.

Grethe had rung before breakfast. 'Sorry, I didn't ring back, Varg, but I slept round the clock,' she had said before asking:

'What are your plans for today?'

'I'm driving out to Jølster. Would you like to join me?'

''Fraid not, I have to be with Silje today, too. And Jan Egil, if need be. Will we see each other later?'

'I'll be in touch when I'm back.'

'Fine. I've got something I'd like to show you.'

'Oh yes?' She had given a low chuckle: 'Yes …'

Before leaving, I dropped by the police offices to hear if anyone had any need of my services. No one had. The KRIPOS officers were going to speak to Jan Egil, they were still waiting for the first results of both the pathologist's and the forensic examinations, and as far as the local police division in Naustdal and Førde were concerned, I could travel to Jølster and further afield without any concerns.

A big, shiny silver milk tanker ensured that I did not break the speed limit before it finally indicated right and turned up into the valley by Årdal. Arriving in Ski, I branched off what was still called the A14. The road on the north side of Kjøsnes fjord was being improved because further along they were building a tunnel through the mountain to Fjærland. But I was not going that far. I turned down to the long, low Kjøsnes bridge, crossed over and bore left to high up on the slope to the south of the fjord.

I rolled down the car window and asked an elderly man standing on the roadside where I would find a farm called Leitet. He gave me a long, thoughtful stare while considering in some depth whether this was a question it would be appropriate to answer. He was chewing tobacco and spat a gobbet some distance into the ditch before half-turning and pointing to some old buildings further up: a grey farm building, a little outhouse and a white farmhouse. I thanked him for his help, and he returned my gaze with a sardonic look, without uttering a word.

I continued and came to a steep, narrow gravel path which seemed to lead up to the tiny farm. I turned off. Twice I had to get out of the car to open and close a farm gate before, at last, I was up in the untidy farmyard. I switched off the engine and sat behind the wheel for a while to see if anyone would come out to receive me. No one did.

Inside the open outhouse stood a red, rust-stained tractor. The white one-and-a-half-storey farmhouse with an attic facing the fjord also looked as if it could do with a spot of paint. From the farm building there was not a sound to suggest animals were housed inside. The barn was overgrown, and the grass had been allowed to grow wild. The whole place seemed abandoned, dead, a derelict monument to the trials of yore by the fjord to the east of Lake Jølstravatn.

As I opened the car door and stepped onto the yard, something happened. The front door opened, and a woman came out. She was wearing threadbare dark blue jeans without a hint of a fashionable cut and a reddish-brown sweater that had not seen a washing machine for many a day. And high green wellies on her feet. Her hair was blonde with broad grey streaks, much greyer than the last time I had seen her. Her face was lean and the network of wrinkles denser, but I still had no problem recognising the Mette Olsen of ten years ago.

She, on the other hand, squinted through scrunched-up eyes and snarled in dialect: 'Who are you? What d'you want here?'

'Veum,' I said. 'From Bergen. I don't know if you remember me.'

Despite not being more than in her late thirties, she looked as though she were well over fifty, and they had been fifty hard years. She had put on weight, although not so much, but what there was round her waist on the otherwise lean body, looked inert and unhealthy.

'Veum?' She closed one eye and looked at me stiffly with the other. 'Ye-es, I remember you ... you were one of those social services arseholes.'

'I'm not there any more.'

She wobbled a little and put out an arm to steady herself. 'What are you doing here then, eh?'

'It's partly to do with ... your son.'

She raised her head and inhaled deelpy through her nostrils. 'Johnny boy?' she said in such a low voice that I barely heard. 'What's up with him now then?'

'You haven't seen the papers?'

'I don't get a paper.'

'Listened to the radio? Seen the TV?'

'Yes, I saw the news, but ...' The significance of what I had asked suddenly seemed to hit home. Once again she almost lost her balance, but it was because she turned her head quickly and stared at the other side of Lake Jølstravatn, at the mountains she had to pass to reach Angedalen. 'It wasn't at that house ... What did you say? How is he? Johnny boy?'

I observed her. The consternation seemed genuine, and even if she *had* read the papers, none of the dead persons had been named yet. On the radio and TV they were even more reluctant to identify the murder victims.

'He's fine,' I said, if for no other reason than to tell her that at least he was alive. Otherwise, it was a dubious choice of words. 'Can we go inside for a moment?'

She looked at me with suspicion.

'It's not exactly summer temperatures outside.'

'Well …' She held out an arm to steady herself again, turned her back on me and stepped over the doorsill. But she left the door ajar behind her as a sign that I could follow.

I walked into a dark hallway where a steep staircase led up to a trapdoor. Two doors led into the rest of the house, one to the kitchen, the other to the sitting room. She had gone into the kitchen, and I followed. She ushered me to the table which was covered with a worn blue and white gingham oilcloth. A very well used coffee pot stood in the middle of the cloth. Beside it, there was a cracked coffee-stained cup. On the worktop in front of the window there were breadcrumbs, a tub of easy-spread margarine, an opened plastic pack of sheep sausage and half a jar of jam. The smell inside was stale, cloying, a combination of food and unwashed pots and pans.

She sat down at the table, grabbed the cup, confirmed that it was empty and filled it from the coffee pot, a pitch black, cold-looking liquid. She offered me nothing. I was glad.

She sat on her chair, crouched over the cup, holding it with both hands. It was only with the greatest effort that she managed to raise her head and look at me, or so it seemed. Her eyes were listless and tired, as if the shock had already left its mark. 'Is it that double murder that's being talked about?'

I nodded. 'Just tell me first, Mette … how long have you lived here?'

'What's it got to do with you?' she said at first, then after a short pause for thought she answered. 'Soon be two years.'

'What made you move here?'

'I wanted to get away from the town!' she said irascibly. 'I should have left many years ago. Perhaps everything would have turned out different then …'

'So your coming here wasn't a coincidence?'

'Coincidence? What do you mean?'

'Well, did you have family here?' I looked around at the greasy, unwashed walls. 'Did this place belong to the family, for example?'

She gave a faint nod. 'Distant family. They almost thrust it on me when I said I was interested. The soil wasn't much to shout about. Just scree and rocks. No one wanted to take it. You're not exactly top of the world if you do agriculture at the moment, anyway, I'm told.'

'But I suppose that wasn't the only reason you came to Jølster?'

'I told you why! I didn't pay a button for it.'

'Wasn't it more that you found out that Jan was living here? In another valley, true enough, but not so far away that you couldn't keep an eye on him.'

She didn't answer; just stared ahead with a darkened brow.

'How did you find out? Who told you where he'd gone?'

' … erje,' she mumbled.

'Terje? Terje Hammersten?'

She nodded in silence.

'And where had he got it from?'

'You'll have to ask 'im yourself!'

'I'll consider doing that. If I meet him. But, at any rate, we can establish that you moved here because you … because Jan lived here.'

'Let's say that then! If that's the way you want it.'

I put all the sympathy I could into my intonation. 'You couldn't let go of him?'

She squeezed the cup with her thin, dry, reddened fingers, the nails chewed right down. The knuckles went white and the gaze she directed at me was dark and angry. 'No, I couldn't! But that's absolutely impossible for bastards like you to understand, isn't it? All that bloody social services shite!'

'I'm no longer in –'

'No, I heard you the first time! But I don't care what you're doin' now. You were in social services when you took Johnny boy from me!'

'I just visited you at home, Mette. In 1970. It wasn't me who took the decision.'

'No, because then everything would've come up roses, wouldn't it? If you'd been in charge.' The scorn was unmistakable, concise and honed after many years of confrontations with bureaucracy and public authorities. 'Don't make me laugh.'

'But listen …'

'No, now you listen. Can you imagine what it feels like, here …?' She placed her hand on her left breast. 'Inside here, when local services come and take away the thing you love most, the most precious thing you possess?'

In a flash I saw in front of me the neglected, apathetic child we had visited at home on the Rothaugen estate that summer day in 1970. 'But you weren't capable of …'

'No, so you said! And no, perhaps I wasn't. Not then. But later, when I'd dried out and recovered from this and that … when I was ready to start afresh again, the whole of my life … where was he then? Well, he was out of your hands, you said. He'd been transferred to a new home. Yes, but I should have visiting rights, I said. Visiting rights, repeated that bitch I was speaking to. You signed the adoption papers, she said. Adoption papers! How was I supposed to remember any adoption papers?'

'You must have signed them if they said so.'

'Yes, but I reckon I must have been doped up at the time! Not in my right mind! I couldn't have just given him away … he was the only thing I had … the only thing I had left. After that …'

I waited. A terrible grief seemed to have taken over her face, a nameless, indescribable grief, greater than all else.

'After that I had nothing else to live for. From then on everything went downhill for me.' Tears ran down her wrinkled, all too prematurely aged cheeks; shiny, transparent tears. Her nose ran too, and with an irritated movement she wiped it all away with the back of her hand. 'Into the depths of hell,' she concluded, almost slumped over the table.

I had a feeling that I had heard this story before, and not just from her mouth. We sat in silence for some minutes. I looked towards the window. The daylight was pale and milky from behind the unwashed panes, a reflection of another world, somewhere far from where we were, in the shadow of a wretched past with little to look forward to.

'Things could have gone so much better for me, I'm tellin' you,' she broke the silence with a weary obstinacy, a doggedness she would never set aside.

'So tell …'

'Oh yes, you'd like that, wouldn't you! I could tell you some stuff, Veum, if I wanted. But …' She got up from the table with stiff movements. She supported herself on the table and walked to the door. I heard her out in the corridor and from there into what had been the drawing room of the house, where those living here only sat on Sunday mornings to listen to the church service on the radio, or on other formal occasions.

On her return, she had a small photo album in her hand. The red cover was torn, and when she flicked through I could see that several of the plastic pockets were empty. She flicked slowly from picture to picture. I glimpsed some black-and-white photographs from a distant childhood and a couple of pink colour snaps from an equally distant teenage period. Then she stopped by one photo, which she took out of the pocket and passed to me.

Despite the drastic change in her appearance, I could see that the woman in the picture was her. But it was still a different Mette from the one I had ever met. It was a beautiful young woman smiling happily at the photographer. She was wearing a colourful patterned blouse with a plunging neckline, and her hair had fluffy blonde curls, decorated with lots of small red and white ribbons, as if for a party. With an arm around her shoulders stood a man with long blond hair and a thin youthful beard, dressed in a white shirt, wide at the neck and hanging loosely from his chest, a Jesus freak smiling at her, in love, some time in the 1960s, I reckoned it would have to be.

'Taken in Copenhagen, summer of '66,' she said quietly.

'Who's the person you're with?'

'... David.'

'That was ... your boyfriend?'

She nodded. 'Yes.'

I hesitated, but I knew I had to ask. 'What happened?'

Her gaze swept along the tabletop as though the answer was scratched into the oilcloth somewhere. Once again I saw how she was gripped by a terrible pain, a grief beyond all words. 'He died,' she almost whispered.

I waited a while. 'How?'

She raised her face again. Stared me straight in the eye. 'We were betrayed. Someone stabbed us in the back.'

I motioned to her to continue.

'We – I had met him in Copenhagen in the early summer – and we fell head over heels in love. We were young and foolish, and we were already talking about moving in together, going back to Bergen and finding a place to live. And then we were offered a chance for quick money. We ... made a deal, packed our bags and took the plane to Flesland. But they were standing there waiting. Someone had snitched on us, of that I've been convinced from that day to this. And ...' She snatched desperately at her cup again, as if it were a lifebuoy. 'We were arrested.' She swallowed several times before proceeding. 'It was worse for David. He was carrying all of it, in a belt round here ...' She pointed to round her waist. 'I didn't have anything on me. But I was taken in as an accessory, and they charged me too, the bastards. Had it not been for my lawyer, I'd have had to do a stretch.'

'Langeland?'

'Jens?'

'Yes.'

She looked at me, perplexed. 'No, it was Bakke. An old boy. But you're right that Jens was there, too. But just as a junior. A superior gofer, I remember, he called himself. Do you know him?'

I nodded, but didn't add anything.

'He said … but you mustn't tell anyone this, right?'

'It'll stay between us, Mette.'

'He said I should deny everything. Bakke, that was. Say I had no idea what David had taken with him. The cops didn't care when I had met David. I should just say it was someone I had met in Kastrup Airport and had tagged along with. And … they would have to accept that. In court at any rate. No one could prove anything different. And David didn't give me away. You could rely on him …'

'But he was convicted?'

'Eight years in clink.'

'Eight years!'

'It was a huge amount we had with us. But the worst of all, do you know what that was?'

'No.'

'Imagine the guilt I felt afterwards. After all, I'd lied!'

'Ably assisted by your lawyers, it has to be said.'

'Yes, but nevertheless … it wasn't true, was it. I betrayed him just as much as someone had betrayed us. And when he hung himself it was like someone had thrust a knife into my chest and twisted it.'

'He hung himself in prison?'

'He suffered from claustrophobia. He couldn't stand it. He'd already told me in Copenhagen: if we get arrested, Mette, take my life. I'll never be able to cope with being locked up. And he couldn't. He held out until the sentence was passed, but then it was over. As soon as he got an opportunity he used a sheet as a rope and tied it round his neck. They found him in the morning. By then he was dead.'

She stretched out her hand as if to say she wanted the photo back. I passed it to her. 'From then it was curtains for old Mette. From then on it could only go one way. Down, to hell.'

She was trembling with sobs now. Her lean body was shaking with convulsions, and she wept uncontrollably. I let her cry herself out. When things had calmed down, I asked carefully: 'And you have no idea who it was who informed on you?'

She shook her head gently. 'It must have been some prick in Copenhagen. Who was jealous that David had cleared off with the Princess.' Before I could say anything, she added: 'Yes, that's what they called me, that summer down there. Princess Mette they called me. Or simply the Princess ...'

'But someone must've lost a hell of a lot of money on that number ...'

'They did, the bastards.'

'You never heard any more?'

'Why should I? I didn't have anything to do with it, did I.' Her voice was saturated with bitterness as she said: 'I'd only just met him, too. That was what they said in court. At Kastrup on our way home.'

'But someone knew you were a couple in Denmark ...'

'Of course! But I never had any trouble because of that. I just hope ...'

'Yes?'

'Well ... they arrested the man who snitched on us.'

'You're sure it was a *he*?' As she was about to answer, I went on: 'It could've been someone who was jealous of you as well? A woman.'

She looked at me blankly, seemingly incapable of following my gist. Again there was a silence between us, as though both of us had more than enough to do with the musing our conversation had triggered. In the end I said: 'But by then you had Jan ...'

'Yes.'

'So you could still have gone on the straight and narrow, Mette.'

'When I had Johnny boy, I was already a dopehead! That was all I had to console myself with. Hash was just the beginning of it. Then it was acid and pills alternately. He was born affected, they told me afterwards.'

'But you were still allowed to keep him.'

'I did everything they said! I did rehab, got dried out, found myself a place to live, out there on the Rothaugen estate. They would get me a job, they said. Help me get some training. But it didn't happen like that. Instead I met Terje. And then I got some help in a different way, if you understand what I mean. It was straight back to dreamland again.'

'Terje Hammersten.'

'Yes.'

'That name has a habit of popping up in the strangest of places.' She gaped at me. 'Really?'

'Tell me, Mette. Terje Hammersten told you that Jan had moved up here. You followed him. Have you ever tried to contact him?'

'Johnny boy?'

'Yes.'

'Well, I … I'll tell you what I did. Yes, I found out where he lived, in that valley.'

'Angedalen.'

'Right. So I caught the bus in one day, walked along the road, tried to have a look in at the farms. But I didn't know which farm it was. Then the school bus came along and some kids got off. A boy and a girl. Kids I call them. Though they were young adults …' She visualised them, without speaking. 'I walked past them. And they looked at me, a bit snouty like. Who's that old biddy then? I met his gaze. I looked straight into his eyes. But I couldn't say anything to him. I couldn't have a chat with him! He doesn't know who I am … he hadn't seen me since he was three years old! And I was so close I could've touched him!'

'But you … how did you know it was him?'

'I recognised him. From his dad.'

'So he looks similar then?'

'Yes …' With a snuffle, she breathed in through her nostrils. 'Later … I made the trip several times. I didn't always see him. But a few times I did. And after a while I found out where he lived. I saw the people he was with. The old boy and his missus. Bloody farmers!'

'They're dead now. Both of them.'

'Yes, what do I care! I didn't do it.'

'Well, the police think … Jan did.'

She looked at me, her eyes black. 'Yes, I suppose they would. But life has taught me one thing, Veum. The police are not necessarily always right. No way!'

'Possible, possible. Are you still in touch with Terje Hammersten?'

'I hadn't been until …' She bit her lip and said sulkily: 'No.'

I waited for her to continue. 'You were going to say something else. You said: I hadn't been until …'

'Oh, for Christ's sake! Can't you stop pestering me!'

'Until …'

'A couple of days ago.'

'A couple of days ago! When?'

She looked at me helplessly, as though unsure. 'Monday – I think.'

'Monday just gone?'

'Yes. I hadn't seen him for … six months. He'd been here before, but I didn't want any more to do with him, so I told him to pack his bags and go to hell.'

'Sounds very sensible.'

'Sounds very sensible,' she mimicked with contorted lips. 'But out of the blue he reappeared … late one night.'

'Monday evening?'

'Yes, I told you! Monday! Forced his way in, although I … Said he had to spend the night here, otherwise he would hammer me black and blue. Yes, he'd done that before, so I knew he wasn't exaggerating. Then ... well ... he had to stay here. But don't you get it into your bloody head that I let him fuck me, if that's what you're thinking!'

'No, but ... did he say where he'd come from, that Monday night?'

She shook her head. 'Just that he'd come from town. The heat there had got too much for him. He was always in trouble, in one way or another. There was always trouble with Terje.'

'He didn't seem, er, particularly het up? Worked up?'

'Het up? Worked up? You know ... Terje's never anything else but up there, high. I can tell you that for nothing. There's no difference between Christmas Eve and any other day as far as he's concerned.'

'So when did he go back?'

'Go back? He's still 'ere, sunshine.'

My spine ran cold. 'Is he here – still?' Automatically I looked towards the window. 'Where?'

'No, no, today he wanted to go and visit his sister. Trude. She lives in Dale, somewhere along the fjords.'

'Trude, yes. She lost her husband, she did. Ten or eleven years ago.'

She shrugged and met my eyes. 'Really! I didn't know ...'

I stood up to go. She suddenly grabbed my wrist. 'You ... Veum ...'

'Yes.'

'If you meet Johnny boy, can you tell him one thing, from me?'

'And that is?'

'Tell him I've always loved him. Tell him his mother thinks of him every single day, as she has done ever since he was born, and which she will do until she dies. Can you tell him that?'

'I don't know if I'm going to meet him face to face any more.'

'But if you do!'

'If ... I'll think about it.'

'Don't think! Just do it!'

'If events allow me.'

She let go of my wrist. Then she pushed me away. 'Go! Just go! I knew it. I can't trust you, either. You're a bunch of arseholes, the whole lot of you! Scram! Sling your hook! Go to hell!'

I took her advice. But I didn't go to hell. I went to Dale instead.

32

Passing Førde, I wondered for a moment whether I should drop by the local police offices to hear if anyone was missing me. However, I had a strong suspicion what the answer would be, so I drove on regardless and was caught in the tailback behind a struggling long-load vehicle, round all the bends from Halbrendslia to the Slåtte hills. After Skilbrei I turned off for Bygstad. In the north-west rose Kvamshesten and Litlehesten, towering mountain formations that left their indelible mark on the surrounding countryside.

I drove past Bygstad and turned inland towards Osen to come round south of Dals fjord. The stretch of road between Bygstad and Osen passed beneath greyish-black overhanging cliff faces that looked as if they might collapse onto the road at any moment. There was something dark and forbidding about this section that reminded me that it had been somewhere round here, down by the water's edge, that Ansgår Tveiten had been found dead, battered to death with a blunt weapon in early 1973.

The inner part of Dals fjord was reminiscent of the Jølster district, even though the mountains were closer to the sea here, with the high fell-like formations that had given the area the name Fjaler from time immemorial. The sun swept low over the mountain ridges and hit the other side of the fjord tributary where the autumn colours frolicked wantonly on the foliage. The road was narrow and relatively well maintained. When I met oncoming traffic I had to pull into a passing place or drive onto the verge to get by.

Not without a touch of eager, child-like anticipation, I drove westwards. Even further to the west, where the fjord opened into the sea, my father had been born and grew up on a tiny farm called

Veum, some way outside Hellevik, before he moved into town and looked for work in the mid 1920s. But this time I was not to drive so far.

By Laukeland waterfall the countryside tapered in again. To the north were the towering mountains Kringla and Heileberget. Between two of the Nishamar tunnels I passed a small incineration plant, and after the last tunnel Dale suddenly appeared in the sunshine. The location was perfect. The mountains towards Eikenes and Dokka on the northern side of the fjord stood like blue silhouettes.

I parked my car by the coach station and got out. The old community centre looked still and peaceful. A couple of drivers were standing in front of the buses smoking roll-ups. Some schoolchildren were on their way home with blue and red rucksacks on their backs. Behind a large window on the corner by the crossroads I glimpsed the faces of a few elderly people peering inquisitively in my direction. Who can that fellow be? they were probably wondering. He's not from around here …

I enquired my way to the post office, which was in the council building down towards the quay, and took a punt that that was where I would get the help I needed. A gentle dark-haired man gave me a sly look through the bars of the post office window when I asked whether he could tell me where Trude Tveiten lived. 'Perhaps I can,' he said and began thereafter to give a detailed description. The upshot was relatively straightforward. I should go back to the main road and follow it to some flats in the building beside the second petrol station I came to.

I thanked him, went to my car and followed his instructions.

The flats were on the first floor with a west entrance. I took the stairs and found a door with her name on it. For a moment I stood listening. I heard voices from inside; a man and a woman. Then I rang the bell, and everything went quiet.

Nothing happened.

I rang once more and held the doorbell this time.

'Alright, alright, alright!' came an irritable voice from inside the flat. It was the man. 'We can hear you!'

The door was torn open, and Terje Hammersten stood glowering at me. 'Who are you? What the hell do you want?' in broad vernacular.

I repeated my familiar refrain: 'The name's Veum. I don't know if you remember me?'

He squinted at me with suspicion. He was ten years older too, and you could see it. His hair was thinner and his neck fatter. But the most visible change was the pencil-line, almost mafia-style moustache he had acquired, although it did little to improve his appearance. He was wearing a white shirt and brown trousers, both garments a bit too tight, and beneath his shirt he had a red T-shirt, visible at the neck. His shirt sleeves were rolled up and dark-blue tattoos adorned his forearms: an anchor on one, a naked Venus on a misshapen shell on the other.

Gradually I emerged from his creaking archive of images. I saw recognition in his eyes. 'Yeah, I remember you. Just. You're in social services, aren't you.'

'Not any more. But I've met you twice before, at Mette Olsen's place.'

'Terje!' came a shout from inside the flat. 'Who is it?'

'But in fact it was your sister, Trude, I came to talk to.'

'Trude? What d'you want with her?'

'To talk to her, as I said.'

He looked back over his shoulder. 'Someone called Veum, used to be in social services. He wants to talk to you, he says.'

'Let him in then! Why are you jabbering outside?'

Hammersten stepped reluctantly to the side and let me in. Through a small hallway I came into the flat itself, which appeared to consist of two rooms and a kitchen. Cigarette smoke hung heavily over the furniture, which was simple and standard, straight from an IKEA catalogue. The windows overlooked the main road. I saw Heile Mountain like a grey wall on the other side of the fjord.

Trude Tveiten was a thin, bony woman, not dissimilar to Mette Olsen, just darker-haired and with a more striking facial structure: high cheekbones and a lean jaw. Her nose was long and narrow, her eyes wide open, blue-black. Her hair was cropped, almost boy-like. It was difficult to see anything of Silje in her. She was wearing faded jeans and a dark-blue cotton blouse. Over her shoulders she had thrown a light-grey machine-knitted jacket.

She had got up off the reddish-brown leather sofa and stood waiting for me to enter. I went over to her, held out my hand and introduced myself. She gave me a limp handshake and looked at me with an expression of surprise. 'What's this about? Has it anything to do with social services?' she said without a trace of dialect.

'No, no. I have nothing to … I work freelance now, as a private investigator.'

'What?!' Terje Hammersten reacted instantly. 'A private snoop? What the hell are you after?'

I turned to face him again. 'I've just come from Mette Olsen. Even though she didn't appear to know, I assume that you are informed.'

'Informed about what?'

'About the double murder in Angedalen.'

'Dunno anything about it. Dunno what you're talking about.'

'Terje!' his sister reproved. 'Don't …' She turned to me again and nodded. 'We know. I was rung up by someone from the local police. Because of Silje.'

'I could imagine.'

'I had a few words with Silje, too.'

'But what I'd like to know is what you've got to do with any of this!' Hammersten burst out.

I kept my attention focused on his sister. 'I think Silje's fine. She's in good hands.'

She sent me a sorrowful look. 'Well … I hope so,' she said softly. 'But … can't we sit down? Let me hear what you came to say. Terje, please get a coffee cup from the kitchen, would you …?'

Hammersten gave a snort of contempt, but did as she said. A mug appeared on the table, and Trude Tveiten poured from a thermos jug standing on the low teak coffee table.

I sat down in one of the chairs, she was on the sofa, Terje Hammersten on the other chair with his glare fixed on me and both hands tensed on the chair arms, ready to spring into action, should the need arise.

'The incident on Tuesday … Did Silje say anything which might shed any light on the matter?'

She lit a cigarette before answering. 'No. I just had a few words with her. All she said was that she was … fine. Things were fine, now.'

'So she didn't say anything about the lead-up to all of this?'

'No.'

'Nothing about – sexual abuse?'

'What! Abuse? In that case he'll have to deal with me! I can promise you that!' Hammersten clenched his fist and banged the table so hard Trude automatically recoiled.

I looked at Hammersten thinking my own thoughts. To Trude I said: 'How much contact did you have with her actually?'

She took a long drag, and her eyes converged on the glow. 'Not a lot. I'm allowed to visit her now and then, but … her foster parents are not very warm, and I never feel welcome there. The whole of Angedalen is like a living hell for me.'

'But when you visit her, do you talk together? Does she confide in you?'

She glared at me, with resentment. 'What do *you* think? She was five years old when her father … died. Since then she's lived in other places. First, a few years in Naustdal, then in Angedalen.'

'What happened?'

'What happened? What do you mean?'

'Your husband died, you said.'

'Yes, and I had a nervous breakdown. Total. And I hadn't been good beforehand.' The hand with the cigarette shook. 'No hard stuff but … pills. And alcohol.' Her lip twisted. 'A bad mixture, especially with a tiny tot in the house.'

'He was killed, wasn't he?'

'Why do you ask if you already know?' she exploded.

I concentrated on her, but from the corner of my eye I could see Hammersten, and there was more than a hint of tension when I said: 'The case was never solved, was it.'

Now her hands were trembling so much that she dropped her cigarette. It fell on the table and she made a determined grab for it, creating a shower of sparks over the scarred coffee table. It wasn't the first time this had happened.

'Pack it in, will you, you prick! You can see how you're torment-ing her, can't you.' Hammersten had half-stood up from the chair.

I met his eyes with strained composure. 'Perhaps you know something about this case, do you?'

He pushed back his chair and drew himself up to his full height. I did the same, and he shrank instantly. He was shorter than me, and it was more his pent-up fury than his size that intimidated. We stood glaring at each other.

'Terje! Don't …' Trude said from the sofa. 'It'll just end in trouble. I might get evicted again. I can't take any more of this!' With which she burst into tears.

His eyes wandered, from me to her and back again. I could see how he was oscillating between the desire to have a go at me and to comfort his sister. With a low, intense voice, he said: 'I had nothing to do with it. Anyone who says anything else is a liar. And the man who lies about Terje Hammersten is in the shit. Mark my words, Veum. He is in deep, deep shit!'

I held my eyes trained on his. I fixed him there, but I tensed my abdominal muscles at the same time, ready for whatever came my way.

'Everyone must've seen that it was just lies!' came a sob from the sofa. 'Ansgår and Terje were best pals! That was how we met. They had been to sea together, they knew each other from the time they were young kids. Terje could never have done anything like that. I told the cop at the time, and I told everyone who came snooping for many years afterwards.'

'But is it true that Ansgår was involved in smuggling alcohol?'

I was still staring at Hammersten, and he answered. 'And so what if he was? Does it matter? With the policy we have on booze in this country – and especially in this bloody county – they're asking for it! It's fuckin' welfare work what they're doing, smuggling booze into Sogn and Fjordane.'

I produced a weak smile. 'I can imagine views are divided on that.'

'Not among normal people! Is it any wonder there was big money in it?'

'Klaus Libakk,' I said abruptly.

A remarkable change occurred in his face. The expression altered at a stroke from active aggression to squinting vigilance. 'What about him?'

'You know who he is?'

His eyes darted away for a moment. Then they were back. 'He's the one who was killed, right? Him and the biddy.'

'You're well informed, I see.'

His temper instantly flared up again. 'And what d'you mean by that?'

'Their names still haven't been made public.'

Behind his forehead, his brain was working at full steam.

'But … but …that's what the cop said, to Trude. Or … she was led to believe …'

'We knew where Jan was living,' the sister said calmly from the sofa.

'Yes, you did know that,' I said, still eyeing Hammersten. 'You told Mette, didn't you. Where did you get the information from?'

'That's got fuck all to do with you!' he barked back.

'But to go back to Klaus Libakk. He was also part of the smuggling racket, people say.'

'OK! That's what you say.'

Trude had stopped crying. I noticed she had raised her face and was staring at me.

'Could he have had anything to do with the murder in 1973, do you think?'

He stared at me, his expression blank, bordering on fossilised. But his eyes were as rigid and smouldering as they had been the whole time. At length he said: 'If so, I'd ...'

'Yes? Have done the same to him as you would've done to the person who abused Silje? And what about if they were one and the same? You're accumulating a nice pile of motives here. Impressive.'

I should have seen it coming. But for a moment I had been a bit too complacent. My attention wandered, and I only just managed to ward off the surprise blow.

His fist swung towards my face, but in a pure reflex action I yanked up my shoulder and the punch glanced off my cheek and left ear instead. The next was more accurate. It hit me right in the chest and sent me tumbling backwards, knocking over a standard lamp; I hit the wall and slowly sank until I was sitting on the floor, dazed and shaken. I felt a dull pain in my chest and a hot, smarting sensation in my ear.

Above me stood Terje Hammersten, ready to lay in to me if I tried to get to my feet. Trude had stood up, too, now. She rushed forward and put her arms around his upper body to restrain him. 'Don't, Terje! I told you not to. I'll be evicted ...'

I looked up at them. Everything was blurred. For one strange, long, drawn out moment they seemed to be one person, a two-headed, androgynous creature from a world where I didn't belong. Then I succeeded in re-focusing. 'It's alright,' I said. 'I won't report you. There won't be any trouble, so long as nothing else happens.'

Terje Hammersten lowered his fists, shook himself free from his sister's grip and walked across to the window, where he stood with his back to us, gazing down at the road leading to Dale town centre.

Still dizzy, I slowly stood up. I felt nauseous and could see dots dancing in front of my eyes. All credit to him. He had a powerful fist on him. I nodded to Trude with a mixture of gratitude and the need to say she shouldn't worry. I wouldn't tell anyone.

'How are you feeling?' she asked.

I rolled my shoulders and rubbed my chest. 'Could be worse.' Without looking at Hammersten, I added: 'I think I'll be off.'

'What did you actually want?'

I studied her. 'To be quite honest, I'm not at all sure any more. But I've made a mental note of some things.'

Terje Hammersten turned round smartly, strode across the floor and came up close to me again. But this time I was prepared. I raised my fists in defence and eyed him stiffly.

'Be careful, Veum!' he snarled. 'Be bloody careful!'

'Unless I want to wind up like Ansgår Tveiten, you mean.'

Between us, Trude gave an involuntary sob. 'Not again!'

The blood vessels in his temple swelled and the knuckles of his fists went white. But he kept himself in check. He didn't lash out this time.

Without letting him out of my sight, I walked to the door, opened it and left the flat. In the corridor outside I hurried towards the staircase, then stopped to check if he was following. But there was no one, and, still feeling physically uncomfortable, I went down the steps and into the bright daylight. A high white sky hung over Dale, like a huge plastic cupola. A handful of gulls sailed on the wind to the steep walls of Heile Mountain, while complaining in grating cries about bad backs, poor catches or whatever it is gulls complain about.

It was beginning to get dark as I drove into Osen where the Gaular waterway plunged like a faded bridal veil towards the fjord. High up above the mountains the moon had appeared, the earth's pale consort, distant and alone in its eternal orbit around the chaos and turmoil below. It struck me that the moon wasn't alone after all. There were many of us adrift and circling around the same chaos, the same turmoil, without being able to intervene or do anything about it. We were all consorts of death.

33

It was six o'clock when I arrived at the hotel. There were no messages for me in reception. I went to my room, found Grethe's telephone number and dialled. No one answered. I rang down to reception and asked if Jens Langeland or Hans Haavik were in. Langeland was out. Haavik was in his room. Did I want to speak to him? I considered for a moment and ended up saying no.

My body felt strangely restless. Maybe it was a side effect of the blow I received in Dale, or else it was something I had heard in the course of the day, a bit of information I still hadn't managed to sift out from all the rest. Something that had invaluable significance for the development of the case, unless, as things were progressing, I should begin to say: cases.

The latter reflection caused me to ring the police offices and ask for Standal. He was in, but what surprised me most was that he was willing to talk to me.

'Yes?' his voice came on to the telephone.

'Veum here.'

'Yes, so I heard. What do you want?'

'Anything new?'

'Nothing you have any right to know, anyway.'

'Well, right … Listen to me for a moment, Standal. I may have something to tell you that you don't know.'

'And what would that be?'

'Have you taken out the old 1973 murder file yet? Ansgår Tveiten. The illicit alcohol business. We touched on it yesterday.'

For a moment the line went quiet.

'We've got the file, yes. But so far we haven't had time to look into the material in any depth. It's quite a pile, Veum.'

'I don't doubt it. But it was shelved.'

'Not shelved. It's incorrect to say that. In active abeyance, we call it. We're still gathering information for the case.'

'OK. Then that's perhaps what you're doing now.'

'And by that you mean …?'

'Let me remind you what the lawyers Langeland and Bråtet told us yesterday. That Silje Tveiten, as she is still called, is Ansgår Tveiten's daughter. And I know that her uncle, Terje Hammersten, was on the police radar at that time, although nothing decisive was to come of it.'

'We know that, Veum!' he said impatiently. 'I thought you said you had something to tell me.'

'Well, listen to this then. Rumour has it that the deceased Klaus Libakk was involved in the same contraband operation. He distributed the goods to people in Angedalen. Did you know that?'

'He wasn't down on our records, at any rate. I'll have to regard this as idle gossip for the moment.'

'Odd. That his name isn't in your records, I mean.'

'It was a complicated case. With lots of ramifications. And when this murder came to light the investigators had to concentrate on that aspect.'

'With not much success, it has to be said.'

'Get to the point!'

'Alright. I'd like to inform you that the said Terje Hammersten is in the immediate vicinity of Førde right now, and has been since Monday evening.'

'Monday evening. Uhuh. Anything else?'

'He stayed with a woman who's lived in Jølster for the last couple of years. Her name's Mette Olsen and she is the biological mother of Jan Egil.'

'Hang on there, Veum. Let me take a note of that. Mette Olsen. Where does she live, did you say?'

I explained.

'And this Terje Hammersten … do they live together or what?'

'They did at some point. Something like that. And he has a sister who lives in Dale. Trude Tveiten, who was married to Ansgår Tveiten. In other words, Tveiten was his brother-in-law.'

'This is beginning to become pretty entangled, I have to say. But I still don't understand what you're driving at.'

'Then listen here. Let's suppose that, just as a theory, of course, let's suppose that Klaus Libakk was involved in the murder of Ansgår Tveiten in 1973. Unless Hammersten committed the murder at that time, that would give him a motive for exacting revenge on Libakk today. On behalf of the family, so to speak. He is hot-tempered and stands on his honour, I can assure you.'

'But what about Kari Libakk? We're not just talking about one murder victim here, Veum.'

'No, but she may simply have been unlucky enough to have been married to the wrong person at that time in her life.'

'And what can you put forward as evidence for all of this?'

'We-ell ... I suppose primarily we're talking circumstantial evidence. But now we have Silje, who has in fact confessed ...'

He interrupted me. 'That confession is threadbare. I would even go so far as to say that the thread has worn through.'

'And now we have Hammersten who could have a motive and who we can also assume to be handy with weapons and, furthermore, the capacity to undertake such a brutal act. Maybe his connection with Mette Olsen is another motive we should examine.'

'And how do you explain away Jan Egil Skarnes grabbing a weapon, taking a hostage and fleeing up to Trodalen as soon as he sees a police officer in the yard?'

'He didn't take a hostage. They both deny that.'

'OK, OK. So maybe they were playing Bonnie and Clyde, were they? Nevertheless. Him clearing off like that is a very strong piece of evidence in our eyes. Not to mention all the forensic evidence we're painstakingly gathering. Let me make this absolutely clear, Veum. At this stage we have already passed the case up to the Public Prosecutor. I would be very surprised if charges are not drawn up by tomorrow. And they won't be in the name of this Hammersten.'

'So you've gone that far?'

'To tell the truth … we've gone a lot further, Veum. Was there anything else you wanted?'

'You should call him in though. For questioning, at least.'

'Who are you talking about now?'

'Hammersten.'

'Yeah, yeah. I've made a note. We're not stupid, Veum. Was there anything else?'

'Not at the moment.'

'Then I'll bid you a good evening, Veum.'

'Thank you and the same to you.'

I rang off. Then I tried Grethe's number again. As she didn't reply this time either, I went downstairs to eat. In the dining room I saw Jens Langeland sitting alone at one of the tables. I went over and asked if I could keep him company.

He brightened up. 'Naturally! And now I hope you have some good cards up your sleeve, Veum, for otherwise I'm afraid things are looking grim, in all ways.'

'I've got something anyway,' I said, fetching a menu, pulling out a chair and joining him.

34

I ordered sea trout in a cream sauce with cucumber salad and Norwegian almond potatoes. To drink, I treated myself to half a bottle of white wine. 'I'll put it on the bill,' I said to Langeland and winked.

He nonchalantly waved the matter aside. It wouldn't be him paying it, anyway. 'Let me hear what you've found out, Veum.'

I gave him a brief summary of what I had been doing, told him about my visits to Mette Olsen and Trude Tveiten, as well as Terje Hammersten in a not insignificant supporting role.

He listened with particular interest when I came to the part about Ansgår Tveiten. 'We can use this, Veum! This is brilliant! A connection between the murder in 1973 and the current double murder, linked by the smuggling in which both Tveiten and Klaus Libakk were involved. And this Hammersten, he turned up in Jølster on Monday evening, did he?'

'Yes, he did.'

'Is it possible to find out when he came to Sunnfjord? And, for example, if he had been there the night before?'

'It's possible to make enquiries, anyway.'

'So let's do that! We need everything that can point in the opposite direction to the path the police chose quite some time ago.'

'Yes, I've just spoken to Standal. He indicated that charges would be drawn up tomorrow.'

'Yes, that wouldn't surprise me. But they can't hold him in custody much longer, so …'

'Are the pathologist's and the forensic reports through yet?'

'I haven't been given them, if they are. But forget that! With what you've unearthed we already have a good hand.' He was positively exploding with renewed energy. 'This will create problems for them. Ha!' He thrust his finger forward in the way that a torero delivers the *coup de grâce* to a bull at the festive table the day afterwards.

'You show an impressive commitment to the case. I must say that ...'

'My goodness, Veum! I've been following Jan ... Jan Egil since he was born, so to speak.'

'Yes, I'd heard you were Mette Olsen's solicitor back in 1966.'

'No, no. I was just a solicitor's clerk then. But I remember the case well. It was a tragic story. Her friend took his life while in prison.'

'Jan's father.'

'What? Oh, yes, exactly.' He ruminated before continuing. 'A tragic story, as I said. Now and then you wonder what makes otherwise talented individuals take such decisions. My God! I think it was close on half a kilo's worth of hash he was carrying when he was arrested. And she ...'

'... knew nothing, you had persuaded her to say.'

'Right.' He raised both hands in defence. 'He was the one carrying all the dope. What purpose would it serve if she also went to prison for knowing all about it?'

'Hmm ... That's one way of looking at it.'

He leaned closer. 'Mette Olsen was not like she is now, Veum. I can assure you of that! She was a gifted young girl, sweet and charming. But she had made a fatal decision, too. She went to Copenhagen, played the hippie and got a taste for – well, this and that. We did what we could to get her back on an even keel. Believe me ... This was one of the very first of my cases, and I was committed to it even though Bakke was in charge. A High Court barrister, if I may ...'

'So you wash your hands of it?'

He splayed them. 'Yes, in fact I do. All that transpired later was beyond our jurisdiction. But tiny Johnny boy, I've always done what I can to help him, right from the very first moment.'

I nodded. 'Well ... that's admirable, that is, anyway.'

'And this business with Terje Hammersten, I'll get the police onto that. They won't get away with it. But you check it out, too, Veum. I'm paying!' He stood up. 'I'm afraid I'm going to retire. I have to make a few calls. This is not the only case I have, unfortunately. I wish you a pleasant evening ...'

He walked to the door. As if on cue, Hans Haavik appeared in the foyer. He and Langeland exchanged a few words as they passed each other. Langeland left and Hans looked around the room, as I had done.

Catching sight of me, he came over to the table. 'Hi, Varg. Can I join you?'

I motioned towards the used napkin on the other side of the table. 'Langeland's just gone. Someone'll come and set the table if you ask them.'

The efficient waiter was already at hand. The place was cleared and Hans sat down with a bump on his side of the table. He ordered the same as I had, except for the wine. He made do with a jug of water. I was now on dessert, a hot blueberry tart with ice cream.

'One thing I'd like to ask you, Hans, since you were a relative of the deceased. Who is the heir? Have you any opinion on that?'

He stared into middle distance, lost in thought. 'They had no children of their own, so if they haven't written a will, I suppose everything will go to the nearest relative.'

'Would Jan Egil qualify?'

'Not as a foster child. Not without being mentioned in a will. He might have been, though, of course. Then, on the other hand ... if he's convicted of killing them, I'm afraid it will be declared invalid. In any case, legal proceedings are bound to be instituted.'

'By whom?'

'Well, that's it. Klaus Libakk and Klara Almelid were brother and sister.'

'Yes, that's right. Silje called him Uncle Klaus.'

'Yes.'

'She called him an old pig, too. Did I ask you about that?'

The food arrived on the table and he waited until the waiter had gone before answering. 'Yes, I heard from Jens that there had been some such suggestion. But it seems quite improbable to me. Did she say straight out that he'd tried it on her?'

'Tried it on her or had his way. The whole thing is extremely unclear. She definitely called him an old pig.'

'Hmm.' He ate.

'Now you know yourself from all your years in social services that this type of thing tends to happen behind very closed doors, Hans. Behind the most decorative Christian façades unmentionable things can happen with small children and young people.'

'Mm, yes, yes.' He swallowed and stretched a hand out for a glass of water. 'I'll buy that. But then it's often with a member of the family. Silje, after all, came from a different farm, which immediately made it a riskier venture.'

'But she was, well, if she wasn't his niece by family, then in a way she was. He'd known her from the time she was small. She visited their farm, was with them in the cowshed, that sort of thing. Trusted them. Trusted him, in this case.'

'So you don't hold Kari liable, I take it?' he said sarcastically.

'I ...'

'She was killed too, you know. What about ...?' He sent me an inquisitorial look. 'If we're letting our imaginations run wild, I mean.'

'Yes? It's not at all unusual for the partner to know but to keep quiet, not to intervene, thus making themselves an accessory to the crime. We've experienced that several times, haven't we.'

He shook his head in disbelief.

'You don't believe this, I can see.'

'Not for one second, Varg.'

'So who do you think did it?'

A sad look crossed his face. 'I wish there were another explanation. That there were some tramps who happened by this farm. I mean … That sort of thing goes on all the time. But generally with people older than Klaus and Kari. On the other hand … it took place at night, didn't it? Burglars? I don't know.'

'That's what Jan Egil claims.'

'However,' he said with emphasis. 'I'm afraid that isn't good enough. I'm afraid the whole business is the way it appears. That it was Jan Egil who did it. But the motive … Look, it may have something to do with Silje, if we assume that your speculation in this regard is correct. It's difficult to see any other motive, though.'

'In other words, that he killed Klaus and Kari because of what Klaus might have done to Silje?'

He stared down at his plate with an expression that suggested that all of a sudden he had lost his appetite. 'Something like that.'

I drained the last dregs of wine. 'But … back to the inheritance. Klara is the nearest heir then?'

He peered up. 'Yes, that's not beyond the realms of possibility. There was another brother, but he died young. Lost at sea while herring fishing one year.' He gave a wry smile. 'So perhaps we should jog the sergeant's memory. Tell him to have a chat with Klara, too?'

'It wouldn't be the first time someone has killed to gain benefits from the will, anyway.'

'But I doubt with such brutality, eh? Klara Almelid with a smoking rifle, standing like Calamity Jane over the body of her brother and sister-in-law? I can't exactly see that … Besides Kari must have some family, I would assume.'

'Yes, of course. Well, I think I'm going to have a coffee with a little something in the bar. See you there?'

'Maybe. Have to see.'

I went into the bar. The number of press people was much reduced from the evening before, probably because the case in the eyes of most was so clear cut that it no longer held their attention.

I ordered the same as the previous evening, coffee and Line aquavit, and found myself an unoccupied table. I had hardly sat down when I noticed the Bergensian from the day before, still as drunk and with his eyes fixed on the base of my neck, as if imagining a tie he could grab onto so as to steady himself. He floated across the room, stood swaying in front of my table and said: 'Could I join you for a bit? I think we have mutual friends.'

I frowned with scepticism. 'And who might they be?'

Without answering, he flopped down on the chair.

The bartender had followed him with a glass of beer on a tray. He placed the beer on the table and looked at me, abashed. 'I hope he isn't bothering you?'

'Let's see how things develop. As far as I can see, he must have had enough several days ago.'

'He won't get anything stronger than this, either,' the bartender mumbled, pointing to the beer glass. 'And that's the last,' he added, eyeing my new acquaintance with severity.

'Yeah, yeah, yeah,' he replied, reaching for the glass. His hair was dark, bristly, combed to make it stand up. His face bore the signs of many years of over-indulgence, and he was struggling to focus. On eventually locating me, he held out his hand and introduced himself. 'Harald Dale,' he said, as if that explained everything.

I shook his hand and said my own name.

'I couldn't help hearing what you and the others were talking about in here last night.'

'I kind of noticed. But you said something about … mutual friends.'

'Yes, perhaps not friends, more …'

'More …?'

'I heard you talking about this double murder. About Klaus Libakk and the smuggling and all that stuff.'

My ears pricked up. 'Right. Did you know Libakk?'

He put on a foolish grin. 'If I knew Libakk? Are you asking me if I knew Libakk? I was his contact person for Christ's sake. The missing link …'

'The missing link between …?'

'Between Libakk and Skarnes, of course!'

That seared through me like an electric shock. 'What did you just say? Not Svein Skarnes?'

'Yes! That's what I said.' Again he held out his hand. 'Harald Dale. Ex-technician for Skarnes Import. I often came here for work reasons – and others.'

The penny dropped. 'Yes, now I remember … you even had a kind of celebration dinner here …' I looked around. 'Here at the hotel, wasn't it?'

'Yep!' he said with a broad grin. 'That was when I met Solfrid. She checked me out here in the bar. Well, after we'd eaten. And she and I, we certainly had mutual friends …'

'Solfrid…?'

'The missus. We got married two years afterwards, and I moved up here. Tveiten, her name was then.'

'Tveiten!'

'Yes, sister to someone called Ansgår who was killed when the whole shebang disintegrated.'

'Right. Little Silje's aunt in Angedalen when …'

'Yeah, yeah. Something like that. But they don't have any contact. Not a lot anyway. So much has happened in that family.' He was grinning so much his loose lips were almost flapping in the air. 'Yes, we don't have much contact any more, either, Solfrid and I, so to speak.'

'Well, I can almost … You're divorced?'

'Se-par-ated,' he said, with difficulty. 'Sepa … yeah. After I lost my job, there was too much … joy juice.'

'I see. But I'd like to go back to … You mentioned Svein Skarnes. Was he involved, too? In the smuggling?'

'That's what I'm telling you! I thought it'd surprise you. I heard you talking about his missus. We called her the dolly. I wouldn't've minded a round with her in the sack, at some point. But she held her nose in the air and never looked in my direction. Svein and I, on the other hand, we were good mates, and both did our own thing.'

'So when he fell down the stairs …'

'You know … There was so much going off at that time. The bubble burst in 1973. First of all, it was the fishing smack that was boarded by the customs officers somewhere at sea. Laden with booze. A few days later Ansgår was beaten to death, and the police here as good as rounded up the whole gang.'

'Not all of them, though, obviously. Klaus Libakk never got a blemish on his record.'

Another grin. 'Nor me. Nor Svein. We were good at covering our tracks.'

'So Svein Skarnes had an important role in the business?'

'An important role! How many times do I have to tell you? He was running the whole bloody thing. He was sitting in Bergen with all his foreign contacts. All his travelling, at home and abroad … it was the perfect cover.'

My brain was reeling. The whole affair was taking on a new perspective. The threads going back to 1974 were even stronger than they had seemed even a few hours ago.

'Well, OK, then,' I said. 'The racket was broken up in 1973, and in February 1974 Svein Skarnes had his dramatic fall.'

'The bitch shoved him down the stairs.'

'At least, that was the official version. Now there's a lot that has to be re-thought, I'm afraid.'

'Don't be afraid, Veum. I've been afraid for many years, I have.'

'Yes, exactly. When did you move here?'

'Well, I met Solfrid here in the autumn of 1973. Svein and I had a sales meeting here while seeing if it was possible to build up something new in the booze market at the same time. I mean … Svein was in a real fix. He owed money for the last load and those waiting for payment were not exactly very patient creditors.'

'No, I can imagine. They threatened to send in Terje Hammersten, did they?'

'Hammersten? Do you know him?'

'Who doesn't?'

'But how did you know…?'

'How did I know …?'

'That Hammersten was involved?'

'He was the one who killed Ansgår Tveiten, wasn't he?'

'Yes, but that … No, I don't know. People here took care of that. That was what blew the whole thing out of the water, for Christ's sake! After that it was as good as impossible to start up again. The whole set-up was compromised, and no one dared touch it with a barge pole! We just had to give up.'

'But you heard from Hammersten as well, I take it?'

He had started sweating. Every now and then he looked over towards the foyer as if fearing that someone he didn't like could enter at any moment. Then he whispered: 'Svein got a lot of calls from him.'

'From Hammersten?'

He nodded. 'For every day he didn't pay, the sum went up. Black-market interest rates. I don't know if you know the system? It's horrendous once you're caught up in it.'

'And if that didn't help, then Terje Hammersten dropped round, was that how it worked?'

Again he nodded, without saying anything.

'So, in theory, it could've been Hammersten who pushed Skarnes down the stairs on that February day in 1974?'

'But his missus confessed, didn't she!'

'Yes, but what if I tell you that some new information has come to light … Someone overheard a row at the Skarnes household, a row between Skarnes and another man …'

'Someone? Who was that?'

'It's not important.'

'But …'

'Then it could've been Hammersten. Why didn't you say anything about this to the police?'

He looked at me as if I were mad. 'And ruin everything for myself? I would have dropped myself right in it. And when his missus had confessed anyway … I didn't reckon she would lie about anything so serious!'

'She must've had her reasons?'

'Yes, they must definitely have been bloody good ones.'

'Perhaps they were. But back to … It was after that that you left everything and came here?'

'Yes, as I said … after Svein died and the missus was in clink the company was dissolved. It was Solfrid who lured me to Førde and I got myself a job, for a while.'

'And you never heard anything – not from Hammersten or any of the others?'

He shrugged. 'Why should I? I didn't owe any money. I was just the missing link, as I said.'

'Right. But time passes, and then this happens: Klaus and his wife are murdered. Didn't that worry you?'

'No, why would it? Isn't it exactly as the papers say, that the case is as good as solved?'

'Maybe. Maybe not. But what if it was all linked with the smuggling business? That that was the motive?'

He gave me a long lingering look. 'It could've been the money, of course.'

'Which money are you talking about now?'

Yet again his gaze wandered off to the foyer. When he answered, he had lowered his voice so much that I had to lean close to understand what he was saying. 'There were some rumours going round, in 1973 … Listen, Veum … Everything went tits up. No one got their money. But the money ended up somewhere, didn't it. Someone was sitting on a pot of gold, somewhere in the chain …'

'And you think that might've been Klaus Libakk? Was there such a large turnover in Angedalen?'

'Angedalen!' He blew out his cheeks. 'Klaus Libakk was organising sales in the whole region. From Jølster to Naustdal. Everything went through him. He was the bloody spider in the web here. That was why it was so bombproof. The whole thing was built up a bit like a resistance group, with small cells that knew nothing of each other, apart from the closest contact-person.'

'But you knew a lot, I can see. You're not scared that you're in the firing line yourself?'

'Me?' He had gone a little green around the gills. I feared he would soon be looking for a suitable place to throw up.

I said quickly: 'But what you're suggesting is that Klaus Libakk might have been sitting on quite a sackful of money on his farm?'

He nodded. 'A fortune, Veum. A veritable treasure chest …'

Now he knew the moment had come. He pushed back his chair and staggered to his feet. He bent forward, grabbed his glass, raised it to his mouth and drained it in one long swig. Then he turned around, and without saying goodbye tottered off towards the toilets.

On the way out he passed a woman. My eyes lingered on her. She was wearing a tight black dress that emphasised her trim figure. Over her shoulders hung a loose coke-grey suit jacket. Her coiffeured hair was arranged in fluffy blonde curls, and it was only when she met my eyes that I saw who it was. Grethe Mellingen, dressed to kill …

By the time she had reached my table I had been standing for quite some time. 'I've been trying to get hold of you.'

'I'm here now,' she said with a pert smile.

35

'What can I get you?'

'What are you drinking?'

'Until now it has been coffee and aquavit. But I can switch to anything.'

'Actually I fancy a gin and tonic.'

'I'll join you then.' I waved to the barman, who speedily took the order.

'How,' we both started, and I finished: '... is it going?'

'With Silje?'

'Yes, for example.'

'Pretty well, I think. She's got very capable parents. Or foster parents, I should say.'

'Do you know them?'

'Peripherally. But I've had Silje on my files ever since I came here.'

'When was that?'

'Five years ago. In 1979.'

'But ... you must have roots here?'

She chuckled. 'Is it so obvious?'

The waiter came with our drinks. We said *skål* and tasted before I answered: 'No, no. But I've heard you break into dialect when you're talking to ... locals.'

'Yes, my mother came from here. But she found herself a man from Østland, so I've spent all my life there. In Elverum of all places.'

'There's nothing wrong with Elverum, is there?'

'No, no. I'm sure there are worse places. But tell me what you've been doing today. How was it in Jølster?'

I told her about that and the trip to Dale. To round off, I told her about the conversations with Langeland and Haavik.

She listened attentively. When I had finished, she said: 'So everything points to Jan Egil being charged, I guess.'

'All the evidence still suggests that it was Jan Egil who did it,' I said. 'Even though a few interesting details have emerged at the end of the day.'

'I don't know if I told you but … Silje was examined by a doctor today.'

'Oh yes? And the results?'

'She's as healthy as a spring lamb. No injuries anywhere. But … she wasn't a virgin, to put it in formal terms.'

'She's had it then, in informal terms.'

'If that's how you speak in Bergen, fine by me. But no signs of abuse, at any rate not recently.'

'Well, well. So now we know that.'

She sipped from her glass, deep in thought.

'What are you thinking?'

'I was thinking … will you come home with me afterwards?'

I met her eyes. 'If you invite me I …'

'There's something I want to show you,' she said with a glint in her eye, as if there was something special she had learnt and wanted to show off.

'Yes, you hinted something along those lines earlier today.'

Nevertheless, she was in no hurry. We finished our drinks, found the way to the night club and spent an hour on the dance floor there, most of the time moving to a gentle rhythm; touching was a natural part of the activity. We exchanged social services experiences and took stock of family circumstances: we each had an ex in the closet, she a daughter of fourteen, me thirteen-year-old Thomas in fitting congruity. She told me she had a seat on the local council, and when I asked for which party, she stepped back and said: 'Guess!' When I went for SV, the left, she smirked but refrained from commenting. In the end, we danced a few slow smooches, she with her arms around my neck and me with one hand between her shoulder blades and the other exploring the lower end of her spine, like a restless chiropractor at a health seminar improving his technique. Her body was warm and soft against mine, and I felt her lips against my ear, like slightly moist petals as she whispered: 'Shall we order a taxi?'

'Mm,' I said into her hair, and with her arm under mine we left the dance floor.

I went up to the cloakroom to collect my coat, and when I came back down, she was standing by the taxi waiting. Lounging at the rear, her arm still under mine, we sat as a silent driver drove us to Hornnes, where she lived in a newly constructed house on the slope above the road to Naustdal and Florø.

Her young daughter, whose name was Tora, was sitting watching TV in the basement when we arrived. She said hello, somewhat shyly, and quickly withdrew to her bedroom.

'What can I offer you?' Grethe asked.

'There was something you wanted to show me,' I said.

'A glass of red wine?'

'I wouldn't say no to that, either.'

She slanted her eyebrows upwards and smiled. Then she was gone. I sat watching TV, lost as to what this was all about. When Grethe returned with two glasses and an opened bottle of wine, she switched off the television and pulled out an LP and started the record player while I filled our glasses. Roger Whittaker resounded around the room with a voice that made me think of ships' tarred planks and a fresh breeze in off the sea.

The ceiling was low. Bookshelves covered the wall around the TV screen. The pictures on the other walls all had landscape motifs: paintings, photos and graphics. I took a seat on the sofa, and she sat down beside me, in the crook of my arm. We tasted the red wine, and some time afterwards she turned to me, with a determined look in her eye, and whispered: 'Kiss me.' I saw no reason not to.

As I began to fumble with the zip on her dress, she laid a hand on mine and said: 'No … Let's go up to the bedroom.' I didn't object then, either.

Standing in the middle of the floor in the cold room, we slowly undressed each other, taking cautious nibbles at whatever appeared. Then we got into bed where we frolicked in a variety of positions until she was writhing deliriously above me, and we buckled into each other in one last sweet exhalation.

Sweaty and hot, she lay breathing against my chest. I felt laughter bubbling up inside me. 'Was that what you wanted to show me?'

She raised her head and looked at me seriously. 'No. Wait here …'

She got out of bed and crossed the floor, naked. Her body was soft and supple, with small breasts and a stomach left with stretch marks from pregnancy that would never go away completely. On her return, she was carrying a large leather-bound book, brownish-black in colour with golden letters on the cover. She switched on the light over the bed, snuggled up to me, pulled the duvet over us, carefully opened the book and slowly turned the first thin pages.

'What is it? A family bible?'

She nodded with enthusiasm. 'A very special one. I got it from my mother when I moved back here. She had been given it by her mother. But what makes it so special is that this bible has followed the women in our family through very different circumstances. My mother and her mother were married, but before them there was an unfortunate succession of one daughter after the other born out of wedlock and given the book.'

'From illegitimate daughter to illegitimate daughter?'

'For several generations, like a kind of original sin. But perhaps that's not so strange when it comes down to it. A woman born out of wedlock was held in low public esteem. Anyone could lay their hands on her and thereby bring more illegitimate children into the world. The unfortunate thing for our family was that the first-born were always girls and thus inherited the rewards of sin.'

I stroked her hair. 'But you've broken the line now ...'

She turned her head, looked at me from the corner of her eyes. 'Oh, we still have a sense of sin ...'

Lying on her stomach, she pointed. 'Look, here you have the whole of the line written down. The first, Martha, writes that she was born in 1799, and that she received the book when she was confirmed in 1816. She married a Hans Olavsson in 1819 and had a daughter, Maria, in 1823.'

'No sons?'

'Yes, but Maria hasn't entered their names. You can see here ... the writing changes. That's Maria entering her name and her daughter's, Kristine. Born in February 1840, out of wedlock. But she enters the father ... look here, as M. A.'

'Uhuh?'

'That doesn't mean anything to you?'

'Not straight off, no.'

'It might be Mads Andersen.'

'Mads Andersen. You don't mean ...?'

'Yes! Trodalen Mads. And look at the birth date. Count back nine months and you come to May 1839. The Trodalen murder, according to lore, took place on June 19th of that year.'

'But ... if your ancestral mother had a child with Trodalen Mads ...'

'She's in fact my great-great-great grandmother.'

'If she had a child with him ...'

'... then I'm a direct descendant of his, yes. Although we've never thought of announcing that in *Firda Tidend*, if I can put it like that.'

'But M. A. could stand for something quite different too?'

'Yes, yes, of course. But this is where oral tradition comes in. The secret inheritance, to use a more formal expression. You see my mother told me, when she gave me the bible, that her mother had told her that her mother in turn had passed down this inherited account of our spooky past, and that she swore with her hand on the family bible that this was how it was, may God himself strike me to the ground if I'm lying … she said.'

'And that account says …?'

She rolled onto her side, put her free arm around my neck, held me tight and looked me straight in the eye. 'Promise me first, Varg, that what I'm telling you now you will never tell another soul!'

I returned her gaze. 'I certainly can't swear on the book and beg God to strike me to the ground if I should lie, but …' I put my hand on my heart. 'I promise by all that I hold sacred, I won't do that. What you tell me here and now will never go beyond these four walls.'

She scrutinised me long and hard, as if searching for lies and ignoble ideals in my eyes.

'But you must've told … Tora?'

'Not yet. Won't be for a long time yet. If I tell you now, tonight, there are only three living people who know about it. My mother, me and you.'

'And to what do I owe the honour? I wasn't that good, was I?'

'No, not *that* good …' she teased with a smile, only to turn serious again straightaway. 'I'm telling you this because in some way or other it may help us to understand what happened here this week.'

'I see! Now I'm even more curious.'

'That was the idea.'

'Tell me then!'

'I'm going to …'

36

She took me with her to Trodalen during the fateful summer of 1839. 'The story about Trodalen Mads, the alternative version,' as she called it, with a tiny smile. She told it in such a vivid way that I could see it unrolling before me, like a film: a flashback of almost one hundred and fifty years.

Mads Andersen was twenty-one years old that year. He was medium-height with a strong build, dark hair and melancholic predisposition, not unnatural for a young man who had grown up on an isolated farm in Trodalen with no one else except his parents, his sister and an adult serving maid. When he went to the priest, he got to know the eldest son of a family from Angedalen whose name was Jens Hansen, and Jens had a sister, Maria, who was four years younger. She was a quiet girl, a willing worker, industrious, who from early childhood had worked with her mother in the fields in the summer. She was at home in the mountains and could, even on Sundays, walk there on her own without any fear of what she might meet. After getting to know Mads, she used to walk all the way to Trodalen; not often, perhaps every other month, and they didn't always bump into each other. How could they? There was no one to whom they could entrust messages, and she didn't dare send a letter the few times the post went all the way up to Trodalsstrand.

According to what was passed down from Grethe's ancestors, a romance sprang up between Maria and Mads that winter and the spring of 1839; and the winter up in Trodalen was long, the snow didn't begin to clear until the end of April, even in June there were still great drifts left along the sunless mountainsides by the black mirror of Lake Trodalsvatn. There was something ominous and compelling about the lake, as though it, even at that time, concealed secrets it would not give up, memories of the past that were forever sunk beneath the depths. Mads often roamed in the mountains, hunting birds, deer or other game. He had set snares which he checked at regular intervals, and on not so few occasions during these wanderings he came to the mountain ridge at the end of the lake whence he could look down on Angedalen, at the farm where Jens and Maria had grown up. Sometimes they met there, he and Maria, and when May arrived and the sun began to warm, they embraced each other tenderly and vowed eternal fidelity …

'…. My mother told me,' Grethe said, still with her hand on the bible, as if the images were growing directly from the thin page where the family line had been drawn up.

'Did she also tell you what happened on that June day when Ole Olsen Otternæs was killed up there?'

'That's precisely the point of all this, Varg, my love. Now listen to the valley drama …

'When there is a confession it very soon becomes the truth, the whole truth and nothing but the truth about past events. But in this case there was another version, hidden and clutched to the bosom of six generations of women, like a secret shame, kept alive by the family's bad conscience about what really took place.

'The second version of the Trodalen murder went as follows. On this particular Wednesday Maria Hansdottir had fled her life on the farm. Perhaps she was hoping to meet Mads again on this beautiful sunny summer's day. The heat was making her blood pump extra hard through her veins, so much so that she could hardly bear being down on the farm, she just had to be up in the mountains where the person who was in her thoughts day and night was to be found. But ill luck was to have it that when she had climbed up to Trodalen and was on her way down to the lake, she bumped into Ole Otternæs, the dealer who only a short time before had taken his leave of Mads Andersen in Trodalsstrand. They stood and exchanged a few words, then she tried to move on. The dealer would not budge. Perhaps it was the summer heat that had gone to his head, too; perhaps it was the long period of abstinence that caused him to make a grab with lustful hands for the young girl. He was strong, strengthened from walking in the mountains. She struggled, screamed for help, the way the Arctic loon screeches at the steep faces of the mountains. But he would not let go. He burrowed up under her clothes with his strong hands until she screamed with fear and pain. Then she seized a rock lying on the ground and brought it down hard on the dealer's head – once, twice, three times! His rough hands let go of her body and he began to slip to the ground. Once again she struck, in fear and fury, until Ole Olsen Otternæs lay lifeless before her.

'Then she was gripped by a fear greater than anything she had ever felt before. She knew now that she had committed a deadly sin, and that the gates of hell would open and swallow her up as soon as her time had come. She was sentenced to eternal unrest, eternal fire, and the fear she felt now was so strong that she thought she would drop down dead on the path she was treading with such quaking feet. There was only one way to go she knew of: down to the water, down to a certain death.

'However, Mads Andersen was coming to meet her. He had heard the cry of the Arctic loon, and he recognised the sound. Now he took her in his arms, held her tight, let her tears flow and ebb, and eventually followed her to where Ole Olsen lay, to see what wretched state he was in.

'She stood at a distance watching Mads examine the lifeless body, and when he came back down to her, she realised from his posture that all hope was gone.

'But then he gave her fresh hope, indeed he redeemed her, took her sin upon himself and said: Let me take care of this, Maria. Just go home. I'll drop Ole Olsen Otternæs into the depths of the lake, and may he never return! Maria left him there and then, and that was the last time they spoke together. Later she was to see him only once, when after five days he was taken to the village by men from the neighbouring farm and from there to Førde with the bailiff and his assistants the following day.'

'He confessed to the murder,' I said. 'For her sake.'

Her eyes met mine. 'Does that sound familiar?'

'What happened then?'

'The rest of the story is well-known. He had taken a few banknotes and valuables from Ole Olsen and they were found on him. He confessed and was given his punishment. Not until many years afterwards, in 1881, was he released from Akershus prison. By then Maria had been dead for twenty-two years. She died in 1859, unmarried and without any heirs, apart from her apparently fatherless daughter, Kristine, who herself had a daughter after what we today would call a gang-bang, in 1863. My great grandmother, who was given the name Margrethe.'

'And Maria never came forward with what she knew about the Trodalen murder?'

'Not to anyone's knowledge. She confided it to this.' She gently patted the opened book with her hand. 'The truth follows our family down from woman to woman.'

'And now to me ...'

'But you swore an oath!'

'Yes ... and I stand by it. So many years afterwards, Mads Andersen's reputation doesn't count for so much, so long as his only descendant ...' With a flourish of my hand I indicated her. '... is happy to leave it like that.'

'But the upshot of this, Varg, did you catch it?'

I nodded. 'Never rely on what is said. A case is rarely what it seems at first glance.'

'Then I've achieved what I set out to do,' she said, closing the book with care and putting it on the bedside table. A fragrance arose from her body like mountain and sun, a scent of mothers past.

'Is that everything?'

She rolled onto her side and slid open her thighs. 'But I could easily handle a repeat performance,' she said with a pert smile, pulling me close.

37

The day after was a depressing contrast, one long unbroken decline from the hectic breakfast at Hornnes, after which Grethe had to drive me in all haste to the hotel because she herself was in danger of arriving late for the morning meeting at work.

At the hotel the mood was one of leave-taking. A press conference had been set for twelve o'clock and the reporters who were still in Førde took the agenda as read. The next item would be the court case and the fixing of a date.

'That's bad,' I concluded as soon as I had had my impression confirmed via a telephone conversation with Helge Haugen from *Firda Tidend*. The pathologist's and the forensics report pointed very clearly in one direction, and Haugen said that a source of his at the police offices had ascertained that in the course of the day Jan Egil Skarnes would be charged with the double murder and held on remand until the case came to trial, incommunicado for the first four weeks.

I thanked him for the information and looked at my watch. There was still an hour and a half until the press conference.

In much the same way that Maria Hansdottir had her Trodalen Mads, Jan Egil had his Silje. It was the last loose thread. I decided to do a bit of unravelling and with the aid of the telephone directory found where Øygunn Bråtet had her office. She had her base in shared office space on the second floor of one of the commercial buildings to the south of the river, east of Lange Bridge.

A reticent secretary told me that Bråtet was extremely busy this morning. I turned on the last remnants of charm I had and against all the odds got to speak to her in the front office.

'How can I help you?' she said in a measured tone.

'I was thinking about Silje. She's something of a key character in this case.'

'Not any more she isn't.'

'No?'

'She's withdrawn her confession.'

'Really?'

'She admitted she'd done it to help Jan Egil.'

'And what caused her to change her mind?'

She looked at her watch. 'A press conference has been called for twelve, Veum. All will be revealed then. You'll have to turn up.'

'Where's Silje now?'

'At home on the farm. But …'

'Yes?'

'Don't try and visit her. She's not talking to anyone.'

'It was more her foster parents I fancied a couple of words with.'

'For what reason, if I might ask?'

'Well … there's the question of inheritance hanging in the air. *Fru* Almelid is, to my knowledge, the only heir to Libakk.'

'And what does that have to do with this case?'

'And there are all the other aspects. The 1973 smuggling business, amongst others.'

'And what was that supposed …?' She broke off and shook her head. 'Tell me … Who are you representing actually?'

'For the time being, your colleague, Jens Langeland.'

'Uhuh.' She didn't seem to appreciate that. 'Well, if you're considering visiting the Almelid family, it won't be without me being present.'

'OK, but … when?'

'It can't be before the press conference at any rate.'

'You were thinking of going, too, in other words?'

'I was, yes. So, if I can get on with the day's business until then, I …'

'See you there then.'

'There will be no avoiding that.'

She nodded and left me with the red-haired secretary, who had not become less reticent as a result of overhearing the conversation between Øygunn Bråtet and myself. I saluted a goodbye and went on my way.

There was not much else I could do but wait for the said press conference. I bought some newspapers and had a cup of coffee at a café by Lange Bridge.

The double murder had moved to the back pages now. *Outcome Awaited* ran one headline. *Double Murder Solved* ran another, without any question marks. No one had picked up on the connection with the murder of Ansgår Tveiten. Only Helge Haugen of *Firda Tidend* hinted at a connection with 'the great smuggling ring that ravaged the district in 1973', without going into any detail about what connections there could be.

Nevertheless, the large meeting room at the police station where the press conference was to be held was fairly full. They had put three tables together for a panel presentation. All the chairs were occupied. I nodded to Helge Haugen who had taken one of the front seats and was sitting ready with his notebook open. Further away, at the table, sat Øygunn Bråtet. I stood by one of the windows, leaning against the frame with my back to the daylight. When Sergeant Standal, a police official and the KRIPOS detective responsible came in, a storm of flashes went off and everyone eyed the new arrivals with excitement.

Standal seemed almost abashed. The police official looked as if he had won the pools. He was a young man with plain glasses and a well-trimmed beard, to all appearances a newly-fledged lawyer. The well-built KRIPOS detective regarded the whole thing as routine and didn't allow himself to be affected.

Right behind them came Jens Langeland. He quickly scanned the audience and then took up a discreet position by the door. Spotting me, he gave a brief nod and gestured that he would like to talk to me afterwards.

Standal raised one hand in the air and the room fell silent. He had a typed statement on the table in front of him. Without raising his voice he read out the decision to charge Jan Egil Skarnes with the murder of his two foster parents and subsequently firing a shot at police officers. Reference was made to the relevant paragraphs and attention drawn to a meeting to be called later in the day to discuss remand. As a basis for the charges, reference was made to the investigation and to the reports, now available, after the pathologist's and the forensic examination. The findings were so clear that the police considered it reasonable to draw up charges. However, Standal informed the gathering that the investigation would continue at full strength with the intention of collecting further evidence until the case came to trial. The KRIPOS detective nodded in approval.

When the floor was opened to questions, Helge Haugen was quick to respond. 'But there was also a hostage drama in Angedalen, wasn't there?'

Standal fumbled for words before saying: 'Until further notice, he is not charged with taking this girl from the neighbouring farm prisoner. The evidence suggests that she went with him of her own free will.'

'Isn't there a chance then that she might be charged with being an accomplice?'

'Not at the present time,' Standal rebuffed. 'But we are continuing our investigation, as I said.'

The police official added: 'At present there is no basis for any charges against this girl. Our preliminary conclusions are that she was unaware of what had transpired at Libakk Farm when she accompanied the accused up to Trodalen.'

I looked at Jens Langeland. His expression gave away nothing, but I could actually see him boiling inside. I would have liked to put up my hand and ask: 'But isn't it the case that this young girl actually confessed to carrying out both of these murders?' I would have liked to see the reactions of the press corps and the high-ranking gentlemen at the end of the table, if such a claim were to be made, but it didn't take me long to repress my inclinations. There were still some people in the room with whom I envisaged friendly relations, and an initiative of that kind would have put an abrupt end to that.

The questions from the floor soon dwindled and thereafter the press conference came to a close. Some radio and TV reporters wanted to ask the usual supplementary questions to the relevant police officials, but beyond that the gathering soon dispersed.

Langeland was waiting for me in the vestibule. I drew him into a corner. 'I have several snippets of information for you, Langeland.'

'Already? My goodness. Come on then! Now I need everything I can get.'

'A source told me yesterday that Klaus Libakk kept a large sum of money at the farm. The takings from the smuggling racket, which, naturally enough, cannot be paid into a normal bank account.'

He viewed me with scepticism. 'A sum of money from 1973? Which he has been able to eat into ever since? How much could have been left of it, do you think?'

'Don't know … But it could support the theory of a possible burglary, or at any rate an attempted burglary.'

'Ye-es …'

'But not only that, listen to this. The main person behind the contraband ring, according to the same source, was no other than Svein Skarnes!'

He stared at me in disbelief. '*Our* Svein Skarnes, as it were?'

'Exactly.'

I hastily retold all that Harald Dale had confided in me the previous evening, and with every turn the story took I could see his brain beginning to churn. Yet his excitement didn't seem to be mounting, and when I came to Terje Hammersten's role in the affair, I understood the reason.

'Hell's bells, Veum. If this is true then Vibecke really should have gone free that time! This is too terrible to contemplate. Now

I definitely will have to have a serious talk with her as soon as I'm back in Oslo.'

'Right, but that's only one side of the matter. Now the police will be obliged to bring in Hammersten for questioning.'

'Mm, I've told them! The problem is that they're so fixated on the reports they now hold in their hands.'

'Uhuh. Have you had access to them, too?'

He looked at me gloomily. 'Yes. And I'm afraid to say, even after a superficial perusal, things don't look good.'

'What! What do you mean by that?'

'First of all, there are the fingerprints on the weapon. His and his alone. And there was a residue of gunpowder on his hands.'

'Yes, but we know he fired the rifle when he ran away from the police.'

'Yes, indeed, and we will have to pump that one for all it is worth. Of course. But to go on … there are his bootmarks at the crime scene, in the blood on the floor, and spores of the same blood under his boots. Both Klaus and Kari were killed with this weapon. There is no sign of a break-in. Quite the opposite. The spare key which hung in a cupboard in the hall was in place. Jan Egil had his own key on him. And then Silje retracted her confession. But!' He thrust an upright finger in the air. 'She is extremely vague in her statement about what happened there last weekend – and especially last Monday.'

'What about the suggestions of abuse from Klaus Libakk's side?'

'Now she claims that that, too, was something she made up, in an attempt to justify what is now looking like a bogus confession. And the medical examination in fact supports her, even if she is not what in the profession is known as a virgo intacta.'

'Yes, I'd been told about that. Her sexual debut was a fact.'

'And to tell the truth I'm not sure it would've been to Jan Egil's advantage if she had been abused by her uncle. If Silje and he were lovers, which there is every reason to assume they were, it simply gives him a strong motive for the killing.'

'Yes, of course you're right there. So … what do we do now?'

'First off, I will insist that the police bring in Terje Hammersten for questioning. I will demand that his alibi for Sunday evening is checked, and the police will be able to do that a great deal more effectively than you or I, Veum. Then we can move on from there. Right now I don't have any more ideas.'

'When's the review meeting?'

'Half past three, I was told.'

'Is it an open meeting – could I go?'

'I haven't been told it's not open. But the press is not allowed to report on review meetings, so if you want to know how the case is being presented you should be there.' He looked at his watch. 'But now I have to go in to see Jan Egil. We'd better talk later.'

We parted quickly, and he hurried back into the police offices. As I came out of the building, I saw Øygunn Bråtet on her way to Lange Bridge. I scurried after her and caught up with her by the pedestrian crossing on the other side of the river. When she saw me alongside her, she sent me a bittersweet little smile.

I didn't waste any time. 'Ready to go?'

She rolled her eyes. 'No! Not yet.'

'Listen … We can do this in two ways, *frøken* Bråtet.'

'It's *fru*.'

'Nonetheless. I can call on Silje and her foster parents on my own, or I can do it in your company. Which would you prefer?'

'Or I can have you arrested by the police.'

'For what?'

That stumped her, and we ended up travelling to Angedalen together, though each in our own car with neither of us feeling much pleasure at being reunited as we parked in the yard at Almelid Farm and got out.

38

Almelid was a well maintained farm, both on the outside and the inside. The walls of the sitting room were white and smooth with just a few pictures up. There was a collection of family photos, an aerial photo of the farm and a landscape picture of the classic kind: a fjord in the evening light with the sun low over the shiny sea.

The crockery Klara Almelid used was white with small pink flowers and a gold edge. Within ten minutes she had made coffee, put out a bowl of biscuits, cut up a small malt loaf and spread golden farm butter and genuine goat's cheese on the slices. She was small with an efficient, ferret-like nature. Her darting eyes took in most of what was happening in the sitting room and the kitchen.

Silje sat by a little nest of tables by the window, sullen. Øygunn Bråtet had taken a seat on the stool beside her while quietly telling her what had been said at the press conference and explaining to her what the next steps would be.

For the first time I had a chance to study the young girl in peace. She was wearing tight, faded jeans and a dark blue V-necked sweater with a short flower-patterned scarf around her neck. Her dark blonde hair was collected in a ponytail, but when I searched for some resemblance with Trude Tveiten, there was not much I could detect; perhaps the way she held her head, that was all, though. She had nodded sulkily when she saw me, before seeking Øygunn Bråtet's eyes like a drowning person desperate for something at hand to grab.

The front door opened, and heavy steps resounded in the hall. Klara Almelid left quickly to explain the situation to her husband. He growled an answer. A door closed and straight after there was a rushing sound in the heating pipes.

When Lars Almelid came in and stood in the doorway, he had taken off his outdoor clothing and changed his trousers. He had house shoes on his feet, a flannel shirt open at the neck and he smelt of soap. His complexion was fresh and red with a distinct pattern of small, thin blood vessels under both ears. His hair was thinning, but he had large, bushy eyebrows. His eyes were blue, determined, as was the set of his lips.

I stood up and we shook hands. He scrutinised me carefully. 'And how may I help you?'

'To be frank, I'd like a little chat with Silje.'

'Frank?'

'Yes, I'd like to hear her version.'

'I understood that, but I believe you said *frank*? From that I conclude there is something else you're after.'

I glanced at Silje and her solicitor. Øygunn Bråtet returned a mocking look. I lowered my voice. 'Can we go into the kitchen?'

He nodded silently. We went out and I closed the door behind me. Klara and Lars Almelid were standing by the worktop on the other side of the room, positioned beside each other as if for a family photo.

I looked at Klara. 'You are the sister of the late Klaus Libakk, I understand …?'

She gave a doleful nod. 'Yes, I was.' She faced the window. 'I grew up on Libakk Farm too.' Her dialect was as broad as her husband's.

'Were there any other brothers or sisters?'

'Yes, we had a brother. Sigurd. But he was lost at sea when he was very young. So then it was just Klaus and I.'

'But Kari, she must have had family, I suppose?'

'Yes, there must be some relatives. But she wasn't from here, you know. She came from somewhere on the Møre coast. She didn't have any brothers or sisters, though. That much I'm sure of.'

'So perhaps it'll be you who takes it over then?'

She glanced at her husband. 'Yes, I suppose it might be. If they don't find a will.'

'How was the relationship between you and your brother?'

'It was good, I think. We weren't very similar, though.'

'In what way?'

'Well, you know …'

'Here on the farm we've stuck to our childhood faith, for example,' said Lars Almelid in a sonorous voice.

'And they didn't at Libakk Farm?'

'At least they never went to … either the church or the chapel.'

'We never spoke about it,' Klara said quietly. 'But we had our own views.'

'What about … it's rumoured that Klaus Libakk was involved in the great smuggling ring that operated in the early seventies.'

Her face scrunched up around a tiny pursed mouth while his face darkened even further. He was the one who answered: 'We've also heard the rumours.'

'But they were just rumours?'

'We never talked about it,' Klara repeated.

'But we saw the vehicles that came to visit now and then,' said Lars. 'And they weren't such small loads he carried in his vehicle, either, a big Hiace, it was.'

'But you never dealt with him?'

'We don't touch that sort of thing!'

'No … but you know of course who Silje's father was.'

Klara nodded. 'Yes, we obviously know that.'

'Could he have been here – at Libakk, I mean?'

She looked at her husband. He shrugged his shoulders slowly and stiffly. 'He might've been,' he answered. 'But that was a long time before Silje came here. He's dead, too, as I'm sure you know.'

'Yes, I do. But the mother popped round now and then?'

It was Klara who answered this time. 'Yes, but not that often. She lives right out in Dale, she does.'

'That's not so far.'

'No, no.'

'Perhaps you don't like her coming?'

She straightened her back a little. 'We don't think it does Silje any good, if I may put it like that.'

'Why not?'

'Because!' Klaus said in a strong, clear voice.

For a moment we sat chewing on that. Then I decided to change the topic. 'Of course you must've heard what Silje said about … Klaus and her.'

Klara had a violent reaction, and I saw her grip the edge of the worktop to prevent herself from falling. 'It's … impossible,' she said in a low, intense voice.

Lars looked at me with fire in his eyes. 'Whatsoever you have done unto these the least of My brethren you have done unto Me,' he quoted.

'And by that you mean …?'

'If what Silje said is true, he's going to burn in hell until eternity!'

'So you don't know any more about it?'

'She never said anything to us,' Klara said. 'Not a single word.'

I nodded. 'Well, perhaps then …' I motioned that we could join the others again. Klara took the coffee pot and began to fill the cups. Silje was asked if she wanted a glass of juice, but she responded with a shake of the head.

Øygunn Bråtet was sitting on the stool with a cup of coffee in her hand. I was sitting at the table with Klara and Lars. Silje was staring at the floor, cowed into silence by this cheerless assembly.

Klara and Lars folded their hands and said grace quickly before Klara passed round a dish of the malt bread sandwiches, then the biscuits.

No one said anything.

I looked at Øygunn Bråtet. She met my eyes; her gaze was measured and cool.

In the end, I spoke up. 'Silje …'

She peered up with a start, then looked down again.

'We met in the valley on Tuesday evening. Since then I haven't had a chance to talk to you. But I'm trying to help Jan Egil as much

as I can. That's why it would be very helpful if you could tell me –
in your own words – what happened.'

She mumbled something indistinct.

'Pardon? I didn't hear what you said.'

'There's nothing to tell,' she said in a quiet voice, but more distinct now.

'You had a lot to say up in Trodalen. And afterwards, too, I'm
led to believe.'

'That was just something I said.'

I leaned forward. 'Something you said? All of it? Or just parts
of it?'

She didn't answer.

As I started formulating a new question, she interrupted me.
'Do *they* have to be here?'

'Do you mean Lars and Klara?'

'Yes.'

I glanced at her two foster parents. Klara looked desperate, Lars
as if he were about to explode. In a low voice I said: 'This is not an
unusual situation. Children or teenagers don't want to say their
opinions in front of their parents.'

'They're not my parents!'

Øygunn Bråtet placed a small, reassuring hand on Silje's arm.

'We can go out! If that's how it has to be.' Lars's voice was
brusque. 'We don't want to impose. We've just cared for the girl,
we have. Since she was five years old and alone in the world.'

'I wasn't alone! I had my mum!'

Lars ignored her. 'Oh yes, she had her mum. And we could all
see what she'd done for her.'

Klara gripped him. 'Lars … Don't … If she doesn't want us here,
that's …'

'Yes, that's what I'm saying. We can go outside. By all means.
Can we take our cups of coffee with us?'

Klara sent us an apologetic smile as she shooed Lars into the
kitchen and gestured that we should help ourselves.

I got up and closed the door after them. 'Now you can speak, Silje.'

'There's nothing to say, I told you.'

'There must be something. Tell me about Jan Egil and you when ...'

She said sulkily: 'We were good friends. We grew up together, didn't we! And then he was my boyfriend.'

'In every sense?'

She straightened up. 'What do you mean?'

'Well, I mean ...' I glanced over at Øygunn Bråtet, who refused to give me any kind of support. 'Had you been to bed together?'

She stared at me with wide open eyes, as if it were inexcusable to ask questions of that nature. Her face went crimson. Then she jerked a nod. 'Yes,' she whispered. 'Many times.'

' ... Mm, did you use any, er, contraception?'

'We did, yes,' she jeered, without going into detail. It wasn't important, anyway.

I responded with a friendly expression, to imply that it was sensible of them. Øygunn Bråtet sent me a condescending glare.

'And last weekend ... Sunday night. Is that right?'

'Yes, it is. They asked me the same at the police station. I don't know what's so ...' She broke off.

'... important about it? Oh yes, you do. After all, a double murder took place that night.'

'Right, but Jan Egil was here with me!'

'All night?'

She nodded.

'Absolutely sure? You were asleep, weren't you? I assume you weren't at it all night?'

Øygunn Bråtet gave an admonitory cough. I thrust forward my chin in an apologetic manner.

'He was asleep, too, I think.'

'But he nipped home before you went to school, he said.' As she didn't respond, I went on: 'Weren't you afraid of being found out? By your ... by Lars and Klara, I mean?'

'They never looked in at night. We heard them hitting the hay, and so we went the other way, through the barn. I've got a room at the other end of the house from them,' she explained.

'What happened then?'

'You know what happened! On Monday we had so much school-work that we didn't see each other, and he didn't go to school on Tuesday. That was why I went to see him at home. But I should never have done that.'

'Did you see them? Kari and Klaus?'

She shook her head.

'But how did you come to say … what you did up there in the valley and afterwards?'

Then the tears flowed. 'It was for his sake! How many times do I have to tell you? I did it for his sake. But that doesn't mean I think he did it. I just … he's my boyfriend. I wanted to help him …'

'And you did that by calling Klaus Libakk an old pig, with all that that might imply?'

She put on a defiant look through the tears.

'*Was* he?'

She didn't answer.

'Had he made approaches to you?'

As she still refused to answer, I said: 'Why don't you answer? Because it was all fabrication? You made it up to explain why you'd done something you hadn't? Or have you realised now … that this, in fact, also gives Jan Egil a motive? A very strong motive, some would say.'

But she had gone into a new mode. For some reason she had decided not to say another word.

I sent Bråtet a quizzical look, but she just shrugged. She had nothing to add.

Was it something I had said? Something she had reacted to?

At length, I stood up and said: 'Well … I suppose then I have no more questions. I hope you get over this, Silje, and I wish you all the best in your life.'

She peered up, tossed her head and stared at me stiffly with tears in her eyes. I waited for a moment, but she had no more to say. I left her in Øygunn Bråtet's hands and went into the kitchen.

Klara and Lars were sitting on opposite sides of the table with a cup of cold coffee in front of them. Neither of them had tasted it, as far as I could see. Lars was staring into the middle distance; Klara looked up nervously when I came in.

'Did you know that Silje and Jan Egil were girlfriend and boyfriend?'

Lars's mouth twitched. Klara answered: 'Yes. No. Of course we saw that they were together a lot.'

'She says he spent the night here last Sunday. In her bedroom.'

Lars's face darkened. Klara said: 'Yes, we've been told. But we had no idea that was going on! We would've intervened straightaway.'

'I hope you won't tell her off for that now. She's been put under colossal pressure.'

She nodded. Neither of them spoke.

'What impression did you have of Jan Egil?'

'I've never liked him!' Lars snarled. 'There was something about him right from the very beginning.'

'When they were small, they played together so well,' Klara said. 'But in recent time they've met in places other than here. I think we lost contact with him over the years.'

Lars nodded in agreement.

Øygunn Bråtet came through the door from the sitting room. She looked at me. 'You can leave, but I'll stay here for a while. I'd like to talk a bit more with Silje.'

The two at the kitchen table nodded.

'I'll do that then,' I said. No one seemed upset to see me go.

No one accompanied me out into the farmyard, either. Before getting into the car, I had a look around. Surrounded by high mountains, Angedalen lay like a paradise on earth, a landscape exuding peace and tolerance, a striking contrast to the dramatic events that had taken place here in the last week.

I contemplated Trodalen and thought about what had happened up there, in the past and now. In a strange way the two seemed to reflect each other, the two unhappy couples: Mads Andersen and Maria Hansdottir in 1839, Jan Egil Skarnes and Silje Tveiten in 1984. Birds floating on the wind, transfixed by the sun, with death as the only way out after a long period of imprisonment for others' crimes; death as the centre around which the whole solar system rotated.

39

Back in Førde again, I tried to get in touch with Jens Langeland. It was impossible. He was with Jan Egil and had made it quite clear that they were not to be disturbed. Not by anyone.

Instead I went for a last offensive against Sergeant Standal. I said I had something to tell him, something that might shed some light on the case. He therefore insisted on having a KRIPOS representative present.

It was the same well-built, cropped detective who had attended the press conference. 'Tor Frydenberg' he introduced himself as, with a robust handshake and a look of curiosity, before taking up a position against one wall with his arms crossed, ready to hear what I had to say.

I told them everything I had discovered about a possible connection between the smuggling affair of 1973 and the events of this week. I told them about Terje Hammersten, the connection with Svein Skarnes and the alleged stash of money Klaus Libakk had been keeping on his farm.

They listened patiently. After I had finished, Standal said: 'You brought this Terje Hammersten to our attention yesterday. I can reassure you that orders have been drawn up to hold him for the purposes of questioning. But we have examined the conclusion they came to in 1973.'

'And that was?'

'He was in Bergen the day the murder took place.'

'Who with? His associates?'

'His alibi was accepted by the investigators at the time. It was impossible to disprove, at any rate.'

'And what about now? Did he also have an alibi last Sunday?'

'We haven't got that far yet. However, as I said, we're picking him up for questioning. We won't leave anything untried. Anything else you wished to present?'

'Let me come back to Klaus Libakk's stash. Have you observed any unusually high spending behaviour from Libakk since 1973?'

'As I told you a day or two ago, Veum, Klaus Libakk was never on our records.'

'Strange. But you agree it could be a motive?'

'If the money really existed, yes. So far, though, we have no evidence of it. And there was no sign of a burglary in the house.'

'Isn't it normal in these parts for people to sleep with their doors unlocked?'

'Not any more. There have been too many unpleasant surprises over the last few years for that, of the kind you're suggesting now. Even the accused has had to concede that the door was always locked at night.'

'The accused?'

'Yes, he will be – officially now as well.'

I stole a glance at Frydenberg. 'And you? Are you behind this decision? Are you happy with the outcome?'

'*Happy* is not an expression we in KRIPOS are given to using, Veum. We collect facts and evidence, then it's up to the police lawyers to consider prosecution. But I can confirm that until anything else is proven, all the facts in this case point in one direction.'

'Veum,' Standal said gently. 'We fully respect your commitment to this case. We know of your social services background, and we know that Jan Egil Skarnes is an ex-client of yours, but …' He took a large, greyish-green box file that had been lying in the middle of his desk the whole time. 'I've been conferring with my colleague here, and even though this is not our usual practice we've agreed that we will show you these …'

He opened the file and pulled out a handful of large colour photographs. Then he selected a couple of them before placing four pictures beside each other on the desk. He beckoned me over to look closer. 'These are the crime scene photos, Veum. And I ought perhaps to warn you. It's pretty strong stuff.'

I slowly dragged my chair closer and leaned over.

I had never seen them alive, but I immediately knew who they were. On a large full-view photo we saw them both: Klaus Libakk lying in bed in a pool of blood with a limp jaw and staring eyes, and Kari, his wife, in a strangely distorted position with her back to the photographer, her face jerked to the side, her upper body bent backward, a clear bullet wound in the back of her head and a big, dark bloodstain on the rear of her nightdress.

The next photo zoomed in on Klaus, from the chest upwards. The bullet or bullets had gone right through the duvet, and he was staring up at the ceiling with glassy eyes, unable to communicate anything other than the impression of an abandoned body, the mark of death in his forehead.

The two last photographs showed Kari. She was well-built, a dark blonde with streaks of grey in her hair. In contrast to Klaus, she had a clear expression on her face, one of infinite fear and despair, a death mask set for eternity and fixed to this glossy paper for all to see. The unnatural position told its own story. She had been hit in the back and hurled against the wall, then she had slumped to the floor, which movement had been halted by a bedpost. Afterwards she had stayed like this, half bent backward, with the lower half of her nightdress ruffled up around her waist and her broad white thighs visible above the edge of the bed.

These were pictures of a slaughterhouse not of a bedroom. I felt a peculiar mixture of fury and horror grow in me, a fury against whoever had perpetrated such a brutal act as this, and at the same time a horror that the person who had done this was unknown but someone I had myself spoken to on one of the recent days.

'We have a clear idea of the sequence of events,' Frydenberg said with intonation suggestive of a football match commentary. 'The first shot hit Klaus Libakk in the chest. He was killed instantaneously. His wife woke up and in total panic tried to escape, making for the window. There she was struck by two bullets, both in the back, both life-threatening injuries, but she did not die immediately. Then another shot was fired into the chest of Klaus Libakk, who was already dead, before the murderer gave Kari what we have to call the *coup de grâce* to the head when he noticed she was still alive.'

'My God!' I burst out.

'You can certainly say that, but … he was probably looking in a different direction at this point,' Frydenberg said drily.

I looked at Standal. 'Why are you showing me these?'

'So that you understand how serious this crime is. So that you have no doubt that we will do everything in our power to have this crime solved. And we're of the opinion that we are well on the way to doing so. I'm a hundred per cent sure that we have the right man behind bars, Veum.'

'A hundred per cent? Not even a smidgeon of doubt?'

'None whatsoever.'

I looked at Tor Frydenberg. His face was expressionless, as though to demonstrate that with him there was no room for faith or doubt. With him only dry facts counted.

Sitting and listening to the submissions made at the review meeting later in the day, with Hans Haavik in the chair next to mine, I almost allowed myself to be convinced.

Point by point, the police lawyer outlined the case for the prosecution, leaning heavily on the interim results from the forensic examination. The most telling evidence was of course Jan's fingerprints on the murder weapon, the gunpowder residue on his clothes and skin, the boot pattern on the prints at the crime scene and the spores of blood under his boots.

'Two days afterwards?' Jens Langeland commented sarcastically without gaining any more than a patronising look in return.

There were additonal references to Silje's confession, which had been retracted now, but which nonetheless gave Jan Egil a very strong motive for the alleged act. A brief and, as far as it went, very superficial character analysis of Jan Egil was given, based on reports from the school medical service and social services, which also drew on his traumatic childhood experiences when he was six.

The conclusion was unequivocal. The prosecuting authority asked the court to approve their submission that Jan Egil Skarnes should be charged with the double murder of his foster parents, Kari and Klaus Libakk, as well as intent to cause actual bodily harm to a civil servant while firing a shot at the police officer who visited Libakk Farm two days later. They recommended that the period of remand should be extended until the investigation was concluded, with Jan kept incommunicado for the first four weeks.

Jens Langeland opposed these allegations with vigour. He showed that the fingerprints on the weapon, the bootprints at the crime scene and the blood spores under his boots could be explained by Jan Egil discovering what had happened when he came home from school on Monday. In shock he had grabbed the rifle, reloaded it and then hidden in the sitting room out of fear that the perpetrators would return. When the police officer turned up on Tuesday he might have believed him to be one of the murderers, or he could have reacted hastily because he feared he would be blamed for something he had not done.

Langeland accepted the claim that Jan Egil had fired a shot at the policeman 'in panic', but argued that this had its roots in the situation in which Jan Egil had found himself, by all accounts one of deep shock.

He would not comment on Silje's role in this tragedy, but he pointed out that there were so many dubious points in the prosecution's recommendation that the court should have 'no hesitation' in rejecting the case for charging Jan Egil Skarnes and release him until the investigation was complete. In this regard, he placed great emphasis on the age of the young boy, only just over the minimum age for criminal responsibility.

In a brief flurry of exchanges the police offical asked Langeland who he was referring to when he said 'the perpetrators'. Langeland replied that in his assessment of the investigation so far, there could very well be one or two 'unknown gunmen' and he begged the police to concentrate their efforts on this aspect of the case as well in the coming time. In this context he called the court's attention to the fact that a 'known violent criminal from Bergen' had been in the district on the day of the murder, a claim which the police lawyer rejected after a rapid conferral with Sergeant Standal: so far no evidence had been found to suggest that the person in question was in the area at the time of the deaths, but the police were aware of the claim, and this person had been brought in for questioning to Police Headquarters and this would be resumed as soon as the review meeting was over.

Not much more was said and the meeting was brought to a close.

At various points during the review I had looked across at Jan Egil. He was sitting slumped over a table, staring down; he only raised his gaze a couple of times. He was sitting as if he found himself in a completely different place and that the events taking place here, in this chilly room on the third floor of the post office building, did not concern him. I couldn't help but see the tiny boy Cecilie and I had collected and taken to Åsane on that February day in 1974. He was still the same boy, just ten years older, thirty kilos heavier and – if we were to believe the prosecution service – a lot more dangerous than he had been.

When the court re-sat, after a short adjournment, it came as no surprise which way the judge had gone. The plea for Jan Egil Skarnes to be charged with the double murder of his foster parents and the intent to harm a police officer had been accepted. The same applied to the prosecution authority's request for Jan Egil to be held on remand until the trial, incommunicado for the first four weeks.

After it was all over, I caught Jan Egil's eyes as he walked out with Jens Langeland beside him. His look shocked and hurt me; it was a look so full of hatred, so dismissive that it pierced me like an arrow of ice. As if I had personally failed him. As if I was the only one.

40

Hans Haavik and I walked back to the hotel together. Neither of us said anything. We were equally depressed.

'Now I have to have something to drink,' he said as we entered the reception area. 'I have a bottle in my room. Will you join me?'

'Why not? Let me just find out if ...'

But there weren't any messages for me in reception. I wondered whether I should try and ring her, but Hans was so impatient, shifting from one foot to the other, that I didn't have the heart to keep him waiting any longer.

His room was identical to mine. There was an open suitcase on the luggage bench. A used shirt hung over the only chair. He took the shirt, slung it in the suitcase and picked up a bottle of Tullamore Dew from which so far only a quarter had been drunk. He went to the bathroom and returned with two plastic beakers. 'You have the chair,' he said, placing the beakers on the table and pouring almost to the rim. I didn't complain.

He took one of the glasses himself, raised it for a toast and we drank. Then he flopped down on the edge of the bed with the drink in his hand. The wooden frame creaked under the weight of his large body.

'Now and then you can just get so damnably bloody depressed, Varg!'

I nodded. 'I know the feeling.'

'Things are so bad you have to ask yourself the question: what the hell are we doing? Are we any use to anyone?'

'You must have seen some positive results over the years?'

'Yes, we have ... some.' Despite his massive presence, it was as if he had shrunk while sitting on the bed. Most of his height was in his legs of course, but the way he held his shoulders, like a mother bird protecting a newly hatched chick, made his powerful upper body narrower and smaller. 'Take a case like this one, though. Jan Egil Skarnes ... Johnny boy whom we've followed almost since he was born.'

'You, too?'

'Yes, don't forget that I studied with Jens Langeland. By the way, he had brilliant exam results, unlike others I can mention.' He grinned. 'As soon as his studies were over, he got a job as a solicitor's clerk at one of Oslo's prestigious law offices, Bakke & Lundekvam. In the autumn of 1966 – it must have been – he assisted on his first case. A drugs case, a young couple were arrested at Flesland Airport with a huge packet of hash in their bag. That is, the man was carrying it all, and Bakke managed to get the girl off because she'd been unaware of what the journey involved. But this girl ... it was Mette Olsen in fact. And I knew all too well who she was.'

'Mm?'

'They called her the Princess in Copenhagen.'

'Yes, actually I'd heard that, but ...'

He gave a flourish with his arm as if to dismiss what I had been going to ask. 'You know what it was like in those years, Varg. Hell, there were lots of us who flirted with hash and other hallucinogenics. My own passage through was not entirely without incident. Was yours?'

I smiled with embarrassment. 'No, I suppose I'd had a few puffs, but ...'

'Yes?'

'Well, my problem was that I'd never smoked. Just inhaling was a challenge for me.'

'Right ... Later, when I started at social services, I met her again of course. Jan was no more than six-seven months old the first time we had her in for an assessment. He was sent for a short stay at an infants home while she was drying out, and then we gave her another chance, a chance she wasted a year or two later.'

'1970,' I said. 'I went with Elsa Dragesund to Rothaugen to fetch him.'

'You see, you're just as bloody involved in his life as I am. You're like me and all the others.'

'All the others?'

'Or no one, if you understand what I mean.'

'Not exactly.'

'Well, listen here …' He studied his glass in amazement. It was already empty. He leaned forward and re-filled it to the brim. At the same time he re-filled mine. I didn't complain this time, either. It was a good Irish whiskey, a rounded taste with a golden colour.

'This boy was brought onto this earth by a mother who was so doped up that she hardly registered it. Right from the very beginning he had poor odds. The first thing that should have been done was to take him away from her for good. Then neither you nor I would be sitting here today, Varg. I'm convinced about that. The injuries a child suffers in the first years of its life can be fatal. You and I know that and so does everyone else who works in this business of ours.'

'True. But there are exceptions. And there are some who travel in the opposite direction, born with a silver spoon in their mouths and take it down the swannee with them.'

'Yes, yes, of course. But then he reappears – how many years is it? – six years later?'

'Three and a half after Elsa and I picked him up from Rothaugen.'

'Yes, but six and a half years old. And he was unlucky with the hand he was dealt yet again.'

'Unlucky, maybe. You knew Vibecke Skarnes from university, didn't you? Was she bad luck?'

'No, but her husband probably was. He had far too many pokers in the fire, and he never gave Jan the stability and tranquility at home he would have needed.'

'Mm. You were pals I remember you saying once, weren't you?'

'For a while. But it came to an abrupt end when he and Vibecke got together.'

'Why was that?'

'Well,' he shrugged. 'That's the way it goes sometimes.'

'Do you know what I found out yesterday? An apparently reliable source told me that Svein Skarnes had played a very central role in the big booze smuggling ring that I think we talked about the other evening in the bar.'

'Yes, but we were talking about Klaus Libakk.'

'Right. But Libakk was only responsible for distribution here. Locally. Skarnes was the main man behind the whole racket.'

'Svein?'

'Yes. He was the one who had the contact with the German distributors, he was the one who brought home the deals with the boats supplying the goods, when they were transferred to smaller boats, fishing cutters and the like, and then they were brought down the fjords, from Sognfest to Selje. But that's not all ...'

He reached for his glass. 'No?'

I gave him a quick shakedown of the case, including the murder of Ansgår Tveiten, the connection with the double murder in Angedalen and the conversations I had had over recent days with Mette Olsen, Trude Tveiten and Terje Hammersten.

He leaned forward. 'I know Hammersten. A brutal bastard.'

'That's my impression, too.'

'He's got a son who's been in and out of our Åsane home. Fourteen years old.'

'A son? Who with?'

'I don't know if I ... Yes, I do, to hell with it. This will have to be the day for openness. The mother is a streetwalker. The father is Terje Hammersten. The boy flits from one foster home to another, and Hammersten is such a pain. The last time was Monday morning – I had hardly got back home from Angedalen – and there he was at my door ready to give me a mouthful.'

I sat watching him. 'What did you just say? Was Hammersten at your place in Bergen on Monday morning this week?'

'Ye-es?' he said, with questioning eyes.

'But then ... oh shit, Hansie, you've given him an alibi. Bloody hell.'

'Alibi. You don't mean that ... Has there been some suspicion that Hammersten ...?'

'Would that be so improbable?'

'He's the type, right enough. But what did he have to do with Klaus and Kari Libakk?'

'He was in on the booze-running at any rate, and according to my source he made threatening phone calls to Svein Skarnes in 1973.'

'Threatening? On whose behalf?'

'Well ...' I threw my hands in the air. 'The big wheels in Germany? What do I know? But ... you'll have to tell the police this, Hans.'

He looked at me with crestfallen eyes. 'Another nail in Jan Egil's coffin?'

'I'm afraid so. Shit! Now and then you could wish ...'

'Yes, you could, couldn't you. If you only knew how I blame myself, Varg! What feelings of guilt I am plagued by ...'

'My God, Hansie! Who could have guessed that all this would happen?'

'True, but we should perhaps have been a bit more thorough.' He took a big swig from the beaker and shook his head with vehemence, as if to spread the alcohol to all the brain cells that might have been open a crack and waiting. 'It's enough to make you despair. We work our bollocks off to help these young kids. And what the hell do we end up with? Double murderers!'

'Now, now. Go easy on the pessimism ...'

We took a break and filled our glasses again. I was starting to feel the alcohol. The lighting had begun to glare a bit and the room had changed character, becoming longer and narrower. Hans was out of the room, peeing. When he returned, I could see he was swaying, too. This time he sat down on the bed so hard it almost broke in half.

'I'm going to tell you something you don't know, Varg ...' He sat forward with his hands cupped around the glass. Suddenly he made a theatrical gesture with his hand, then gripped the glass again. 'The Story of my Life, as told by the one and only Hans Haavik Pedersen,' he said in English.

'Pedersen?'

'Yes, didn't you know? My mother was called Haavik. I took her name when I was sixteen. I had nothing to thank my father for. Nothing at all!'

'You don't need to ...'

'Yes, I do! Now listen to this. My father, Karl Oskar Pedersen, was a notorious alcoholic. I can only just remember him. He died when I was four years old. What I remember best is the repressed sobs, the strangulated screams of my mother, when he came home from drinking and started beating her up. I was so young that I don't remember if he ever laid a hand on me. But she was made to suffer, night after night, day after day. That was why I grew up with a mother who was a living corpse, a human wreck who took increasingly large doses of medicine, was admitted to hospital every so often and was hardly in a state to take care of a child. We were also very poor. Terribly poor. As poor as it was possible to be in Norway in the first years after the war, before they had got the welfare state properly going.'

'What did your father die of?'

'Booze. He was forty-nine years old, much older than my mother. I suppose that was part of the problem. He was so jealous, she told me in confidence, on one of the few times I had ever got her to talk about those times. She died herself in 1954, only thirty-eight years old, worn down after all the psychological downers. I was fifteen, and I swore I would never be the same when I was older. I would never be poor, never be so drunk ...' He glanced down at the glass he was holding in his hand. 'Never be so cruel to those with whom I had chosen to live my life.'

'Well, I don't think I've ever ... but you have a family?'

'Family!' He smiled sadly. 'No, I've managed to avoid that. When it didn't come to anything with Vibecke either, then … yeah, well.' He waved his hand to dismiss it. 'Jens was the one she chose – and later others. She never looked in my direction, Varg. Believe me. I was part of the furniture.'

'Well, well … but you can hear for yourself. You come from a difficult background, but you came out on top. You even chose to devote your life to helping … children in similar situations. That shows there's hope for everyone. Also for Jan Egil.'

'For Johnny boy?' He stared ahead, perturbed.

'Who helped you when your mother died?'

'There were so many episodes, even before then. But I had my family around me, on my mother's side, that is. After she died I was allowed to live with an uncle and aunt of mine until I finished school, started university and could move into digs. Afterwards I managed by myself, with a study loan, doing part-time work in the evenings and living off other sources of income.'

'That's what I'm saying … You came out on top.'

'Hmm, on top, I don't know. It feels pretty skewed right now, I'm telling you.' He grabbed the bottle and poured himself another full glass. He offered me some, but this time I succeeded in saying 'No, thanks'. Perhaps he should have rammed the cork in, too. His eyes were beginning to glaze over. 'I'll tell you something, Varg. When I get back to Bergen … I'm going to hand in my notice.' He was swinging his arm around helplessly. 'Hand in my resignation.'

'What? You don't mean that. That's just something you're saying because you're drunk.'

'Drunk? I'm not bloody drunk!'

'Of course not, that's why you're falling off the bed.'

'I mean it! This case … this failure of all the things we're doing … it has persuaded me. I'm stopping. I'm getting out. I'll find myself something else to do …'

'What?'

'Don't know, but I'll find myself something …' He leaned closer as though to tell me a secret confidence. 'You know, Varg … all these government regulations, all these laws and rules … it would be bloody great not to take any notice of them for a few years. Tell it as it is. Call a spade a spade and …' He laughed at his own comment, but it was a low, mirthless laugh.

'You're tired and upset now, Hans. You won't think like this when you get home, I'm sure of that. You can't exist without what you've worked for over so many years. You have to be positive. Think of all those you've helped, all of those who send you a Christmas card every year …'

'Ha! You've put your finger on it. Shall I show you how many of the people I've helped, as you call it, who send me Christmas cards? Eh?' He held up his right hand and formed a zero with his thumb and index finger. 'That's how many, Varg. That's how many.'

'I don't get many more if that's any consolation.'

'Thank you. Bloody great consolation.'

He sat rocking his head. Sitting on the edge of the bed, he resembled a huge teddy bear, an overgrown cuddly toy, one a child who was now well into adulthood had left behind at his institution, abandoned by someone who no longer needed that sort of thing. He was immensely drunk, and I noticed his eyes were beginning to blink.

I slowly got to my feet. 'I think I'll move on,' I said, with a furry tongue.

His eyes floated in my direction. 'OK. Thank you for keeping me company, Varg. I think I'll try and have a snooze.'

'Do that, Hansie. See you tomorrow – or at the next crossroads.'

He waved one arm. 'G'bye!' he slurred.

'Goodbye,' I replied, still able to express myself in full syllables.

He stood up, not to show me the way out, but to stagger into the toilet. Before I had closed the door behind me, I could hear him vomiting. That didn't improve my mood.

When I came down to reception, there was a message waiting for me: *Ring me when you get in. Grethe.*

41

I did more than ring. After exchanging a few words with her, I arranged to drop by, ordered a taxi and went outside into the cold night air. I leaned backwards and stared up at the sky. High above me in the black heavenly vault some pale stars had taken up position for a few fleeting moments, as rare guests to Sunnfjord as the sun I had glimpsed the previous day.

In Hornnes I was forced to concede that my body was not in perfect equilibrium as I pushed on up the steep slope to her house. She had seen me from the window and was standing in the doorway waiting, but I had hardly said anything before, with a glare, she asked me: 'Tell me, have you been drinking?'

I rolled my head and tried to find something funny to say. But inside it was empty. Empty and dark. Hans Haavik had turned off the light when he left.

I don't think I won any gold medals that night. I remember quoting Emil Zátopek's wise words: 'If you want to win medals, run a hundred metres. If you want to learn about life, run the marathon.'

She replied: 'If you want to run the marathon you'll have to be in better shape than this, Varg.' She had already given up.

The following day arrived with a throbbing head, farewells and departure. She was friendly enough, yet I sensed a sudden distance; or else she was stricken with the same collective feeling of guilt, the same depression that had driven both Hans and me into the dingiest mental back streets the day before.

She drove me to the hotel. After parking outside, she turned to me and said: 'Are you going home?'

'Yes. There's nothing more for me to do here. Not for me. And no one's paying for my stay now.'

For a second or two I entertained the thought: You could invite me to stay with you perhaps … but either she didn't have the same thought herself, or she didn't like it, for all she did was lean forward and kiss me on the cheek and say: 'Maybe we'll see each other another time then, Varg …'

I stole into her line of vision, still with my tail between my legs. 'I hope so, Grethe …'

But it didn't turn out like that.

In reception I asked after Jens Langeland, but he had gone back to Oslo, I was informed. I tried to ring him at his office, but an answering machine replied. It asked me to ring back during office hours from Monday to Friday. I called directory enquiries and was given his home number. No one answered there, either.

I packed the little luggage I had, settled my account at reception, got into my car and left. On one of the highest bends on Halbrendslia I stopped the car for a moment and sat looking across. From there I could see right up to the furthest end of Angedalen valley. I saw Førde lying in the morning mist between the high mountains. I saw the residential quarter in Hornnes, the huge dockyard beyond the tiny airstrip, the new industrial buildings and businesses. I saw the old white church, sighed and thought to myself: Everything is changing. Nothing stays the same as before. What's the purpose of it all, of all the things we do? Then I pinched myself and said: 'No, none of that, now you sound like bloody Hansie Haavik. Pull yourself together, man! There are still things to do …'

I rammed the car into gear and drove to Bergen without stopping anywhere apart from those places nature intended, by the ferries in Lavik and Knarvik.

Two images fought for a place in my head during the drive: Grethe Mellingen who so brazenly gave herself to me a day and a half ago, and Jan Egil who glared at me like a wounded animal as he was led out of the courtroom.

42

After the narrow, restricted space of Førde, Bergen seemed like open countryside. The fjord wound gently through the town towards Askøy and the light rain drizzled on the surrounding mountains forming a veil of glistening silver. I drove straight home, took a long, hot shower, went down to the harbour and bought myself a decent lunch, walked back, lay down for a nap and slept like a log until the next day, which was Sunday.

In the afternoon I strolled down to my office and checked the answering machine. There were the usual sighs and snorts before someone slammed down the receiver, annoyed that I was not sitting and gawking at the telephone, waiting only for them to ring. There was a woman who, in broken Norwegian, had sent a long and partly comprehensible message about a partner who had run off, and she very much wanted me to bring him back to the fold. And there was Marianne Storetvedt who wanted to talk to me. I called her private number, but she was busy with a family meal. We agreed I would go to her office after work the next day.

Then I tried Jens Langeland again. This time he was at home.

'Veum … I tried to contact you at the hotel, but they couldn't find you.'

'No, I was … probably sitting in Hans Haavik's room drinking.'

He chuckled quietly. 'Really? Did you take it so badly?'

'Didn't you?'

'No, no. I hadn't expected anything but an extended period of remand. The big battle will be in court. First of all, I'd very much like you to find out everything you can about this Terje Hammersten and his movements.'

'That's just it, I'm afraid I have bad news on that front.'

'Oh, yes?'

I told him what Hans Haavik had told me about his confrontation with Hammersten in Bergen on Monday morning.

'At his place? In Bergen?'

'Yes.

'That's a sod.'

'That was my reaction, too.'

I could hear him thinking aloud. 'Nonethless, Veum. I still want you to carry on with your enquiries. Concentrate on Hammersten. That's by far the best card we have.'

'You'll still cover my costs?'

'Naturally, Veum. We'll pass this onto the police anyway, so take the time you need.'

After ringing off, I sat looking out of the window. We had all heard about solicitors' bulging wallets, but this was more like pockets stuffed with wads of notes. My creditors could look into the future with confidence, if this carried on.

The day after, it rained. It was mean, probing rain and made me turn up my jacket collar that bit extra; another reminder that winter was around the corner. The light was lower, the days shorter, and it was a long, long time to next summer. That didn't matter all that much. I had more than enough to be getting on with.

The first thing I did was to call Vegard Vadheim, the detective at Bergen police station I got on best with. I told him I had some information for him about several earlier cases to do with the ongoing investigation into the Angedalen double killings. I asked him to dig up the files of two of them from their archives: the case against Mette Olsen and a man called David from the autumn of 1966 and the case against Vibecke Skarnes in 1974.

'And what do I get in return?'

'I've got some info, as I said. I think it will interest you.'

'Oh yes?'

'Especially if you dig up all you have on Terje Hammersten at the same time.'

'Hammersten? It's never been easy to pin anything on him.'

'I've noticed. If you have any files on the big seventies alcohol smuggling ring in Sogn and Fjordane, I may have something for you there, too.'

'Doubt we have much on that lying around.'

'Then I have something to tell you about it.'

We agreed I would drop round the police station after lunch.

Before that I met Cecilie Strand over a cup of coffee and a roll at the café in Sundt. From the corner table looking over Torgallmenning, the main square, it was possible to imagine we were the mother and father of the whole town, with a full perspective of everything that went on down there. We had no idea how wrong we were; or perhaps we did.

Cecilie sat listening attentively to everything I had to tell her from Førde, restricting myself to things directly relevant to my investigations. I only mentioned Trodalen Mads in a subordinate clause, although it didn't seem to make much of an impression, and I referred to Grethe Mellingen as 'our social services colleague there'. There were tears in her eyes when I told her about the time I met Jan face to face, and once again I was reminded of the close, intimate, almost family situation she, I and Jan had found ourselves in during the spring and summer of 1974, with Hans Haavik as a kindly uncle.

'But ... do they really think he did it?'

'The Public Prosecutor definitely thinks so. And the evidence against him is compelling, I have to admit.'

'But why would he do it? Such a brutal thing?'

I shrugged. 'This girl, Silje, claimed she had been subjected to sexual abuse by her foster father. That may have been enough.'

She sent me a doubtful look.

'By the way ... something new about Svein Skarnes came to light while I was there too.'

'Svein Skarnes?'

'Yes, just listen.'

I told her about the link between Skarnes and the smuggling, the murder of Ansgår Tveiten and Hammersten's role in both affairs, as well as his appearance in Sunnfjord the day after the double murder.

'The day after?'

'Yes, and his alibi in Bergen is no less than Hans Haavik.'

I told her everything I knew, and in the end she looked as bewildered as I was becoming. In a way, it seemed as if everything and nothing fitted. Threads led in all directions, but none of them met, and the pattern was still a mystery, even for a trained observer like myself. But I was convinced there was a pattern.

'Anything else new?' I asked, drawing the session to a close.

She shrugged and drained her coffee cup. 'No, I suppose by and large everything is the same here. But when you hear things like this you wonder about what we do. Whether we're having a beneficial effect at all.'

'That's exactly what Hans said the other day in Førde. So I'll say to you what I said to him: Yes, we are. You are. You might slip up a few times, but you're successful many more times. Aren't you?'

'Mm ... but then you dropped out.'

'I didn't drop out, Cecilie. I was gently given the boot. And I've continued in the same area, in my own way.'

'As a private investigator.' She smirked.

'Yes.'

We took the broad marble stairs down to street level again. On two of the floors we were met by our own reflection in the same chequered mirrors that had been there since my childhood, in the days when taking the escalator up to the top of Sundt was the closest a little Bergensian got to an amusement park. We both looked somewhat disillusioned, like a disgruntled couple who had just agreed that there was no way of avoiding separation and divorce after all.

I gave her a quick hug on the pavement and went for a walk around a small lake called Lungegårdsvann and over to the library to kill time before meeting Vegard Vadheim. At the local branch I found the newspapers from 1974 on microfiche and refreshed my memory of the Vibecke Skarnes case, though I didn't end up much the wiser.

Just before one o'clock I announced my presence at the police station and was met by Vadheim at the desk. When we arrived at his office, he knocked on the adjacent door, popped his head round and a female colleague of his, Cecilie Lyngmo, joined us.

'Cecilie was the officer responsible for questioning Vibecke Skarnes at that time, so I thought it would be a good idea if she came along,' he explained, and I nodded.

I said hello to Cecilie Lyngmo, whom I had met before but I had not been introduced. She was in her early fifties, a strapping woman, but she didn't give the impression of being overweight. Her hair was greyish-brown, no sign of it having been dyed. She beamed when we shook hands, a firm grip.

'A few years ago now, isn't it?' she said. '*Fru* Skarnes must have been out for some time.'

I nodded. 'She lives in Ski, just outside Oslo, I've been told.'

'She's no danger to her surroundings, if you ask me.'

'So, in your view, she could have gone free at the time?'

'No, no. Even an unpremeditated murder is murder. But she found herself in an unhappy situation, as so many women do.' We all sat down, and she continued: 'Inside the sheltered walls of home they're subjected to systematic violence, direct or indirect, for years. And the one time they defend themselves, it ends in – murder.'

'But that was taken into account during the trial, wasn't it?'

'To a certain extent. But one character witness after another spoke up for the husband. The Counsel for the Prosecution had done a very good job there.'

'Sounds to me as if you'd have preferred to work with the defence.'

She said drily: 'Now and then it can be like that, when you've seen all the nuances. We investigators are victims of the case; we're much closer to the case than the lawyers. And among other victims of the case I include the accused just as much as the real victims.'

'Yes, I can remember several of the witnesses myself. I was in court for a couple of the days.'

Vadheim cleared his throat, to join the conversation. 'You said something on the phone about new information, Veum.'

'Yes, listen to this.' In broad outline, I told them what I had heard about Svein Skarnes and the smuggling racket.

They listened attentively. In the end, Vadheim said: 'But all you have is allegations made by this Dale, an ex-employee of Skarnes. No concrete evidence, no documentation.'

'Would he have any reason to lie though?'

'Maybe not. But you never know. An ex-employee, conflicts in the workplace, chance to get back at ...'

'Yes, but Skarnes has been dead for ten years. How can you get back at someone who's been in his grave since 1974?'

'No, you're right, of course.'

I turned back to Cecilie Lyngmo. 'When you questioned Vibecke Skarnes long ago ... what sort of impression did you have of the marriage?'

'As I've already said, and the main point of the defence's plea was that Vibecke Skarnes was an abused housewife who happened to push her husband down the stairs and accidentally kill him. She painted a very credible picture of a tragic marriage. They didn't have children, either, until they adopted one. And he was a pretty restless chap. She had little to be happy about and received minimal understanding from her husband. On top of that, she hinted that he had committed a number of infidelities without covering up any more than he was absolutely duty-bound to do. I remember she was very suspicious of his secretary.'

'A classic affair, in that case. I met her by the way. The secretary. *Fru*, or was it *frøken*? Berge or Borge, I think.'

'Well, all this is history now. She was sentenced, and the appeal was unsuccessful. Now she's out. So what use would any new information be?'

I shrugged. 'Justice is a word in my dictionary,' I said.

'Yes, but what's the point? The husband's dead, as you said. The wife's served her sentence. The son …'

'Exactly. The son, or the adopted son, to be accurate. He's alive, and right now he's locked up, charged with a double murder in Angedalen.'

She glanced at Vadheim. 'Yes, you mentioned something about that.' Then she turned back to me. 'And this is the same boy?'

'One of the many parallels between these cases.' I went through the case for them, including the connection between Klaus Libakk, Svein Skarnes and the smuggling ring. 'And one more thing,' I concluded. 'When I was talking to Jan Egil, we eventually touched on what happened in 1974. And then he said something which never came out at the time, neither during the police questioning nor at the trial.'

I had their undivided attention.

'He claimed that while he was sitting in the lounge playing with his toys he heard the doorbell ring. Then someone arguing with his father.'

'Yes, the mother,' Vadheim said.

'But she didn't need to ring. She had a key.'

'Yes, yes, but if she knew her husband was at home anyway.'

'No, it doesn't make sense. At least there's an element of doubt here. Someone might have visited Svein Skarnes that day. It could've been Terje Hammersten, for example.'

'Hammersten! So that's why you wanted to know what we had on him.'

'At any rate, this Harald Dale claims that Hammersten physically threatened Skarnes several times in 1973 in connection with the debt he was left with, after the smuggling business fell apart in Sogn and Fjordane earlier that year.'

'But why didn't all of this come out at the time?'

'Because Dale was too scared to risk his own skin, of course. And, if we are to believe the rumours, Hammersten had shown what he was capable of when he did Ansgår Tveiten in. But, as you said on the phone earlier today, Vadheim: It's never been easy to pin anything on him.'

'And the same applies now. As long as all this is pure speculation. Here at the station we need tangible proof.'

'I know. So what have you got on him from the past?'

Vadheim sighed and held out a thick file. 'Look. This is our friend Terje Hammersten's record. Fat, heavy and not very delectable. Most of it's trivial stuff, frequent use of violence in connection with threats. He's what they used to call a torpedo in America, a heavy.'

I opened my palms. 'There you go!'

'But never anything big. Just minor matters. He's had a few relatively short prison terms.'

'Yes, I can remember he got one in 1970.'

He nodded, distracted. 'The longest stretch he had was two years.' He flicked through the pile of papers. 'From 1976 to '78. I see there's a lot of material about the Bygstad killing, too, but he had a cast-iron alibi in Bergen, so nothing there.'

'The alibi was drinking pals, wasn't it?'

'Yes, but there are several … neighbours. The man who ran the grocery where they bought beer. A prostitute he'd been with.'

'Easy enough to get if you lean hard on the right people. Or if you have some cash to wave around. But you didn't manage to crack the alibis, I see.'

'No, not that time. And now it's definitely too late.'

I nodded. 'What about the other case I asked you to dig up? That's even older.'

'Yes.' He took out another file, considerably thinner, and opened it. 'The case against David Pettersen and Mette Olsen, November 1966. He was given eight years, she was acquitted. He topped himself after the sentence was pronounced.'

'Yes, I know. But … were they picked up at customs by chance, or were there grounds for suspecting them?'

He began to flick through.

'She thought they'd been set up,' I added.

He took out the documents from the case file and flicked through to the end. Then he nodded. 'Yes, that's right. An anonymous telephone call, it says here. August 30th, 13.05. The same afternoon they were nabbed.'

'A telephone call? Where from? From Copenhagen?'

'Nope. From Bergen.'

'From Bergen! Was any attempt ever made to trace the call?'

He nodded again. 'It would certainly have helped the defence during the trial. But they never got any further than one of the telephone booths at the railway station.'

'But who the hell would want to inform on them in Bergen? I assume the drugs were coming here?'

'Here, and maybe travelling further. We'll never know. But think back, Veum. This was in 1966, right at the beginning of the new drugs boom. It was still tied up with dope romanticism and hash heaven, sex 'n' drugs 'n' rock 'n' roll. No one knew about the consequences, what tragedies and misery it would lead to for coming generations.'

'What are you driving at?'

'Well, I mean … there was big money to be made with hash at that time, and there were lots of dogs after the same bone.'

'You mean … it could have been someone competing in the same market?'

'Someone. Anyone. What do I know?' He thrust out his arms. 'Anyway, there was a telephone call, and the police rang customs. They were stopped at customs, and the rest we know.'

'So what's the common theme here, Vadheim?'

'Your guess is as good as mine.'

'But can't you see it? The theme is smuggling.'

'Smuggling?'

'Yes! From Mette Olsen and this David Pettersen, who are apprehended at Flesland airport, to Ansgår Tveiten, who is killed in Bygstad, to Svein Skarnes, who falls down the stairs in Bergen, and to the Libakk couple who are killed in Angedalen almost exactly a week ago.'

'Aren't you jumping to conclusions now, Veum? You can interpret all of this in a completely different way, too. The common theme for the first two cases is smuggling, that's right. But the first one's about narcotics, the second alcohol, which at that time were two very different markets. And as far as Svein Skarnes is concerned … he falls victim to a marital dispute in which the theme might just as easily have been abuse or infidelity.' He looked to Cecilie Lyngmo for help and found it in the form of an affirmative nod. 'This Angedalen double murder seems to have been triggered by sexual abuse, in other words, it's a family affair. You could just as easily say that all of this goes off in a variety of directions. Hard to say what we can do, in my opinion.'

'But Hammersten may have been involved in all of the cases.'

'May have been? All we have is vague rumours about some connection with the Tveiten murder in 1973.'

'And he lived with Mette Olsen!'

'After she got into drugs, yes. But in 1966 she was with David Pettersen.'

I leaned forward. 'At least do me one favour, Vadheim. As soon as he's back in town … bring him in for a – talk. Have a chat with him.'

He viewed me with scepticism. 'With Hammersten? On this evidence? Hardly, Veum. Hardly.'

'Then I'll have to do it myself.'

'Would you take the risk?'

'If no one else dares, then …'

43

Marianne Storetvedt received me at the same office as in 1974. Bryggen Museum and the new SAS hotel had been up a long time on the other side of the bay, but apart from that the view was the same. She hadn't changed much, either. She still reminded me of a Hollywood star from the early fifties, glamorous and with the slightly old-fashioned, glossy hairstyle: Rita Hayworth in a role she filled to perfection, to everyone's surprise. But her attire was not very provocative and the clear signs of wrinkles on her face would hardly have been accepted by Columbia Pictures.

She listened without interrupting while I told her about Jan Egil and all the other developments in the case since she had treated him in 1974. A couple of times she jotted something down in the notebook on her lap.

When I had finished, she nodded her head in acknowledgement as if I had passed an exam. 'A classic tale, I'm afraid,' she said.

'In what sense?'

'The art of creating a psychopath.'

'You're thinking about – Jan Egil?'

She lowered her head in affirmation. 'I think we talked about this last time. He was already exhibiting clear signs then of early emotional damage, what we in the profession call a reactive attachment disorder. If parents only knew how important the first years of life are for their children, Varg!'

'In this case, neither parent was even present. Well, one was, but not a hundred per cent. The mother was on drugs when he was born.'

'Even more typical. Here it's the frequent shifting of carers that creates the problem, on top of the primary carer – in this case the mother – not being stable enough, being on drugs, at least for long periods. A child like this will develop its own primary personality based on rejection. It becomes the fundamental emotion this child will feel most at home with, even when grown up – and then often with tragic consequences.'

'I see. So if you were to be a character witness in the case against Jan Egil ...'

She interrupted me. 'I wouldn't be able to do that, of course. I haven't followed his development for the last ten years. I'm only giving my opinion in general terms, Varg. But, by and large, it's not so unusual for children with this kind of background to perform criminal actions at a very young age. Often directed against adoptive or foster parents who in a way are there in *loco parentis*, ones who, voluntarily or involuntarily, failed them.'

'But not in such a dramatic manner as this, I hope?'

'No, but it could be hooliganism, it could be theft – of cars, for example – or other anti-social actions. Such as smashing up the foster father's car. Sometimes with a fatal conclusion for them both, or anyone else they might meet on a joyride. If people only realised ...'

'Doesn't sound like you'll be invited to the witness box by his defence counsel, anyway. More likely by the prosecution, sad to say.'

'We'll have to see what the investigation turns up before we make our final judgement...'

'For Jan Egil, of course, it's a big problem that the murder weapon has no fresh prints on it other than his. Could it be that he wasn't aware of the consequences of his actions?'

'You mean if he wasn't the murderer? That he might conceivably have come to the crime scene after the murders had taken place and picked up the weapon without thinking? Then taken it with him when escaping from the police, out of fear of being blamed?'

'Something like that.'

'Being governed by sudden impulses, and therefore capable of carrying out imprudent actions, would not clash at all with the picture of the personality I broadly sense here, no.'

'Right. Well, at least there's some light in the tunnel, if I can call it that.'

We sat for a while in a somewhat uneasy silence. I noticed her scrutinising me. 'You look troubled. Is there something bothering you?' she said.

'Nothing apart from the fact that I have a son myself, thirteen years old, who I might not have been a hundred per cent present for in the first years of his life. I don't know if you remember, but we ... split up when he was two years old.'

She smiled gently. 'Have you had any problems with him?'

'Not that I've been aware of, no.'

'So why the concern? My God, with all the divorces we have nowadays ... and all the children of divorced parents! We would've had an avalanche of psychopaths if they'd all had reactive attachment disorders. I'm talking about relatively few unhappy souls, Varg, and we must not forget that some of this is genetically determined.' She laid her hand on mine and patted it comfortingly. 'So you can relax. Your son will be absolutely fine.'

'But I'm not only concerned about him. I can't get Jan Egil out of my mind, either. I've met him at three stages of his life. As a helpless little child, as an apathetic and aggressive six-year-old, and now as an unbalanced and somewhat complicated teenager. The period in 1974 when Cecilie, Hans and I looked after him like ... well, like a married couple and an uncle, we were all of the same opinion ... that he could have been our own child, Marianne! Our common foster child.'

'But then remember what I said. The reactive disorders emerge during the first years of life. An adopted child you know nothing about can be a time bomb. We see this most clearly with foreign adoptions, children from slum areas or – even worse – a war zone. But then you know the child's background and you know it's bad news. If the mother was on drugs during the pregnancy, it means he will be born with withdrawal symptoms, if I can phrase it like that. Suddenly he no longer has access to what the tiny body was used to in the mother's womb. There is no father at hand, and he has a mother who either isn't there – because he's in a clinic for infants – or when she is there, she's barely capable of looking after him properly.' She leaned forward and locked her intense eyes on mine. 'Neither Cecilie, Hans nor you could have done anything for Jan Egil, Varg!'

'That is a terribly defeatist view of life, Marianne.'

She looked at me sadly. 'I'm afraid not. It's statistics. And experience.'

'Hans feels the same way. He told me … I don't want to be indiscreet, but he's decided to give up. He can no longer face all these failures, all these never-ending projects, all this work that appears to be in vain.'

'But there are lots of successful treatments, too.'

'That's what I said. But he's given up, as I said. He wants a total break.'

'Well …' She threw up her hands. 'We all feel like that at some point. How's your business going, by the way?'

'As a private eye?'

'Yes.'

'I'm into my tenth year now. And I haven't gone bust yet, even though it's been a close thing a couple of times.'

She smiled again and nodded with sympathy. Then she stood up. 'Should you need me again, you know where to find me.'

We gave each other a friendly hug, and I left. On the way downstairs I wondered how she was, actually. But that was probably one more of those questions I would never find an answer to.

44

We were getting nowhere.

For a week or two I played detective at the state's expense. I paid a call on the grocer who had given Hammersten the alibi in 1973. He had become a pensioner in the meantime and pretended he didn't remember a thing, neither about Hammersten, nor about what he had said or hadn't said eleven years ago. I tried to trace the prostitute who had also given him an alibi, but she had vanished off the face of the earth a few years afterwards, without anyone worrying too much on her account. 'One of those deaths that receive scant scrutiny and are then shelved,' Vadheim confided. 'Christ, Vadheim! She was one of the key witnesses in the Hammersten investigation.' 'I doubt if anyone made the connection in 1976, Veum ...' Finding the drinking pals from that time proved to be just as fruitless. Some of them were dead; others had decimated their remaining brain cells with persistent over-indulgence over a long, wasted life. The only one I managed to get to speak to me, a dried-out alcoholic by the name of Peder Jansen, was so frightened when I mentioned Terje Hammersten's name that he sat trembling for the rest of the conversation, as if afflicted by unbearable withdrawal symptoms. Casting doubt on his alibi at this time proved, not unsurprisingly, to be impossible.

Jens Langeland's telephone feedback on the police interview with Hammersten, first of all in Førde, later in Bergen, was even less uplifting. Hans Haavik's confirmation that he had had a confrontation with Hammersten in Bergen early in the morning after the night of the Angedalen murders gave Hammersten an alibi that while not a hundred per cent watertight did, however, based on the ferry companies' night routes, make it in practice impossible for him to have travelled from Førde to Bergen for that time. 'Unless you have any better cards up your sleeve, Veum.' 'Not yet, I'm afraid.' 'Hmm, that was what I feared ...'

When Hammersten was back in town, a week and a half later, I made an attempt to make him talk. All that produced was a black eye, which took a further two weeks to heal. By way of a parting shot, he had said that if I continued to stick my big nose into what he was doing, he would give me such a thorough pasting that I would never stand on two legs again. I gave Ansgår Tveiten a thought and took him at his word.

At length, I ate humble pie, phoned Langeland and said I had reached the end of the road. There didn't seem to be any fresh leads anywhere. He took note without giving any kind of audible reaction. 'How's Jan Egil?' I asked. 'Not too good. It's all we can do to get him to talk. Even to me,' he added, before concluding the conversation and with that the commission. I sent him an invoice, which was paid promptly, unlike most other invoices I sent.

In the winter and spring of 1985 I followed the case, first of all at Gulating, the West Norway law court, and then – in late May that year – in the newspapers, after both sides had asked for the High Court to deliver the sentence.

While the trial was on at Gulating, I visited the courthouse as often I was able. I followed attentively when one of the police weapons experts was in the witness box. He held the weapon Klaus and Kari Libakk had been shot with in his hand. It was a 1938 Mauser, 7.62 calibre, and there were five bullets in the magazine. The forensic examination of the bullets and cartridges left no room for doubt that it was this weapon that had been used at the Angedalen double killing. All the bullets had been fired. It gave you a special feeling of horror to watch the dispassionate police officer stand there with the rifle in his hand and demonstrate how the safety catch was released, the bolt was pulled back with the handle and the rifle was loaded with cartridges, one by one. 'Does it have to be loaded after each shot?' Langeland wanted to know. The policeman nodded. 'We think that Klaus Libakk was shot first, in the chest, and that his wife woke up and tried to escape. She was shot twice in the back, then the gunman turned on Libakk and shot him once again, also in the chest. Finally Kari Libakk was also given the *coup de grâce*, through the back of the head.' There was a deathly hush in the heavy air of the vast courtroom as the brutal actions were presented in such a down-to-earth, factual fashion. Only a few weak, nervous coughs could be heard from the gallery as the most gruesome details were stated. The atmosphere was not lightened when the policeman concluded his presentation by showing a series of slides based on the same crime scene photographs I had been shown in Førde. The powerful pictures caused a shock wave to surge through the courtroom, and when the court took a break afterwards, there was a noticeably gloomy mood among the spectators collecting outside in the corridor and the internal galleries overlooking the courthouse's central lobby. I made small talk with a court reporter from one of the town's newspapers. He was convinced that this had been the kiss of death for Jan Egil Skarnes. I couldn't produce any cogent counter-arguments. For once in my life I kept my mouth shut.

When the break was over, Langeland immediately went on the attack. He wanted to know if several people could have been involved in the crime. The police officer had turned to the defence benches and, with the rifle half-raised in front of him, had said: 'No weapon other than this was used, and only the accused's fingerprints were on it, apart from those of the deceased.' 'Klaus Libakk's?' 'Yes, but they were of an earlier date.'

Langeland, however, still did not give in. Looking intensely at the officer in the witness box, he asked: 'But what if the guilty party wore gloves? Is there any reason whatsoever not to consider that?' The policeman returned his glare, as if to tell Langeland he hadn't been born yesterday. 'There were no traces of glove fibre on the rifle.' 'What about plastic gloves?' The officer sent him a condescending smile and shrugged his shoulders: 'Not impossible, of course. But not very likely.' 'Why not?' 'Because in our opinion there is no doubt who the guilty person in this case is.' Everyone's eyes turned to Jan Egil, even mine. He sat with his eyes directed into the distance, the way he had sat the whole time. 'No doubt? In other words, you as a group were prejudiced?' Langeland went on. 'The forensic examination has swept away any doubts, to be more precise then,' said the policeman, and I saw the judge note something down on the pad in front of him.

But still Langeland would not give in. It was easy to see that he had an uphill struggle on his hands, which the faces of the ten jurymen made manifest with abundant clarity. The three judges listened with professional sensitivity, but not even they displayed any sympathy for his arguments. His summary of Jan Egil's unhappy life, the first years and the sudden departure from Bergen in 1974 after the tragic events in his foster parents' house, seemed to be having the opposite effect to its intention, not so different from the testimony given by one of Marianne Storetvedt's colleagues, in which I recognised the thoughts and terminology from the assessment I had been given some months before. Langeland had decided to call Silje as a witness, but it was the prosecuting counsel who gained most from her, too. When the prosecutor produced the undocumented claims of sexual abuse on the part of Klaus Libakk, Silje had to concede that she had made this up in the heat of the moment to help her boyfriend. 'I see. Wasn't it also the case that you at some point confessed to being the killer?' 'Yes, I did, but …' Silje burst into tears: 'That was just somethin' I said to help 'im.' 'So you, too, thought he had done it, in other words,' commented the counsel, turning to the jury in a telling fashion, but without any further comment. It was obvious that the prosecutor had triumphed in the duel. Even though Silje's testimony had made an impression on the jury and the allegation of sexual abuse also caused a degree of sympathy to spread through their ranks, a realisation that he had had a kind of motive for the brutal act cemented the notion that it was he and no one else who had to be the guilty party.

Langeland's attempt to point to other potential explanations fell on stony ground, since the police investigation had not uncovered anything to corroborate them. The alleged burglars who had broken into Libakk Farm at night had not left a trace of any break-in, and there was not a single testimony from the neighbours or anyone else pointing in that direction. Next Langeland touched on Klaus Libakk's involvement in the local alcohol-smuggling activities of the early seventies, intimating that the killing might be tied up with the hitherto unsolved murder of Ansgår Tveiten, a supposition which the prosecution counsel flatly rejected in his response, saying that, for his part, they were dealing with the specific crime of October 1984, not dragging up criminal cases that were more than ten years old.

Langeland's final summing up was brilliant, a masterpiece of rhetoric, but in the final reckoning no more than a scintillating precis of the arguments he had brought to bear earlier. After the jury had retired, it was difficult to see who had had most impact: Langeland with his masterly eloquence, the prosecutor with his rugged stating of facts or the judge with his sober review of the salient points.

When Jan Egil was led out of the court again, he cast a first glance at the benches in the gallery. Once again our eyes met, and once again I felt the incomprehensible hatred I thought I could read there; as though he laid all the blame for finding himself in this situation at my door.

The next day the jury was ready with its verdict. Jan Egil Skarnes was found guilty on all counts of the indictment, and the judges retired to consider the sentence.

I exchanged a few words with Langeland in the corridor that day. I thanked him for his efforts and asked whether he had any opinion as to how long Jan Egil would be imprisoned. 'Impossible to say, Veum. Anything from five to fifteen years, closer to the latter in all probability, I'm afraid.' 'Fifteen!' 'Yes, I'm afraid so.' The high-flying lawyer had turned away with a downcast expression, as though this was such a terrible defeat for him personally that it was hard to bear.

Jan Egil chose not to appear when the jury announced their verdict. As the sentence was read out, he sat on his seat without raising his eyes once. Langeland bent down to him several times and spoke in a low voice, probably to explain what the often complicated legal formulations in fact meant. He was sentenced to twelve and a half years' imprisonment, with his time on remand to be deducted. From Jan Egil's blank face it was clear that he had not understood a word of what had been said, and when the court rose for the last time, as the panel of judges left the courtroom with a long final stare at the convicted felon, only a squeeze to his shoulder from his lawyer could rouse him from his chair.

During the trial at Gulating the case was reported comprehensively in the press with new photographs of the farm in Angedalen, artists' impressions of what had happened in Klaus and Kari's bedroom and anonymous-looking drawings of the accused. It was only when the High Court had taken its decision and stipulated the final sentence, in line with the previous court's decision, that the convicted person was named in the media. In the wake of the judgement there was a great deal of discussion in the papers; many commentators considered the punishment much too mild, yet more evidence of the lenience with which today's legal system treated serious lawbreakers.

Jens Langeland wrote a letter countering this, in which he stressed the tender age of the accused and the fact that in many people's eyes, including his own, there was still substantial doubt about what had actually happened in Angedalen during that fateful night between the Sunday and the Monday of the penultimate week in October last year. *Are we so sure that the guilty party or parties is not still walking around free?* the letter concluded, sowing another dose of disquiet in my head; a disquiet which had never been extinguished, but had lain there smouldering, until it burst into flame again on that September day ten years later when Cecilie Strand phoned me at my office, asking me to meet her in Fjellveien.

45

Over all these years my thoughts had regularly returned to Jan Egil. I had never managed to reconcile myself with the claim that we had got to the bottom of the matter. A couple of times I had been on the point of ringing Jens Langeland, who I assumed was still his solicitor, but had then rejected the idea. 'What's the point?' I had asked myself.

And now here she was, Cecilie, sitting on a bench in the sunshine by the sub-station in Fjellveien, looking at me through her round glasses and saying I was on his death list.

I sat looking at her. 'Can we run through that one more time?'

She nodded. 'By all means.'

'Jan Egil is out?'

'On probation. He was let out in May, after serving ten years.'

'They waited a long time before letting him go. Were there problems?'

'He wasn't exactly a model prisoner. Several times he overstayed his home leave and his parole was delayed accordingly as a punishment.'

'So, what's he doing?'

'Well, I suppose that's part of the problem. The Probation and Aftercare Services found him a job, which he soon began skipping. At a car workshop. Later he had the occasional part-time job here and there, but I'm afraid it's the same with him as most of the others who do time … The relationships they form behind locked doors pursue them on the outside, and I fear he already has contacts inside the semi-organised crime circle in Oslo.'

'OK. Go on,' I said with impatience.

'He stayed in a hospice in Eiriks gate in Tøyen. A kind of private social initiative, run on idealistic guidelines. In fact the person running the place is an old friend of ours, Hans Haavik.'

'Hansie! So that's what he did. He couldn't quite hang up his profession, either.'

'No, but let me get to the point. On Monday this week a man was found dead in this hospice. Killed over the weekend.'

'Right, but what has that got to do with Jan Egil?'

'One of the other inmates found the body and reported it to Hans, who in turn called the police. Just as a matter of routine the police officers went from room to room in the hospice, first of all to see if anyone had heard or seen anything recently. Jan Egil wasn't in. But they found something else in his room ...' She hesitated before continuing: 'A bloodstained baseball bat.'

'That's an unpleasant reminder of something I've heard before.'

She nodded gravely. 'Furthermore, it was to transpire that the dead man was someone Jan Egil knew. In other words ... all the signs are that he's in a serious fix. For the moment they're conducting internal enquiries, but it won't be many more days before it's in the papers.'

'Well ... alright. I'll have to find out more. But what were you saying about a – death list?'

'Right, death list. Perhaps it was a little drastic to call it that, but the woman he's had a child with told me.'

'A child! He's had ...'

'Result of an earlier home leave. But the mother ... well, they're in care.'

'Sounds familiar.'

'As he was when he was a child, yes.'

'This bloody vicious circle that is so difficult to break! This woman ... is she reliable?'

'It's Silje.'

'Silje! Not the same Silje who ...?'

'Yes, I think so.'

'Wow, she's been loyal. I have to give her that. What did she have to say?'

'She said Jan Egil had said several times that there were at least two people he had decided to do in. The two people who, more than anyone else, had made him into the person he was.'

'Made him who he was! But, for Christ's sake, I never ...'

'You were there when he was taken from his mother, weren't you? The very first time?'

'Yes, but I wasn't the one who ...'

'So I suppose you've become a kind of symbol for the hated social services system, which once again has started to take control of his life because we were following the progress of his child with eagle eyes. Hans thought we should warn you, anyway.'

'You said – two people.'

'Yes. The other person was killed a couple of days ago. Clubbed with a baseball bat until he was ...' She shuddered in the sunshine. 'Almost unrecognisable.'

'But he was identified, I take it?'

'Yes, he was.'

'And who was it?'

For a moment her gaze wandered off to the fjord beneath us. Then it returned, accompanied by a determined expression around her mouth. 'You know him, Varg.'

I could feel the alarm mounting in me. 'Yes? Come on! Who was it? Not ...?'

'Terje Hammersten.'

46

The following day was a Friday, and we took an early flight to Oslo. The cabin crew served breakfast with a smile, and Hardanger Plateau lay beneath us like a patchwork quilt of grey, blue and brown.

Cecilie sat sipping from her mug of coffee when she burst out: 'That time in 1984, up in Førde …'

'Mm?'

'Did you get to know a colleague of mine – Grethe Mellingen?'

'Yes. For as long as it lasted. But I never saw her again. It was only the once.'

'The once?'

'Yes, the days when …'

'She said nice things about you.'

'You've met her?'

'At a seminar a few years back.'

'Right … You know how it is. Some people you meet again. Others you lose track of. And suddenly ten years have passed, and then it's all too late. Getting in touch after such a long time would be embarrassing.'

'Don't say that.' She glanced at me out of the corner of her eye. 'Are you still … on your own, Varg?'

'Are you asking me if I …?'

'You don't need to answer. I was just wondering.'

'Yes, but in fact I am. I didn't find her in Førde, and she hasn't popped up in Bergen, either. The dream princess, I mean.'

'I didn't mean to …'

'Not at all. I understand. But she told me an interesting story when I was there, Grethe did. About someone they called Trodalen

Mads, and who was convicted of a killing he may not have committed – at least if I'm to believe what she told me.'

'But …'

'Yes, too late then, too. He was convicted in 1839 and imprisoned for forty-two years afterwards.'

'Forty-two!'

'The justification for it was apparently that he had sworn to avenge himself on the parents because it had been their testimony – and especially the mother's – that had led to him being convicted. That was why he was kept in Akershus until both parents were dead, and it lasted so long, with the accrued interest, if I can put it like that. I can't help thinking that this is reminiscent of Jan Egil and his story.'

She looked at me in surprise. 'In what sense? Not that he was innocent surely?'

'No one knows if Trodalen Mads was innocent. Though, maybe they did. And this revenge business. The only difference is that nowadays murderers aren't given forty-two years. With good behaviour they are soon out on the street again. Sooner than people like to think.'

'But … you didn't answer my question. Do you really think he was innocent? That he was convicted of something he didn't do? Johnny boy?'

'And his mother.'

'The mother? Are you thinking of Vibecke Skarnes or …?'

'Yes, Vibecke. The foster mother. What if she took the blame for her husband's murder, what if it was never an accident and she thought that Jan had done it?'

'So she went to prison for his sake, you mean?'

'Yes. What if someone else was guilty then as well?'

'Then … *as well*?'

'Yes.' I sent her a defiant look. 'I was never convinced that Jan Egil was really behind that double murder in 1984. I've always had the feeling that something was overlooked at the time.'

'But the police had pretty substantial forensic evidence against him, didn't they?'

'Yes, they did, Cecilie. They did that.'

We had started the approach to Fornebu Airport. The cabin crew were clearing up after the meal, and we were requested to check that our safety belts were properly fastened.

'And you, Cecilie? Has the dream prince walked into your life?'

She smiled. 'If not the dream prince then … Yes, in fact I have got a partner. We've been living together for the last four years.'

'Perhaps I should move to Oslo, too. If that's where you find them.'

She giggled. 'Maybe.'

'So that means I can't reckon on sleeping on your sofa when I'm there?'

'I'm afraid that might be a little unpopular.'

'OK. I'll have to sweet-talk Thomas then.'

'Your son?'

'Yes, he's still at university. I'll have to take my chance with the corner of his sofa.'

She smiled. 'Then everything's okay?'

'Not everything, perhaps.'

'No, you're right. Not everything.'

We hovered over Oslo in a slow glide, the Royal Palace on our right with Karl Johans gate like a filthy grey carpet edged in green rolled out from the palace steps right down to the central railway station, then Frogner Park, the tree tops autumn-dappled, before landing with a cautious little bump in Fornebu, which would soon be signing off as an Oslo airport. We were let out of the plane in single file, and it wasn't long before we were sitting on the bus bound for Oslo town centre.

She looked at me with a frown. 'How are you going to tackle this, Varg?'

'Somehow I'm going to have to find Jan Egil before he finds me.'

'You realise that could be dangerous though?'

'Yes. But what's the alternative? Sitting on my arse in Bergen and waiting for him to appear, with or without baseball bat?'

'I have to show my face at work, but … where will you make a start?'

'First I'll drop off my bag at Thomas and Mari's. Afterwards, I'd like to find out a bit more about the murder. Is Hansie the right person to contact?'

'He can show you round the hospice anyway. Whether you'll be allowed to go into the flat, I have no idea.'

'Doubt it.'

'Just a mo …' She opened her handbag, took out a wallet and produced a little business card. 'This is Hans's card. It's got his mobile number and so on.'

'Great. Thanks. And yours?'

'OK, I can write my number on the back.' She fished out a biro from her bag and jotted it down.

I took the card, checked the number was legible, nodded and stuffed it in my inside pocket. We got off at the National Theatre, and we stood on the pavement for a moment. She was serious. 'Take great care, Varg!'

'I've been in tight spots before,' I said. 'Even in Oslo.'

She nodded and gave me a quick hug before leaving. Then she headed towards the Town Hall. After phoning first to see if anyone was at home, I took a taxi to Frydenlundgata, where Thomas and Mari had moved since I was last in Oslo.

I rang the doorbell and Thomas came to the intercom before I had finished ringing. Then the door lock buzzed. I walked up the stairs to the second floor of the large block. He was in the doorway waiting. He had hardly said hello before adding: 'Would have been good if you could've given us some notice before appearing on the doorstep. I'm supposed to be at a lecture now.'

I smiled an apology. 'Yes, I'm sorry, but this came up with no warning. And I don't have a client paying for it either, so …'

He nodded indulgently. 'Could you sleep on the sofa again? Course you can. Come on in!'

They had moved from one room and a kitchen in Bislett to three rooms, kitchen and a bathroom close by St Hanshaugen. Thomas gave me a quick run-through on the amenities, fetched a spare key from the bedroom and said we could convert the sofa into a bed when I was ready. I nodded thanks and he hurried off to university, on his bike in the wonderful autumn weather.

As soon as I was alone, I called Hans Haavik.

'Varg! So you decided to pop over ... did Cecilie contact you?'

'Yes. Once again it's about Jan Egil.'

'The eternal problem child, Johnny boy.'

'I hear you're in the same business?'

'Yes, but this is on a private basis now, Varg, and with no other ambition than to help with the little I can. It was tough getting over all the things that happened then, up in Sunnfjord.'

'And it's not finished yet, it seems.'

'You're referring to ...'

'Yes, the murder. Jan Egil. And it happened at your hospice, I gather?'

'Yes, it's terrible.'

'Do you mind if I come round?'

'To the hospice? Not at all. No problem.'

'Have you got access to the room where it happened?'

'Not in principle.'

'In principle?'

'Yes, no one has taken the key off me. But we can talk about that when you're here. Have you got the address?'

'Yes, Cecilie gave me your card.'

'Right. Well, see you there then ... at one o'clock. Is that OK?'

'Should be alright.'

We said goodbye and rang off. I took the spare key with me and left the flat.

47

I took what I had worked out to be the shortest route to Tøyen. From Ullervålsveien I went up Akersbakken to Gamle Aker church and from there down Telthusbakken with all its wooden houses. In the allotments by Maridalsveien there were some Oslo-ers of foreign extraction preparing their herb beds for winter. I crossed the River Akerselva on the footbridge by Kuba and made my way through the Grünerløkka area. At the terrace restaurant by Olaf Ryes plass the tables were packed with a motley bunch of people, some with half-full beer glasses in front of them, others with infants on their laps and a coffee cup at an arm's length. In Hallén's dress shop on the corner of Thorvald Meyers gate it was as if time had stood still since 1950. They displayed dresses for mature women in an interior so worthy of preservation that the Central Office for Historical Monuments must have been a regular customer there.

I crossed up to Jens Bjelkes gate and stayed in that street, passing the Gråbein flats, named after their tight-fisted builder, and the Botanical Gardens. After passing Sørli plass and the sad remains after the clearance of what had once been Enerhaugen I was at my journey's end, Eiriks gate.

The straight stretch between Jens Bjelkes gate and Åkerbergveien consisted of four-storey apartment buildings painted rust-red and off-yellow, many of them embellished with exquisite details on the façade, arches over the windows and classic columns under the roof overhang. At the end of the street was the Police HQ in Grønland, like a massive barrier facing Bjørvika, with so many windows that it gave me the acute sensation that I was under surveillance. And I was not at all sure that this was a good sensation.

It was now five minutes past one. Spotting me from a black

Mercedes parked on the opposite side of the street, Hans got out. He crossed and gave me a firm handshake and a broad, good-natured smile by way of a welcome. 'Nice to see you, Varg. You haven't bloody changed an ounce.'

'Mm,' I said, running my hand through my grizzled hair. 'Nor you.'

'Oh no? Not a bit bigger maybe?'

He might have been right. Hans had always been a well-built fellow. Now he had added a few extra kilos and was on the verge of appearing overweight. His hair was thinner, but the smile was as broad as it always had been, and the bitter purse of his lips I thought I could remember from Førde had been erased. Now there was an expression of real concern on his face as soon as the initial polite formalities had been exchanged.

'It's a helluva story, Varg! The boy must've been born under an unlucky star.'

'Have you kept in regular touch with him? While he was inside, I mean.'

'No, no. Not at all. But I've got a notice on the Salvation wall, and some time in May he suddenly showed up here to ask if I had a room for him. I think he was just as surprised as I was when he saw me in reception.' He turned towards the house. It was one of the yellow ones, and relatively recently decorated. 'I have a little office here on the ground floor where I administer the whole thing. Porter, bookkeeper, spiritual adviser – just like in the old days.'

I looked up at the house front. 'But you own it?'

'I do.'

'You must have come into some money.'

All of a sudden he seemed almost ashamed. 'It was the ... inheritance, you know.'

'You inherited it?'

'No, no ... My God, Varg! The damned farm in Angedalen ... It turned out Kari and Klaus had left it in their will, to me of all people!'

'To you?'

'To me who never had the least interest in becoming a bloody farmer! I'm sure it was done to pull a flanker on her sister and husband. You remember – the people at Almelid. They were dyed-in-the-wool Christians, and Klaus was pretty much the opposite. Klara was the closest heir of course, and anyway the farm had to be run as a going concern, so … it all culminated in them buying me out. I used the money I was paid to buy this block here and a bit later a few others, from the security on this. That's what you do in big towns.' He grinned, but soon reverted to being serious. 'But to be quite frank … the whole business left me with such a bad taste in my mouth that to offset it I decided … I would at least try to help someone. That was why I started this hospice, with the lowest possible rent for people being rehabilitated into society. Alcoholics on the wagon, ex-cons, drug addicts on rehab, you name it, I've had it. Anyway, it provides an old social worker with a sort of meaning to his existence.'

'You could've done the same in Bergen?'

'Yes, of course. But I had so much baggage there. I needed to get away. A long way away!'

'And your definition of a long way is over the mountains to Oslo?'

'This is far enough, anyway. I had all too many bad memories of Bergen.'

'So do I.'

'Then I suppose we're different, you and me, Varg.'

I shrugged and twisted my mouth into a smile. 'I suppose we must be …'

Before going into the building, he took a good look around. It struck me immediately that it was not just the look of concern that characterised him. It was more like a form of fear, as if he were on Jan Egil's death list, too.

We went through the gateway. The front door was to the right. He held the door open for me, and I stepped inside. There was a smell of fresh paint. A broad staircase led up to the higher floors. On the right hand side, KONTOR had been painted on a door into what looked as if it had once been a shop, but was his office. He unlocked and led the way. We came into a small room with a desk in one corner, a sofa and chairs in the other and on the wall opposite shelves full of files, local reference books and a volume of *Norwegian Law* bound in red leather. On the windowsill there was a large green plant with its dusty leaves stretching towards the sunlight outside. Above the desk hung a calendar advertising a local car dealer and a collage showing a representative selection of Mercedes models from 1926 through to today.

'You can't live off this, can you?' I said, flopping onto the sofa.

'Not without a government subsidy, no. It's the income from the other properties which finances this one.'

'I see. Tell me about Jan Egil. What actually happened?'

Again a flicker, as though of fear, flitted across his friendly face. 'Well, what happened? As I mentioned to you on the phone … he turned up here in May, and he's stayed here ever since.'

'He was supposed to be working at a car repair shop, I heard.'

'Yes, but it went badly. He couldn't get up early enough in the morning, and the jobs he was given there were not particularly demanding. So he took odd jobs here and there.'

'What sort of odd jobs?'

'Well, removals, bit of loading and unloading for transport firms … I'm not entirely sure. Anyway, he paid his rent as regular as clockwork. There was never any trouble about that.'

'He had contacts with the criminal fraternity, didn't he?'

'Who told you that?'

I shrugged. 'Most people who've been inside do, don't they?'

'Yes, I'm afraid so. From that point of view, modern prisons function as first class training establishments,' he said with a wry smile. 'But maybe he did. I haven't noticed anything of that kind myself.'

'Are you here all the time?'

'No, no. I have office hours from ten to twelve every day, and so I can be contacted if there are any problems of a practical nature – water, electricity and so on. But part of the point is that residents should manage on their own as far as possible. And I have a deal with a security firm who look in regularly to protect us against various kinds of public order offence.'

'So you're free for the rest of the day?'

'If only I was! No, the rest of the day I run my other properties. Pure business, but quite profitable actually.'

'And you're happy doing that?'

'Yes, but wasn't it Jan Egil we were going to talk about, not me?'

'Yeah, yeah. We got distracted. He's become a father, I've heard.'

'Cecilie did a good job of getting you up to speed, I can hear.' As I reacted with no more than a nod, he went on: 'Yes, he has, and with this Silje, whom I'm sure you remember from 1984.'

'Goes without saying.'

'Yes, I don't know much more than that. They have a little boy whom social services are keeping a bit of an eye on.'

'Have you met her?'

'No. She's never been here. Neither her nor the boy.'

'And if that wasn't enough, you had Terje Hammersten living in the house, of all people, as well.'

'Yeah. Jan Egil showing up was a coincidence, but Terje came because he had heard I was running this place.'

'Terje? You were on first name terms?'

He smiled in a good-natured way. 'That's probably something you don't know, Varg, but … Terje Hammersten had been converted.'

'Converted? What to?'

'He had found Jesus, as he put it.'

'Christ! Who would have thought that? Whenever I met him, he generally threatened to beat me to pulp.'

'You know … there was a powerful personal reason. He lost his wife. Mette. I'm sure you can remember …'

'Did they get married? Mette Olsen and him? Jan Egil's mother?'

'Yes, but then she died. She had cancer of the womb and it spread so fast it was impossible to operate. They treated her with cytotoxin, but she was already so weakened that the end was a foregone conclusion. It was while she was ill that he found Jesus. That was how he explained it.'

'And they also lived in Oslo?'

'No, in Kløfta. Jan Egil was banged up in Ullersmo, and I suppose this ran through her life like a leitmotif. Wherever Jan Egil went, she followed. And up there she was given permission to visit. I think she was the only person he had left. His foster mother had been out of his life for a long time, and the foster parents had been killed – by him, if we're to believe the court.'

'Vibecke Skarnes lives here too – I seem to remember. At any rate she moved here after leaving prison.'

'That's possible but … I've never heard that there was any contact. But there was a relationship between Jan Egil and his real mother for the first time in their lives. It was worse with Terje. I don't think Jan Egil could ever accept that Terje and his mother had become a couple, and even worse, when he was finally given parole, that only Terje was left. And that the mother he had got so used to as his very own was also suddenly gone. For good.'

'When did she die?'

'Last autumn. She was buried up there. In Ullensaker. The end of a long and tragic life. Another homeless soul,' he said with a heavy sigh, half standing, half sitting on the edge of the desk.

'So how did he react when he came here and found that Hammersten was living here, too?'

He nodded thoughtfully. 'I realised I would have to take the bull by the horns, so I told him straight out, in case he would prefer to live somewhere else. But he didn't, and afterwards I introduced them to each other, made them shake hands and swear to be good neighbours. Of course I could feel there were no warm feelings between them, but I would never have guessed it would go this far!'

'Can you tell me what happened?'

'Not in any detail. After all, I wasn't here when it happened. It must have been some time over the weekend. One of the other residents found him.'

'Mm?'

'Norvald Kristensen's his name. He realised he hadn't seen Terje since the Saturday. He knocked and listened at his door, which was unlocked. And when he opened ... well, I can assure you, Varg, it was not a pretty sight. Norvald rang me and I drove down immediately, but I knew straightaway that I would have to call the police. There was no hope for Terje Hammersten.'

'How ...?'

'He was lying on his back. Someone had battered his face to mush. If I hadn't recognised his clothing and his torso, it would have been impossible to say who it was. Blood was spattered all over the floor, and next to him lay his Bible, open but face down.' When he saw my quizzical look, he added: 'You never saw Terje without the Bible in his hand. Every single time I dropped by to talk to him he was sitting and flicking through it. Absolutely had to read out to me a new bit of the scriptures he had found, some words, like manna, that would give him comfort and forgiveness for all the misdeeds he had committed over a long life of sin.'

'Mm ... he didn't confide in you at all about any of these misdeeds, did he?'

'No, but he complained a lot about what a bad father he had been to his son in Bergen. I don't know if you remember I had some dealings with him, too?'

'How can I forget that? That was how Hammersten got his alibi back in 1984.'

'Yes, but you can just forget all that. Jan Egil has paid the penalty for the double murder, and now he's got another damn murder on his hands ...'

'Are the police confident this time as well?'

His brow darkened. 'They found a bloodstained baseball bat

in his room, Varg. And the boy has vanished into thin air. At first they didn't know about his background. But then they made a few phone calls, to Førde and Bergen, and that was when all the alarm bells started ringing. I gave them Silje's address. He wasn't there, either. But they've got a full-scale search for him under way, and it can't be long before they catch him, I hope.'

'Silje's address, can I have it, too? Is her name still Tveiten?'

'Yes. I noted it down on his registration card when he moved in. It's always good to have tabs on … relatives.' He turned round, pulled out a drawer from the desk and lifted out a small grey card-index box. He flicked through to a card, checked it, leaned over and passed it to me.

'Søren Jaabæks gate?'

'Yes, it's up in Iladalen. Right by the church.'

'OK. I'll find it.'

'But what …?'

'I only want to have a few words with her.'

'I meant to ask you … What's the point of this? Are you on some kind of investigation?'

'No, this is more in the way of a preventive measure.'

'Preventive?'

'Yes. Didn't you say you had a key to the room … where the murder took place?'

He looked at me, troubled. 'Yes, I've got one. But theoretically it has been sealed off by the police.'

'Properly sealed?'

'No, just with plastic tape. But we can't … I can't let you do any more than stand at the doorway and peer in.'

'It would be great just to have an impression of the room.'

'But I still don't understand … This is very much a police matter, Varg. There's nothing you or I can do here.'

'No, but you know what we've felt for the boy, right from the time he was Johnny boy to us.'

'Yes, I do.'

'Do you know if Jens Langeland is still his solicitor?'

'No … I suppose he's climbed a bit too high up the greasy pole for us mere mortals now. I guess you must have followed him in the press, too, haven't you? The stellar barrister who goes from one momentous case to the next. Detached house on Holmenkollen ridge, chalet in the mountains, by the lake, you name it, he's got it. Hats off to him. But you can seek an audience, if you've got some business to do.'

'I might do that.'

'Good luck.'

'Well, shall we have a look at the flat?'

'OK then … I've got the key here.' He opened a drawer, took out a key and motioned to the door. 'But I don't know if I like this.'

I didn't, either. But I went with him up the two floors to the scene of the crime.

48

On the second floor we came to a halt in front of a door closed off with police tape. But there was no seal on the lock, and when Hans bent over the plastic ribbon and inserted the key, it was just a question of turning it, pressing down the handle and pushing the door, then we had standing room at the theatre where the drama had taken place.

The door between the tiny hall and the room inside stood open, and through the doorway we could make out a spacious furnished sitting room. What caught my eye was the outline of a man on the floor, marked with white tape, and the big, dark stain on the wood where the head had been. There was a pattern of smaller spatter stains around the large one, and we could follow the trail of blood with our eyes to the hall where we were standing.

'The murder weapon must have been dripping blood,' Hans said. 'That was the detective's comment anyway.'

'They should have every chance of finding bloodstains on his clothes too, by the look of it.'

'Yes. He must have been literally spraying blood.'

'Did anyone see him? Arriving at or leaving the crime scene?'

'Not as far as I know.'

'What about this Norvald Kristensen? Is it possible to grab a chat with him?'

'If you can find him, that is. He went on the piss and hasn't been seen since Monday.'

'Another missing person, in other words?'

'Norvald will turn up again, I reckon. All his things are here.'

We stood staring at the large patch of blood for a while. I didn't even need to close my eyes to visualise the massive blows or Terje Hammersten, who had collapsed after the first of them, and then the flurry of blows that followed as he lay there, lifeless on the floor, being beaten to an unrecognisable pulp by someone who must have hated him with a vehemence it was hard to imagine.

'Hatred – or fear,' I said to myself.

'What did you say?'

'The only thing that could make someone do something like this. Hatred or fear.'

He nodded. 'Have you seen enough now, do you think?'

'Yes.'

I turned away while he carefully closed and locked the door without touching the tape. We walked back down in silence.

Hans accompanied me to the ground floor, stepped outside and cast a long look up and down the street before turning back to me. 'And now your plan is to …?'

'I'll have to try Silje. We're old friends, as you know.'

He looked at me sternly, then shook my hand and said: 'Well … if there's anything else you want to discuss with an old colleague, you've got my number. Good luck!'

'Same to you,' I said, waving goodbye and leaving.

Perhaps it was just the atmosphere of the scenario upstairs that was playing tricks on me, the unpleasant feeling of contemplating a crime scene, as if you were standing on the edge of something indefinably dark, the pull of a deep, apparently bottomless, precipice, but from the moment I left the house in Eiriks gate I had the oppressive sensation that I was being followed. I craned my neck round several times on the way from Tøyen to Grünerløkka, but I didn't see anything remotely suspicious, neither on the pavements nor in the traffic. The vague sense of unease however didn't leave me, and straightaway it was as if the town around me was changing character from being a medium-large, not particularly impressive capital city in a country with an overblown opinion of itself to something quite different and much more dangerous which it was difficult to put a name to …

Søren Jaabæks gate lay at the top of Ildalen and the address I had been given had an entrance right next to a humble mustard-coloured brick church with a rectangular spire. Silje Tveiten lived on the basement floor, straight through the corridor and to the right. I stood at her door listening. Inside I could hear a child crying.

I rang the bell. Immediately I heard movement, and the child's crying came closer. After opening up, she stood there with the tiny tot in her arms. Its face was burning red, its mouth wide open, but the crying was beginning to shift into desperate sobbing, like a kind of realisation that there was no point anyway, there was no one who could provide solace and everyone was busy with their own whimpering soul.

Silje's eyes widened and she moved to slam the door shut in my face, but I wedged a foot in the crack and stopped her.

'What d'you want?'

'You remember me, Silje?'

'Course I bloody recognise you! What d'you want, I asked!'

'Just to talk to you. About Jan Egil.'

'You've done enough harm to Jan Egil and me as it is! I don't wanna listen to you.'

'Yes, I gather he … bears me a grudge.'

Her face hardened. 'You can bet on that!'

'But let me in anyway! We can't stand here … It's not good for your child.' I indicated the infant with my head. It suddenly went quiet as if it were listening to what was being said.

She exploded with a small inarticulate outburst. Then she turned her back on me and retreated into the flat without a second glance. I closed the door behind me and followed.

It wasn't a large flat, a room with a kitchenette and a sleeping niche where a curtain was half drawn. Outside the curtain was a narrow cot, almost a camping model. On the bed there was a pile of toys; it must have been used as a playpen during the day. The furniture looked threadbare: a burgundy sofa with grey sides and worn edges, a well-used leather Ekornes chair, creased with wear, a coffee table with a maze of circles from glasses, bottles and beer cans thrust down at will. But the only things there now were an eggshell-coloured mug with a red pattern and a coffee stain round the rim, plus a child's plastic mug with a lid and spout.

'A boy?'

She gave a surly nod.

'What's his name?'

'Sølve.'

'Nice name.'

She grimaced. 'You didn't come here to chat, though, did you.'

'No, I didn't. Can I sit down?' I indicated the leather chair.

She flourished an unoccupied arm and plumped down on the sofa while holding Sølve to her breast. He was beginning to roll his eyes and make a few small chugging sounds now. 'He's got colic,' she explained, as if I was conducting an inspection for social services or some other public department.

'He seems happy here,' I said without much conviction in my voice.

'Yes, fancy that – so he does!' She flashed a defiant glare, as though used to being contradicted.

'The last time we met was almost eleven years ago.'

'I haven't forgotten, believe you me!'

'No, I'm sure you haven't.'

I looked at her. She would have to be twenty-seven now, a grown-up woman. I recognised the girlish features I had only come face to face with a few times before, and perhaps I could see more of her mother in her now: that slightly aggressive, jumpy nature that can afflict people whose lives have been placed under council care. The ponytail was gone. Her hair had been cut short and given a sort of shape. It emphasised the narrowness of her face. Her mouth bore a disgruntled set, and her eyes flashed, blue and bitter. She did not seem very happy with her existence.

'Would you tell me about Jan Egil and yourself?'

'Why should I?'

I leaned forward. 'I'm here to help you, Silje.'

'That's what you said last time! But you lied, like all the others.'

'I didn't lie to anyone. I did what I could. But I'm afraid it wasn't enough. The evidence was too strong, and there was nothing I could do about that.'

'Jan Egil says you let him down. He should've shot you down while we were in Trodalen, he said. Then there would've been one less bastard in the world. It was your fault he was arrested.'

I felt an unpleasant tingle between my shoulderblades. 'Goodness me, he can't blame me for that. Think of all the police there were. He would've been arrested whatever happened. He was the one who asked them to get me from Bergen.'

'Yeah, precisely!' Tears appeared in her eyes. 'Because he trusted you from that time in Bergen when you'd been like ... like a father to him.'

'Oh yes?'

'And then you – more than anyone else – let him down.'

'But, my God ...'

'Yes, you'd better start praying if you believe him. I wouldn't like to be in your shoes when Jan Egil finds you!' Through the tears her mouth twisted into a taut grimace, a parody of a smile.

'I've spoken to someone called Cecilie,' I said. 'She told me he had a kind of ... that he told you who he was going to wreak his revenge on?'

She studied me with her lips pursed and a glint of triumph in her eyes, as if relishing the hold she had over me. 'Maybe,' she whispered, so low that it was hard to catch.

'What was that?'

'Maybe, I said! You hard of hearing or what? He was gonna nail both you and that Terje Hammersten who was sleeping with his mother! And he didn't have much time for the guy running the hospice, either.'

'Hans Haavik.'

'Yes, the one who buggered off with all the money that time, who inherited Libakk Farm.'

'Right, do you mean … he was on his list, too?'

'List?'

'Yes, of the people he would take his revenge on.'

'There was no list. They were just loose ends he had to tie up!'

'He's already dealt with Hammersten, I understand.'

'So what. He'd killed others before, as far as I'm informed.'

'You know about that?'

Her eyes flashed. 'My father in 1973. Jan Egil told me that.'

'Listen, Silje. Tell me … what actually happened between you and Jan Egil? Why has he set out on this … this mission now of all times?'

Her face was blank. 'I don't know anything about a mission. All I know is that when I was twenty I moved east to be close to where Jan Egil was. I knew he was in prison. When he started to get days out on probation, he came home to me, and we … we've always got on well, Jan Egil and me. We're the same. Two of a kind. Nothing to hide.' An expression of tenderness and wistfulness fell over her sad face. 'Then … about two years ago I became pregnant. Sølve was born, and Jan Egil had yet another reason to behave properly, to get out and lead a normal existence, maybe for the first time in his wretched life. But it was not to be …'

'Did you plan to live together?'

She shook her head. She said quietly: 'No. He didn't, anyway.'

'Why not?'

'Ask him!'

'But he was here, and he visited you, didn't he?'

'A few times. Not as often as I would've wished. I don't know but … he seemed to be afraid. Afraid of being together with him, afraid of being in the same room as him.'

'As … Sølve?'

She nodded furiously. 'Yes! As his own son!'

'He might've been afraid of … he didn't have the world's greatest experience of fathers.'

'And he was so restless! Fidgety. As though there was something he had to do – as if there was someone or something somewhere else. At any rate whatever it was, it wasn't with me. In the end I was so tired of it that I was just glad if he went! I had been waiting for him here for so long, and when he finally got out he couldn't settle to anything. He had to move on, somewhere else …'

'So that was why he went to the hospice in Eiriks gate?'

'Yes, he went there and met this Hammersten. You might not know this, but his mother had died. She died a year ago.'

'Yes, I heard that. Did you have any contact with her?'

'Not at all!'

'But she lived up there, in the district, too. You must've bumped into her when you were visiting him?'

'I saw her once. But when I asked him who it was, he just answered: Someone from the Red Cross. What was I s'posed to say to that? There was always someone from various organisations visiting the prisoners. It was only when she was dead that he told me who she was.'

'I see. Let's hang on to that thread for a moment. Hammersten. He met Hammersten again, you said. What did that lead to?'

'You already know. He did him in – they say. They've been here too, the plods, of course.' She gazed into the distance as if to recreate an image for her inner eye. 'He came here late on Sunday night.'

'Really, last Sunday?'

She nodded. '*I just wanted to talk to him,* he said, completely out of his mind. *Who?* I asked. *Hammersten! But he was dead and couldn't tell me anything.* I asked what had happened. And then he looked at me in despair: *It wasn't me, not this time either! But no one'll believe me! – Yes, they will, Jan Egil!* I said. *No one! It'll be just like last time,* he answered. And that was when he suddenly changed tone: *But I'll kill them, every one of them!* And then he reeled off the names of all the people he would get.'

'And that was when he mentioned me?'

'Yes, you and …'

'Were there several on the list?'

'Yeah, yeah … but right now I can only remember you.'

'Jens Langeland, what about him?'

'The solicitor?'

'Yes, was he on the list?'

'No, no, no. Course not! He's still his solicitor and has always helped him.'

'But he said that … it wasn't him this time, either?'

She nodded silently. I looked at her. The tiny boy had gone to sleep against her breast. For some reason a refrain from a Beatles song went through my head: *Lady Madonna, children at your feet – wonder how you manage to make ends meet …*

Our eyes met. I said: 'Tell me … where did he go after dropping in here?'

'On Sunday?'

'Yes.'

Her eyes wandered off. 'Dunno. He didn't say anythin' to me.'

'Sure?'

'Yes!'

'Silje … If he gets in touch, then …' I took out one of my business cards, wrote my mobile phone number on the back and pushed it over the table to her. 'Ask him to ring me on this number. I've got my mobile with me at all times. Say I have to talk to him. Tell him I can help him.'

She studied the card with no interest. 'Might do. Best to leave it like that, I think.'

'Just ask him to get in touch. Say it's important.'

'Tell me … are you so keen to die? Are you in such a hurry?'

'Yes,' I said. 'I am. Enough people have died in this case already. It has to stop at some point.'

'In this case?'

'In this case, yes.' I could feel the fury rising in me. 'Haven't you understood? Haven't any of you understood? Everything is connected, right from the very first moment. You, of all people, should think about that …' I shifted my focus down from her face. 'You with a little baby to take care of.'

Again our eyes met, hers defiant and moist, mine smouldering with anger.

'Right!' I stood up. 'I can't do much more for you just now, Silje.'

She didn't move from the sofa. 'You've done more than enough! Out with you! I never want to see you again! Never!'

'Wonder where I've heard that before?' I mumbled under my breath as I buttoned up my jacket and made for the door. There, I turned and sent her a last glance. *Who finds the money when you pay the rent? Did you think that money was heaven sent?*

She was deliberately ignoring me. I shrugged and left.

Out on the street, the sun's rays angled over Iladalen. My eyes fell on the church with its famous spire.

All of a sudden, the doors on both sides of a parked dark grey Volvo swung open. Two men got out and rushed over to me. I knew who they were long before they displayed their badges. They were classic undercover police in leather jackets and jeans, with two-day old stubble on their chins and hair down their necks.

'What was the name?' one asked.

'Why do you want to know?'

'Show us some ID,' the other demanded.

I sighed out loud, rummaged for my driver's licence and passed it over.

One studied it closely. The other had his eye held firmly on me.

'Veum? Varg Veum?'

'You can read, I see.'

'Would you mind accompanying us to the police station?'

'Would it make any difference if I refused?'

'No.'

'So, what are we waiting for? Let's get it over with. The sooner, the better.'

49

Inspector Anne-Kristine Bergsjø was sitting behind a large desk with fingertips pressed against each other and a sour glare behind the frameless glasses. Her hair was a little shorter than I remembered it, but her clothes were just as conservative: a plain white blouse, nice blue culottes and a tailored grey jacket. A classic blonde of the competent variety.

She was wearing a trademark smile with tight lips curled at the corners, almost like a cartoon character. 'Varg Veum, private eye,' she said with biting acerbity. 'I had hoped I would never see you again.'

'That's a hope I never shared, I'm afraid.'

She raised her eyebrows sceptically. 'You didn't?'

'We had such a cosy time when we last met, didn't we?'

'No, we didn't. Unless I'm much mistaken you brought death and destruction last time, too. I hope you're not on the same mission now.'

I splayed my hands. 'To tell the truth, I hadn't been considering a courtesy visit to the police station, either. It was these colleagues of yours who absolutely insisted.'

She sighed. 'You were observed leaving a flat we're holding under surveillance. Could you first tell me what you were doing there?'

'If you could give me a good reason.'

She looked at her telephone. 'Of course we could send you down to the basement and let you mull over the question there for a few hours.' She looked up again. 'But it would be so much more enjoyable if we could resolve this in a friendly atmosphere, don't you think?'

'Over a drink maybe?'

She forced a wry smile. 'Coffee?'

'From the machine you have in the building? No, thank you.'

Her expectant gaze lingered.

'Well, I can't see any reason not to … I was visiting a woman called Silje Tveiten. She has a child with a former client of mine.'

She leaned forward. Her eyes were alert and direct, her eyelashes unmoving. 'Jan Egil Skarnes was a client of yours? When was that?'

'While I was still in social services. Twenty-one years ago.'

'Uhuh. I see.'

I gave her a rundown of my life with Jan Egil, from when he was three years old until my last sighting of him in court, a good ten years ago, and why I was in Oslo this time.'

'He was going to kill you?' She looked at me, her eyes disbelieving. 'She didn't tell us that.'

'I suppose she didn't want to add fuel to the fire.'

'Maybe not.' She looked at me seriously. 'I'm going to have to give you a warning, Veum.'

'A warning?'

'Or, to be more precise, I have to warn you.'

'I understand the difference.'

'You're mixing with the fringes of a nasty group of individuals. They're dangerous.'

'Dangerous people? What are you talking about? Jan Egil?'

'I'm afraid to say that we've observed him several times in what I would call bad company since he was let out on parole. I can tell you in confidence that he's been very close to being banged up again.'

'Right! On what grounds, if I might ask?'

She eyed me coldly. 'Tell me … Do you know that organised crime is on the up in this country, Veum? Especially in the capital.'

'I've had an inkling.'

'Whether you're on the inside or outside does not matter much.

You're part of the set-up anyway. Reports we've received from Ullersmo suggest that during his incarceration Jan Egil Skarnes nurtured close links with a very unsavoury bunch based here in Oslo. He'd been on our radar several times before he was released.'

'Before he was released? What's that supposed to mean?'

'Mm ... It's not at all unusual for inmates out on leave to be used to carry out jobs. They have a kind of alibi, at least at first. We don't always check who's on leave or not when there's a robbery, someone is beaten up or something even more serious.'

'Murder?'

'That, too. Inside the fraternity, that is. Internal showdowns, quarrels between various factions. Big money's involved. Drugs. Contraband alcohol. Prostitution. And behind all of this – the backers. Yes, some of them are even under lock and key and steering the whole thing from prison. Ullersmo Executive, as we call it. I could give you a number of names. Others conceal themselves behind respectable façades. Business people, restaurant owners, entrepreneurs. And you won't find what they earn from this on any tax register, if that's what you thought.'

'No, I didn't think that. We've got them in Bergen, too, though on a smaller scale.'

'At the moment, Veum. At the moment. Norway is virgin territory for organised crime of this calibre. The worst is yet to come. Mark my words.'

'But ... you're maintaining that Jan Egil is part of this?'

'We have substantiated evidence that he is. In a sense, prison is the best school you can attend.'

'So what shall we do with them? The ones who deserve to be there?'

She sighed. 'It's a weighty issue, Veum. Either they have to invest more in preventive measures, including precautionary surveillance of criminal milieus. Or else we'll just have to lock them up, chuck the keys and walk away. One of the two options.'

'So, in reality, there's just one.'

She smiled weakly. 'I suppose so.'

'Are you suggesting that the killing of Terje Hammersten was a hit job?'

'It could be. Hammersten was himself a link in the criminal network.'

'He'd left it, my informant tells me. Rumour had it he'd been converted. He was holding the Bible in his hand when he was murdered.'

'Yes, a Bible was found at the crime scene. That's right. But we stick to what we've got on Hammersten in our files, and a good part of that comes from Bergen. If he'd converted today, there would've been a lot to pay for from the past. And this criminal fraternity can bear grudges for a long time. Deliberately, so that the punishment is not linked too closely to the actual deeds.'

I sat pondering what she had just said. Then something clicked. 'Tell me … You said you were holding this flat in Ildalen under observation, that was why you brought me in.'

'That's correct.'

'So it wasn't you following me from Eiriks gate then?'

'Not as far as I know. Do you think you're being followed?'

'Perhaps.' I had a sinking feeling in my stomach, a warning sign that something was brewing, something I wasn't going to like.

'Another reason to look at least twice before crossing the street.'

'So … what would you recommend I do, Anne-Kristine?'

She showed with the utmost clarity that she did not appreciate my familiar tone. 'Go back home, Veum. The sooner, the better. Oslo is not a healthy place for you to stay.'

'I found that out a long time ago for myself, but …'

She breathed in through her nose, raised her head a fraction and peered at me through her shiny glasses. 'Yes?'

'There's an old friend I just feel I should visit first.'

'And that is?'

'Langeland, the solicitor. Jens Langeland.'

50

Twilight had begun to fall as I got off the Holmenkollen line train at Besserud, and after a bit of a search, but without falling into any traps set for me, I found Jens Langeland's huge detached house in Dr. Holms vei. A solid brick wall separated the property from the passing peasantry, and the lock mechanism on the gate was so complicated to work that I considered shimmying over instead.

The house stood screened against prying eyes by thick, well-established elm trees. The architectural style was a strange mixture of national romanticism and functionalism, rustic red with vast flat surfaces. From the plot, the view was beyond what money could buy, at least for all those of us who didn't have millions handy in our inside pockets, a dizzying drop to the fjord below.

I followed the gravel path to the solid, green front door, pressed the bell and announced my arrival.

The woman who opened was small, nimble and of Asian origin. She was wearing a plain turquoise dress of shiny material. She smiled gently and said in a somewhat sing-song voice: 'Yes? How can I help you?'

'Is *herr* Langeland at home?'

'One moment,' she said, and tried to close the door, but I had been in fancy areas like this before and already had my foot in the door. I pushed the door firmly and stepped inside; she was powerless to prevent me.

She glared at me, and for a second or two it went through my head that, for all I knew, she could do kung fu and karate, with dreadful consequences. I said quickly: 'I'll wait here.'

She stood still for a second. Then she turned her back on me with no other comment than a chill smile. I watched her cross the spacious hallway and start ascending the stairs to the first floor with springy steps and small, firm buttocks.

Not long afterwards she came back down, followed by Jens Langeland. He cast a glance at me from the top of the stairs and frowned, then, still a good distance away, called: 'Veum?'

'Correct.'

'What on earth are you doing here?' he asked, crossing the floor.

'I'm sure, with a moment's thought, you know.'

He gave a routine nod, as if in court. 'Jan Egil.'

'Jan Egil,' I said.

'Let's go into my study,' he said, pointing west with a sweep of his hand. 'Lin can take your coat.'

Lin took my padded jacket with a deep bow, placed it elegantly over her arm and carried it to a wardrobe as if expediting a royal cape.

Before we got as far as the study, we were interrupted by a woman's voice from the top of the stairs. 'What's this about, Jens?'

We both looked in her direction. She was standing on the landing, slim and graceful in a short black skirt and light grey silk blouse with a black print, like the casual brushstrokes of a bewitched artist. She had very nice legs, and her hair was arranged in a studied casual fashion, steel grey with dark streaks.

'Business, my dear,' said Langeland. 'This way,' he said to me with an imperious gesture.

But it was too late. I had recognised her.

My eyes held hers, even from this distance. 'Vibecke … Skarnes?' I said with a conscious pause before her surname.

She continued to descend without speaking.

'My wife,' said Jens Langeland, quite superfluously.

It was twenty years since I had last seen her, and the only time close up had been that late afternoon when I had met her at Langeland's place in Ole Irgens vei.

'Haven't we met before?' she asked, searching my face.

'Yes, in Bergen the time your first husband … died. I was in social services and … '

'Oh, yes, I remember you now,' she interrupted. She shook my hand. 'Vibecke Langeland.'

'Varg Veum.'

'Pleased to meet you,' came the toneless response. She was still something of an everyday beauty, with attractive regular features and a lovely smile. But her eyes were pensive and distant, and time had drawn two bitter furrows on each side of her mouth. She stroked her steely grey hair with a graceful movement. 'What is it you wish to discuss with my husband?'

'It's ….'

'Is it about Johnny boy?'

'Yes, I can't … '

'Then I want to be present as well!'

Langeland threw his hands in the air in frustration. 'I suggest then that we go up to the living room,' he said. 'It's cosier there after all.' He turned to the Asian woman who had stood in attendance in the background like a shadow. 'Lin? Could you brew us up a pot of tea, please?'

'As you wish, *herr* Langeland,' Lin said, swiftly withdrawing.

On one wall in the hallway there was a stuffed elk head. 'Did you shoot it?' I asked Langeland as we passed beneath.

He shook his head. 'Came with the house. None of the heirs wanted it.'

Despite being on the losing side in both court cases I had witnessed, Jens Langeland had had a meteoric career in the last decade, which his des res on Holmenkollen Ridge confirmed. His lean figure was unchanged, but his hair had suffered deep inroads and the strains of grey were stronger, and there was an air of fatigue about his face that I could not recall having seen before. Then again he was one of the most popular defence counsels in the country and appeared in the newspapers as often as the Prime Minister.

The living room we entered could have held the whole of my Bergen flat, and I would still have had room for a little garden outside. The parquet floor was only partly covered with very exclusive furniture arranged in a variety of formations. The bookcases were in classic empire style, and behind the glass fronts there was hardly a paperback to be seen. Broad windows revealed a dusk landscape with scattered gleaming lights and Oslo fjord lying like a blue-black silk drape casually discarded between Nesodden and Bærum. Far beneath, we saw an aeroplane taking off from Fornebu, as soundless as in a silent movie. It was only later that the faint echo of jet engines at full throttle reached us.

Vibecke Langeland led us to a small coffee table, also in classical style, burgundy and dark brown, and so polished that we could see our reflections in the wood. 'Sit down, Veum,' she said, indicating one of the four high-backed chairs. On the same finger as the thin wedding ring she wore a diamond ring, two distant relatives, one rich and one poor, out promenading. A plain jewel, vaguely triangular-shaped, set in a precious stone at least as exclusive, hung from a gold chain around her neck, from the very spot where her pulse was throbbing.

We sat down; she with her elegant legs slanting to the left, Langeland sitting in a more casual fashion, or as far as it was possible in such a chair, with his long legs sticking out at the side of the table. I felt as if I were being interviewed for the vacant gardener's post.

'That was a surprise,' I said casually, essaying a tiny smile.

Langeland eyed me in silence.

Vibecke said: 'Oh, you mean us two? I can explain that.'

'Vibecke,' Langeland said.

'Of course, of course … We have nothing to be ashamed of, have we.' She patted him affectionately on the knee. Then she turned her gaze back to me. 'Jens and I have known each other, well, ever since university. We were also together for a while then, in fact.'

'Yes, I seem to remember someone saying.'

'But then, well, we wandered apart for a few years. I got together with Svein, and then all the disastrous events came at once. But in 1984, when Jens came back from Førde after all the happenings there, and looked me up to tell me everything, …' She smiled sweetly. 'Zing went the strings of my heart! Since then it has been just us two.'

I glanced at Langeland. 'That was how it was?'

He put on an expression of indifference. 'Does it matter? Has it got anything to do with you? I assume you did not come here, unannounced and uninvited, to delve into our private lives?'

'No, the cause is of course, yet again … what do you call him? Johnny boy?'

It was Vibecke who answered. 'For me he will never be anything else. They started calling him … the other name in Sunnfjord.'

'Have you ever met him?'

She recoiled in surprise. 'What do you mean?'

'No, I mean, naturally enough, have you met him since … 1974?'

She slowly shook her head, as though remonstrating to a small child. 'No. Never. You have to understand. He …'

'Yes?'

'Well, after what happened at that time. I ended up in jail, Veum, don't forget that! Had it not been for Jens then …' Her face had suddenly cracked, it was open now. Sheer despair was written all over it.

'So …'

'Veum!' Langeland sat up erect in his chair. 'What the hell is all this? She told you she hasn't seen the boy since he was six and a half years old. Everything that has happened since then is … history to her.'

Lost in thought, I looked at him. 'That's just it, Langeland. The roots of this case go way back. A very long way.'

'This case! Which case?'

'You know he's wanted by the police?'

Vibecke's eyes widened and she looked up at her husband in

amazement. He gave a brief nod to her before focusing on me again. 'And so?'

'He's suspected of having committed another murder, this time here in Oslo.'

'A murder?' Vibecke almost whispered. 'Who was it?'

'Someone by the name of Terje Hammersten. Does that mean anything to you?'

She shook her head. 'Nothing at all! Who is he?'

A clinking sound came from the staircase, and we were interrupted by Lin who came in carrying a silver tray crammed with teacups, saucers, spoons, an elegantly shaped teapot, sugar in a bowl and a plate of fresh lemon slices. As if by a flick of the fingers, Vibecke switched into the perfect hostess, helped Lin put out the cups and saucers, offered me sugar and lemon and told Lin, after she had poured tea for us all, that we could manage fine on our own now, thank you.

When Lin had left, I faced Langeland. 'But *you* remember Terje Hammersten, don't you?'

'Indeed I do. But we never managed to get anything on him, at least not in connection with the cases that concerned Johnny boy.'

'No, we drew a blank there, I regret to say.'

'Probably because there was no connection.'

'Are you still convinced about that?'

He eyed me with raised eyebrows. 'Aren't you?'

'Did you ever meet him?'

'Not face to face. I had to attend a police interview with him once, behind a two-way mirror – that was the closest I came. He was never taken to court because of the damned alibi.'

'Exactly. And now he's been killed, in all probability by Jan Egil. I don't suppose he's contacted you?'

'Jan Egil? No.' He shook his head firmly.

'When did you last speak to him?'

'Veum … in fact, I've been visiting him regularly. Because it was important that he should have contact with … someone. On a private basis, in other words. But of course I had a finger in the pie when he applied for parole this spring. But that was also the last time I saw him. When he was released, I mean. Some time in May.'

'In other words, you're ready to help?'

'I'm still his solicitor, yes, if that's what you mean.'

'Which is what you've been all his life.'

'All?'

'Yes, you were even his mother's solicitor, before he was born. I think you yourself told me that on one occasion.'

'Hmm.' He sent me a dismissive glare.

'And you definitely lent a helping hand when he was adopted by Vibecke and Skein Skarnes in 1971, didn't you.' I glanced at Vibecke, who was nodding agreement.

'Yes, but that was because I knew them both – from university, as I mentioned. Well, I knew Vibecke better. And, as you yourself said, I assisted his mother with a ... spot of bother.'

'And were you sure he was going to a good home?'

'As I said, I knew Vibecke, didn't I!'

I shifted my attention back to her. Her eyes wandered for a moment. Then they were back, shiny and reserved. 'Yes?' she said.

'Was it a good home?'

'Veum!' Again Langeland interrupted us. 'This is none of your or anyone else's business. This is water under the bridge! Forget it!' he turned to her. 'Don't reply to everything he asks you!'

He continued, facing me now: 'I didn't officially become *his* solicitor until 1984, when I was called to Førde.'

'Yes, that's right ... but I believe you'd followed his progress, from a distance at any rate, in the meantime, too.'

'Because I felt responsible for him, yes. Both to ... his real mother, and because of what happened in 1974 with Svein and Vibecke.'

'We can come back to that but ...'

'Yes?'

'But let's concentrate on 1984 first.'

'What are you actually getting at, Veum?'

I ignored him. 'As you know, it was a dramatic case, and what emerged about his foster parents, or foster father anyway, Klaus Libakk, was hardly trivial.'

He glanced up, resigned. 'You're thinking of these rumours about alcohol smuggling?'

'Yes, and about the police interest in Terje Hammersten eleven years earlier over another brutal murder. Perhaps set up by Klaus Libakk, or someone else from the same ring.'

'Another?'

'Yes, and we found that out at the time. But you didn't make anything of it at the trial. Why not, Langeland?'

'You're thinking of ...' He was sitting upright in the chair now, and I could see he was uncomfortable with the direction the conversation was taking.

'What are you talking about now?' Vibecke burst out.

'You've never told her?' I said.

'Told me what?' she asked.

I half-turned to her again. 'Didn't you have a clue ... didn't you know that your husband at the time, Svein Skarnes, was one of the main men behind the smuggling racket, mostly in the Sogn and Fjordane district?'

She stared at me in disbelief. 'What are you talking about? Smuggling?!'

'Svein Skarnes was the boss. He had contacts in Germany, sorted out the deals with the boats smuggling the goods in, organising the local machinery in Sogn and Fjordane, ably assisted by his office equipment rep, Harald Dale, and he earned big money, of course.'

'Big money! And what happened to it then? Can you tell me that?'

'No. But you two were rolling in it, weren't you.'

'No more than anyone else. This is completely new to me!'

'But your husband here, he's known since 1984.'

She turned on Langeland. 'Is that right, Jens? Have you known all this without saying a word to me?'

'I ... wanted to spare you, Vibecke. Besides, this was never documented.'

'Nevertheless ...'

'The whole business was full of uncorroborated claims that ...'

Her eyes filled with tears, and her lips were trembling. 'I just can't believe it! That you could keep this hidden from me for so many years, Jens! How could you?'

They stared at each other with a distance in their eyes that increased as the seconds passed.

'There may be more you haven't told each other,' I said.

Now they both turned towards me.

'About things that went on in 1974, for instance.'

I had their undivided attention.

51

'What are you blathering on about now, Veum?' Langeland exclaimed with annoyance. 'Haven't you caused enough trouble yet?'

'Trouble! All I'm asking is for people to stop lying. And to stop taking the blame for other people's misdeeds, however honest it may seem.'

I held her eyes with mine. 'I assume Langeland took this up with you back in 1984, but nevertheless I feel obliged to remind you of what Jan said when I was talking with him at Førde police station at that time. Of what he remembered from the day Svein Skarnes was murdered.'

Langeland stood up. 'Veum! I think you should go now!' I didn't move. Nor did Vibecke. She raised an arm to her husband and said, in a quivering voice. 'Don't … Jens. I want to hear what he has to say.'

Langeland remained on his feet.

I said: 'He did tell you this when he came back from Førde, didn't he? To me he even said it was a basis for re-assessing the case. We're talking about *your* case now.'

'Yes, he did, but I said that … that I couldn't remember … all the details any more. And Jan must have made a mistake.'

'And that … was perhaps not quite the whole truth?' I said warily.

She hesitated. Then she said, so quietly that it was barely audible: 'No, it wasn't.'

'What!' Now it was Langeland's turn to be amazed. With an incredulous expression in his eyes he fell back in his chair while staring at his wife. 'But you've always …'

'It was you who insisted that I should confess, Jens. You said I would receive more lenient treatment from the court if we could convince them that it was involuntary manslaughter.'

'And you did! But, my God, I didn't expect you to confess if you hadn't done it!'

She swallowed hard. As she spoke, she was having trouble finding the right words, and what she said came in slow staccato: 'T-tell me again … what did Jan say?'

'It's so long ago now that I can't remember the precise wording, but the main gist was that he had been alone with his father, well, your husband. The foster father. He was sitting and playing with his train. Then he heard the doorbell ring. Your husband went to open the door and he heard a loud altercation with someone. A man, please note. Then everything went still. Later he went into the hall and … in fact I don't know whether he found him or that happened when you came home. I don't recall whether he told me that or not. The main point, however, was this: someone came in, argued with your husband, and left again. Who?'

She did not look at either of us, but somewhere in-between. 'You … both of you know why I did it.'

I leaned forward. 'Did what?'

'Confessed.'

'I've always had my suspicions …'

'Because I was sure Jan had done it. To protect him against … this monstrous act.'

'But there was one thing he said to me that day. And it was this: *Mummy did it!*'

'Yes?' For a moment her eyes seemed to be flashing sparks. 'I said that to him when he was standing by the cellar stairs, as stiff as a poker. I crouched down in front of him, looked him straight in the eye and repeated several times: 'Don't feel sorry, Johnny boy! Mummy did it …'

'Mummy did it,' I repeated, the way the sentence had resounded in my head for all the years that had passed since that February day in 1974.

She looked at her husband with tearstained eyes while nodding in silence.

'I see,' I said. 'But then the question is … Can you tell me what really happened?'

'No. No more than anyone else can.'

Both Langeland and I waited for her to go on.

'I … had been out. At the doctor's. When I came home, I unlocked the door and … the first thing I saw was Jan standing in the hall, in front of the open cellar door. He was standing with his back to the wall, on the opposite side of the door, and there was something strange, something lifeless and apathetic about his face, as though he had lost all form of expression. Because he had done something terrible.'

'Done, or seen?'

'My perception was … he had once done something similar, in blind fury. Gone for Svein and bitten his hand so hard that he drew blood. Svein went ballistic and gave him a belting after-wards … but Jan refused to say anything. He didn't say a word to me, neither that day nor …' Again tears flowed, and she looked straight at me. 'That was the last time I saw him! Do you under-stand? I could never take him in my arms again, never try to help him with all the rest, all the pain in his life which had made him what he was. I lost him that day. Lost him!'

'You unlocked the door, you said?'

'Yes, I did! I didn't ring the bell. Or if I did, no one opened up. And I didn't have a row with Svein, either. Not that day. I did not do it. There was never a clash between us which resulted in him falling down the stairs.'

'You just made that up to make the death sound credible, is that it?'

She nodded mutely.

'He hadn't been brutal to you, either? All the character wit-nesses refused to believe that.'

She whispered: 'No, that was lies, too. A pretext.'

'Lie after lie after lie,' I mumbled. 'And your solicitor ... what did he think?'

Langeland exclaimed: 'I took her at her word. I always trust my clients!'

I turned back to him. 'But you and Vibecke had been on intimate terms since university. Are you asking me to believe that she didn't tell you what really happened, not even you? Or did you choose to trust her blindly, out of consideration for Jan? You too?'

'Out of consideration for ...?'

'Yes? After all, he was your son. Was he not?'

The large room fell quiet. Vibecke stared at me. 'What was that you said? I didn't quite catch ...'

'I said to your husband that, after all, Jan was his son,' I said in a low neutral voice, as though telling her the weather forecast for the following day. 'In a way that explains his commitment to this case, as I said, from the time Jan was born!'

She turned to Langeland with a face like one large, open wound. Again we could barely hear what she whispered: 'Is this true, Jens? Are there any other things you haven't told me?'

'Vibecke, I ...' All his eloquence was gone now, all his defence mechanisms destroyed. All I could read in Langeland's face was deep, bottomless despair. 'I couldn't ... tell ... couldn't tell anyone! I've never told ...' He swung round to me again. 'How this fellow worked it out ... I just can't fathom!'

I studied him. 'I remember,' I started, 'seeing you together in court, during the review meeting in Førde and later in Bergen ... it struck me how similar you were. The same gangling stance, the same toss of the head. You can never completely disguise genetic traces, not a hundred per cent.'

He brandished an arm, as if to reject everything, but I was past the point where I would let myself be stopped. 'I seem to remember ... the description you gave of Mette Olsen the first time I visited your Bergen office ... young and sweet, you called her, and there was a sort of elation about the way you said it. But there was more. What really put me on the trail was the time aspect.'

'The time aspect?'

'When I visited Mette Olsen in Jølster in 1984, I committed the folly of believing that the man she was arrested with in Flesland, David Pettersen … was Jan's father. But Jan was born in July 1967, and David and Mette were arrested in Flesland on August 30th the year before. Unless they had an unguarded moment at court, which I consider highly unlikely, it is simply impossible for him to be the boy's father.'

I let this sink in before carrying on: 'So which other men was she keeping company with at that time? And don't forget that she was in remand right through till November when the case was brought before the court. But she must have met her solicitors, I suppose, without police supervision even, if I'm not mistaken …'

He looked at me with an expression of blank resignation on his face. Vibecke had stopped crying. Her eyes flitted from me to him and back again.

His voice was now almost as hushed as hers had been. 'I couldn't … first of all, I had infringed the solicitors' code of conduct, and this was one of my very first cases, Veum. I wasn't even … Bakke had the case. Bakke was a barrister, my superior. But when she became pregnant … it didn't come out until she had been released. I tried to persuade her … but she insisted on keeping the child. I said to her: 'But there can never be anything serious between us two.'

'Why not?' Vibecke snapped, like the crack of a whip.

'Because … she wasn't the right one. She didn't have the right …'

'Status, shall we call it perhaps?' I said. 'A little hippie girl on her way home from Copenhagen in very unseemly company. And God knows who she might have been with over there … or how many … was that how your mind was working?'

He half-stood up. 'Anyway, that's how things stayed. We made a deal. I was never registered as the child's father. In recompense I've helped her and Jan, as far as I've been able all the years since.'

'Have you now?'

'As well as I've been able, I said,' he mumbled despondently, almost to himself.

'And she kept her mouth shut all these years ... Mette, I mean?'

He looked up again. 'Well, did she?'

'She never banged on the door asking for money?'

'No, she did not!'

'I can understand her,' Vibecke broke in with a bitter timbre to her voice. 'At least *she* had retained her pride!'

'And what help have you been exactly?' I persisted. 'You didn't manage to prevent his foster mother doing time for a murder she had not committed. You didn't manage to prevent Jan being convicted for a double murder it is highly questionable that he committed.'

He eyed me with increasing desperation. 'So who did commit them?'

I met his eyes with defiance. 'Yes, who did? Who the hell do you think? Terje Hammersten?'

'Hammersten's dead. You told me that yourself.'

'Now, yes.'

My mobile phone suddenly rang. Vibecke gave a start, Langeland looked around, confused, and I made a grab for my inside pocket as if I was having a heart attack.

I got up and walked over to the window. It had grown dark outside. The sun had long gone down, but the lights from Ullerntoppen and the gleam of the floodlights round Oscarshall Palace orientated me as to where I was, high above the peasantry. I lifted the mobile to my ear and said my name.

His voice came in fits and starts, as if he too was having problems finding the right words. 'I've spoken to Silje. You said you wanted to meet me.'

It was Jan Egil.

52

'Where are you?' I asked.

'In town. Where are you?'

'With your solicitor, Jens Langeland.'

There was a silence.

'Are you still there?'

'Yes ... Ask Langeland if you can borrow his car.'

Langeland and Vibecke were following the conversation closely. I lowered the phone and said: 'It's Jan Egil ... he's asking whether I can borrow your car.'

'My car!' Langeland held out his hand. 'Let me talk to him.'

I raised the phone to my mouth. 'Langeland's coming.'

Langeland took the phone and said: 'Jan Egil! What's going on? ... But why haven't you contacted me? It's at times like this you need a solicitor! ... Yes ... No ... But what do you want with him? ... In that case I'll come, too. ... Why not? ... But, I'm already involved. I'm your solicitor, for Pete's sake! I have been for all these years.'

I looked at Vibecke while Langeland was speaking. The answers we guessed he was getting from Jan Egil seemed to be reflected in her face, like rapidly changing cloud cover.

'OK then! But I don't like the sound of that! I repeat with the uttermost clarity: I do not like this. I don't even bloody know if the man has a licence ...' He cast a sidelong glance at me, and I responded instantly with a nod: *Oh, yes, that much I did have.* He glowered in return. 'OK, Jan Egil ... I'll put him on. Take care.'

I was given back my mobile and raised it to my ear. 'Me again.'

He wasted no time. 'D'you know where Ullevål Stadium is?'

'Yes, more or less. I'll find my way there, anyway.'

'Across the street there's a Mercedes showroom. Park in front and get out of the car. I'll be there as soon as I'm sure you're alone.'

'When?'

'Soon as poss.'

'I'll give you a call back.'

'Just come, Varg. That's the main thing.' With that he rang off.

I looked at Langeland again. 'Did he say anything else to you?'

'Just that he had something very important to discuss with you personally. You heard me insisting I came along too, but he said …' He threw his arms in the air, desperate. 'He told me not to get involved. But I'm already involved, I said.'

'Yes, we heard that.'

'Does he know?' Vibecke asked in a clear voice.

We both glanced in her direction. 'Know what?' Langeland said.

Her eyes widened a fraction. 'That you're his father!'

'No! No one knew … until now.'

'Except for Mette Olsen,' I said. 'And she died a year ago. Could she have told anyone?' As neither of them answered, I went on: 'Terje Hammersten, for example?'

He stiffened. 'Not as far as I know. No one has ever confronted me with it before today.'

'And your superior at that time, Bakke, did he get to hear of anything?'

He shook his head.

'Well … then I'll have to take my chances and meet him face to face.' I felt my nerves jangle inside me as I spoke. 'If I can borrow your car, that is.'

He threw up his arms. 'I agreed to that. Goodness me! The boy is wanted by the police and here I am, knowingly letting …'

'If so, it's not the first time you've violated professional ethics, Langeland.'

'Watch your mouth or I'll withdraw my offer!'

'Offer?'

He pursed his lips and stood up. 'Come with me.'

I joined him. Vibecke remained sitting, still half in shock at all she had learned over her elegant teacups.

I tried to catch her eye. 'Goodbye, *fru* Langeland. See you again perhaps.'

'Not if I have anything to do with it,' Langeland mumbled.

She raised her head, but her eyes never reached any higher than my chest. 'See ... you.'

She was sitting by the large window like a little mermaid on the bank of the rest of her life, without the slightest confidence that she would ever be venturing out to sea again. She was stranded for good.

Langeland led me downstairs and asked me to wait in the hall while he went to his study to fetch the car key. From somewhere behind the wall panelling, tiny Lin scuttled out with my coat held in readiness, as if she had known for some time that I was leaving. Langeland returned, and we left the house together. He pressed a remote control and the broad garage door swung upwards.

There were two cars inside. One was a huge four-wheel drive, a Range Rover, the other a natty little Toyota Starlet.

'You'll have to take Vibecke's,' he growled, nodding to the tiny Starlet. 'More your style, I would guess.'

'I'll be right at home,' I said. 'No problem. I'll even be able to find the brake pedal.'

He didn't smile, just pressed the key fob and the alarm was switched off. He opened the car door and peered in, as if to make sure there weren't any personal effects left there. 'I trust you will return it safe and sound, Veum.'

'If that's within my powers,' I said, taking the key and sitting behind the wheel. After pushing the seat back a couple of notches I started the engine. The radio came on, a local station playing thump-thump-thump music. I turned down the volume and peered up at Langeland. 'Then I'll be saying "see you" to you, too.'

'I wish it were avoidable, but we have to have the car back. Listen, Veum ...' He leaned forward, with a sudden insistent expression on his face. 'Try to bring Jan Egil back with you. Whatever he's done, it's important that he and I talk.'

'As solicitor and client or as ...?'

'Yes, yes! And I trust you'll keep your mouth shut about the other business. If ... when he finds out, I want it to be from me. Understood?'

'Understood. Quickest way to Ullevål Stadium is down to the ring road, then head east, isn't it?'

He nodded. 'Good luck ...'

'Thank you.'

I put the car into gear and carefully manoeuvred my way out of the garage. He walked ahead and opened the gate. I raised my hand as I passed. Then I was on my way.

As I swung into Dr. Holms vei and down towards Besserud, I noticed a large black car with darkened windows parked a bit further up the road. The muscles in my midriff tautened instinctively, and my mouth went dry. But it was impossible to see if anyone was inside, and for as long as it was in my rear-view mirror, it didn't move.

I adapted quickly to the car. It wasn't very different from my Corolla, but I would have felt more like the king of the road if he had lent me his four-wheel drive. I kept glancing in the mirror at regular intervals. When I was almost in Slemdal I suddenly noticed a big black car barely a hundred metres behind me. At that distance it was difficult to tell if it was the same one, but the feeling in my stomach did not improve.

The black car followed me right down to the ring road. I lost sight of it in the traffic build-up behind me. It was impossible to see if it was still there. When I saw Ullevål Stadium rise before me, I took a right and pulled over. I sat waiting, totally composed. After thirty seconds a big, black car drove past heading east towards Tåsen without turning off the ring road.

I waited for a few more minutes, but it didn't reappear. Reassured, I drove off again. After passing the stadium, I turned off towards a petrol station on the right and pulled into a large, at this moment, unused car park. I pulled up outside the Mercedes showroom, switched off the engine, opened the door and got out. A bit nervous, I strolled around the car without stopping in case someone had me in their sights. I was uneasy.

From the ring road I heard the sound of traffic, a regular pulsating rhythm. The lights from the town contaminated the evening sky with jaundice, and from high above me I heard the throb of a plane on its way to Fornebu.

I heard the sound of his footsteps on the tarmac. He came round the corner from the back of the showroom as if on a quick evening run out with the dog. But he didn't have a dog, and he came straight towards me.

He was wearing a baseball cap pulled down over his eyes, and his body had grown since I last saw him. In Førde – and the last time in the courthouse in Bergen – he had still cut a gangling, immature figure, not unlike the man I now knew was his father. During his prison stay he had obviously killed lots of hours in the gym. He was bigger and bulkier and definitely looked more dangerous than he had before. Coming to a halt in front of me, he radiated an edgy, pent-up strength that, if released, could have trashed me in the space of a few short seconds.

Under the peak of his cap, he was staring at me through wide-open dark eyes. Without changing expression, he nodded towards the car. 'Get in.'

I did as he said, leaned over and opened the door on the opposite side. He dropped in so heavily that for a moment it felt as if the whole car would tip over. 'Drive,' he said.

'Where to? Shouldn't we – ?'

'Just drive!' he ordered roughly, and I didn't feel it was the right time to object.

53

On the ring road, I tried again. 'I have to know which direction we're taking.'

'We're just going somewhere we can have some peace and quiet. I'll tell you.'

I cast a sideways glance. 'What is it exactly you want with me?'

'You know what.'

'No, I don't! Wasn't it enough with Hammersten?'

We passed a turn-off, but he just pointed ahead. 'It wasn't me who killed him!'

'Wasn't it?'

'He was dead when I found him.'

'When you ... but what did you want from him?'

'I was shoppin' in the street when I met him. I knew of course that he ... he'd been married to my mother. My real mother.'

'Yes, you met her again, I gather. She visited you at Ullersmo Prison?'

'I recognised her soon as I saw her.'

'You recognised her? But you were just three when you ... were taken from her.'

'Not that time, you idiot!'

I was suddenly ill at ease. 'So when was it?'

'It was when we were comin' home from school in Angedalen. Silje and I. We walked past a woman walkin' along the road, and I can still remember her gawping at us. At me most of all. Afterwards we had to laugh at her, and Silje said: Did you see the old biddie! She must be completely crazy, and then we laughed even more. And when she turned up at Ullersmo I recognised her at once. Not as my mother of course, but as the crazy woman from Angedalen.

So, we had been laughing at my mother, my own real mother. I wonder if you can imagine how that felt! I could've cried, a grown man ... and it was the likes of Hammersten who had turned her into what she was. I understood that from what she told me later.'

'But what – ?'

'And then I knew what I'd been missin' for all those years.' His voice was trembling, as if it was hard for him to speak, harder than any bench presses. 'The other so-called mothers've never loved me, not like her, who had to live without me for all that time. And who came after me, through the prison gates. But we had a few good hours anyway, at the end of her life.'

For a while we sat in total silence. The impression I was left with from what he had just said was so strong that I found it difficult to continue the conversation. It was Jan who resumed. 'He said I should drop by to see 'im.'

'Hammersten?'

'Yeah. He had something to tell me, he said.'

'Something to tell you?'

'Something very important for me ... and many others. He'd become a Christian, and now he wanted to clear things up. But when I went to see him that evening, he ... was just lyin' there. Unable to speak to anyone. Killed, and with such brutality that there was blood everywhere.'

'But how did you get in?'

'Door wasn't locked.'

'But if it wasn't you who knocked the living daylights out of Hammersten ...'

'It wasn't me, I told you!'

'OK, Jan Egil. I believe you. But who was it then?'

'He was just paid back for all the torment he had caused me.'

'Hammersten?'

'He killed my first foster father, in Bergen, and it wouldn't surprise me if he hadn't taken out Kari and Klaus in Angedalen as well!'

'Do you know that?'

'Does anyone know anything at all? I've had to do time for it!'

'Do you know that he killed your foster father in Bergen, I mean?'

He didn't answer, just stared into the distance.

I went on: 'But … at any rate it wasn't your foster mother, and she has also paid a debt to society for a murder she didn't commit.'

He took his eyes off the road and stared straight at me. 'How do you know?'

'I spoke to her earlier today. Do you know where she lives?'

'No.'

'But you know she lives in Oslo?'

'I couldn't care less where she lives! She was out of my life a long time ago.'

'But you must be interested to hear what she had to say?'

'Course! So what did she say?'

'She said she arrived home that day in 1974 and it had already happened. You were standing in the hall, paralysed. Nothing else. She didn't know anything else. She did think …'

'What? Who did she take the blame for?'

'For you, I guess.'

He blinked. 'For my sake! I refuse to believe that.'

'It wasn't for Terje Hammersten's sake anyway.'

'How long was her stretch?'

'You don't know? Has no one told you …?'

'No!'

'She was out again by the time of the Angedalen murders.'

He was grinding his molars now; I could literally hear the scraping of worn fillings. 'Right!'

'And you still maintain it wasn't you who … in Angedalen?'

'That's what I've been tellin' you all these years! But none of you believed me.'

'I believed you. But it was impossible to find good enough evidence to break down their case. Or any kind of evidence. If only you hadn't picked up the murder weapon!'

'I had to protect myself, didn't I! I knew who would be blamed ...'

I snatched a sideways glimpse. The way he was sitting and staring, big, heavy and well-built, he was still a replica of the defiant youth I had spoken to at the police station in Førde. But there was something new about him too, which had not been present before: the pent-up fury I had observed from the moment he came towards me in the car park by Ullevål Stadium.

I returned my attention to the traffic. And said: 'There's one thing I have to ask you, Jan Egil. Why are you so angry with me? I've always tried ...'

He interrupted me, still speaking his dialect. 'How can you ask! You and Cecilie'd been like a mother and father to me. The best time of my life was the six months with you. Why d'you think, when I was holed up in Trodalen, pursued by the sergeant and his men, that I asked for you to come to Sunnfjord? And do you remember what you promised me? I shouldn't be afraid, you said. And I wouldn't be cuffed, either. But the first thing the cops did when I got down to them was to launch themselves at me with handcuffs, and from then on I could hardly have a piss without them. You failed me, Varg, you and all the rest. But you pretended to be my friend. That's why you were the biggest fraud of the lot!'

'But ... I've never thought you did it, Jan Egil, not for one moment!'

'That right, eh?' he almost bellowed. 'So why am I sitting here, after ten years in Ullersmo? Can you tell me that, Varg? You who think you're so clever.'

'No, I can't, Jan Egil. It's a tragedy, a tragedy so great that I have no words for it.'

We were approaching Økern now. He pointed east. 'Turn off here! In that direction.'

I did as he said. And looked in the rear-view mirror at the same time. The shock surged through me. *Wasn't that ... two, three cars behind us ... the same black car that had been following me down Dr. Holms vei?*

I accelerated. All the cars behind us kept up, but none of them seemed to want to overtake.

'Take the right at the next crossroads.'

I did as he said. The two nearest cars continued straight on, along Østre Aker vei. The black car turned off and took the same route as us.

'I have a sneaking suspicion we've got someone on our tail,' I mumbled.

'What?' Jan Egil twisted round in his seat and reached for his inside pocket. 'Shit!'

Then the black car was right behind us. We were heading for a large industrial area. On both sides of the road we saw warehouses, access ramps, containers and parked long-haul vehicles. On the ridge facing us we could make out the tall blocks of Tveita.

As we approached a roundabout the black car came alongside. With a bang it sent us slithering into the first exit. For a second or two my mind went back to Jens Langeland's concern about what might happen to his car. But I wasn't given any more time to pursue the thought. I had more than enough trouble steering the car.

The road we were on now was in much worse condition. There were great pot-holes in the tarmac. At the next roundabout I tried to drive right round, but those in the car behind guessed my intentions, swerved into the other carriageway and came to a screeching halt across the road, forcing me to skid down another exit.

Jan Egil was writhing like a snake beside me. 'What the hell's going on?'

The black car had sped after us and was bumper to boot now. I tried to see who was at the wheel, but it was too dark, and I had my task cut out keeping our car on an even keel.

Bump!

They drove into us again, this time from the rear, and with such force and precison that the lightweight Starlet lurched forward. Again I cursed Jens Langeland for not lending us the four-wheel drive.

'Bloody hell!' Jan made a sudden movement beside me, pulled a handgun from his inside pocket and pointed it at the rear window as if intending to shoot through it.

'Jan Egil! Don't …'

'Just drive! Drive for all you're bloody worth!'

Bump! Bump!

A clatter came from the back, as though something had been loosened. We lurched forward, hit the post of an open lattice gate, scraped alongside it and landed with a bang on the inside of the fence. I scanned round quickly. We were in a container depot; dark blue, grey and red containers. I swiftly changed down and shot forward, desperate to find a way out.

Suddenly the tarmac came to an end. Now we were on a gravel road, as bumpy as a switchback. Behind us the tyres of the black car screeched as it skidded after us.

'What the fuck are you doin'? You've driven us straight into a trap!'

'You wanted to go to a nice quiet place, didn't you,' I snarled back.

I looked around, swung the wheel, tried to reverse. Once again the large, black car rammed us, this time from the side, shoving us even further into the corner we were finding ourselves ensnared in. I changed gear and accelerated in an attempt to by-pass them, but they followed us as if stuck to our side and pushed us deeper and deeper into the gap between five or six large containers, with a huge loading ramp in the middle and a barbed wire fence at the end. The bonnet of the Starlet got jammed up against one of the steel supports of the ramp. For an instant all the warning lights on the dashboard flashed, then they went out, the engine died and all we could hear was the faint but insistent hiss of a punctured tyre.

Jan Egil smashed open the door on his side and ducked his head, still holding the blue-grey pistol in his hand. Then, bent double, he got out, with his eyes on the car behind.

I peered into the cock-eyed side mirror. The black car had

positioned itself like a barrier between us and the rest of the world. Around us lay the district of Groruddalen, dotted with glittering lights, as distant as the stars in the sky above us. White smoke drifted from a tall chimney, giving off an acrid smell, as if from burning waste. The only light to reach us came down from two tall pylons, filtered by the darkness. The two men who got out of the car behind – with the same caution and wariness as Jan Egil – were barely visible, no more than two large, dark silhouettes. But the matt gleam from their hands spoke its own unambiguous language. They were not coming to the party with empty hands, either.

One of them called out: 'Out of the car, both of you!'

Since Jan Egil was already outside I calculated that it must have been me he was referring to. I heaved a heavy sigh and felt a sense of inevitability in my stomach. Then I pushed the battered door to its full extent, swung myself out, placed my feet on the gravel and slowly exited the car, copying Jan Egil's example by holding the door in front of me like a shield.

'Freeze!' shouted the man. He turned to the other who already had a mobile phone to his ear and was talking.

'What the hell do you want from us?' I shouted.

'Shut up!'

'Who are you phoning?'

'Shut up, I said!' answered the man, brandishing with menace a considerably larger weapon than Jan Egil's. From this distance it didn't look very inviting, a machine gun of the variety that sold like hotcakes in the organised section of the criminal community, in tiger-town Oslo and elsewhere.

They said something we couldn't hear. I turned my head to Jan Egil. 'Any idea who they are?'

'Not the cops, that's for sure.'

'No, I'd worked that one out, too.'

He wasn't letting the two armed men out of his sight. Standing there – with his top-heavy body, weapon in hand, cap down over his forehead, the little hair I could see shaved tight to the skull – he reminded me of a bully boy, a threat to everything in the vicinity, me included. Anger and pent-up violence radiated off him, and it was not difficult to recognise the disproportionately muscle-bound frame and the vacant look as belonging to someone who had overdosed on anabolic steroids for much too long.

Inside me, I still carried the image of the small, tearful boy on the Rothaugen estate that hot July day of 1970 when Elsa Drage-sund and I had gone to pick him up, and it struck me: had we done this to him? Was this the result of twenty-five years of public service commitment, trying to make him a different and better person, or at least trying to secure him a place in society that both he and we could tolerate? Was this the best we could achieve, the sum of our success?

'What the hell are you mixed up in, Johnny boy?'

'Don't call me that!'

'Sorry, but … is it me or you they're after?'

Suddenly one of the men by the black car shouted. 'Didn't we tell you to keep your mouths shut over there?'

I swivelled round. 'What the hell's wrong with you? Are you feeling left out? You're warmly invited to take part in the conversation, if you like!'

He hoisted the gun to his face and pointed it at me. 'Shut up, I said!'

'Shut your mouth yourself!' Jan Egil snapped. 'I've got you in my sights! Move one centimetre this way and you're a dead man!'

For a moment the whole picture seemed to freeze. I prepared myself for the worst, then the situation suddenly changed. We heard the sound of a car before we saw it. Round the bend from the gate it came, a large black Mercedes which soon slowed down when the driver caught sight of us. As quietly as a panther, it drew up at an angle beside the two armed men and the other black car.

The door slid open, and in the gleam from the tall pylons I

glimpsed a silhouette as he got out. He was a tall, powerful man, and even before the light from the distant headlamp hit his face, I knew who it was. Now I could see the pattern that I should have seen eleven years ago.

54

'Nice to see you again, Hansie!' I shouted.

'I think I'm the one who should say that, Varg,' he replied with a tight-lipped smile. He kept a wary eye on Jan Egil and his gun. He whispered something to the two others.

'So it was you they rang!'

'Who else?'

I moved to the side, around the open car door and a few steps forward. From the corner of my eye I saw Jan Egil twitch.

'Varg! What are you doin'?' he said.

'Take it easy, Jan Egil. We're out in open countryside now.'

'Open countryside! What the hell d'you mean by that?'

A gun belonging to one of the men twitched, too, but Hans raised an authoritative hand and gave a brief command.

'Stay where you are!' he shouted to me.

'OK,' I said and stopped. 'Does that mean we can talk?'

'What about?'

'You know every well. About everything.'

He eyed me with a stony face, mute.

'I should have known in Førde, eleven years ago, when you were telling me about your childhood with such passion, about poverty and how you never wanted to experience the same again.'

'Should have known what, Varg?'

'How ruthless you'd been to avoid winding up in a similar situation again.'

'I haven't a clue what you're talking about! This is a local score we have to settle, between Jan Egil and us.'

'Between ...?'

'Between two groups. It was foolish of you to get involved in this. Now we'll have to – '

'Gang warfare, is that what you're trying to make me believe? Don't give me that bollocks! You're petrified you're on his black-list, and you should be higher up on the bloody list than I am.'

'You talk too much, Varg. But you've always been like that. Waffling on about all those brainless ideas of yours.'

'Oh, shut up, Hans! Do you want me to extract all your lies from you, one by one? I suppose that was what Hammersten threatened to do as well, being the born-again Christian he was. He wanted to do penance and renounce all his sins. Especially with regard to Jan Egil, who had to pay for them. The snag was that it wasn't only his sins he would have to do penance for. He had an accomplice. No, wrong. Not even an accomplice. You were the Mr Big, Hans, right from the very outset.'

He took a couple of steps closer. I did the same. Our eyes were locked; we were like two cowboys in the final scene of a western.

'You talk too much, Varg! This is rubbish. You must be able to hear that yourself.'

'Listen to my reasoning then!'

'I don't have the bloody time to –'

'We can start from a few days ago. Hammersten told you he could no longer keep all he knew to himself. And, worst of all, he wanted to tell Jan Egil. You beat him to death with a baseball bat, and when Jan Egil legged it, you took the opportunity to put the bat in his room. Yet again, damning evidence.'

'Yet again?'

'I'm thinking of the rifle in Angedalen.'

'For Christ's sake, I had nothing to do with the murder of Kari and Klaus.'

'No?'

'I think the turnip on your shoulders is beginning to go rotten, Varg. You might recall that I was in Bergen when it all happened.'

'We-ell. In theory, on your way to Bergen perhaps, but …'

'Which Terje Hammersten was able to corroborate, unless you've forgotten.'

'Not any more, and besides … very convenient that was. You and Hammersten giving each other an alibi in a kind of mutual alliance, since you were both in Angedalen that night.'

'You can prove that, can you?' The sarcasm lay thick on his vocal cords.

'A little detail that has always buzzed around my head is the key to the Libakk farmhouse. The spare key hanging in the hallway cupboard. No one broke in that night the murders took place, and that was part of the circumstantial evidence that pointed to Jan Egil. But you … you'd left the house, according to your statement, a few hours earlier and could have taken the key with you. Later that night you went back, either alone or most probably with Hammersten, you unlocked the door and committed the atrocity.'

'Oh yes!' he jeered. 'And what on earth would my motive have been?'

'You would inherit the farm afterwards.'

'Right, and what benefit was that to me?'

'Enough money to establish yourself here in Oslo! But that was not the whole reason. The keyword here is booze – and the much talked about seventies smuggling racket, with Klaus Libakk as one of the central distributors. Klaus owed you money. Big money. And you knew where he kept it, hidden somewhere on the farm. Ultimately, there was only one way to get at it, and it meant killing both of them, Klaus as the main victim, Kari because she was unlucky enough to be married to him.'

'Really? You can see yourself how thin your arguments are, Varg. To be frank, I … '

I interrupted him. 'You couldn't foresee that Jan Egil with his lack of self-control would end up in such a mess, but you certainly knew how to fan the flames with even greater zeal. You had used Hammersten before, to kill Ansgår Tveiten in 1973, and he must have been your and Svein Skarnes's well-remunerated henchman since the mid sixties, I would guess, when you hatched up the scheme.'

'The scheme?'

'You and Svein Skarnes, one of you desperate never to be poor again, the other desperate to earn quick money. It started with hash. Later it was booze. The only problem you had was that a woman stood between you. Vibecke Størset.'

'Vibecke was never a problem!'

'No? Never? What about that February day in 1974 when you paid a call on Svein Skarnes, got into a fight and pushed him down the stairs, breaking his neck? Wasn't it Vibecke you were quarrelling about?'

'No, it wasn't! That was about money, too.'

With a half-hearted sense of triumph, qualified by the situation we found ourselves in, I left his last statement hanging in the air between us. I could see how much he would have liked to retract the words. Now they were out, though, he was forced to continue: 'He also owed me money. Everyone owed me money! It was hell.'

'Exactly. Because when it came to the crunch, it was you who had started the whole thing. You were alone when you began. Your old university pal, Svein Skarnes, didn't pop up until later, and he provided a perfect network with Harald Dale as the agent. It was a perfect cover, too. But when things started going awry in Sogn and Fjordane because Ansgår Tveiten had gone to the police, it was you who sent Hammersten in. Perhaps you had Hammersten with you on that February day in 1974, too? I think I can almost visualise it! Hammersten hanging around outside the gate while you drag Skarnes to the window and point: Look who's outside waiting, Svein. Shall we invite him in perhaps? But you didn't get your money after all. Because you acted hastily and pushed your old pal down the stairs.'

'It was an accident, for Christ's sake! The heat of the moment, just as …'

'Yes, what was that you were about to say? Just as Vibecke said? Vibeke who had to serve a sentence on your account?'

'Is it my fault that she chose to take the blame for this?'

'No, it isn't. But you know very well why she did it, and you could have given yourself in at any point, if you had had the backbone. And she wasn't the only one unfortunately. The other scapegoat is here.' I vaguely indicated behind me.

His eyes wandered to Jan Egil and back again.

'But I suspect your guilt regarding Jan Egil is of a much higher order, Hans.'

'And what's that supposed to mean?'

'In fact, he can thank you for becoming the person he is. You were the one who ruined his mother's life, Mette Olsen.'

He sent me a wan look. 'Me? Ruined her life! What the hell are you talking about now?'

'It's no wonder your sense of guilt was so heavy that you were climbing the wall on the last evening in Førde eleven years ago.'

'I still don't understand ...'

'You told me yourself you'd met her in Copenhagen that year. She'd always had a suspicion a rejected suitor had blown the whistle on them. But wasn't it competition in the hash market that you feared most? Because the telephone call that betrayed them did not come from Copenhagen, but from Bergen in August, 1966. You said yourself you had dabbled with drugs, and the step from dabbling to dealing is not so large. Especially not for someone who was on the lookout for a way to secure his finances.'

His eyes narrowed, and I didn't like what I read there. I knew that every word I said was sealing my fate. But it was too late to stop now. I had to see the whole thing through. 'Mette Olsen got off thanks to her solicitors, but her boyfriend David Pettersen killed himself in prison. The year after, Mette Olsen had a child. And the boy who was born, under an extremely unlucky star, was ... Jan Egil. From even before he was born you'd shaped his destiny, Hans. Three times he has paid the price for your actions. The first time while in his crucial first years with an unstable mother. The second time when you deprived him of both the new parents he had been given. And the third time when he was blamed for the double murder that you committed. But now it's over, Hans! He won't pay any more.'

He fixed me with heavy eyes. 'And how are you going to prevent that?' He tossed back his head. 'You can see the guys there. They obey my every order. They get paid well to do that.'

I looked over at the two armed men who had been standing too far away to catch all of what we had been discussing. 'Yes, they're good, I'll give you that. You put them on my tail from the moment I left your hospice in Eiriks gate. But it wasn't me you were really after, it was Jan Egil.'

He suddenly raised his head. I did the same. We could both hear it now. Another car was on its way into the area.

We looked at the gate where a white car with a taxi sign on the roof came into view. When the driver spotted us, he jumped on the brakes, causing the tyres to squeal. The two armed men instantly turned in that direction.

Behind me I heard Jan Egil. 'You bastard! You're to blame for everythin'. Now I'll fuckin' give …'

And then all hell broke loose.

55

One of the rear doors of the taxi opened.

Hans called out: 'Guys! Don't ...'

Jan Egil shot first, but the range was too great. He missed. Hans Haavik threw himself to the side and down, and by that time the two men had managed to turn back in our direction. Two continuous salvos sounded like a sudden crackle of fire in the darkness.

I heard Jan Egil groan before I could swivel round. He toppled backwards, hit in the chest by one of the shots. Instinctively, I continued in the same direction, as if to reach out for him, when I was hit myself, a sledgehammer blow in one shoulder. I was spun round, I slid down the side of the car and landed on the ground with a thump, where I lay on my back staring into the air. I could see stars, but they were in the sky, high above. For a moment I felt nothing, as if my whole body were numb. Then came the pain, it was like a chainsaw cutting through me from my left shoulder down to my heart. The whole thing could not have taken more than a few seconds.

From afar I could hear the sound of a car door being slammed shut and then running footsteps.

'Careful,' I heard Hans shout, but the footsteps just continued. They were coming closer. Now they were by me. Light steps, like on cotton. The stars grew, to become suns, but they were no longer in the sky; now they were in my head.

I heard her voice. 'Varg! Oh my God! This was never meant to happen. I never knew ... He tricked me too, from beginning to end!'

I tried to see her through the sun dance, but all I saw was a reflection in her round glasses. 'Ce-cilie?'

She turned away, her face a white pallor. 'Ring for an ambulance! Do you hear me, Hans? You ring! Now!'

'What's going on? What are you doing here?' I heard the echo of my own voice.

'It's all a terrible misunderstanding. I thought Hans was seriously worried about you.'

'But …'

'It wasn't until this evening that I realised who I … what sort of person I have … You have to believe me, Varg! I had no idea what he was doing on the side!'

'Doing … you don't mean … you and Hans …'

She nodded vigorously. 'Hans and I have been together since we met again in Oslo. He convinced me that Johnny boy was a danger to you and him, and that was why I … but when I overheard the conversation about where he would meet you two …'

'Overheard …'

'And overheard him say that on no account must either of you escape alive … I demanded to go with him, but he refused point blank! He just shoved me away, refused to let me come. It was then I realised how completely he had pulled the wool over my eyes … I've rung the police, too …'

'The police?'

'Yes, it's over now, Varg. It's all over …'

I tried to focus on her. But she seemed to float slowly up and away. It was becoming harder to see her. The pain inside me was growing. It filled the whole of my body now. I felt something hot and wet against my cheek. At first I thought it was blood. Later I realised it was tears. But they were hers, not mine.

'How's Jan Egil?' I mumbled, but she didn't answer.

Now I could hear the sirens, a long way off. But they had nothing to do with me. I was beginning to sink, slowly, calmly, as if I was lying and floating on an upward airstream. I was being lowered into a vast, dark void. I rolled over and lay face down. The pain was receding, and everything felt nice and cosy. Far below I saw the circular light, glittering silver water, which I was on my way towards in the first, and only, perfect swallow dive of my life.